C000163670

Becoming
Lady Darcy

A Pemberley Story

Sara Smallman

Reviews for 'Becoming Lady Darcy'

'The concept is unique, the characters complex, flawed and vital. Smallman has created something special here.'

'...totally enthralled by the author's weaving of all the various characters and timelines. It has made for a highly entertaining read.'

'Oh my god...my heart is singing. What an absolutely gorgeous story!'

"The characters are so real, the backdrop so immersive... I didn't want it to end."

'The characters...are flawed, deeply human and utterly lovable, and that is what makes the story so special.'

'Tiny Dancer' – ©Elton John, Bernie Taupin, 1971

Copyright © Sara Smallman 2019

All rights reserved. This book or any portion thereof may not be reproduced or used in any manner whatsoever without the express written permission of the publisher except for the use of brief quotations in a book review or scholarly journal.

All characters in this publication are fictitious and any resemblance to real persons, living or dead, is purely coincidental.

Also available as an eBook.

First Printing: 2019   Cover Design: Elspeth & Ink   Instagram: @sarasmallmanwrites

For Thomas.
Gentleman/Explorer.

Author's Note

Lyme Park, the ancestral seat of the Legh family, is the very real inspiration for the fictional Pemberley depicted in this story, as well as one of the filming locations for the BBC adaptation of 'Pride and Prejudice' starring Colin Firth. Some of the historical stories told in 'Becoming Lady Darcy' are based on real events that occurred at Lyme, and a great deal is owed to my fellow National Trust volunteers who lovingly and reverently shared these tales with me so that I could tell this one.

DARCY
ONE MADE OUT OF MANY

It is a truth universally acknowledged...

Seeds

The horse thundered on through the countryside, the quickening thud-thud thud-thud of hooves on firm ground pounding through the rider, each punctuated by his own breathing as he held tight to the beast who had been ridden hard.

As he powered on past an outcrop of trees, a herd of agile does and tottering fawns rushed into the small and protective wood which garnished the hillside; their burnished tones blazing across the muted green of the landscape where the soft whispering grasslands faded into an outcrop of thick rock at the base.

This ancient hunting ground had been gifted to him by a benevolent monarch, grateful for his valiant and brave services on the battlefield; its location scratched out on a faded piece of parchment. Piers D'Arcy had followed the gentle curve of the terrain to this spot as marked.

So, he thought, this was Pembarlegh.

1810

The carriage rumbled over the cobbled outer courtyard, clattering as it did so, the heat and smell from the torches drifted over as the clock in the tower struck eight o'clock. She was gently resting her head on his shoulder, the feather on her bonnet tickling his nose.

"Lizzy."

She stirred, lifting her head, her face illuminated by the light from the beacons.

"Have we arrived?"

He nodded, smiling down at her, finding that his expression was mirrored. The carriage stopped, a small jolt as the four horses were brought to a halt outside the stone porch. Offering his hand, he helped her to descend from the carriage and directed her towards the house where Mr Staughton, Mrs Reynolds and the rest of the servants were waiting to greet them, all eager to catch sight of the new Mrs Darcy in her finery.

Elizabeth climbed the steps to the entrance, stopping outside the large wooden door, hesitant to gesture to the footman to request permission to enter as if she were still a passing traveller requesting entry whilst the master was in town. It was a fact that she was still finding hard to comprehend. Pemberley now belonged to her, and she to it.

"Of all this I am mistress…"

"Yes, Mrs Darcy," he said, leading her inside. "Welcome home."

The newly married master spared no expense in making Pemberley as comfortable as he could for his bride, indeed everything he did was for Elizabeth, including the renovation of the library, for he dearly knew how much she loved to read. It was a beautiful modern room hidden away at the far corner of the building. The solid oak floors gave way to soft, wool rugs, led into ornate cream panelling, beautifully patterned fabrics, gilded coving and rows upon rows of books. It had been newly painted in a warm yellow and on days when the winter sun shone brightly over the hills and the whole room became illuminated in glorious gold, she could imagine herself back in her father's study at Longbourn.

In the first few months of marriage, Elizabeth found that on occasion she ached to be back in Hertfordshire, because there were some days when she felt that being Mrs Darcy, mistress of Pemberley, was a role that she felt she would never be able to perform with any level of accomplishment – that she was not as refined as she was expected to be, that she would never be able to run the household and organise the servants. It was on these days that she would close her eyes and imagine herself back at home, where she was Miss Elizabeth Bennet and that person only. Mrs Elizabeth Darcy was a completely different person, and she wasn't quite sure if she knew who she was yet.

Darcy had never dreamed that he would have found such a happy situation in life, never thought that he would find a wife who was so like him - who tested and challenged him daily, with no regard, well not in a real sense, for his rank or fortune. They had argued before he had left for London on business – strong words about her management of her lady's maid, Ellen – how she dealt with her in a less than formal manner and how she needed to be aware of her station. Elizabeth had snapped back at him with a few choice phrases and had refused to apologise or acknowledge her fault.

Already late to depart, he had left without properly saying goodbye and even though God had joined them together he wondered, albeit briefly, if he would have had an easier life with one of the society beauties who knew three languages and their place. He had travelled to London by horse but his anger, which had been so vehement the night before when he had stopped in the inn at Grantham, had abated and he sent his wife a small missive, containing an apology.

A response arrived for him two days later when he returned to Derbyshire House after completing his business. Even though it was stated that Mrs Darcy had accepted his apology, a hint of frostiness in her phrasing still remained which put him on edge and reminded him of the cold response to his first failed proposal.

Fitzwilliam Darcy understood that he was a proud man, it was one of the fundamental keystones of his character, laid in his personality when he was very young by his parents and teachers. Although his love for Elizabeth was much stronger than his predisposition for pride, it was sometimes hard to overcome this core characteristic, being as it was, so rooted in him and the position which he held. But he knew now, time away from his wife revealing to him this truth, that it did not matter to him that she had behaved with an unbecoming familiarity towards her maid, or that she cared about the family servants. Pemberley was a large and expansive estate, but the people who lived there were very much human, especially his wife who was perhaps the best example of her sex. Despite having a day of appointments remaining, he saddled his horse and began the journey to Derbyshire, not wanting to spend another hour away from home.

Arriving at Pemberley he handed his horse over to a stable hand, running through the courtyard, up the stairway, and into the entrance hall. The sound of Georgiana playing on the pianoforte echoed large and loud in the air, the candles illuminating the concentration on her face. He stopped momentarily as if to stop and embrace her, she shot him a knowing glance, acknowledging his return as she continued to play.

He found his wife stood in the library, surrounded by papers and books on household management.

"Mrs Darcy."

He realised this was more formal than usual, but he was unsure as to where the land lay and decided to err on the side of caution.

"Darcy!' She smiled at him broadly, "you have returned earlier than expected?"

"My business was cut short," he lied. "I decided to return home more promptly than first arranged. If this vexes you in some way I apologise."

"Why would I be vexed because my husband is home early from town? Mr Darcy, you have strange views on what vexes a woman. Here, let me fetch you a glass, you look half frozen."

She poured from the decanter, placing a tumbler of brandy in his hand before returning to the table and her work.

"And how was London…did you see Jane at all? Mama wrote and said she was due a visit to Upper Grosvenor Street. Your presence may have leant a little respite for Charles."

Darcy shook his head as he walked to the fire to warm his hands; he realised that he had not removed his overcoat or boots. He stood in the middle of his library looking almost like a savage. The smell of the journey loitered on his skin and he drank quickly before placing the tumbler down. He needed to ask her something, something that he needed to ask to resolve it promptly, one way or another.

"Do you regret your match with me, Mrs Darcy? Am I not, despite the large fortune that your Mother found so desirous, what you require in a marital partner?"

He said it fast, almost not sure what he wanted to say before it was said and out there, loitering in the air. Darcy looked up quickly to see her eyes searching for his questioningly.

"Fitzwilliam?"

"Do you regret this…this *marriage*? Do you regret our hasty engagement?"

Elizabeth walked purposefully over to her husband and placed the back of her hand on his forehead; he pulled away, but she insisted. He could smell the gentle scent of violets and bergamot, the perfume she had bought as part of her trousseau. It instantly transported him back to those weeks spent in the Lake country for their wedding tour. He closed his eyes, shaking his head slowly before slumping onto the settee.

"Fitz, are you sick? Do I need to call Dr Jeffries?"

She sounded genuinely concerned and hastened to move the books and papers, taking a seat next to him, reaching for his hand.

"Do you wish you hadn't married me, Lizzy? I am asking you a direct question and I would appreciate a direct response."

He couldn't look at her, but she studied his face for the briefest of moments.

"Darcy, we disagreed on an issue," she said plaintively. "You had one idea of how something would happen, and I had another, but this does not mean that... well, I don't know what you would think it would mean."

"The tone of your letter, Mrs Darcy, suggested that you no longer wished to assume the title of wife."

Elizabeth may have forgiven her husband for their argument, but she had no intention of yielding to his opinion on this.

"I *was* cross with you, and with quite good reason too, but when I came to apologise in the morning and find a resolve, you had already left for town. I had so many questions about the Ball to ask you about and you had *skulked off* before I could ask you any of them."

Ah yes, the Lady Anne's Ball – why had he not remembered about this. Held on the anniversary of his mother's birthday, the Ball was one of the most important events in the Derbyshire social calendar –a massive undertaking for any woman and even his Aunt, Lady Fitzwilliam, had struggled with the arrangements in previous years.

"I am sorry my letter sounded ill. It was written in haste and I fear it may have sounded angrier than I actually felt."

Darcy glanced over at his wife, her eyes showed the concern for the worry she had caused him.

"Oh, Elizabeth, I am a fool."

He hid his head in his hands and gently laughed, relief coursed through him. How idiotic for him to think that his wife would declare their marriage a failure after one disagreement.

"Yes, Fitzwilliam Darcy, you are."

She gently kissed his temples and placed her hand on his cheek, stroking the roughness of his sideburn until it was smooth.

"I am sorry, my love."

"As am I, but I understand now. My family are not as refined as yours – our arguments are all out in the open. My parents argue in front of their children and their servants; it was a natural thing for the residents of our home to see them bicker and then resolve their differences."

"Darcys have never really done that."

"But *I* am a Darcy now too, and whilst I understand that there are all these unspoken rules that I must follow, I need a little time to acquaint myself with it all. You have had your whole life and I have had but a few months."

He knew that she was a long way away from her family, in both miles and manner, and he understood now too. He nodded, pleased that harmony was now restored to his household.

"Now as your wife, I must ask you to please go and bathe…before you stink out the whole house with your stench!"

He grinned – partly to cover his mortification, but partly because it brought much happiness to him to have someone who knew him well enough to tell him he stank with such candour. He got up, kissing her on the forehead as he did.

"No, you are seriously vile! Go and wash, I implore you!"

Darcy practically ran to his dressing room, where his valet Brown had already lit the fire and heated the water.

When he returned to the library, now smelling of soap and cologne, Elizabeth was drawing out a plan on a piece of parchment – which was more difficult than she had obviously anticipated. The paper curled up at the corners, causing the ink to splash on her favourite yellow gown, he knew this would annoy her and made a mental note to have a replacement made.

"The problem, you see, is that we have closed off the entire South wing and so we have five bedrooms that are unable to be used, and the new saloon will not be ready by then – so where do we put everyone? We have over one hundred people who have already confirmed attendance and I have Mrs Reynolds demanding answers!"

His wife looked up at him exasperatedly, her hair falling out of its pins and falling down her back. He remembered the first time he had unravelled her hair, the first time they had been gloriously alone, undressing each other slowly in the quiet privacy of their chambers. He had brushed her hair that night as she took a seat in front of the mirror, naked excepting for a thin, soft chemise, the outline of her figure temptingly close as she pulled him into her and kissed him fervently. A feeling of love and contentment washed over him as he remembered. He was so very lucky.

"What do you find so amusing, husband?" She questioned. "Is it my horrendous seating plan or the ink on my gown that entertains you so greatly?"

"I think you look rather fetching when you are planning things, dearest wife." He placed the errant curls behind her ears and kissed her gently, impatiently, on the neck, breathing in the scent of her. "I should let you plan things more often..."

"Mr Darcy, we don't have time for any of that nonsense right now. As you know I am a very important lady and have-"

His firm kiss on her lips silenced her for a moment, the quill now still in her hand.

"I apologise, you were saying…"

She looked up at him smiling, he really was insatiable, she thought, and incorrigible, and incredible. He leaned in, the warmth of him pressing softly into her neckline, gently moving down…

"Mr Darcy, I have a desire to know your opinion on white soup to start."

"Mrs Darcy, as you well know I love white soup, but could this wait until the morning? It is late, and I have been away from you for far too long…"

Elizabeth's eyes flashed mischievously and teasingly she pushed him back at arm's length, loosening his cravat she leaned up to softly kiss behind his ear and nuzzled his nose.

"Maybe, but what would be another hour? Patience, my darling; you know good things always come to those who wait."

"Alright, we need some supper and then, madame, I am taking you to bed."

"Promises promises…" Elizabeth laughed as she turned her attention back to her plans, knowing full well that her husband didn't remove his gaze from her once.

One

She slouched down in the water, the hot water resting on her top lip. It was dangerously close to her nostrils and she knew that one mistimed breath in would result in water up her nose, and a very ungraceful coughing and spluttering fit blowing her cover. Concentrating hard, she listened intently to the voices outside in the corridor. This was *not* happening today. It had taken nearly forty minutes to run this bath, relying as she did, on hundred and fifty-year-old plumbing and a heater that had been installed at least a decade before Hitler invaded the Rhineland. The water was gloriously hot and bubbly, poking her toes out of a mound of foam, she was surprised when they bobbed out glittery, forgetting the sparkly pedicure that had come courtesy of her daughter the night before.

Half-submerged, she could hear the bass tones of what she guessed was an older man, and then the higher-pitched tone of a woman. Movement outside the door now, the scrape and shuffle of people and bags against plaster and paint, and she gripped her hands on the side of the bath, ready to submerge like a fleshy submarine.

The voices were loud.
Getting louder.
American, maybe…
Yes, American.

Reluctantly she eased herself out of the claw-footed enamelled bath and grabbed herself a towel from the back of the door, tying up the wanton mass of brown curls high on top of her head. Cautiously, she opened the door and peered out into the hallway. A large, stocky man with a rucksack on his back and a small, rotund woman wearing a sun visor wrapped around a massive bouffant, were currently gazing at the pictures on the wall, flicking through the guidebook to see exactly what they were looking at, confused at not seeing the collection of eclectic postcard prints documented in the glossy pages.

"I think you might be lost."

She announced her presence cheerfully, walking out with all the confidence of a gameshow host, the fluffy towel wrapped tightly around her. The large gentleman turned quickly, almost hitting his companion across the face with his bag.

"Oh, hello there," he exclaimed, moving toward her with his hand outstretched, and which she shook firmly. "I think you might be right. Can you point us in the right direction?"

"You need to turn straight about and out the door, then turn right and back down the stairs", she pointed out the directions, checking his understanding. "Don't worry, it happens quite a lot…"

He nodded quickly, shooting her a relieved look, she could almost see him working through the route in his head trying to figure out where on the tour they had gone so wrong. He had never been to England before, had never really been outside of Texas, and now he had gotten lost inside of a house.

"That's mighty fine of you," his accent was thick like molasses, "thank you for your assistance, Miss-?"

She hesitated for a moment, feeling it catch it her breath, the words hanging there before stating firmly and with a rehearsed smile.

"It's Elizabeth."

The woman perked up immediately as if she has been pricked with a needle. Her eyebrows raised, looking at her husband with a surreptitious glance, a suppressed beam etching itself across her face.

"Excuse me," she said almost furtively, "I hope you don't mind me asking, but are you one of the Darcys that live here?"

She studied her carefully, and then immediately became flustered, her face now matching the same colour as the flamingo on her t-shirt, her hands rolling the stiff pages of the guidebook into a baton.

"Oh, sweet mother of Jesus, you're Lady Elizabeth Darcy, ain't ya?"

"Yes…Yes, I am," Lizzy said in a hesitant voice, offering a friendly handshake to the woman, who was now desperately trying to curtsey.

"I've just been reading about you!" She began flicking frantically through the guidebook she had purchased at the gate. "But I never for one moment thought that… this is truly spectacular… Oh my gosh… wait until I tell the girls back home that I have met a real-life English Lady, my friend Evangeline McMeans will eat her hat!"

She grabbed her phone out of her pocket, and then hesitated a moment.

"Would it be terribly rude to ask you, Lady Elizabeth, to scoot on in here for a photo? She won't believe me otherwise."

"Of course not!" Lizzy laughed. "I like a selfie as much as the next person! You must think me ever so rude, but —"

"Oh, you must think I have forgotten all of my manners! My name is Crystal. This here is my husband, Hank," she poked him with an acrylic-tipped finger. "We're the Treachers from the good old U S of A."

She leaned forward and gave Lizzy a big, US-style embrace as she snapped pictures for posterity.

"Well, I'm so glad you decided to visit us here at Pemberley today."

"We wouldn't have missed it for the world, I just need Mr Darcy to pop out of the lake and my day will be complete. You know, if you are ever in Texas, you should most definitely call and visit us."

"I would most definitely come and visit you," she grinned. "I hope you do a good line in barbecue!"

"Oh my, you mean you would?! We do the best barbecue in Katy… don't we Hank!"

"We sure do!"

Hank immediately became animated at the suggestion of food, and he started to describe the slow-cooked brisket in intricate detail.

"Hank," Lizzy pleaded with a flirtatious feather to her voice. "You're making me so hungry, stop it!"

Crystal grinned again, with a smile that made her look as if she had slept with a coathanger in her mouth, her bright orange bouffant bouncing up and down as she jiggled with laughter, her eyelashes fluttering.

"Well, Lady Elizabeth, we will be on our way," she announced, "but meeting you here has made our day."

"It has been so lovely to meet you," Lizzy beamed.

Crystal squealed and gave her another hug, as Lizzy hoped that her towel would stay in place. After thanking her again profusely, the Treachers turned around, making their way down the corridor and to the right as instructed, talk of the imminent green-faced envy of Evangeline McMeans escaping from their lips. Lizzy watched as they walked to the large oak door that led back to the grand staircase and the rest of the house.

Lizzy shouted upstairs towards her daughter's bedroom, her voice carrying up the twisting wooden staircase and to the third floor where the sixteen-year-old would be hiding under the duvet, pretending that she didn't have to get up and go to work.

"HARRY!!"

Harriet Darcy awoke with a jump upon hearing her mother's shriek echoing throughout the flat, and then stubbornly closed her eyes and tried to fall back to sleep. It was early – super early, *well* before eleven – she knew because of how the sun shone through the curtains and where it landed on the wall, illuminating but not quite reaching the smouldering face of Heathcliff on the Wuthering Heights poster that was directly opposite her bed. It was Saturday, and she had already heard her mum
clunking the old plumbing to life, making coffee, doing laundry, watching crap telly. She just wanted to sleep.

Lizzy came in without knocking and walked over to the window and opened the curtains, the early spring sunshine blazed through. Her daughter hidden under her Harry Potter duvet, with only a fluff of her hair was visible, and a be-socked limb poking out of the bottom of the bed. She pulled the sock off her daughter's foot, before tickling the bottom gently, Harriet's toes curled, and she pulled her foot back under the safety of the cover.

"You need to get dressed, your shift starts in half an hour and there are people in the house already." Lizzy put a pile of clothes on the chair next to the dresser, grabbed some cups and dishes. "C'mon, Harry, don't be a shirker, be a hard worker!"

"*Really*, Mum. Really??"

Harriet squashed her pillow over her head, giving a silent scream as her mum clomped heavily down the stairs. She *was* a hard worker – you had to be when everyone knew who you were – but she disliked working in the tearoom, especially as she had to dress up in regency costume and serve afternoon tea, complete with cake stands and fancy teapots, to foreign tourists who wanted to take her picture for Instagram, and tip her with currency that she wouldn't be able to spend. Her friends from school thought it weird that she lived in a house that you could pay to visit, they all lived within five minutes of each other on the housing estate in Lambton that was filled with medium-sized pre-war semis with names like Rookwood, Wodehouse, and Meadowside. Sometimes she wished she lived in one too, instead of in the flat at the top of Pemberley, which was always bitterly cold in winter and roasting hot in summer.

It could have been worse though, she could have been shoved off to boarding school like her cousins, Tom and Josh, or forced to some Swiss finishing school like her mum's sister, Imogen, who was only four years older than her and had already appeared on Babes of Bayswater and a whole cacophony of celebrity websites, dressed in skirts so short you could practically see her cervix. She didn't really see Imogen that much, but she knew that she would look down on her brown waves, un-plucked eyebrows and ability to get out of cars without flashing her underwear.

Dragging herself out of bed, she cleaned her face with a wipe from a pink packet before sighing deeply; Harriet could say with absolute certainty that her aunt would never be forced to get a Saturday job, she didn't think Imogen would gratefully accept six pounds an hour for any kind of manual labour, especially after seeing her three day stretch on 'Filthy Rich and Farming' where she was voted off after a hysterical meltdown caused by a rogue cowpat. But then again, she didn't think her infamous Aunt would be locked in a strategic bidding war on eBay for a 1930s embroidered clutch bag that could only be won when she received this week's wages. She was so close to winning that to give up now would be foolish, and she couldn't wait to receive the bag through the post, wishing away the days. It was so close to being hers that she could practically feel the soft threads of the floral design under her fingertips.

Her handbag infatuation started with the gift she received from Great-Aunt Sybil on her birthday the year before. It was made from a sturdy, yet supple leather; lined with bright blue shot silk, it smelled like rolled tobacco and the faint musky smell of something forbidden and exotic. This particular bag had belonged to her suffragette great-great-grandma, who had known the Pankhursts and been arrested more than twelve times. It had been given to Harriet on her sixteenth birthday by her great aunt, who proclaimed that all Darcy women should be in possession of a beautiful bag. Sybil, with her liver-spotted hands and translucent skin, had pulled it from a faded green dustbag, marked with ornate branding of a fashionable Parisian fashion house, and held it close, before handing it over slowly as she entrusted something precious and irreplaceable to the teenager with the frizzy hair.

Handbags were so personal and so unique to each owner; you could tell a lot about a person from their bag. Her mum carried a big old leather bag with only one inside pocket filled with change and jewellery she discarded throughout the day, and a faded designer label which would have been impressive when it was new about fifteen years ago. It held everything that she could possibly need for the day, but everything was thrown into it and you had to rummage about to find what you needed. It was organised, but messy, a bit like her mum.

Aunt Maggie had a smaller blue fabric bag, that was well-structured and had plenty of pockets for all those bits and pieces that she kept squirrelled away. It was like Maggie, in that respect. And Joyce; well, Joyce had a wonderfully beautiful Hermes Birkin, which she used every day and treated with care and respect. She had told her once that she had saved up for it for years, invested in something she really wanted. The brown leather bag would never go out of style, would never kowtow to fashion and trends. Harriet thought this bag was a good reflection of the woman who ran Pemberley, and it helped to support her theory.

The youngest Darcy lady didn't know if she would ever live up to the reputation of Millicent's handbag – she had been a formidable woman who had lived so many lives - but she found that the more she used it, the harder she tried, her great-great-grandmother's memory pushing her on to achieve what she wanted, and stray from the beaten path. Harriet Darcy was the latest in a long line of obstinate, headstrong girls who had roamed the halls of Pemberley House and she was going to do as she pleased. Strong women seemed to run in her family and she fully intended to carry on the tradition.

1811

The early morning sunrise crested over the summit of Cage Hill as the last carriages of guests pulled away from the front of Pemberley. Elizabeth stood at the window in the drawing room. The fire, which has burned so furiously the night before was now embers, and the air was still and cold. Upstairs her houseguests were all still tucked away in their chambers and she suspected it wouldn't be too long until a flurry of maids woke from their rest and began work in the kitchens downstairs, preparing food for breaking the fast later that day. Darcy had been up since dawn the day before, helping her prepare, supervising and giving his firm instructions to Staughton. The food, despite her concerns, had been well received and the illustrious pineapple – complete with its own pewter stand – had been the talk of the night. Emily Warner, who lived on the neighbouring estate, had even asked if she would be able to borrow it for her own event the following month. Elizabeth had agreed, of course, and this had started what to all intents and purposes was a waiting list for the loan of the pineapple.

"I say, Lizzy, that wretched fruit has a more eventful social life than we do – why I think it will be dining with four and twenty families before the evening is over," Darcy said quietly.

She had given him a gentle nudge in the side before returning to sit with her mother, who was complaining most heartily to all that despite living some distance away, she too would like to procure the fruit for a dinner she planned to host upon her return to Meryton.

"Dearest Mama, it is your birthday soon, maybe we could buy you a pineapple as a gift and send it down to Longbourn by carriage," Elizabeth said, with humour.

Her husband, still standing within earshot, guffawed loudly, but managed to disguise this breach of manners with a well-timed cough, even if it did not go unnoticed by his wife.

"Oh, Mrs Darcy! My dearest Lizzy, I knew that you would put your riches to good use to guarantee the happiness of your Mama. You are such a good girl. My daughter," she said to her audience. "Mistress of Pemberley and all you can see here today!" She waited for the collection of middle-aged women to look impressed. "Well, go on, Lizzy, stand up..."

Elizabeth rose to her feet and did a polite, if mortifying, curtsey for the assembled ladies before quickly making her excuses. She made a beeline for her husband, who was trying to casually disguise a knowing grin as he passed her a glass of wine.

"Dearest, we need to procure a pineapple for my mother." She took a longer gulp of the wine than was proper in company. "Maybe we can sell some silver to finance it. We don't need all those plates that have been in the family for centuries, do we?"

"No, no, not at all. Useless heirlooms, gathering dust, creating more work for Staughton. Best rid of it all, I'd say." He paused for a moment, "do you have any idea how much that wretched thing cost? We can't even eat it, apparently. Does it have to be a pineapple? Can we not placate her with a nectarine or maybe some exotic apples?"

"Dearest, I am very much hoping that my mother will continue to imbibe wine at her current rate, resulting in her recollections of the evening being less than accurate."

The Darcys watched the result of their months of planning coming to fruition, Fitzwilliam reached for his wife's hand and gave it a tight little squeeze. She grinned from ear to ear, and he moved his hand to her waist pulling her in close. Two younger girls, who Elizabeth recognised as friends of Georgiana's and newly out this season, tottered past and twittered at this public display of affection, they were resplendent in their brightly coloured and be-feathered turbans, the rustle of satin and stiff new gowns following them.

The whole room was filled with people and music and colour, muted green and reds with the odd dazzling blue or gold. The six-hour candles – expensive but, according to Mrs Reynolds, necessary for the occasion - were flickering away happily around the room and everywhere gaiety and merriment were apparent. Darcy spotted his sister over by the pianoforte, happily engaged in conversation with Colonel Fitzwilliam.

Georgiana had always been a little shy, and whilst his own reserve presented itself as a haughty arrogance, hers sometimes overwhelmed her, causing her to seek retreat rather than attempt to fight it. It was here that the presence of Elizabeth had benefited Georgiana the most; she was blossoming into a confident young woman who knew her own mind and her own heart. Darcy found himself bullied and teased by the two enemies in his very own camp; they would mock his majestic moods, enabling him to laugh at himself and his occasional pomposity which would manifest itself whenever he failed to keep it in check. Georgiana loved how Elizabeth made her brother smile, Darcy loved how she increased his sister's self-confidence and it was common knowledge within their society that they made a very happy threesome at home in Derbyshire.

Elizabeth spotted her father walking to join them from the other side of the banqueting hall and waved him over. The stress of living with two of the silliest girls in England, or three if you counted Mrs Bennet, took its daily toll on Mr Bennet and he eagerly anticipated spending the next few days having conversations that did not involve talk of soldiers, ribbons or sermons. As much as it pained him to not have her close, he could see how adored his Lizzy was here in Derbyshire, how effortlessly she had adapted to be the mistress of a great estate.

"Elizabeth, what is all this I hear of your mother being gifted an expensive tropical fruit from Mrs Darcy herself?" He gladly took a glass of wine from Darcy and with a sardonic smile sighed, "How will I ever afford the upkeep of such a precious delicacy?"

Elizabeth missed the playful banter and easy wit of her father, the company of her mother being a fair price to pay to be back in his presence even if just for a few nights.

"What about a painting of a pineapple? Or maybe an embroidered pineapple? I'm sure you could turn your hand to embroidering a pineapple for your mother, Lizzy."

"You know as well as I, Papa, that any embroidery from me would not be a gift that one would want to receive."

"I can testify to that," Darcy murmured, shooting a knowing glance at his wife.

"I am very sorry, Papa," she stated with faux solemnity. "But I am afraid we have committed to the purchase. Besides, I think we all know quite well that Mama has probably already sent a letter by post to Mrs Philips and by now surely everyone in Meryton will be fully aware. Would you like to be the one who tells her that you have declined the gift?" she teased, arching her eyebrow.

Mr Bennet looked at Darcy, who looked at his wife, who looked at her papa. He sighed and finished his wine, before kissing his daughter on the cheek and shaking the hand of the host.

"I'll be in the library," he said. "If you see your mother, please don't tell her where I am."

Darcy held Elizabeth's hand and squeezed it gently. She glanced up at him for a moment and beamed, before turning her attention to the dancing, which she watched with glee. Darcy thought his wife the most beautiful in the room that evening, looking positively resplendent in a blue satin gown with a gold brocade trim, surely it appeared to be the most perfectly cut gown that she had even worn, excepting her wedding dress, and he must thank his Aunt for recommending such an adept and talented modiste. Her hair had been placed in curls with jewelled flower clips holding them in place, the look reminiscent of a Grecian goddess and her long neck elegant, almost regal. He wished that he could take this image and preserve it forever, keep it locked next to his heart to remember this vision of beauty.

As she stood next to him wearing his mother's diamond and sapphire necklace, the gems sparkling and glowing in the candlelight, he could see the attention that it drew from the ladies as they walked passed or thanked their hosts for the evening, and he smiled to himself as Mrs Darcy received the recognition she deserved and accepted it graciously. His wife had received an education befitting that of a gentleman's daughter, she had not been schooled by a governess in the unspoken and complex rules of the aristocracy, and he knew that her composure often belied an underlying anxiety of being unable to stand her ground amongst the ladies of high society. But tonight, she had been formidable – gracious, generous, funny, and attentive, and he knew, probably knew better than she did herself, that she had no need to be worried about anything.

Elizabeth watched the dancing and clapped her gloved hands. Observing others gave her time to think, her current thought being that she must have tried too much of the food over the last few weeks as her dress felt much tighter than she remembered it being when she went for her final fitting in town with Lady Matlock. But never to mind, she could survive a few more hours of discomfort if it meant that Darcy would continue to keep looking at her like he did. Darcy and Elizabeth usually kept separate chambers, but the cramped conditions at Pemberley this weekend meant that they were breaking with social protocol and sharing for three nights. It was a glorious inconvenience for Elizabeth, who loved waking up with her husband, and an even better one for Darcy who secretly loved playing the ladies maid, helping her remove her attire with all the playfulness of a naughty schoolboy.

The evening passed in a whirlwind of introductions, reunions, laughter, and food. Jane and Bingley had arrived earlier that day and happily confirmed with their closest friends and relations that they would be expecting a new addition to the family sometime in the autumn. Elizabeth was thrilled for her sister and excited about the prospect of becoming an aunt. Married life suited Jane and this happy event had made Bingley even more decided to relocate from Netherfield and further north. They had found a solid estate called Dunmarleigh in Cheshire and planned to move there before the baby was born. The distance between the sisters would now be a lot more manageable with good roads between the two residences.

The whole assembly became aware of the good news once Mrs Bennet was informed, and no-one had seen a woman happier that evening – although Elizabeth did not know if this was a result of the baby or Darcy's pineapple centrepiece. Either way, her mother's nerves had absconded for one evening and this had made her company a great deal more pleasurable for all concerned.

Elizabeth watched as the final carriage disappeared around the bend of the driveway. How beautiful her home appeared in the early days of spring, she thought. From the front of the house, she could see down into the valley below and how the colours of the forest were turning with the seasons. She made her way to her chambers, slowly opening the door so as not to disturb Darcy who had retired to bed at just past four am. The clock in the room chimed to signify that it was now quarter to six, she removed Lady Anne's necklace and placed it in the chest on her dresser, it was too early, or late, to call for her maid Ellen who would still be asleep, so she lay on the bed to rest, just for a moment. It had been such a wonderful night.

The household began to stir, maids waking from their rest, splashing their faces, pinning their hair and running down the curling staircases of the tower, ready to light fires and prepare food for the family and their guests. Darcy awoke to see his wife sprawled out on the bed, her hair had become loose in the night spreading out over the pillow. She was still fully clothed, her dress crumpled. He did not know how she could sleep laced in her stays, but it had been a long day. Leaning over gently, he stroked her face, she stirred a little, turning over so that she faced him. He adored these early morning moments that they shared.

"I love you in this colour blue," he murmured.

Elizabeth awoke but did not open her eyes. She hoped that he would go back to sleep and let her rest.

"This blue... it's beautiful."

He must still be drunk, she thought.

"Beautiful Eliza Bennet in blue..." he said, gently tracing his finger behind her ear, tenderly pulling her to him with a hand on her waist. She opened her eyes to see him looking at her with a look of love and wonder. He kissed her tenderly, and she responded to his gentle persistence.

"Darcy, the dress is indigo. If you are going to be painfully annoying, at least be accurate about it and make my lack of sleep worthwhile."

"I will be accurate about taking you out of this damn dress, for beautiful as it is, I would much rather see you out of it."

Quickly, potently, he kissed his wife with vigour, his hands were all over her body as he attempted to unlace the dress, Elizabeth giggling as his still-tipsy fingers fumbled over the fastening.

"There is no need to mock me, Lizzy, I am a desperate man!" Defeated, he left the lacing and fell back on the bed exasperated.

"There will be plenty of time for that later!"

She kissed him firmly so that he knew she meant it, confirming it once more by looking into those dark grey eyes that could captivate her from across a room.

"Also, dear heart, do not forget that you danced with my mother last night," she giggled, before getting out of bed and walking over the window. "I was expecting you to be more than a little delicate this morning."

The drapes were still closed, but she opened them in a dramatic move that let mid-morning sunlight spill into the room.

"Oh, oh good god in heaven, I danced a reel." He placed his head in his hands. "With your mother." He turned to face her, looking absolutely mortified. "Did Georgiana laugh?"

"Hysterically, particularly as you forgot the movement more than once," Elizabeth said. "But I suppose I will forgive you for being such a liability on the dancefloor, as you are so very good at so many other things."

Darcy attempted to pull his wife towards him, but she pushed him back on the bed, "there will be time for that later! You forget that we have guests to entertain and a full afternoon of leisurely pursuits planned – and I'm sure I can recall that you promised my mother to dance another set with her this evening after dinner."

Elizabeth disappeared into the dressing room, pulling the bell to call for Ellen, glancing back around the door frame she grinned at her husband with his tired face and ruffled hair. Darcy fell back onto the soft feather pillows and groaned. He pulled the blanket over his head and resolved never to drink again.

Two

The girl stood in the porch dwarfed by her huge suitcase. It seemed as if one wrong word would cause a waterfall of tears to cascade down her face, but she had a resilient little lip that stuck out firmly, and she held her breath, scared to make a sound in case those sad little sobs and sniffles escaped without her permission. In her hand she held Jane, stroking the golden polyester locks of her dolly as if they were rosary beads and she was absolving herself of a great sin. She didn't know where her other dollies were. Grandad Duke took her hand and squeezed it gently, leading her up the stone steps, through the big rattling door into the entrance hall and then up more stairs into the crackling, musty warmth of the drawing room. She had never been here before without Mummy, or Daddy, or Charlie. The room was dark, but the windows sparkled like jewels from a storybook. Grandad Duke passed her a cup with Vimto in it. She liked Vimto. Mummy liked Vimto too. Where was Mummy? Her lip wobbled and the cup fell to the ground with a smash.

Maggie Wickham watched the new arrival from her position on the bright gallery where she was furtively spying on the new girl. What a wild-looking thing, she thought, with her curly hair and her mismatched clothes...and she had wellies on. Yellow ones. Maggie was nearly ten and considered herself to be very grown-up indeed. She had already decided that she would look after Elizabeth Darcy, whether she wanted looking after or not, and got very cross when Winston and her mum found it funny. Jumping down from the ledge, she nudged against her little brother who was racing cars down the wooden floorboards.

"Come on, Matty," she ordered, grabbing his hand and pulling him off the floor. "Let's go and meet our new friend."

The room at the back of the house was light and airy and it had, at some point in the past, been the head housekeeper's room, although it had been the 'shop' for as long as Maggie or Lizzy could remember, Mrs Reynolds always preferring the small snug next to the estate office, from where she could see everything and get everywhere quickly. She walked over to where Lizzy was busy packing away her Lady Darcy tour information, sticking her tongue out as she concentrated on squeezing too many leaflets back into the purple plastic box.

"Here you go, your ladyship!"

She handed her a large mug of coffee emblazoned with Colin Firth's face and 'I Love Mr Darcy' on it.

"Thanks, Mags. I am absolutely parched!"

Lizzy took a large swig and grabbed her bag from behind the counter, rummaging about in its murky depths.

"If you are looking for your Jammie Dodgers my wonderful niece stole them when you were out doing a meet and greet with the Barnabus group," Maggie grinned, rearranging some guidebooks that weren't in their proper places and tidying up a display in the centre of the room.

She paused for a moment to take stock of the day; it had been the busiest of the season so far, and they had been rushed off their feet since the gates had opened. Poor Harriet had been serving afternoon tea all day in full regency costume and had suffered in the underground heat of the tearoom on this uncharacteristically hot Saturday in April.

"Don't worry though, I sent her upstairs early with two pieces of chocolate fudge cake."

"Which she will have eaten all to herself," Lizzy chastised, before posing dramatically on the ticket desk, hand swept over her face like dramatic heroine. "Nobody suffers like I do, Miss Wickham. No-one."

"Wow," Maggie said straight-faced. "And get your bum off the desk, you're meant to be setting a good example!"

"Crikey, who to? Anyone who thinks I'm a good example must be mad!"

"Well, that's what I thought…" Maggie handed her an official-looking envelope. "This arrived for you today."

Lizzy jumped down off the ticket desk and stared at the envelope, her heart pounding out of her chest. The envelope felt thick and heavy, with the official mark of the publishing house she had sent a short story to a few months before.

"Is it what you have been waiting for?"

She nodded, and ripped into the envelope, pulling out the paper and scanning the words. Her face immediately fell.

"Is it a no?"

"Thank you for your submission, but unfortunately we are not accepting new manuscripts for publication at present."

"Oh, Lizard…" Maggie reached over and took the letter. "Which story?"

"Trick of the Light."

"Well, I liked it, apart from the bit where his mum turned out to be his sister…"

"His mum wasn't his sister," she shrugged. "But if I can't get you to read it then I obviously have no chance getting an editor to read it, do I?

The walkie talkie blared from behind the counter with the code 'Oscar Isaac', Maggie took a deep breath and sighed.

'Oscar Isaac' meant that someone somewhere was very unhappy and wanted to vent their frustrations to a figure of authority. She hated dealing with guest complaints, especially when people were shouting, as they often did.

"Don't worry," Lizzy said, placing her cup down and grabbing a Pemberley postcard, "I'll go."

Relief swept throughout Maggie's whole body, she wasn't the best at dealing with any kind of confrontation, taking every criticism against Pemberley as a very personal slight.

"Are you sure?"

"Of course, you know Lady Darcy always impresses any cantankerous customer. At least it will give Joyce fewer points to poke me with," she took a final slurp of her coffee. "Don't worry, Mags. I'll sort it out."

Maggie smiled to herself, Lizzy Darcy could be about fifteen different people in one conversation, but she always so fantastically Lady Elizabeth when it mattered. She watched as Lizzy charmed the elderly lady with a serene smile and a coupon for a free cake, before taking some photos with the rest of the party, telling them information about the house, and hugging and laughing with them as if they were old friends. She could always rely on Lizzy to smooth over any guest issues with a Darcy smile and a few kind words, and she wondered what she would do if at some point in the future they weren't working together.

The moon was high in the sky as Maggie and Lizzy finished their second bottle of wine and nibbled the cold remnants of their takeaway, eating as they did on the small slope directly in front of the south front of the house – the Pemberley View, immortalised in countless paintings, pictures, and on film. It was wonderfully warm, the fragrance of the coming summer held in the air like a promise and small fairy lights, leftovers from a wedding the previous weekend, twinkled in the bushes to the right of them.

"I can't believe this is our last pizza…" Lizzy sighed, coating the final slice of thin-crust Hawaiian with garlic mayo and folding it over, the greasy sauce dribbling down her fingers.

"I hope you've enjoyed it," Maggie replied, popping a garlic mushroom in her mouth. "No more takeaway deliveries to Pemberley, it said. It doesn't work with the aesthetic!"

Lizzy sniggered, how ridiculous; she knew full well that this rule had come straight from the top, from the Boss Lady with the angry face and the strict observation of the rules.

"She should eat some pizza once in a while," she said bitchily. "Needs a little bit of fun in her life to quell the upsurge of wrinkles."

"Lizzy…" Maggie rolled her eyes, "you know she is only doing her job."

"Her job is not to boss me about though, is it?"

"Her job is to look after all of this! You need to cut her some slack occasionally."

"I don't know what Joyce's problem is. It's not like I'm going to whip my boobs out and start running through the flowerbeds."

"Are you *not?*"

"Of course not! Well, not *again* anyway…" Lizzy harrumphed. "But if she is looking for historical accuracy then every Darcy I have ever read about always thinks it's a brilliant idea to dance on the front lawn," she slurped her wine.

"I agree with you. Even Mr Darcy used to get drunk occasionally…judging by his wine ledgers anyway."

"He also looked nothing like Colin Firth."

Maggie shook her head. The portrait of the real Fitzwilliam Darcy, painted by an artist when he was in Rome, hung on the grand staircase. It showed a young man with a furrowed brow, dark eyes and a chin you could cut glass with. Whilst he wasn't an unattractive man – and Maggie secretly had a bit of a crush on him – he wasn't as handsome as casting directors wanted the public to believe.

"They still haven't moved that painting of Colin Firth from outside my front door."

"You can put it in my bedroom if you like!"

Maggie remembered the height of Darcymania, the shrine that had appeared around the portrait of the fictional Mr Darcy that Winston had convinced the production team to donate to the house.

"You will have to prise it out of Joyce's cold, dead hands, I think! That's the thing, isn't it? A book is life with the boring bits taken out, but Austen took out some of the more dramatic bits. The bits that come after the happy ending."

"Do you have proof of these dramatic bits?" Maggie asked teasingly.

"I might do."

Lizzy folded her arms, her chin jutted out and she sat on the rug, indignant, the true Darcy inheritance streaking across her face.

"Come off it, Lizzy, if there was any evidence of Darcy and Elizabeth doing anything particularly extraordinary then we would have known about it long ago."

"Not necessarily."

"All those researchers from Austenation squint over the archives every year trying to find some more information about them. The only thing they found of any interest was that Darcy spent three grand on a pineapple, which he didn't even eat!"

Lizzy loved the story of the pineapple, which had been passed down as family lore for generations, and finally confirmed by receipts, housekeeping journals and the discovery of a pewter pineapple stand in one of the rooms off the service tunnel.

"You know what," said Lizzy, still laughing. "I bet I fell asleep one-night reading Jane Austen fan fiction and got all confused. It sounds like something I would do, doesn't it?"

She got up from the rug on the lawn, collected the rubbish in the carrier bag she had brought with her, after fighting to remove it from her trouser pocket, and began the short walk back to the house.

"I'm off to Bedfordshire," she said, turning. "Goodnight, Miss Wickham."

Lizzy did a little curtsey and began laughing again, her loud, boisterous boom echoing against the sandstone walls, ricocheting down into the ravine, piercing the silence. Maggie watched as Lady Darcy stumbled towards the house, clanking the gate loudly, singing a song, finding herself hilarious. Maggie wondered if there were actually any letters at all; she grabbed her bag, slipped on her shoes and made her way through the rose garden and back to the flat above the stables.

In the topmost room of the Wyatt Tower, Lizzy sat on her bed. She reached under the metal frame finding what she was looking for. A small, engraved wooden box. She carried it gently downstairs and placed it on the coffee table. It was small, insignificant; not really something that anyone would look for, but inside were bundles and bundles of letters, fastened with a yellow ribbon, and sealed with the stamps of Mr and Mrs Darcy. She unpacked the contents carefully and laid them about before her.

Running her finger over the seal of Fitzwilliam, she could feel that the stamp still firm and assured; the bull wearing his coronet with pride, the initials FGD intertwined underneath. The metal felt cold and heavy in her hand and the wooden handle smooth and worn. She wondered how many letters he must have written, how much of his life he had committed to the page, how many times he had dripped wax onto paper and pressed down hard to seal it. She traced her finger over the seal of her namesake, the twisted metal initials 'ED' underscored by an elaborately embossed feather; the wooden handle was lost to the ages, but the stamp itself still left a mark on her skin as she pressed it deeply against her palm.

Lizzy had spent her teens reading the firmly regimented scrawl of Darcy, the curved dreamy marks of Elizabeth – all their love, all their disagreements, everything that had made their marriage work – and she had kept them safe and hidden. As she placed the letters back into the box carefully and hid it carefully in plain sight on the large oak bookcase in the front room, Lizzy knew that she was a very tiny offshoot at the end of the long branch that made up her illustrious family tree.

1780

In the late 1700s, George Frederick Darcy had remodelled the north front of his Derbyshire estate for reasons only known to himself. He had employed the services of one of the Wyatt brothers who found some of the more Elizabethan aspects of the house not exactly pleasing to his eye. George, whose wife Anne was in town and due to give birth to their first child within the next few weeks, left the venerated architect in charge.

Eight months later he returned to the county of his birth with his wife and son – a strong little boy called Fitzwilliam - to see that the bellcote which had once stood proudly atop the frontispiece had been removed and rebuilt on a small incline to the east of the house. George was now in possession of a three-story folly with a spire which Wyatt had named 'The Lantern'. His wife laughed at how remarkably in fashion they were and how she was convinced that her sister would now commission something even grander to be built in the gardens of Rosings Park.

One evening as the Darcys walked the short distance to their new garden feature, George presented his wife with the traditional gift given to each lady of the house following the successful delivery of her firstborn son. The necklace consisted of an intricate interlocking chain crafted by a local silversmith, and from it hung a pendant made of diamond and pearls. The pearls themselves were Darcy heirlooms having been in the family for at least three generations.

Although no one was exactly sure, it was Pemberley lore that these pearls had once belonged to Mary, Queen of Scots. Nobody knew the truth, the facts of which had been lost to history a long time ago, but regardless of their origin, the Darcy Pearls were an important gift to give. After the birth of a Darcy heir, three of the gems were carefully removed from the tripled-stranded necklace, remounted in gold, and encased with diamonds, before being returned to the family vault for another generation; each pendant was unique to its owner and no two were the same, each husband having the final say in the design that would best suit his wife.

Anne received her pendant with the greatest of pleasures, and the Darcys remained in the hollow folly at the top of the hill for the longest of times, until the lit beacons signalled to them that it was time to return home.

A few years later, whilst running down the hill with her son on a sticky summer night, the necklace snapped, and the pendant fell to the ground bouncing on the stones and disappearing into the meadow. Fitzwilliam fumbled around on the ground until he found it, concealed in a clump of grass. He was always very good at finding things and he handed it to his mother proudly. She ruffled his hair, before tucking it into the pocket of her dress, and taking her son by the hand as they walked the remaining distance back to Pemberley. It was only when she placed the necklace back in her jewel box that Lady Anne noticed that one of the pearls was missing, and she planned to look again the following morning. The weather broke that evening, the storm over Derbyshire lashing the ground with thick, heavy rain; the earthy smell of cold water on the warm, dry soil filling the air. The ancient pearl was absorbed into the topsoil, disappearing into the earth, falling through the cracks of time.

Over a hundred years later, a tall, fair-haired boy with a curl to the nape of his neck was digging in the soil, hiding in the grass from a girl with blue eyes who was desperately trying to find him. He rubbed the dirt off and tucked it into the pocket of his trousers for safekeeping, fully aware that he had found something rare and beautiful.

Lady Imogen Darcy dazzles in diamonds at celeb-filled Porttos launch

The reality tv star, 19, currently dating Adam Gould, 26, from reality pop band, Smash, has released her own clothing and lifestyle brand, Porttos. Lady Darcy wowed fans outside the event in a floor-length Stella McCartney gown and a sparkling Harry Winston diamond choker. The blue-blooded stunner, who is a direct descendant of Mr Darcy – played by Colin Firth in the BBC adaptation – oversaw the glittering launch at The Dorchester in London's swanky Mayfair. Lady Imogen, daughter of the Duke of Derbyshire posted pictures of the party on her Instagram @ladyimogenoflondon, where she has over 5 million followers. She captioned '*I am so excited for the new Duchess range launching TOMORROW on my website! I hope you are all as excited as I am.*' Porttos will be available in John Lewis stores nationwide from November.

Three

The late spring sunshine was beating through the tin roof of the sports hall. Harriet yawned widely, she was now three-quarters of the way through the GCSE Maths paper and fully aware that she was failing wildly. She was glad that her mum had chosen to send her to Lambton High, a small average comprehensive school with middling exam results and a toadying headteacher, rather than the boarding school in Hertfordshire that her grandad had offered to pay for, although she always wondered what it would have been like to wear a straw boater and play lacrosse.

"Pens down."

There was a collective sigh from her year group and the immediate scraping of chairs along the floor and she sighed with… *relief*, maybe? Or maybe just the thrill of escape. It was her last exam and now she was free, from school at least. Collecting her phone from the plastic tray held by a tight-mouthed invigilator she switched it on, taking a minute to wave to Summer, who rolled her eyes from across the room, tossed her blonde curls and gestured that she would meet her outside. The phone beeped four times:

Mum
Mum
Mum
Dad.

Dad? She sent her mum a quick confirmation text and made a mental note to reply to her dad later, before walking down the school corridor and out into the amazing freshness of the May afternoon.

Lambton's newest coffee shop 'Lydia Teapot' looked out onto the main road through town, where a row of shops stood squished together vying for trade with their quirky signs and inviting windows. A collection of Darcy themed gift shops were neighbours with Fitzwilliam's, Pembertea and Miss Bennet's Emporium being the most popular. Harriet watched the latest coachload of visitors venturing in and out, gathering an ever-increasing collection of printed paper bags as they did so. Summer languished on the squishy sofa in small café, her legs thrown casually over Harriet's, whilst Caitlyn sat opposite sucking on the unyielding straw of a decadently syrupy iced latte. Harriet munched on a brownie, enjoying each mouthful as she licked the chocolate off her fingers, much to Summer's disgust.

"My mum agrees with you anyway," Summer admitted, her blonde curls spreading over the couch arm. "But she thinks it's messed up that you fancy your grandad."

Caitlin snorted. Harriet's obsession with Mr Darcy was very strange, especially considering that they were related.

"I don't fancy him," Harriet retorted adamantly. "I admire him!"

"Admire his Regency bulge!" Summer blurted, looking at Caitlin as they burst into laughter.

Harriet blushed; she didn't have a crush on Mr Darcy, but she supposed it was a bit odd. Fitzwilliam Darcy was such an imposing figure at Pemberley that you couldn't help being a little bit in awe of him, and that stupid portrait of Colin Firth in the hallway outside the flat, 'for storage' Joyce had said, but it had been there since she started high school. She supposed that it was a little weird that sometimes when she needed advice, she would air her thoughts and feelings to her imagined ancestor, standing on the top landing corridor and looking for answers in the handsome face, as he stood to attention in his oil-painted glory.

"Anyway, my mum said that Matthew Macfadyen is the better Darcy, from the looks point of view at least," Summer continued.

Summer's mum, Moira Sinclair, loved her daughter being friends with Harriet, always inviting Lady Elizabeth round for gin and cake under the pretence of organising things for the girls, and then posting it on Facebook. Aunt Sybil thought of her as the worst type of social climber; rather like the Delanceys, who she also vehemently disliked, telling her great-niece her opinions on the subject frequently.

"My mum likes Matthew Rhys," Caitlin chipped in, "she likes how shouty he is."

"Well," Harriet began, and her friends both groaned.

"No, we don't need to hear about historical inaccuracies again! Matthew Rhys is a *brilliant* Darcy, but the argument is between Firth and Macfadyen," said Caitlyn firmly.

"You can't discount Firth because he's old now," Summer said, "he wasn't old then, and they did actually film it at Pemberley, and not bloody Chatsworth."

Harriet nodded in agreement and took the Frappuccino off Summer, slurping a large icy mouthful, "my Grandad Duke gets really cross about it, and my mum thinks Winston spins in his grave every time we watch the 2005 version."

"I like Chatsworth," Caitlin stated a little unsurely and found herself immediately glared at by the other two. "What?" She cried defensively, "they have a really good shop... and, y'know..."

"Traitor!" Harriet said in a sinister tone.

Summer leaned over to thwack Caitlin with a magazine.

"You deserve that!"

The rivalry between the two great families of Derbyshire had been ongoing for centuries, when previous Dukes had become embroiled in a dispute over the red deer herd, and it had been the ultimate betrayal when Chatsworth had been chosen twice over Pemberley itself to portray the great Darcy estate.

"Shush," Harriet said firmly, "okay, so we're going with Firth then?"

"Shouldn't we wait and see what Benn Williams is like before we make any final decisions?"

Caitlyn thought that out of all the actors she liked him the best, especially seeing as they could probably meet him in real life.

"Ugh," Summer shuddered. "He's old enough to be your dad, Cat, don't be so grim."

Summer had already decided that Colin Firth's wet-shirted Darcy was going to win, she just needed to convince everyone else that it was their idea.

"So, Harry, we've decided on Firth yeah? My mum keeps going on and on about it so she can order the cake toppers off Etsy or whatever."

"Wait!" Caitlyn exclaimed as if she had been stuck with a pin, "what about the Zombies Darcy? He counts too!"

"Bugger off!" Summer shrieked. "Even I know that Zombies Darcy doesn't count, regardless of how good with a sword he is."

She said goodbye to Summer and Caitlyn with a multitude of hugs, even though they would be snapchatting all the way home and meeting in town the following morning, before climbing into the car, passing her mum the skinny latte that acted as payment for the journey home. It was only a short journey from Lambton to home, but there was no bus stop outside Pemberley, and Harriet found that she had to rely on either

her mum's good nature or guilty conscience for a lift, or else it was a long trek up the driveway.

Lizzy pulled up outside the main gate punching in the entry code. The car was emblazoned with 'Pemberley Estates' and the shiny gold crest of the Darcy family. She had managed to coerce Donald, the grumbly groundskeeper who lived at the main gatehouse into letting her borrow it on the proviso that she left it tidy. Her own ancient Mini had been slowly deteriorating over the past few months and she was getting tired of it deciding to strand her halfway down the main drive when the engine would fail and refuse to sputter back to life. She had found herself in trouble during the weekend of Mr Darcy's Regency Christmas when the car, loaded with Christmas shopping, had stopped dead at the ticketing kiosk, holding up the three coaches and stream of visitors who were desperate to see local actors re-enact scenes from Pride and Prejudice, whilst eating millefruit biscuits recreated from a recipe that had been found in the archives.

The car shimmied and dipped over each bump in the mile-long road, as they passed over the bridge and jolted over the cattle grid, before settling onto the long, grand sweep of the drive. The flag was flying on top of the Cage, signalling it was open, and a few straggling visitors were slowly making their way down from the hunting lodge, the bright colours of their jackets and wellies popping against the subdued spring hues of the ancient deer park.

"How did it go?"

"Maths, innit," Harriet sighed. "It just has to be a C."

"It just *has to be a C*?"

One eyebrow was raised; Harriet groaned, she wasn't in the mood for one of her mum's lectures about grades.

"*Yes*, Mum! I only need a C for AS Levels, you know this."

She sighed loudly and focused her attention on the constantly flashing phone in her hand, before turning the radio station over even though it was the middle of Women's Hour.

"Oh, Dad said to tell you that he's home this weekend."

Harriet noticed the change in her mum's mood immediately and, somewhat wisely, changed the radio station back to Women's Hour. They pulled up at the north front gate, parking the car in Donald's signposted space where he would collect it later. Walking silently together under the gateway and around the circular outer courtyard, Harriet nudged herself into Lizzy's shoulder and the two Darcy ladies hurried inside for a Netflix binge, a microwave biryani and copious amounts of chocolate cake.

1811

It was a fine evening when Mrs Bennet was informed by her eldest daughter that she was to become a grandmother. This news had been all she had hoped for in the months since she had seen her two oldest daughters married. Secretly, she did not think it would be too much longer before Lizzy would be making her own announcement and she looked forward to the days when she could pronounce the birth of the heir of Pemberley to the captive audience of ladies in Meryton. She was so fortunate to have two daughters so fortuitously wed and Lydia... well, Lydia would be alright, she would make her own way as she always had. The mistress of Longbourn fell back into the warm bed in the turquoise bedroom and congratulated herself on a job well done.

Jane Bingley was first to rise that morning. It had been the same every day for the last few months, up with the crow and vomiting into her chamber pot. She felt guilty, as the poor maid who had taken it away to empty it each morning also visibly retched. The young girl was no older than her sister, Lydia, and yet their lives would have been markedly different. Mrs Wickham was now happily ensconced with a regiment in Newcastle, where she was able to flirt with officers and make a fool of herself with little embarrassment or negative reflection on her family. There was inevitably requests for money, but the older Bennet girls had obliged their younger sister – who was unable to manage a budget or her husband – with occasional gifts from their own purses. The Wickhams were not welcome at Pemberley and, despite the protestations of both Lydia and her mother, an invite to the ball had not been forthcoming.

Charles Bingley knew that his wife was bearing the brunt of this pregnancy in her amicable way, but for the most part, she was putting on a brave show of it. For the last few months, she had been sicker than he expected, and he hoped that her nausea would soon abate so that she could enjoy her bloom. Jane caught glimpse of his worried face as she turned around on the bed and then settled back into the warmth of the sheets, gently kissing his brow to allay any worries. He returned her embrace, and the Bingleys settled back into their slumber, aware that the residents of Pemberley would probably not be rising until noon.

Mrs Reynolds was always a flurry of nerves in the week leading up to the Lady Anne's Ball; it was a massive undertaking, even for an experienced woman such as herself, and that morning she congratulated herself with a small glass of port from Staughton's cupboard and prepared to thank her staff for a job well done. Mrs Darcy had looked beautiful and acted with all the grace and decorum of a lady with twice her breeding. Of course, the Darcy's housekeeper had been aware months before the official engagement announcement that her master had a predilection for this Hertfordshire Miss, her impromptu visit a few summers earlier had sparked something in Fitzwilliam Darcy that Mrs Reynolds had not seen before, and she had wondered how long it would take before Elizabeth Bennet returned to Pemberley as his wife. Now as the evening of the Lady Anne's Ball had passed without setback or drama, Mrs Reynolds helped herself to a leftover biscuit and rested her feet for a while whilst her kitchen staff busied themselves with preparing breakfast for the waking guests.

Elizabeth was frustrated. Her dress fit most ill, even with lacing, it looked wrong. She was annoyed as the daring crimson morning dress that she had chosen for the post-ball lunch had been her absolute favourite item this season, and she had been looking forward to wearing it since the first appointment with her dressmaker in town. Money was no longer an object for Elizabeth, as the mistress of Pemberley it was expected that she would have the best gowns in the finest fabrics, but ever the country gentleman's daughter, she had stuck close to her budget and used fabric that she had found in her new home, hidden away in the crates and trunks that Darcy had brought back from the continent after his Grand Tour. The sheer, shimmery fabric, interwoven with a thin, delicate gold thread in patterns of diamonds and flowers, was spectacular.

She knew that Caroline Bingley would make a derisive comment about the dress, but it did not matter, for she would not be wearing it for the unappreciative glances of society ladies, but the admiring glances full of longing that her husband would direct across the table. Darcy loved her in bold colours, and red was his particular favourite. But the gown did not fit – not even slightly. Ellen pulled out the new dress that had arrived last week, a replacement for the one still bearing the indigo battle-wounds of preparing for the ball, Darcy would have to settle for his wife in yellow this morning. But if time and guests permitted, she thought, he might be persuaded to take her out of it that afternoon.

A few of the larger State Rooms were still closed off as Darcy's elaborate restorations took place, so Elizabeth found herself taking a shortcut down through the servants' staircase, saying hello to Betsy – one of the younger maids - before crossing the courtyard and entering again through the front door.   As she traipsed across the house, Elizabeth acknowledged to herself that she had been walking a lot less now she lived on the estate. She could not simply march the five miles to Lambton through the endless rolling hills that surrounded her new home, and even though she and Darcy had walked the twelve miles to Kympton a few months back, she had to admit to herself that her lack of exercise, coupled with the vast array of new and delicious foods had probably contributed to her expanding waistline. Never to mind, she would wear the dress soon enough.

Darcy found his wife's father in the library that afternoon, sipping on coffee and eating Prince of Wales biscuits leftover from the night before. He wondered if it would have been more pleasing to Mr Bennet to place his bed in the library for the duration of his stay as the gentleman was found in here more often than elsewhere, preferring to eschew the typical country pursuits for a comfortable afternoon spent with Marlowe or Keats.

"Darcy," said Mr Bennet, as he took a bite of his biscuit. "How are you feeling this morning? Sore feet?"

The humour of the situation was not lost on the congenial host, who laughed gently to himself before pouring a cup of coffee and joining his father in law in front of the fire.

"I have been informed by your most amused daughter that I may have filled your wife's dance card toward the end of the evening."

"You most certainly did, and most appreciated it was," Mr Bennet poured himself another cup of coffee from pot engraved with the intertwined initials of his daughter and her husband. "Why, the problematic issue of taking a wife who is decidedly younger than oneself, is that one often does not wish to dance, whilst one's spouse does. This can cause a veritable cacophony of dramatics, where a gentleman is forced to choose between a display of nerves or a show of vexation. Indeed, Fitzwilliam, I find that often it is easier to escape the whole situation entirely and leave the dancing to the younger generation."

Mr Bennet raised his eyebrow at his son by marriage and smiled wryly. Darcy found that it was the exact same mannerism that Elizabeth displayed when she was teasing him, and it pleased him that his relationship with her father had reached a level of intimacy where this could be enjoyed. As much as Darcy had found Mr Bennet's parenting skills lacking somewhat, he hoped that he would have the same easy-going bond with his own children when the time came, although any Darcy offspring would, unquestionably, be reared with a slightly firmer hand than the Bennet sisters had been.

The Darcys and their visitors enjoyed a long and leisurely afternoon, with the gentlemen taking to the lake for fishing, whilst the ladies enjoyed a meander around the gardens before Elizabeth and Georgiana took out a phaeton and ponies for a jaunt around the grounds. Jane retired indoors, not wanting to risk the high-speed trip around the park, and her sour-faced sister, Caroline, joined her.

Miss Bingley was preparing for her wedding, due to take place the following month. Her betrothed was a noble, if impoverished, Scottish laird, and she would be spending winter in Edinburgh before taking up residence in a remote highland castle. Caroline did feel apprehension regarding the move, she would be so far removed from all of her friends and relations, and whilst she would be elevated to the ranks of Scottish aristocracy and become Lady Caroline Dalhousie, she was not entirely convinced that she would be able to persuade Lord Dalhousie to relocate to London on a more permanent basis and was struggling with the thought that she would be confined within a very small society for lengthy periods of time.

Either way, Christopher Dalhousie's estate, and title held much more prestige for Caroline than she would have ever attained by marrying miserable Fitzwilliam Darcy and being shackled to Derbyshire for the rest of her life. She had done well indeed, and the next time she found herself invited to Pemberley she would expect the proper deference due to her rank and the second-best bedroom.

Elizabeth made her excuses at supper that evening and returned to her rooms early. She didn't know if it was the exertions of the day, the heat of the summer night or the long hours that she had been keeping of late, but she felt exhausted and despite knowing it was bad form to leave her guests without the presence of their hostess, she knew it would be even worse if she fell asleep in the soup.

As she walked through the house, Elizabeth gradually realised the reasons for her ills and thought herself hare-brained indeed. Back in her rooms, the yellow and gold suite that had once belonged to the Lady Anne herself, she unbuttoned her gown and stood to look at herself in the mirror. She noticed the change in her body, a rounding of her hip, a fullness of her bosom – how could she have been so blind, how could she have not realised!

There was a quiet knock on the door before it opened, and her husband appeared with a slice of pie.

"Darcy," she said warmly, before taking the plate from him. "Did we spend so much on the ball that we no-longer have servants?"

"Well, if the lady of the house refrained from promising pineapples to all and sundry then maybe I could have asked a servant to bring you refreshment." He pulled her towards him, "although I must admit that visiting your rooms does have additional benefits."

Darcy kissed his wife gently on her neck, breathing in the smell of her. She smelled like soap, and warmth, and home.

"Here, take a bite of your pie – it's very good, in fact, I might even go back to our guests and have some more."

She laughed at his teasing, and then obliged his request, taking a seat on the chair next to her dressing table. Dressed in her chemise and robe, and with her hair unpinned, she looked positively radiant. He felt a rush of sudden desire for her.

"My dearest," she started, keeping him at arm's length. "I have something to tell you."

Her face was serious, and a wave of nauseous anxiety passed over him.

"Lizzy?"

She stood up and walked towards him slowly, her gaze never wavering.

"Elizabeth, what is wrong?"

"We may need to make different plans for these next few months hence."

She took his hand in her own, and kissed it, before gently placing it on her slightly rounded belly.

The slow build-up had been worth the exquisite pay-off – Darcy's face was incredulous, and as he processed the words, the realisation of the news spread all over his face, resting on his lips in the biggest smile. He pulled his wife into his arms and kissed her all over her face, before holding her in front of him, looking down at her belly again, and embracing her.

This was the most amazing news that Fitzwilliam Darcy had ever received in his entire life. He was going to be a father. Daddy. Papa. Yes, he would be Papa. He was going to be all these things to this little miracle of life that they had created between them. The Darcys held each other for a long time that evening, talking, kissing and laughing until the sun emerged over the horizon of the Cage once more.

Four

Lizzy walked into the party taking place in her backyard, she was wearing a black top, bright red cardigan and an amazing printed vintage skirt. With her mother's Darcy Pearls pendant adorning her neck and her hair tied up with a relatively fashionable printed scarf, she felt that she would be able to hold her own in this party full of off-duty starlets and B-list actors.

She wasn't exactly sure who had managed to convince Joyce to hang fairy lights from the gallery windows on each side, but she was glad they had, as it had resulted in an electric constellation lighting up the sky above the courtyard. The whole house felt alive with people, and she loved it when Pemberley was like this. It made her think of Cecily Darcy's infamous Edwardian house parties and how vibrant the house would have been filled with people, music pouring out of every window and every room ablaze with illumination.

Her brother Charlie was already here, braying in the corner with his terrible public-school hoo-ha and a group of his friends from the City, who were all double-barrelled Tories; Aunty Julia, who had been in and out of rehab so many times that everyone had lost count, was chatting animatedly to a stocky member of crew, and the current Duchess, her step mum Carol, who was being feted by the assistant producer, Phil, and loving every minute of it. He called her 'Your Grace' at every possible opportunity and she giggled with flirtatious glee.

Maggie was on duty tonight, answering questions about the house to some random members of the Press who had been invited for advance publicity, Lizzy waved to her and she waved back subtly, whilst explaining something to an excited Japanese journalist. Tottering across the checkerboard tiles of the courtyard in a pair of super-high heels that she had indulgently ordered the night before, she made her way to the bar, which was hidden away in the cloisters. If she had to deal with her stepmother, she would need the copious amounts of free alcohol on offer.

Benn Williams skulked in the corner, drinking his San Pellegrino and looking nothing like Mr Darcy. He had recently grown a beard for a three-week run of 'Our Country's Good' at the West Yorkshire Playhouse, where he had been wracked with nerves each night and required two shots of vodka before he could even step foot on stage. He hadn't shaved it off yet as he discovered it gave him a certain level of anonymity that he found comforting. It was, he thought, quite method of him to be playing Mr Darcy and standing around looking disagreeable at a party and, even though this wasn't any part of his preparation technique, it was the reason he would tell any journalists if they asked.

He would rather have been watching television in the comfort of his hotel room than spending another minute making conversation with over-familiar crew members who he vaguely remembered or pretending to be interested in the vague stories being told by the twenty-year-old actresses, who he was acutely aware should be playing his daughters rather than his love interests. Walking over to the buffet, he hoped for a cheese scone or a bit of cake but was handed a small plate with chicken and some cucumber. 'We can't have a flabby Darcy', he had been told, and the studio had shipped black boxes full of pre-prepared meals, and an aggressive personal trainer to his hotel to hone his 'dad-bod' into something more androgynously sexy in breeches.

"You should try a cheese scone," came a small voice.

He saw a face he didn't immediately recognise.

"I beg your pardon," he said in a stately manner, whilst thinking that this Darcy thing was going to be easier than he thought.

"The cheese scones. They are really good."

As if to prove a point, she picked up the savoury, sliced it in half, smeared it with chutney and placed half back on his plate. He looked at it, with a look that he knew was dripping with disdain, then slowly removed it and placed it back on the table.

"I can't eat that."

He didn't mean for it to sound like he said it with a sneer, but that's how it came out and whilst he immediately regretted it, he knew full well that the sneer was now across his face. She had a quizzical expression on her face as if she couldn't quite understand what his problem was.

"Harriet," another voice chastised. "Leave Mr Williams alone, he's probably not allowed any carbs for the next three months!"

He glanced over to see a face he instantly recognised, Lady Elizabeth Darcy, dressed as what he assumed was some kind of homeless Frida Kahlo tribute – the aristocracy were always a bit barmy, born with silver spoons in the mouths and sticks up their arses. He recognised the girl now as little Harriet, Matthew's daughter – he hadn't seen her for a while, the last time was about three years ago if he could remember correctly. His memory was getting worse.

"Harriet! Of course, I remember you now. You were on set with your dad for Wuthering Heights."

"Yes! That was me."

Her face lit up and he swore she did a little dance at the recognition.

"Yes," he grinned, returning the smile. "Did we take some selfies?"

"Yes! Yes, we did… and then I tagged you in them and you commented on my Instagram!"

"That's right," he agreed "I remember."

He didn't want to tell her that he had a social media person who posted and tweeted on everything on his behalf and that he didn't even know the login for his Instagram account, let alone how to comment on anything.

"I knew you would! I'm working on set tomorrow, so I will see you then, Benn."

Harriet shot her mother a look tinged with smugness, and then walked off towards a gaggle of girls who he guessed were her friends. They all grouped together before turning around in unison to look at him, giggling before walking off under the main gate to the forecourt.

"I am sorry about that. I'm Lizzy, by the way," she said, holding out her hand, which he shook reluctantly.

"Yes," he said. "I know who you are."

"I did ask her to leave you alone, but she was helping out the catering team in the house this morning and feels somewhat personally responsible for the cheesiness of the scones."

The first thing she noticed was his height – much taller than she thought he would have been, and broad, but in a way that she could imagine him picking her up and carrying her over a threshold, not that she wanted him to carry her over a threshold, it was an observation, nothing more.

He smelled of a familiar cologne that she couldn't quite place, and freshly washed clothes, and there was a hint of minty freshness about him. His sideburns were puffy and blonder than she thought they would be, and his beard was not a good look, even though she could tell he had really tried with it. She pondered asking him for a picture to show Deb but decided that it would be very uncool. He sipped his water and she drank her 'Mr Collins' – a cocktail thought up by the production team and consisting of rhubarb gin, lime, and soda – through a straw.

Benn could feel her looking at him as they stood in awkward silence, and he tried to avoid accidentally catching her eye by looking out into the crowd. He gazed out onto the small gathering grouped around the courtyard; over by the bar, languishing handsomely, stood Franklin Hughes, an incredibly posh and well-spoken actor who had only recently graduated from RADA and would be taking the role of Bingley – they had screen-tested together well and the rehearsals in London had helped him to build up a rapport with the man who was fifteen years his junior. He noticed that Matthew Wickham was sitting on the steps that led up to the front door of the house, chatting to Harriet and her three friends who were too excited to listen to anything he had to say; their eyes darting around the courtyard searching for anyone even slightly more exciting. This was his fifth time working with Matthew in some capacity or another, but the first time that he felt like an outsider.

"The actress playing Jane is really good, I saw her in a play in London a few years ago."

"Nancy? Yes, I worked with her on Shellstone."

"Oh."

"Tamsin over there," he gestured towards the tiny blonde actress. "They just killed her off on Casualty."

"The one on the escalator? Ugh, that terrified me!"

"Me too."

He felt himself soften a little bit, felt the tension in his whole body relax. Since watching it the thought of the incredibly long escalator at Angel tube station had made his stomach turn a little and he avoided it as much as possible.

They watched the group of Bennets who were dancing and doing shots wearing tight jeans paired with big hair, swaying along to the music and calling out whenever someone they vaguely recognised walked past.

"You were right," he said, finally deciding on what to say. "I'm on a carb ban until my trousers fit."

"Well, for what it's worth, I think that you would look rather dapper in a pair of breeches just as you are." She took a massive bite of the chutneyed and abandoned cheese scone, "and I can tell that you are very jealous of me and my scone right now," pieces of the pastry tumbling from her hand and falling to the paving stones.

He gave her a once-over whilst sipping on his Pellegrino.

"I think most people could benefit from a carb ban every once in a while, don't you? Cleansing."

She pretended to ignore the sly dig but pulled down the back of her dress self-consciously anyway. There was another moment of awkward silence, as they both watched the party cranking to life, the laughter and giggles of strangers intimately thrown together for a concentrated period of time.

"Do you enjoy working on period dramas?" She asked as she sucked up the last remnants of gin through the end of the pink straw.

He nodded never averting his gaze from the crowd.

"Occasionally."

"You were rather good as Heathcliff, I must admit."

He nodded again, saying nothing.

"I'm really looking forward to seeing what you do with Fitzwilliam, he is –"

"Lady Elizabeth," he said somewhat contemptibly, staring at her as if she were the offensive cheese scone. "I know full well who Fitzwilliam Darcy is and his connection to you."

Leaving his plate on the table he walked away, just as Matthew started his speech and called for the presence of Mr Darcy to the sound of cheers and claps from the party guests. He disappeared into the gardens, ignoring the shouts to come up on stage; his absence soon forgotten after a drunken gaffer shouted out.

"His diet pills haven given him the shits – he's on the bog."

Lizzy didn't understand why he felt the need to act so very rudely, but she did see the almost unnoticeable shard of sadness that momentarily crossed his face as he retreated, and she began to think that maybe he was simply misunderstood.

"Lizzy, how the devil are you, old girl?" Charlie grabbed her in his embrace and gave her the biggest hug, practically lifting her off the tiled floor. "I say, it has been a bloody long time since I have seen you outside of weddings and funerals."

"I know, I miss you!"

She genuinely had. Despite growing up in different parts of the country, they had always kept in touch via letters and phone calls, then emails and IM, before it became Skype and WhatsApp – Winston had always made sure they visited Charlie on St Andrews Day at Eton, and he always made sure that he gave her the pre-requisite birthday punches that he owed her from the month before. She kept her arm wrapped around him, as they walked over to the bar.

"Have you not brought Emma with you?"

"No, of course not, she is at a retreat in Geneva with Mufty and Portia, and then she is off to Norway for a few weeks."

He swigged at his whiskey, waving at a pointy looking red-haired girl with a sour look on her face, before handing her a large glass of something pink as they squeezed past some baby-faced ingenues and a few faces she recognised from past productions.

"She will back for a fortnight before the boys are back at school and then we're all off to the villa to stay with Dad." They pushed past people trying to make their way from the bar, "are you and Harry coming too?"

"Yes, of course," Lizzy laughed, "we're always there for the last two weeks of summer. Idiot." She rolled her eyes at him, "How's Imogen been?"

"Back in rehab, not sure what for. Dad has managed to keep it all out of the press so that's a relief," Charlie downed his whiskey, "he just doesn't want her to end up like Aunty Julia."

"How many husbands now?"

"Four. The latest is some Count from Bordeaux."

"After her money, obviously?"

"They always are. She's done more for European relations than the EU."

"At least they don't write about her in the papers anymore, not now they have Imogen to gossip about."

The older Darcy siblings had always been publicity-shy, never truly understanding their little sister's desire to always be in the spotlight, and she became a frequent topic of conversation between them.

"Promise me you will come to town soon. I want you to come and see the boys. It all would have been so much easier if you had married that chap from the City and moved into the old house like you wanted to, I could have seen you so much more if you were in Chelsea."

"You could see me plenty if you ever answered my FaceTime calls. Besides which, don't you see enough of everyone else?"

"I do, but it's not the same, is it? We're the originals, me and you. Joe and Imogen are good kids, but they're kids, they never spent time at Pemberley as we did. They don't get it."

"No, they don't."

They walked under the porch, sitting on the stone seats, gazing down the driveway. The view never changed; to the right were the majestic Victorian stables with their squeaking weathervane, to the left the formal gardens were gated off and suitably stately, straight-ahead lay the Cage, the deer herd, and the way out. Still the same as when they were children, it had been here that they waited for Winston to bring

out kites in the early bluster of autumn before Charlie went back to
school, or in the long, hot summers when Mrs Reynolds would carry
trays of clinking glasses filled with ice and lemonade.

"I took the flowers for Mum," he said. "The ones from Dad were
already there. Roses, as usual. It looked nice, as nice as it can look, I
guess."

"Thank you for doing that."

She snuggled into her older brother, remembering all the times
when
they had held each other close, how much she missed him.

"I'm starting to forget her," she said.

"I'll help you remember if you want," a tenderness in his voice as
he put his arm around her shoulder, pulling her cardigan in tight against
the cool breeze sneaking through from over the moorlands.

"Old enough to not quite remember, but not small enough to
forget."

"You were very little, Lizard."

Once again, it was as if they were small children, motherless and
alone, clinging to each other in confusion, where he had plastered on
his public-school bravado and put on a brave face for his little sister. It
was what a Darcy did, he was told, so he never really stopped, except
for moments like this when he felt that he could.

"Right, Lady Liz, enough of this. Let's go and get you a massive
cocktail!"

"Sounds like a plan, Lord Darcy. Nobody loves a free bar more
than a member of the aristocracy, especially impoverished ones who live
'above the shop'."

"Quite rightly! Speaking of which, is the esteemed Duchess drunk
yet?"

"Leathered."

"How wonderful, I hope Dad has booked her a car because she
isn't sharing mine."

"Where *is* Dad? Did he not fancy it?"

"An evening with Carol? Not likely!"

Inside the courtyard, she could see Matthew talking to Benn
Williams, who has reappeared and looked furious. He gestured in her
general direction causing Matthew to look at her somewhat angrily.
Lizzy felt annoyed at this hostile move, but inside her head, she laughed
it off. Silly arrogant man, she thought, before taking her brother by the
hand and returning to the dancing, laughter, and singing.

1811

The last month of the year was passing in a flurry of excitement and activity, with Mr, Mrs, and Miss Darcy eagerly anticipating playing host to their greatly extended family. This was Elizabeth's second Christmas as Mrs Darcy, the first spent away in the Lake country in a blissful honeymoon state, where the newlyweds had little regard for any festivities apart from each other. However, this year was different, and Darcy was determined to make Elizabeth's Christmas at Pemberley a most joyful occasion, especially as the birth of their first child was imminent. For Georgiana this would be her own first Christmas spent in the embrace of her new family, and she was excited to spend time with people her own age, as well as those that she truly loved.

The Bennets, including Kitty and Mary, who had recently become engaged to a well-spoken, well-read pastor from Kent, were to arrive on the twentieth, with the Bingleys arriving a few days later. Charles and Jane had spent the last few months busy with introducing their new daughter to relatives far and wide, and everyone who met the strawberry-blonde haired babe declared her as beautiful as her mother and as affable as her father.

Jane found that she enjoyed motherhood and could not think of a time when her days had been better spent, Lydia wrote to her second eldest sister to say that she had never seen Mrs Bingley look so well and it made Elizabeth ache for the arrival of her favourite sister. The Darcys were yet to meet little Charlotte Bingley and, despite letters being sent and received almost daily, Elizabeth and Darcy were both eager to see their new niece in the flesh.

Fitzwilliam had taken it upon himself to supervise the preparations for the Christmas feast, as he did not want to place any undue strain on his wife. He had spent most of the last eight months fruitlessly trying to convince her to rest, which had forced Elizabeth to call Dr Jeffries who confirmed that walking, and lots of it, was good exercise for the mother-to-be and would also help with an easy birth. Elizabeth did not like to be still, he found.

"Mrs Darcy," he enquired as he watched her marching down the courtyard steps with an easel in the early months of October. "Where on earth are you going? Pray, let Stewart or Owens take that for you..."

He tried to take the structure and the accompanying paintbox from her but found that she resisted with a strength he had not witnessed before.

"Mr Darcy," she scolded. "I am not an invalid, there is no requirement to treat me as such."

"Elizabeth," he said, as the under-butler came scurrying over to take the offending equipment. "I do not suggest that I merely ask that you exercise caution due to your condition."

"I understand that Fitzwilliam, but surely I am able to manage a short walk up Cage Hill to take in the bracing air. If you insist, I will allow Owens to carry the easel, but you must not worry as much."

Darcy looked down at his wife, she stood a head height shorter than him and later, when they were safely ensconced in the privacy of their rooms, he would pull her into his arms and the shape of her would fit perfectly into him; the babe a burgeoning wonder between them. But for now, under the gaze of their servants, he would look at her knowingly, a smile playing on his lips.

"Wife of mine, you will surely be the death of me..."

"Maybe," said she. "But what a blessed life we would have had."

Elizabeth turned on her heel, the sound of cotton and muslin swishing as she swept across the courtyard, the feathers on her bonnet blowing gently in the breeze as Owens struggled to keep up.

"Mr Darcy, Sir, would you like to try the millefruit biscuits before we box them up?"

Mrs Reynolds gestured at the decadent, fruit jewelled biscuits that she was holding on the tray in front of him.   Darcy could smell cinnamon and cloves, the rich, sweetened smell taking him immediately back to childhood. He remembered vividly sitting in this same room as a small boy, cuddled up on his mother's lap as she read stories to him in her gentle, melodic voice, stroking his dark brown curls until he fell asleep sated, content and safe.

"They were your mother's favourite if I remember..."

"Yes," he nodded. "Yes, they were."

Mrs Reynolds studied the gentleman before her, she had known him since his childhood and knew that he felt the loss of his mother most keenly during this season.

"Forgive me if I speak out of turn, Mr Darcy," she said hesitantly. "But I understand why you are nervous about the next few weeks."

Darcy glanced up at the woman who had cared for him in those dark days after his mother's death and gestured for her to sit, which she did before continuing.

"Sir," she uttered softly. "What happened with your mother was very rare, and very quick. There was nothing that could have been done that your father did not do, he would have moved heaven if he could have brought her back."

"Mrs Reynolds, I am..." he started before biting his lip and rethinking. "I am aware that childbirth is a risky, yet necessary event."

Darcy's statement tried to disguise his inexperience; his only knowledge taken from the day that Georgiana had been born. He had been twelve years old and the sounds and cries from his mother's chambers had terrified him. He had gained a sister that day, but his dearest Mama was gone.

"I cannot promise you that everything will be alright with this birth, Mr Darcy, but the mistress is strong, and you have ensured that she has received the best care." She paused for a moment, trying to make him look to the future, rather than remember the past. "What I can assure you is our new young master or mistress will be so spoiled by the whole of Pemberley, as we are all of us so eager to have children in the house again."

She tentatively placed her hand on his knee, he covered it in his own and held it for a moment. It was a comfort. Darcy was unable to explain his underlying anguish to Elizabeth, nor was he able to disguise it from her, which meant that she had believed him to be in a foul mood for the past few months. He could not explain to her that he was filled with the insurmountable dread that in the act of bringing their child into the world, she would be taken out of it

"Thank you, Mrs Reynolds," he said quietly. "Your words have been much appreciated."

"You're welcome, Mr Darcy," her voice was reassuring and as she stood, she comfortingly placed her hand on his shoulder. "Now, I think it's time for tea."

Elizabeth listened to her remarkably accomplished sister practice for the Pemberley tradition of carol singing on Christmas Eve, the drawing room fire was ablaze, and the room filled with servants decorating. She had been watching the preparations all day and felt exhausted at the observations. Greenery and foliage had been being prepared in the courtyard to be brought in on the twenty-fourth, whilst the smells of spiced fruits and sweet delicacies hung in the air, the drawing room had been dressed in holly, ivy, and mistletoe, and all around there was a feeling of merriment and festivity. Pemberley was getting ready to welcome guests and even though she was cumbersome with child, Elizabeth was just as excited.

"Lizzy, would you like to join me in a duet? It will sound better if you play with me," Georgiana stated boldly.

"Georgie, you know as well as I that I will play the wrong notes and then try to cover them up," Lizzy grinned, as she walked over the pianoforte to look through the sheet music. "When one has four sisters it is a rare thing indeed to be able to practice as much as one would wish."

"If I had many sisters as you, Elizabeth, then I would never have practiced at all! There is something very lonely about being the only child in a house such as this," Georgiana paused reflectively. "You must promise to have a whole host of little Darcy children to fill these rooms with laughter."

"I think I should probably concentrate my efforts on this one first before making any plans for further additions."

She placed her hand on her belly, now large enough to prevent her from getting into the bath without assistance or fasten her boots by herself. Georgina observed her as she wobbled uncomfortably on the chair, a hesitant question on her lips.

"Can I touch it? Is that odd…can I ask that or am I being terribly rude?"

Her brow creased in the same way that Darcy's did, Elizabeth noticed. Surprising how two people could be so similar and different at the same time.

"No, of course it's not odd – it's perfectly normal, in fact," Elizabeth reassured the younger woman, taking her hand in her own and laying her palm flat on the most prominent part of the baby bump, "if we press here very gently, I think we will disturb him, and he may say hello."

Almost on cue, the youngest Darcy responded from inside the womb with a firm kick. Georgiana pulled her hand back, shocked by the gentle force.

"Oh my! That was so strange! Elizabeth, I am all astonishment that you even manage to walk about with such a commotion going on in your insides."

Elizabeth laughed at Georgiana's shocked face and embraced her gently. It had been wonderful to spend the last few weeks in her company, and she looked forward with eager anticipation at the months to come.

The snow fell on Christmas morning, coating the grounds with a fine dusting of white powder. Downstairs the Pemberley servants were preparing a feast for their guests – they would have their respite tomorrow when Mr and Mrs Darcy would present them with the boxes for St Stephens Day and a full day's holiday. The night before the families of the estate workers and tenants had queued up for joints of beef, presented to each of them by Mrs Darcy herself and Darcy had travelled into Lambton with hampers of food for the local tradesmen and their families. Fitzwilliam prided himself on rewarding hard work and he saw to it that everyone could enjoy the festivities of the season, not just his own family and friends.

Darcy awoke to find Elizabeth standing by the window, they were now sharing the bed in her rooms often, and he delighted in seeing her first thing in the morning. The heavy drapes, which had been hung in preparation for her lying in, had been opened slightly and he could see the bright winter sunshine glinting through. He watched her for a moment; rounded and beautiful, she meant everything in the world to him, but he tormented himself with the innate fear that he was not deserving of lasting happiness.

The room was chilly, despite the fire smouldering away in the hearth, her skin cold to touch, and he enveloped her in his embrace. He didn't know if he was trying to warm her up or if he was holding onto her as tightly as he would allow himself, scared that she might slip away. Sensing the tension in him, she kissed him gently on the nose. He closed his eyes, somehow scared to open them in case she had gone. She intertwined her fingers in his; his hands were much larger than hers, and she always felt delicate when he took her hand in his as he had done now. He held her hand firmly as if the slightest move to relinquish his hold would cause him to lose her forever.

"Are you alright, my love?"

"Of course, my dearest."

"Fitzwilliam Darcy, you hold the livelihoods of hundreds of people in your hands, and you are not yet thirty years of age."

"I find I am at a loss in understanding your meaning."

"How can I explain," she said, wondering how to best phrase this without causing offence. "When people hear of Mr Darcy of Pemberley in Derbyshire and his ten thousand a year, they are instantly of the understanding that here is a wealthy gentleman who has so great a fortune that there could be nothing else able to trouble him."

"You had similar thoughts too if I remember correctly."

"Aye, but that was before I realised that you were all too human."

"Perhaps to a degree of failing, I fear."

"No," she pulled him closer to her. "I want you to know that whatever your worries are, you do not have to face them alone."

"Certain worries are too large for a gentleman to share with his wife."

"They are never too large. Darcy, I know that you are apprehensive about the birth of our child. I am too, but I know that it affects you more keenly because of the loss of your own mother."

"It would not be about the child, Lizzy, children are resilient, children can overcome such a loss," he stopped, unsure of how to intonate his feeling, "but how could *I* live without you?"

She was filled with an immediate rush of love for this complicated man who she shared her life with. Turning to him, with his sad grey eyes and his mournful look, she pulled him into her, letting his head rest upon her chest as she stroked his hair and held him close.

"You would live without me, Fitzwilliam, and whilst I would expect a respectable level of mourning and sadness, I would not want you to pine for me for the remainder of your life. You, above all people, need someone to laugh with, pull you out of your moods and remind you that there is always something to be thankful for and enjoy, even on Sundays when you are bored and monstrous!"

She stood up and tried to drag him to his feet, struggling a little with the weight of her belly and the imbalance it caused.

"Anyway, all this worry is for naught," Elizabeth stated jovially, still tugging on his arm as he playfully resisted. "I have no mind to die young and leave a tragic footnote in history, and neither should you, for even though I would be able to live without you, I would rather not."

He stood up and engaged her arm in his, a smile returning to his face, all melancholy gone for the moment, and the Darcys began their morning routine, laughing and teasing each other as they did.

LUCK BE A LADY!

Socialite Imogen Darcy, 19, currently the main squeeze of Babes of Bayswater co-star Jonty Winchester has been spotted partying and gambling in the luscious Mandalay Bay hotel in Las Vegas. Currently resting after a recent bout of pneumonia, invincible Imogen, youngest daughter of the Duke of Derbyshire, was later seen sneaking out and into a plush Range Rover with her best friend on the show, Abigail Delancey-Fothergill, before filming begins next week for the USA Spring Break episode of ITV's ratings hit. Both girls seemed to be in the middle of a winning streak and left the pleasure palace in the early hours with a stack of chips and two handsome admirers. We don't know about you, but we are looking forward to the new season of Babes of Bayswater to see what surprises the Vegas Special has in store!

Five

The small Italian restaurant in the centre of Lambton was quieter than it usually was on a Monday. With its bare brick walls, painted scenes of Tuscany and Sicily, and the red candles half-melted around Chianti bottles standing proudly on the red and white checked tablecloths, 'La Piccola Pasta' hadn't changed since at least 1975. Lizzy always remembered eating 'sketti meatballs' with Winston when she had been very young, returning to Pemberley smelling of garlic and cracked black pepper, with a dish full of tiramisu for Mrs Reynolds.

"So," Maggie asked casually, "are you ready for a month of filming?"

Lizzy rolled her eyes and ate a mouthful of pasta, slurping down the spaghetti, dropping blobs of sauce onto her top which engrained themselves in the lacy fabric like a bloodstain.

"I'm always ready for a month of hot Hollywood actors and regency romping," she said, wiping the sauce off herself with the napkin.

"I can't wait to see Benn Williams in a pair of tight trousers, do you think Joyce will organise a meet and greet?"

"I can guarantee it, although I wouldn't expect much of a greeting from him. He is very miserable," Lizzy laughed. "But you know how crazy she is for Darcy; we might even have to peel her off the courtyard!" She took a sip of her wine, let the alcoholic warmth of it slip down her throat, then casually the words slipped out, "did you hear about the job?"

Maggie look at Lizzy with a puzzled look on her face, "what do you mean?"

"There are never any surprises at Pemberley, you know that..." she laughed softly.

Nothing could ever be a secret at Pemberley, she was certain that everyone knew Sam, the senior curator, was pregnant before she had even peed on the stick; and everyone knew that Maggie was getting ready to fly the nest, she was surprised that it hadn't been pinned up on the noticeboard or emailed out on the weekly newsletter.

"I haven't heard yet," Maggie fiddled with her napkin. "I should know by the end of the week."

"Austenation will be absolutely bonkers if they don't offer you whatever you want...."

As much as Lizzy disliked the organisation and their complete domination of any vaguely related to do with Austen and her novel, she knew that being there would make Maggie happy.

It had been hard for the last few years, especially after Jean Wickham had died; it had been a merciless battle with lung cancer that had left them all reeling from the loss, but Maggie most of all as she had nursed her mum in those last frantic days. Even though Lizzy knew that she would miss her ridiculously, she also knew that she was desperate to make her own stamp on the world without the shadow of Pemberley.

"Are you cross?" A look of nervous hesitation passed across her face.

"Why would I be cross?" Lizzy grabbed a spoonful of the risotto from Maggie's plate.

"I feel like I'm abandoning you, and Harriet, and even Joyce... I feel like I'm just walking away."

"Abandoning us?" She swallowed the mouthful of rice, "don't be silly! You have to live your own life, Maggie... Pemberley has been around for centuries now and I'm sure it will continue to stay there as long as we keep finding money to fix the roof."

Maggie smiled at her friend, it was such a relief. She has been so nervous about telling her that she was intent on leaving her job of nearly seventeen years and the home she had lived in all her life to move down south to be with a man. Strictly speaking, it was against her feminist principles.

"I'm hoping this film will pay for a good wodge of the repairs this winter, to be honest, I know that Matthew promised us a great payment, but I'm not sure what they settled on in the end."

"Aren't they dealt with by HQ? I didn't think we had much to do with it at a local level."

"Technically, Lizzy, you don't have anything to do with it – you know how annoyed Joyce got when you wrote that letter about volunteer expenses." Maggie chastised her friend.

"Well, Mary deserved that £15.87 and she just wouldn't ask for it."

"Yes, but you have to let Joyce deal with it. That's what she gets paid for. No wonder she gets so pissed at you."

She poured another glass of wine and called the waiter over to ask for the dessert menu, even though they never ordered anything off the menu anyway. Luciano knew the ritual and it was always worth paying extra attention to the girls from the big house, who were generous tippers. He stood behind the bar and opened another bottle of Pinot in anticipation. Lizzy took a moment to order the mascarpone and figs that hadn't been on the menu since 2012; Maggie had the brownie and they ordered another bottle of wine, which appeared on the table within seconds.

"Is Matthew okay? I haven't heard from him."

"He's in the midst of a mid-life crisis if you call that okay." Maggie took a large gulp of the fruity white wine from her glass, "when was the last time you two…"

"Erm… I can't remember." Avoiding the subject, she took a large swig of her wine, the acidic sharpness catching on her throat. She could never lie to Maggie, but she could avoid the subject.

"Yes, you can."

She placed the glass down, "yes, of course, I can…It was about a month ago when I went to London for work, he came to Longbourn for dinner. Uncle Jeremy was very disapproving," Lizzy laughed into her wine. "He said that he was quite happy for me to be the scarlet woman as long as I didn't get named in any litigation. Said that he wouldn't be my counsel if it all went to court. He refused on moral grounds."

"Jeremy refused on moral grounds? That's a first!"

"You know he's been strange since Victoria ran off with Vilda."

"Poor Jeremy!" Maggie pondered on it, "he knows Cara's dad though, doesn't he? That could be awkward for him if it came out."

"Everybody knows Andrew Dalhousie! It's such a musty, fusty old club down there…You would hate it! Remember the time you came with me to that ball that my dad made us go to? And all of those horrible girls!"

"That bunch of bitches!"

"They're all still the same, just older and richer – and that horrible Sarah Delancey who, by the way, I found out she used to go out with Benn Williams at Cambridge – well, she's even more horrible now she's divorced from her hideous middle-aged old banker husband, has a face full of fillers and about a hundred million quid to spend."

Maggie finished her glass and poured another.

"What was Benn Williams doing with her?"

"Probably cheating on her with someone younger and blonder I reckon."

"You are wrong about him! Benn Williams wouldn't do that. He's too gentlemanly."

Maggie had a bit of a thing for Benn Williams. She never quite believed that he would throw off his wife of ten years for someone almost young enough to be his daughter.

"Maggie," Lizzy said softly, "do you think I am a terrible person?"

"For sleeping with my brother?" She shook her gently, "no, I think you are possibly a little bit blind and sometimes very stupid, but not terrible... he's not happy with Cara, he hasn't been for a long time and the fact that he sees you all the time, and other girls too – you know about the others – suggests to me that he is the one that should feel terrible."

"I think he's just scared."

"Do you want the truth, Lizzy?"

She nodded, filled her mouth with a spoonful of mascarpone and a sweet fig, swallowed hard. Maggie was always very wise, but she was also very blunt.

"Matthew isn't going to leave Cara. Ever. It's easy to stay with her. It's easy for him to pretend that they have a glamorous life, and it's easy for him to meet you and do whatever it is you do-"

"We obviously just play Uno and drink tea," she said dryly. "I have no idea what else you think we would possibly do in a bed naked."

"Elizabeth, that is my little brother you are talking about – please don't." Maggie struggled not to laugh and then recovered. "Look, it's easy for him to play Uno with you when you are sitting around waiting for him to stop drinking tea with everyone else."

"I think I need to find someone else to play Uno with."

"I think maybe you need to start drinking coffee!"

The public areas of the house were all strictly out of bounds once they had closed for the day unless given permission by one of the management team. Usually, she had to wind her way through the corridors and back passages, but tonight she knew the top door would be accidentally left unlocked by one of the tour guides as it always was on Monday. Thank you, Diana, and your predictable forgetfulness.

She skipped through the bright gallery, past the stern portraits of the elderly Darcy matriarchs, their unblinking eyes ever watchful and attentive. The cupboard still wobbled, teetering on a loose floorboard and she scared herself a little as the vase on top rattled and echoed in the quiet night. It was cloudy, but the moon peeked through to cast shadows on the wall as she made her way up the gentle turn of the grand staircase, designed for delicate-footed ladies in their vast gowns.

It always made her think of the White Lady of Pemberley, the resident house ghost – the loitering spirit of Lady Hortense Holland-Darcy.

Winston had delighted in terrorising Lizzy and her friends when they were younger, teasing and grumbling as they hid under duvets and pillows. He would sit on the chair by the fire with a torch under his chin, the plaster busts on top of the bookcases casting eerie shadows around the room, the moonlight peeking through the gaps in the heavy red velvet curtains that covered the creaking sash windows.

"Lady Darcy, it has been told,
Did not have a heart of gold,
And because her soul was painted black
It is said that the Devil took it back.
With her finest jewels and her foot e'er slight,
She wandered through the lonely night.
Down the hall and up the stair,
Bejewelled, she walked without a care,
But with each fateful step she took,
It was clear that she was out of luck.
Over the bannister she fell,
And Lady Darcy went straight to hell,
Dead on the floor ne'er more to roam,
She departed this earth with a mournful groan.
As she stood before the unholy throne,
She asked why he had called home,
'Twas not I', the Satanic Beast did cry,
'Who caused your earthly soul to fly.
Lady Darcy, you led a troublesome life
Twas your husband who thought you a disposable wife!'
Returned as penance to the site of her doom,
She wandered through each darkened room,
A soulless spectre, a ghostly bride,
To view her meant an ill betide,
And until her soul from its prison can flee,
She will remain the White Lady of Pemberley."

They would all scream and hide under the covers and Winston would retreat upstairs, leaving Mrs Reynolds to wrangle the teenagers by bringing them lemon biscuits and hot chocolate and telling them all to settle down and be quiet. They never were, laughing and giggling past midnight, counting down until morning as the clock in the room next door rang out its centuries-old melody every hour.

Cyril Darcy's first wife had fallen over the low bannister that ran along the top corridor to her death. There was still a blemish on the wood that marked the spot where the woman landed on the hard surface, her skull cracking and the blood pumping out of her onto the floorboards, staining them forever. It was never known whether Cyril was responsible for his wife's death, but he had married Henrietta Morley with rather unbecoming haste. The story of the unlucky Lady Darcy has always been a favourite when she was younger, but now it felt rather macabre to think of the poor woman dying alone, crying out for help to an empty house.

BANG! She jumped and turned; poking his head through the door at top of the staircase, looking tanned and expensive, was Matthew Wickham. His manner was gracious, relaxed almost, as he padded across the landing in his Ralph Lauren socks, his hand curling around hers as he pulled her up from the step. Lizzy wrapped her arms around him, the familiar shape of him fitting the indentation on her own body. He kissed her gently on the cheek before whispering softly in her ear, a frisson of anticipation shooting its way down her spine.

"Did my sister fill you full of Pinot G and send you home, because I never normally receive this kind of welcome."

"Yes, pretty much," she giggled into his shoulder. "When did you get here? Was London good?" She walked past him and through the door leading to the flat. "I'm ravenous, fancy some toast?"

Smirking, he closed the door with a firm tug after checking the landing to ensure that no errant spirits were still loitering.

"Yeah, we got back about five," he watched her confusion at the bunch of flowers on the table, studied her as she sniffed them. "Harriet was knackered so I..." he caught the smile on her face, "Lizzy, you're pissed, aren't you?"

He laughed at her, which made her frown at him as she reached into the kitchen cupboard and grabbed a loaf. He reached into the fridge, passing her the butter, as she knocked the large basket of peonies and daisies drooping their scent and pollen over the counter.

"Did you bring me flowers?"

"Might have done..." he fingered the lace on her top, noticing the spaghetti sauce blotches. "Or maybe you have a secret admirer."

She batted his hand away, but he grabbed it and pulled her close; there was no space between them now, and he moved nearer, his hip touching hers as they leaned against the worktop.

"Your eyes have always amazing." He raised his hand and ran the back of it down the side of her face. He could feel her breathing get heavier; she felt the heartbeat in her chest flutter. "They're like the dark side of the moon."

"You're getting good at this," she said with more than a hint of sarcasm, "who have you been practicing with?"

"I've always been good at it."

He moved close enough for her to feel the heat of his breath on her cheek and as she turned, she felt her lips graze his for the tiniest of moments. This was always dangerous, she thought, always too hard to resist. It was too easy to fall into it when really, she should be picking herself up and dusting herself off. The toast popped in the toaster, and the spell was broken.

"Don't try and seduce me, Mr Wickham," she whispered. "I am not Lydia Bennet...I will not fall prey to your wanton acts of seduction."

He took a bite of the toast she had just buttered, planting a kiss on her neck, "so if I decided to keep you company this evening...."

She turned, "you would be staying on the couch."

"You know full well that I have never stayed on the couch," he grabbed the last piece of toast from the counter. "Anyway, I should be having very stern words with you about harassing my actors. Upsetting my leading man terribly, you naughty little madame," he crunched on the toast, "asking him lots of questions and making him feel *nervous*."

There was a look and they both burst out laughing. Matthew was grateful that his years of working with temperamental creatives had enabled him to deal with Benn Williams' frankly ridiculous tirade a few weeks earlier. The fact that he had managed to do it with a straight face led him to secretly believe that he was a far superior actor to the troubled star of his new film. He had known Benn for a long time now and suspected that his overreaction was more due to his home life than anything Lizzy could have done.

"He was being a ridiculous arse! He is much nicer when you get to know him, I promise you."

"I don't think I *want* to get to know him," she pouted stubbornly. "I'm planning on staying out of his way for the next few weeks."

"That's a shame," he grinned. "You got him so riled up that I am convinced he fancies you."

"He does not."

"Well, there's no accounting for taste."

They sat together on the couch, watching some terrible reality show involving screaming half-naked woman and a lot of inflatables.

Instinctively she leaned her head against his chest, and he rested his arm around her shoulder, before nuzzling into her neck, kissing the soft curve between her shoulder and ear gently. He could smell the warm ginger and cinnamon perfume lingering on his skin. She had worn this for years now, and the merest hint of it sent him careering back through time.

A hundred memories.
A hundred moments.
Lizzy Darcy smelled like home.

1811

The fire had caught just before midnight, silently climbing its way through the entrance hall and up the newly finished grand staircase, catching light to the dried foliage and greenery decorating the banisters, creating a trail of destruction. At the stroke of twelve, Staughton and the other senior male servants ran through the house waking up the residents, leading them to safety and ensuring that all members of the household, regardless of status, were accounted for.

Elizabeth and her family watched in their nightgowns as teams of men from all over the estate formed a bucket brigade to put out the fire. Darcy, his face covered in soot, was at the front – trying to control the flames. At just after midnight, the fire was out; the scorched remains of a medieval tapestry still smouldering in the early hours of St Stephens Day as the toll of the courtyard clock chimed into the night.

Mrs Reynolds organised for the guests to be moved away to rooms in the west wing of the house, the furthest point away from the scene of the fire. As usual, she noticed that Mrs Darcy's mother was on the verge of hysterics and made arrangements for her to be administered with large amounts of brandy and a sedative.

When her husband was confident that the fire was now out, he found Elizabeth in the servants hall, a coachman's jacket wrapped around her, pouring out small ale for the young men who had helped him to fight the flames. She looked exhausted, he thought. Through all of it, his main concern had been her.

"Is it over now?"

He nodded and, with no regard for decorum, held her close to him, pressed to his heart, in front of anyone who could see, whispering prayers of gratitude that no souls had been lost that day. Darcy was not a particularly religious man, but he decided there and then that God, who had deigned to save all of those most precious to him, was worth thanking indeed.

"The fire is out, but we will have a lot of work to do."

His face was pensive as he thought about the heat of the flames, the smell of burning wood and paint.

"Lizzy, I think we should go to Grosvenor Square until the baby has arrived."

"Leave Pemberley?" Her face turned to a frown, "I understand your reason, but I cannot agree."

"Mrs Darcy," he said firmly, "I think I must insist."

"You may be happy travelling to town in the winter, but I most certainly am not. We will stay here until the child arrives."

"Lizzy…" his voice warned, but she had already crossed her arms against him.

"Fitzwilliam! I will not say another word on it, the baby will be born at Pemberley. At home."

The youngest Darcy confirmed his agreement with kicks and thuds so fierce that Elizabeth was convinced her son was going to be a great sportsman. She hoped that this boisterous babe was a boy, partially due to Darcy's innate longing for a son and society's expectation that she provide an heir as soon as possible, but they had discussed the possibility of a girl and he was similarly delighted at the prospect of a headstrong daughter with fine eyes.

This horrible incident taught Darcy that he was just one person, in a team of slightly over a hundred, who worked tirelessly to ensure that Pemberley continued to thrive and grow. He gave permission for the following day to still proceed as the annual day off for his staff and authorised the distribution of the sum of one pound to be paid to each upper servant and 10 shillings each to be paid to the rest.

Mr Staughton, the butler who had been in charge since before Darcy was born, had resisted this, stating that the servants of the house were only doing their duty and that there was no requirement for additional reward outside of their own wages, but Darcy insisted, most adamantly. He knew that, if he had the taste for gambling, he could easily lose that total amount in half an hour on the tables at his club in Bermondsey, but he was aware that this small gift would make a significant difference to the lives of the Pemberley family and he wanted to show his utmost appreciation for their efforts.

It was Twelfth Night, but the annual day of celebration was muted this year. Elizabeth retired early, before dinner, causing a level of concern amongst her husband and Jane, who knew it was most unlike her sister to miss out on any fun, especially when in the company of her father, and she took it upon herself to see how she fared. She gently opened to the door of her sister's room and saw her sitting up, bedclothes thrown back, the stench of vomit in the air.

"Lizzy," she exclaimed as she hurried towards where her sister sat in obvious discomfort. "What has happened, what is the matter?"

"Jane," Elizabeth said pitifully, "there is so much pain. So much, I can't bear it."

Mrs Bingley put her arm around her sister, holding her close to her, she was acutely aware of what was happening. Elizabeth's nightgown was drenched from the waist down, the pallor of her face, the pain radiating through her - Jane knew, from her own experiences, that the eagerly anticipated Darcy baby was preparing to make an appearance.

"Lizzy, it's time."

"No," she exclaimed. "It is too early, it cannot be…"

Her voice took on a wailing tone and she grasped Jane's hand tightly as the wave of pain came over her again.

"I must call for Fitzwilliam, Lizzy," she said softly, removing her own hand from her sisters and ringing the bell for attendance. "It's going to be alright…you have ten times the resilience I have, and I managed perfectly well. I found that if you concentrate as the pain washes over you, you can –"

She was unable to finish as Elizabeth screamed out in agony. Ellen knocked on the door and entered as Jane yelled at her to fetch her master. Even though she was concentrating on the wave of pain as advised, Elizabeth noted that she had never heard Jane yell at anyone before.

Darcy was enjoying a game of billiards with Bingley and Mr Bennet when the under-butler advised that this presence was requested upstairs immediately. As he reached the landing, he could hear his wife, obviously in great amounts of distress; it was so reminiscent of the haunting cries of his own mother that he felt immediately nauseous fearing the worst. He paused for a moment before recovering his composure and entering the room.

"Is it now? But you said February… surely this is too early, is it too early?" he pleaded with Jane for confirmation.

"They say that it is not an exact science…" she reassured. "But for the sake of Lizzy and the baby, you need to call for your doctor or ask the servant girls if they know of a local woman who can get here quickly."

Darcy was holding onto her so tightly, helping her move and breathe and tolerate this immense pain. It was almost as if she was being wrenched in two, and she did not know how she would bear it.

"Lizzy, what can I do?"

His brow creased, and he looked scared half to death.

"Just stay, please. I need you here."

Ellen came in with hot water and clean linens, she placed them next to her master and observed her mistress writhing uncomfortably on the bed. Elizabeth's maid was a girl of not quite twenty, but she had seen this before, and she wanted to help. Mrs Darcy was always kind to her – treating her with great respect and appreciating the work that she did – and Ellen was grateful to have a senior position with the family when most girls her age were working as under maids. Being the oldest of seven in a household that could not afford a doctor, Ellen had seen her share of births and she knew that she could make it easier for her mistress, could even deliver the babe if she needed to.

"Excuse me, Mr Darcy," she said hesitantly. "Please forgive me if I speak out of turn, but Mrs Darcy needs to stand. It will help."

Darcy nodded; he did not know why he was trusting the advice of a servant in the matters of childbirth, but he felt so helpless that any assistance was well-received. They helped Elizabeth to her feet, Darcy supporting the weight of her on his shoulder, her legs buckled again as her body shuddered with the intensity of another contraction and, as she cried out in pain, Ellen could see tears of fear and frustration running down her master's face.

They had been in this room for what felt like hours now; the yellow walls and heavy drapes felt like they were closing in on him and he felt claustrophobic with panic. He had taken a seat and a shot of brandy as he watched Ellen press cold flannels to Elizabeth's forehead and whisper words of encouragement. He understood now why men were not usually present during the birth of their offspring; not because of decency, but because this was horrifying – any man subjected to this would surely never want to impregnate his wife ever again and he sincerely hoped that his wife would be happy with just the one child.

"Mr Darcy, the baby is nearly here," Ellen prompted. "You need to get Mrs Darcy to push when I say."

"Push?"

"Yes! Stand there," she said pointing to the head of the bed. "When I say push," she said to Elizabeth. "You need to push, Mrs Darcy. You need to push really hard."

Elizabeth nodded, taking his hand she squeezed it tightly, looking in his eyes for confirmation that all would be well. He was scared witless but trying to hide it.

"Mr Darcy! NOW!!"

Fitzwilliam Edward, named for his father and grandfather, entered the world screaming loudly as if announcing his arrival. The quick delivery of their son had astonished both Darcy and Elizabeth, but despite being perfect in the eyes of his parents, there was nothing to hide the fact that he was incredibly tiny and at least a month early, indeed Ellen had never seen a baby so small, and she swaddled him in cotton and blankets to keep him warm on this cold January night.

"He will be alright, Mr Darcy, sir," she said as she passed the boy to his father. "He is strong."

He looked down at the small pink bundle; how was it possible that someone so tiny could change your entire world.

"My son has the Darcy countenance, don't you think?"

"Master Darcy is a very handsome boy, sir."

He held tightly to the newest member of his family. He was Papa now. Elizabeth beamed at him from the bed and he walked over, gently placing the baby in her arms.

"Look what you have made," the love and complete wonder in his voice were evident.

"Who we made."

She seemed so vulnerable and so unlike his normal resilient Elizabeth that he felt a sudden rush of tenderness and feeling, wishing that he could hold her inside his heart and keep her there forever. Master Fitzwilliam Darcy was tiny; barely bigger than a pup, but he would be strong, and he would be loved beyond measure. Elizabeth gazed at her husband with a look that he had never seen before; it was the contented love of a new mother. She nuzzled into him and he kissed her gently as they gazed at the pink perfection of their baby for a long time.

Darcy went downstairs to inform the waiting party of the arrival of his son and heir to discover that everyone had gone to bed; excepting his sister, who was uncomfortably asleep and perched on a chair, and Bingley and Jane who were asleep on couch, their heads resting on each other in a display of comfortable matrimony. Internally he scolded himself for ever doubting the sincerity of Jane's affections towards his friend. They were the most content and amiable couple that he had ever had the pleasure of spending time with and he delighted in seeing Bingley so happy in his marriage.

He walked over and poured himself a glass of port – it had felt like a long night, however, after checking the clock on the mantelpiece he could see that it was a little after three am. The whole process had taken just over six hours, and in that time, he had become a father. It was an exceptional feeling and one that he felt overwhelmed by. For all his emotional reticence in public, or in the presence of strangers, Fitzwilliam Darcy was a passionate and caring man who loved his wife, his sister and now his son to levels of extreme. Standing at the window, looking down on to the snow scattered lawn, he shed a small, significant tear of happiness for his fortunate position in life.

Jane was the first to hold Master Fitzwilliam and declared him absolutely perfect, followed by his Aunt Georgiana, who promised, after observing his long fingers, that she would teach him how to play pianoforte to such a high standard that he would be the most accomplished gentleman in England, as well as being the most handsome. Mrs Bennet found herself predisposed to grand-motherhood, much more so than raising her own children.

"Of course, it is much easier to enjoy your children when you both have such generous incomes."

Jane subtly rolled her eyes at Lizzy, who offered her son to her mother to hold. Mrs Bennet admired the tiny boy who was wrapped in cotton, his brand-new features visible for the world.

"He looks very much like Mr Darcy, does he not, Lizzy? Yes, he will do very well indeed."

Maybe it was the way his Grandmama looked at him or the way she held him, but Fitzwilliam began to scream and there was no comforting him. Mrs Bennet passed him back to his mother, who removed him to the nursery.

"Well," the older lady harrumphed. "Did you ever see a child so spoiled?"

"Jane! Come and look!"

Georgiana Darcy was beside herself with excitement as she witnessed Charlotte Bingley sitting up on the floor completely unsupported.

Her mother arrived too late, and the baby fell over, crying out as her face landed on the chenille rug. Jane laughed and gathered the child up into her embrace, whilst Georgiana was mortified.

"I am so sorry, Jane," she apologised. "That was all my fault."

"Not to worry, a little falling over hurt no-one and Charlotte is perfectly alright. Do not concern yourself, Georgie, you did nothing wrong."

Georgiana smiled and retired to the chair, where needlework was waiting and demanding her attention.

Jane and Elizabeth were discussing their mutual plans to visit Hertfordshire for Mary's wedding the following month. It was also decided that the Darcys alone would call to visit their Aunt De Bourgh and take the newest family member to be introduced to their formidable relative.

"I must say, Lizzy, you are very brave to visit Lady Catherine," Jane stated, whilst sipping tea and rocking Charlotte on her knee.

Elizabeth smiled mischievously as she reached for a lemon biscuit, "why not at all, Jane. I find that Lady Catherine is a very pleasing sparring partner once one has married into the family and already polluted the shades of Pemberley."

Mrs Bingley laughed at her sister's good humour; she did not envy Lizzy for the visit – Lady Catherine terrified her, and her first meeting with the noble mistress of Rosings Park had left her stomach in knots. Georgiana too felt similarly wary of her Aunt and her sudden demands for attention and gratification; it was because of this that she asked Jane if she were able to reside with the Bingleys for the duration of the Darcy visit to Kent to which Jane kindly obliged, the younger Darcy lady content that her remaining time away from Pemberley would be spent in their happy home.

After their wedding, which Lady Catherine had refused to attend, Elizabeth had taken it upon herself to make amends with her husband's relative, accompanying Georgiana whenever she was summoned to Kent and eventually charming the self-appointed family matriarch with her steady wit and restrained flattery. Darcy had refused to make amends with the lady after her treatment of his betrothed and his refusal to yield had maddened his wife to the point of exasperation.

"Kitty," Georgiana rose from the settee, "would you care to accompany me in a duet?"

"Only if I can play, Georgie!" Kitty had recently become much improved, "I received some new music today from Mr Worthing and I am eager to hear it."

"Mr Worthing?" Georgiana whispered excitedly as the two women walked across the drawing room, and through to the hall, "has he been writing to you again?"

Kitty nodded, blushing a deep pink; Georgiana took her by the arm, and they disappeared out of earshot for private chat and secret sharing.

"Well, I am happy that we are all so fortunate to be together after a tumultuous few days," Mary stated, in a bold new voice that she had been practicing and everyone agreed that, for once, she was completely accurate in her assertions.

Darcy was in the nursery, his waistcoat removed, his cravat loosened, his shirt pulled loose, his boots off, and he was sitting in the rocking chair in his stockinged feet, cradling his son in his arms whilst simultaneously telling him an incredible story of pirates and shipwrecks.

Fitzwilliam cooed at his father, which caused him to smile to himself. The boy was getting stronger every day, the frightening nature of his early birth assuaged by his good-tempered nature. He was, Darcy thought, the most amenable child that he had the fortune to meet, and he counted himself very fortunate that he belonged to him.

"You can put him down, you know."

Elizabeth was standing at the doorway, dressed for dinner, her new Darcy Pearls necklace shimmering at her throat.

"I don't think I want to."

"You must, for we have guests and you are half-dressed," she walked over and ruffled his hair. "Don't let becoming a Papa make you forget your obligations."

Darcy rose to his feet and pulled the bell for the nursemaid.

"Do we have to entertain tonight, dearest?"

"Yes, Mr Darcy, we absolutely must."

"What if I were sick?"

"Fitzwilliam…"

The nursemaid entered, silently removing the boy from his father's arms. Elizabeth took a moment to kiss him gently on the head, inhaling the soft milky smell.

"We are very fortunate, Mrs Darcy."

"We are, but you will be less fortunate if you keep my mother waiting for dinner. Now, go and get dressed."

It was later when their guests had retired and the corridors were dark and dimly lit, that Elizabeth decided to walk the short distance to her husband's chambers to wish him goodnight.

"Good evening, Mr Darcy," she whispered, perhaps a little more loudly than she thought given the amount of wine she had consumed with dinner.

"Elizabeth, get in quickly, you must be freezing."

He threw back the covers, and she slid into between the cotton sheets. She held him tightly feeling the warmth of him through her nightgown. Outside she could hear the whipping wind gathering force as it invaded from over the Peaks and she pulled him closer.

"This is a rather delightful garment," he said, the hint of port on his breath, a look in his eyes that she recognised all too well. "I really appreciate the needlework of your seamstress… can I get a closer look?"

"I think you may have had one too many glasses of port this evening, husband."

"I think you may have had too much wine, wife!" He pulled on the sleeve her nightgown, "but I'm not complaining if it means I get to wake up with you in the morning."

"I may have had more than a glass…"

She leaned in; it had been a while since she had felt the softness of his lips on hers and she felt overwhelmed as he moved his attention from her mouth to her neck.

"Lizzy, we should have more babies…"

"Would you like to start right now?"

"I wouldn't complain," he ran his hand over her shoulder and down to her hip, "in fact we should have enough babies to fill every room at Pemberley…"

"Fitzwilliam, that's over twenty-five rooms!"

But as he kissed her slowly, almost reverently, and passionately for the first time since the birth, she knew, submitting to his desire as well as her own, that she would happily have as many children as he wanted, and fill their home with laughter, love, and life.

2000

Lizzy Darcy and Matthew Wickham had grown up together at Pemberley. Closer in age to each other than to the very sensible and bossy Maggie, they had made natural playmates and could often be found running up and down the halls or up the hill to the Cage, looking for conkers underneath the massive horse chestnut tree that stood next to it.

Maggie and Matthew lived with their mum, Jean, who had acted as Winston's secretary for years before she accidentally fell in love with the kindly steward John Wickham, and promptly married him. Unfortunately, he had dropped down dead two days before his fortieth birthday, and it fell upon his wife to raise her young daughter and baby son in the small apartment above the stable block that they had once shared.

Matthew was always a little bit in awe of Lizzy. He wanted to tell her that she was squishy in all the right places, but he knew enough of women to know that squishy was not the right word to use. Her head was covered in a bird's nest of curls, sometimes she straightened them, but she couldn't be bothered with it for the most part, and they hung frizzy and unbrushed around her face. When she smiled, two dimples appeared on her cheeks, and she had a soft, pink mouth that curved upwards, even when she was angry. In fact, you could only tell she was angry when she frowned because her eyes turned from a soft grey to a dark, melting lead and she metamorphosed from a calm summer day to an oncoming storm.

The problem was that Lizzy didn't really notice him like that until after they had left high school and gone to separate colleges – where he suddenly became cool, bringing back giggling girls to the house in his Ford Fiesta, parading them around the lawn right under her nose and whispering sweet nothings to them in the Orangery.

Lizzy watched with green-eyed envy, filled with something she thought was love for the boy who lived next door, powerless to do anything except watch and wave as he sauntered about with his baggy jeans and his Ben Sherman shirts, casually slouching with his beaten-up converse, music playing and an illicit cigarette hanging from his mouth.

There was a burst of freckles that ran across his nose when it was summer, and they remained there until the last leaves fell from the trees. His eyes were brown, but she knew that really, they were a beautiful chocolate eclipse, surrounded by a circle of gold, like a Jaffa cake gone wrong. She tried to remember what he smelled like close up. His hair had grown out from his standard short back and sides, despite his mother's protestations, and there was the heavy undergrowth of facial hair covering his chin. He still hadn't got the chip on his tooth fixed, gained playing rugby in year ten, and he was still wearing the same coat.

But on Sundays, he would still appear in the porch as the last visitors left for the day and they would sit in the long gallery, eating roast beef sandwiches and roast potatoes, old films whirring through Winston's projector as he snored away on the armchair in the library, oblivious to their presence. Lizzy would snuggle into him, quite unaware that he would smell the subtly expensive perfume she wore and try to not think about kissing her. Even though she saw him with lots of girls, she never asked him if he had a girlfriend. She was always too scared to ask, just in case he said that he did.

Exams came and went; university applications were completed and offers accepted. Lizzy, under the guidance of her grandfather, was off to Manchester to study Law, and Matthew was off to London to study Film. Whilst Winston didn't think it a valid enough subject to warrant a bachelor's degree, he offered to support John Wickham's son through university out of kindness to the man's widow. It was only four weeks into the new semester when Matthew Wickham met a wonderfully rich, bohemian girl called Cara Dalhousie, who smelled like patchouli and had read the Bhagavad Gita. He promptly moved into her squat in Bermondsey and grew out his hair.

Lizzy moved to Manchester, assisted by Winston who insisted on helping pack boxes of things into the little yellow Mini that he had bought her for passing her A-Levels. She made fast friends with the group of girls in her halls of residence and they were frequent visitors back to the house in Derbyshire. Occasionally she would look for the red Fiesta outside the stables, her heart twitchy with anticipation until she noticed its absence.

DAD: 12 Missed Calls
DAD: Lizzy, please phone.

DAD: Call me when you get this.
CHARLIE: Have you spoken to Dad?

She stood outside the lecture hall, Emily and Josh waiting for her. The phone took ages to connect, but she knew. She knew because her dad never called her.

"Lizzy!"

"Dad, what's wrong?"

Then silence.

"Dad?"

"It's Winston…"

"Is he gone?"

"You need to come home."

"Dad. Please. Tell me."

That silence again, the one that lasts for an age, the one that can swallow you whole.

"Yes, he's gone."

Josh saw her legs buckle and grabbed for her before she fell, Emily held her as she sobbed on the pavement; curious passers-by stared, wondering what on earth was going on. She drove Lizzy the thirty-eight miles back to Pemberley, not knowing what to say as she watched her friend stare out of the window.

Hugh was there already, teary and sad, but stoic in the way that he was expected to be. He pulled his eldest daughter into a tight embrace, kissing the top of her head and commenting on how skinny she had become. His wife, Carol, was sitting on the shabby drawing room couch holding tightly onto Imogen, whose podgy toddler limbs poked out from her expensive red woollen coat.

She could feel the heat of the fire burning against the cold of her face, see the angry face of James II glaring at her from his portrait, she stumbled backward. It was too much to take, too much all at once; she couldn't breathe, the fire was stifling, the smell of the wood. She took quick, short breaths trying to stop this feeling, but it washed over her like a tidal wave, and she felt herself falling.

The last thing she heard was the booming voice of her brother, and the clatter of the tea tray before everything went dark and she landed on the threadbare Victorian chenille rug with a thud. Her great-grandmother's teacups shattered. Slivers of porcelain slipping between the cracks, falling into the gaps, disappearing between the heavy floorboards. Vanishing forever.

BREAKING NEWS: The Duke of Derbyshire dies at 84

The Duke of Derbyshire has died at his country estate at the age of 84. A spokesman at Pemberley said the Duke died on Tuesday morning with his companion, Mrs Winifred Wharton, by his side. In accordance with the Duke's wishes, Pemberley – the country seat made famous by Jane Austen in Pride and Prejudice – has been bequeathed to the Historical House Society who will fully open the house to the public in a five-year plan. The Duke, Winston Fitzwilliam Darcy, served as an Officer in the RAF during WWII and earned the George Cross for bravery after completing a record number of bombing raids over occupied Europe. The illegitimate son of suffragette Millicent Darcy, the Duke was legitimised by an act of Parliament after the death of his uncles during WWI, inheriting the title at the age of seventeen. He was the longest holder of the Derbyshire Dukedom, which was restored to Fitzwilliam Darcy in 1838 by Queen Victoria. Married in 1953 to renowned comedy actress, Sylvia Pratchett, the couple had three children before divorcing in 1966. The Duke also leaves seven grandchildren. His eldest son, Hugh, will inherit the title. Jemima Marshall of the HHS said, "we have been working with the Duke for a number of years now to ensure the legacy of Pemberley and the Darcy family. As one of the most famous country houses in the world, we are dedicated to preserving the house in the memory of Winston Darcy, who has given such a precious gift."

Lizzy finally packed up all her belongings from the room that the new guidebook referred to as 'The Knights Bedroom'. She wasn't sure what the new custodians would think of the blu-tac marks on the 17th century wooden panelling near her bed, where posters of Liam Gallagher and his sneering brother had once hung, and she was fairly confident that the distinctly modern splodge on the floor near the fireplace was nail glue from a manicure set she had bought from Superdrug. Good luck removing that, she thought.

She glanced her fingers over the familiar nooks and crannies of the figures on her four-poster bed, it had been placed in nearly every position in the room and she did not know how much damage she might have done to the delicate frame as she shoved it back and forth over the misaligned floorboards. She remembered how Winston had tucked her into bed every night when she was younger, the fairy lights twinkling around the headboard; how when she was older, he had always popped his head around the doorframe as he shuffled off to his room down the hall.

"Night, lie down, sweet dreams, sleep tight..."

"...don't let the bed bugs bite your toes tonight."

He would always blow her a kiss and she would always catch it and throw it back. They had done this every night since she had been five; scared and lonely in a strange place, she remembered the salty tears falling into the stiff cotton pillowcases, and the warm, bracing hug of Winston, who had felt scratchy but who had stroked her chin until she fell into sleep.

'Everything will be alright', he had said, 'everything will always be alright in the end.'

She couldn't bear to stay in the house when the stocktakers had gone through every room cataloguing each item, however small, and had thrown herself out into the grounds, walking for miles around the estate, taking herself to the very edge of Darcy land at all four corners before standing in the Lantern and waiting for the rain, watching the house – somehow no longer her home – until night fell.

After the inventory had been taken, she had been allowed to walk around the house and choose items that had been tagged NHI – *No Historical Importance* – and she had picked a few pieces of furniture that she loved, including the drawing room couch and Winston's old chair. She also pillaged boxes of battered old books from the library that were destined for the skip, piling them up at the top of the grand staircase before shuffling them along the landing and through the generously proportioned door, which would now always remain locked.

All over the estate, there was a feeling of loss, as if Pemberley itself was mourning the passing of its master. Winston had been the Duke of Derbyshire since he was seventeen years old – his tenure had seen massive changes in the house - and now his final goodbye meant that even though a Darcy would still live here, she would be the lady of the manor in name only, all the decisions and choices now made by nameless managers in the London head offices of the HHS.

As she grabbed the last of her belongings, Lizzy realised that she would never again wake up in this bedroom or look out of this window first thing in the morning or last thing at night. She stood still for a moment, noticing how ornate the mouldings were, ran her finger along the tall stone fireplace that still stood taller than she was; she was trying to remember it all, embroider each little aspect into her memory because she knew that from today things would never be the same again.

She was no-longer Elizabeth Darcy, student. Now she was 'Lady Elizabeth', living at Pemberley as the Darcy in residence playing a role she never auditioned for.

Matthew wasn't looking for Lizzy, hadn't expected to see her sitting in the window of the Lantern, her legs swinging, a Marlboro Light balancing off her lip as she drank beer from a plastic pint glass. They talked and reminisced and drank, falling back into their childhood friendship as if it was the easiest thing in the world. Eventually, overwhelmed with grief and remembering, they made mad, frantic love in the folly at the far end of the garden.

"What about your girlfriend…" she asked, as he pulled her t-shirt over her head and kissed her neck.

"I don't have a girlfriend..." he assured her, failing to add that he now had a fiancée.

The days passed by in a hazy reality, nothing felt normal anymore. Before she even realised, Winston had been gone for six months, and she was throwing up her breakfast with alarming regularity.

"Have you thought that you might be…"
"Please don't say it."

It was the end, and everything was not alright.

Six

Joyce Hutchinson had taken the job of Senior Curator at Pemberley shortly after the Historical House Society had acquired it, and she could say with absolute certainty that she loved her job. Growing up reading Jane Austen novels she always got a tingle of excitement reading the paragraphs where her hometown was mentioned and when the big house on the hill was described in detail and she longed for a chance to walk where Elizabeth Bennet had walked or sit where Mr Darcy had sat.

She was twelve when the Duke of Derbyshire, encouraged by his mother, started opening the house for public visits on a more formal basis, which basically meant that he was now charging fifty pence for entry and there was a small tea-room and a little shop. She would never forget the smell of the house – history, tradition, and scones all mixed into one, along with the merest hint of tobacco and a sprinkling of laughter and hyacinths – could never describe it accurately, it was as if it was less of a smell and more like a feeling.

Marjorie watched as her daughter, surely the most serious twelve-year-old in existence, took a seat at the small writing desk by the window, watched as she touched the inlay, carefully read the sign that said this desk had belonged to Elizabeth Bennet-Darcy and had been brought from the house at Longbourn after the death of her father. They shared a scone and pot of tea before walking around the gardens, taking pictures with the Instamatic camera that Joyce had received for her birthday the week before.

On the way out, she bought herself a thin, papery guidebook written by Lady Sybil Darcy with the last of her birthday money. That night she devoured it page by page in one sitting; pouring over the information about each room, each former resident. By midnight, Joyce was fully in love with Pemberley. She had visited at least once a week after that, riding the trolley bus from the entrance gates after walking from her home above the grocers in the centre of Lambton.

"How old are you now, Miss Hutchinson," Winston Darcy asked her one Saturday afternoon as he took her ticket.

"Sixteen now, Your Grace," she said primly, dipping a little curtsey as her mother had shown her.

"No need for all that nonsense, Joyce," he handed back her clipped ticket. "You're here more than my own children, you're practically family."

"Thank you, Your Grace," she smiled. "It's an honour."

"Joyce. Call me Winston."

She was unsure.

"*Winston.*"

"It is my name after all," he walked through to the courtyard with her. It was empty on this brisk autumn day and she had been the only visitor to the house so far. "Would you like a job, Miss Hutchinson?"

Her eyes went wide, a strange excitement filled her, "a job here… at Pemberley?"

"Of *course,* a job here – it wouldn't be too much money to start off with, and only on Saturdays – cleaning the house and dusting and what-not. When my children are back from school you would need to show them what to do."

Joyce would have no trouble telling the spoiled Darcy children, with their famous mother and their boarding school accents, exactly what to do. Especially Julia, who was the rudest of them all. Winston was more down to earth than all three of them, with his second-hand wellies and wearing the same tweed suit she had seen him in for years. He looked more like a jovial farmer than a Duke, with a fluffy moustache and hair smoothed down with Brylcreem, but he had a barrelling laugh that could be heard across the lake and, in the evenings, he was rarely seen without a cigar.

"I can do that," she exclaimed. "I would love to work here."

"Well," he said with a smile. "That's settled. You can start on Saturday week, go and see Mr Wickham in the office, and he will sort you out."

Joyce glanced up from under her flippy Charlie's Angels fringe, "Mr *Wickham?*"

"Don't worry, you don't have to elope with him straight away!"

The Duke walked back out to the front of the house where a few other visitors had gathered next to his makeshift ticket booth. Joyce Hutchinson squealed with excitement before running up the steps and into the house.

Joyce was now the General Manager for the whole Pemberley estate. It hadn't been easy. She had worked hard before getting her post, studying part-time for a master's degree in museum studies whilst working as a curator at Dunmarleigh House in Cheshire, raising two children and nursing her mum, who had early-onset Alzheimer's and a tendency to wander off. But she loved it here. Joyce was always firmly of the belief that Pemberley held a special kind of magic and, as far as she was concerned, she was the one responsible for making sure it kept hold of as much of it as it could.

Sitting down at her desk in the office at the front of the house - the room that had once been the study of Fitzwilliam Darcy – she heard the crash and clatter outside, and she cringed wondering which part of the house the production team had damaged now. Despite all the publicity and extra visitors that would ensue when the film was released, and the injection of cash that they had already received from the production company, she was still having to cut costs across the board to maintain the property at its current level, the huge visitor numbers still not quite enough to fully meet all of the requirements of a huge estate; she was even covering for her Senior Curator, who was on maternity leave, to save a few extra pounds. Extra damage was all she needed today. Getting up, she swigged her cup of tea and made her way outside with an angry, pinched look on her face, her walkie-talkie blaring away at her hip.

Lizzy clambered out of the minibus and thanked Steve profusely for the lift before grabbing her bag and jacket before run-walking as well as she could in heels. She tottered past the small group of paparazzi who had gathered to try and get shots of Tamsin McLeod with no make-up on, or Benn Williams looking sad and depressed since his pretty wife left him. None of them deemed her of any importance, apart from Harold – who must have been eighty by now – he shouted, 'Lady Liz' and took what could only be called a 'pity pap' as she did her most gracious smile before hurrying on her way.

She was determined that one day she would not be late for work, the small practice of Winchester, Sparrow and Jones in Lambton was only ten minutes away from the estate by bus, nestled amongst the row of small shops in the centre of Lambton, but it was arduous when carrying everything that she needed for the day. Blundering through the door, she nearly knocked over Angela's spider plant with what Harriet called her 'Law Bag' – a huge old leather satchel that used to be Winston's and still had a faint whiff of cigars and the British Empire about it.

"Bloody hell, Lizbot, you look a bit flustered this morning," shouted Rob Sparrow from his desk at the back of the office. "Stick the kettle on, will you?"

She sighed and threw her bag down on the cluttered desk that was piled with books and papers; the satchel slipped and sent a pile of buff folders ticker taping to the ground. For all she was disorganised on her desk, Lizzy was organised in her head, but it did drive Deb, a feisty Geordie with fifteen years of paralegal experience and a sharp tongue, to distraction – especially when her own desk was laid out with such a perfect symmetry that it nearly bordered on obsessional.

"Liz is not putting the kettle on, Rob!" She yelled down the corridor outside the office they shared. "If you want a bloody coffee, you can make it yourself!" She shut the office door behind her. "Arsehole."

"You do remember that his dad is your boss, right?" Lizzy reminded, switching her computer on, "and, like, my boss and the man who owns the firm?"

"He needs to remember that he is perfectly capable of making his own drink! He needs to get up off his arse and do it," she said, obviously irritated. "Don't worry, I got us both a caramel latte from Starbucks, my treat."

"I'm sure it's my turn," she sighed, even though she was grateful for the sugary hit of caffeine.

Lizzy slouched down in her office chair and began picking up the files off the floor, she had been working on a complicated inheritance case involving multiple heirs across five countries and she was hoping for a resolution before the end of the summer.

Probate had not been something she had longed to do when she completed her degree and dragged herself through the LPC, but it seemed apt at the time, but however much she tried to gloss over it in her head, it was dull. Even the interesting juicy cases weren't particularly appealing, or maybe she had just been doing it for too long – nearly twelve years of dealing with the recently dead was always guaranteed to put a dampener on the working day.

"What happened at your star-studded party on Saturday, any shenanigans that I should know about. Did they have that prosecco with the gold leaf in it?"

Lizzy, still facing her monitor, swivelled around on her office chair and raised her eyebrow. Deb caught the look and knew full well that something exciting *had* happened at Pemberley; Lizzy didn't really venture out to events often, preferring the quiet solitude of wandering through the park after the gates had closed for the night or spending her evenings half writing novels that she never finished. However, when she did go out, there was always a story, always something wondrous and exciting.

"What did you do?" she said excitedly, emphasising the words.

Lizzy rolled her eyes. "Nothing!"

"Groped by a grip?" Deb raised her eyebrows suggestively.

"Sod off! If you are going to joke, then I don't even think you deserve to know."

"Erm, you spent the evening snapchatting with your new bestie Jenny Graves, and snogged Philip Thomson?"

She wasn't in the mood for guessing games this morning. Both of her girls had driven her halfway up the wall on the way to school and she turned back to her screen, taking a big gulp of the much-needed coffee.

"Well no, but I did get some selfies with Franklin Hughes, and I did sing Dancing Queen with Mariella Jones," she said nonchalantly. "Oh, and I met Benn Williams...is that's exciting enough for you."

Deb spat out her latte all over her desk, droplets of Starbucks dribbling down the wall and her new pink file folders from Paperchase.

"Are you joking'? *The* Benn Williams? But I thought you said he was only coming for a few days."

"I don't know how long he's here for, but he's staying at the Armitage," she caught the look on her friend's face. "I have *not* told you that!"

There was a knock on the door and Harris Jones popped his head around the doorframe. He was a small, ginger man with almost translucent skin, and he reminded Lizzy very much of a dormouse.

"Elizabeth."

"Harris."

"Do I have to mention about the shoes again?"

He gestured to the bumblebee wedge shoes that were peeking out from underneath her desk.

"I'm sorry, it was a genuine mistake this morning. I overslept."

"Yes, that's the other thing. Timekeeping. You've been late three times this week already."

Lizzy tried her best to look contrite, "I didn't mean it. I promise it won't happen again."

"Okay," he seemed placated, never wanting to tell off Lady Darcy, whose name alone was enough to generate ample business for the small firm and scampered away down the corridor.

Deb snorted into her coffee again, setting her off into a fit of uncontrollable giggles. Lizzy laughed louder than a woman dealing with death probably should, they turned the radio up and danced on their chairs to her ABBA playlist for the rest of the morning, much to the annoyance of Harris, whose shouts down the corridor were promptly ignored as usual.

1988

The girl had sneaked off from the library, where groups of old people were making noise about nothing. She had reached up on her tiptoes, her hands glancing across the polished walnut wood, the scrape of her dungaree clasp against the handle of the dresser.

The room was cold, dark, only partly illuminated by the light escaping from the room next door, the faint chinks of moonlight pushing through the heavy shutters that had been closed earlier that evening. She always expected to be scared walking through the grand staterooms when no-one was about, but she never found the house scary. When the shutters were closed, and the curtains were drawn, she felt as if it were simply resting for the night, giving out a creaking yawn and settling down for an evening's slumber.

"Lizzy," the voice was stern, it came from nowhere. It made her jump. "Be careful with that!"

It was Grandad Duke. She ran towards him, holding onto his legs tightly. He was dressed in his dancing suit; it smelled like outside and smoking. She grasped onto his hand and pulled him towards the dresser. The box had always held a strange fascination for her. Plain and unassuming, it seemed out of place in the ornate room where it lived. She reached out and placed her hand on it.

"Grandad, what is it?"

Winston had found that despite himself, he had come to adore the little eight-year-old with her loud opinions and determined manner. She had only meant to stay for a few months, a year at most until she had been old enough to board at St Margaret's in Bushey as all the Darcy girls did; but she had never made it to Hertfordshire. Instead, she had lived here for three years now, running through the house like a whirlwind, breathing fresh air into his home, resuscitating Pemberley for a new generation.

"It's a box of something very precious."

Elizabeth reached for the wooden box, carefully holding it in her hands. It was smooth and solid, heavier than she imagined, and she placed it down on the rug. Sitting cross-legged on the floor in front of it, glancing up at her grandad with expectant eyes.

"What's inside? Is it jewels? Is this where you 'ide the all the 'eirlooms"

Winston frowned a little, sending his granddaughter to the local primary school in Lambton had resulted in more than a hint of a Derbyshire accent, and a plethora of dropped aitches.

"Do you really think we would hide our jewels in the house, Lizzy?"

"You can 'ide them in plain sight," she said knowingly. "When Charlie was 'ere..."

"Elizabeth," he interrupted, "if you insist on continuing with this story then you need to speak properly."

She paused for a moment, eyed him under her curls, and then very seriously in a cut-glass accent that he swore was identical to that of his ex-wife, she enunciated very clearly.

"When Charlie was here, he said that the best place for one to hide one's precious things is in plain sight," she was very serious. *"Your Grace."*

She performed an awkward bow from her position on the floor and beamed at him with a cheeky toothless smile. Her front teeth had both fallen out within days of each other, and she had left a list of demands for the Tooth Fairy under her pillow, which included a tiara, a wand, fifty pence, and a Milky Way. He had, in his capacity as Tooth Fairy, happily obliged, fully aware that she had him wrapped around her little finger.

Trying to hide a smirk Winston shook his head, "all of the jewels are in the vault at the bank. We're not pirates, Elizabeth!"

Disappointment crossed her face and he could see the slight shudder of her sulky lip, he lowered himself to the floor, using his ever-present cane, and sat in front of her.

"No jewels?" her voice aching with disappointment. "What is in here then? It must be very precious."

"What is in here is much more precious than jewels, in here is a whole life."

"That doesn't sound as exciting as jewels, grandad."

He reached into his pocket, shuffled about a bit with a few bits and pulled out a small key, unlocking the box. She noticed the smell first; musky paper, smoke and, faintly, an orangey smell that she didn't quite recognise. These were letters, well they looked like letters, all tied up with a yellow ribbon.

Winston sensed her disappointment, knew that she couldn't realise now what he was showing her. But one day, when she was grown up, she would know.

"You see, Lizzy, we are simply guests in this house. It is our duty to look after it and care for it, for when we are gone, we will join those who have gone before us."

She shook her head, her curls falling loose from the red bow that tied them up and she closed the box shut, satisfied now she knew what was inside.

"But why are you keeping old letters?"

"Well, these happen to be very important letters."

"Is it because they are old?"

"They *are* old. Over one hundred and fifty years old, and they were written by a lady who used to live here a long time ago," he had piqued her interest. "She was a very special lady. Shall I tell you why?"

"Yes, please!"

"Her name was Elizabeth Darcy too, and she was so special that another very famous lady wrote a book about her."

Lizzy wasn't sure about the existence of another Elizabeth Darcy – especially not one who lived at Pemberley.

Surely, she was unique in her Elizabeth Darcy-ness.

Mrs Reynolds often said, *'there's only* one *of you, Elizabeth Darcy, and thank the heavens for that!'* and Mrs Reynolds was never wrong.

"A book about Elizabeth Darcy like me? And she lived here too? At Pemberley?"

Winston nodded, sure that she would be impressed.

"And, was she *real?*"

She eyed him with great suspicion. Grandad Duke liked telling fibs.

"Yes, she also happens to be your great great great great great great grandmother."

Lizzy stared at her grandad in complete and utter awe, her mind wasn't sure how to wrap itself around this whole idea.

"That's a lot of greats."

"She was an especially great lady."

"These are very special letters then, aren't they?"

"They are," he paused for a moment. "When I am gone, Elizabeth…"

"Gone? Where are you going?"

"I'm not going anywhere. Lizzy. Listen. A long time from now, when you are a big girl, you must promise me that you will take this box and keep it safe."

She wasn't quite sure what was being asked of her, but she nodded. She would remember.

He ruffled her hair and she grinned up at him. They placed the box back on the dresser and walked through to the library, where guests and tea and biscuits waited for them.

"They're all here you know, grandad," she said as she pulled him into the warmth of the yellow room

"Who?"

Lizzy took a seat on the settee in front of the fire and took a large slurp of tea from her teacup. In the bay window, she could hear the quiet, well-enunciated chunner of the ladies from the WI who came over with lemon biscuits, knitted cardigans, and opinions on her education, and the warm northern tones of Mrs Wharton floating over it all.

"The other Darcys who have lived here before," she reached for a biscuit, shovelling the crumbly shortbread into her mouth. "They're here in the stories, or the pictures, in the things they bought or made." She slurped her tea again, "every time you touch something they touched, it's like we touch them. It's like we're time travellers, Grandad," she said boldly. "We just don't know it."

Winston realised that in the seventy-three years he had lived at Pemberley, he had never thought about it that way, but she was right.

"Yes," he smiled, his eyes crinkling at the edges. "We're very lucky, aren't we?"

Lizzy sunk back into the velvet damask, the sound of conversation and the comforting heat of the fire surrounding her and nodded.

LADY IMOGEN ARRESTED

Lady Imogen Darcy, 19, was arrested at the family home in Belgravia during the early hours of Saturday morning for breach of the peace. The naughty noble, great-granddaughter of socialite suffragette Millicent Darcy, was cautioned by Police and released on Sunday. There was no comment from the Darcy estate.

Seven

The front door was up a small flight of stone steps, with a cast-iron railing on each side before a tall and imposing door with six glass panels and brass handles opened and led into the epic grandeur of the entrance hall. Mr Darcy was sitting fully dressed in his Regency splendour, and there was a flurry of activity surrounding him as production assistants and crew prepared for the scene, their voices and the noise echoing around the square courtyard at the centre of the house. He had been driven to Pemberley early that morning and sent for a run around the park with Patrick, the persistent and perky coach who had pushed him hard for the last few weeks until his breeches began to fit comfortably, and his six-pack began to re-emerge.

Lucy finished styling his hair; they had worked together for a long time and she could confidently state that she knew every pore on his face. She was currently brushing out his sideburns and smoothing them with wax, they tended to puff out when he got hot.

"I'm glad you shaved the beard off," she said.

"You are?"

He had thought he looked good with the beard, even buying a beard comb and some expensive oil from Neal's Yard.

"I thought beards were 'in' now."

He was sure they were, he had read a *'50 Hottest Beards Right Now'* article in Star Goss and been convinced to take a foray into facial hair. Lucy, the sun shining from behind and casting her bright red hair into a scarlet halo, had a scrunched up look on her face.

"You *genuinely* thought it looked good?"

Slightly offended, he pulled a face.

"It *did* look good!!"

"Who told you this?"

"Erm," he struggled to think of an example. "A-ha! The Daily Mail! People on Twitter!"

Lucy laughed out loud, her perfectly winged eyeliner creasing as she did. Benn looked quite indignant but felt totally crestfallen. He had been very proud of his facial hair.

"It's not a good beard, not like a hipster beard or one of those lumberjack beards. It's... well... it's..."

She shook her head quickly, not wanting to say anymore, continuing to curl his hair.

"Go on," he pressed.

"It looks a bit pubey."

Benn looked at her, astonished at her frank defamation of what he personally thought was rather a good beard.

"Pubey, you say?"

She nodded as she powdered his face.

"So, you're telling me now, *five months later*, that I have been walking around looking like a giant fanny?"

She tried hard to stifle a laugh as she removed his paper bib.

"Fuck me, Luce, thanks a lot! I expected more from my *sister in law*, I really did!"

The laugh burst out of her, "but you were so proud of it!!"

"I was! But next time, please tell me if I'm walking around with Linda Lovelace's bush on my face, won't you?"

"I promise!"

"Did Sean think it was shit?"

"We *all* thought it was shit."

He looked thoughtful, "even my mum?"

Lucy nodded.

"You're all bastards."

She threw back her head laughing, "but we all love you, with or without your shit beard."

Dabbing his nose with a final brush of powder, she released him on his way, still laughing as she packed away her equipment.

Walking out to the front gate he went to join the rest of the main cast for a pre-arranged publicity event, pacing through the entrance porch and out onto the driveway. The new boots were rubbing his heel slightly and he stopped for a moment to adjust them – there was already a sizeable crowd waiting on the front driveway, too many people perhaps. He took a deep breath, inhaled his public persona and let it cover him like a cloak. He was ready now, stepping out with a broad smile.

He wasn't sure if it was being out of London or seeing the positive feedback he had been getting online – apparently, Colin Firth and his wet shirt paled in comparison to Benn Williams in his tight trousers – but he was feeling pretty good right now. A few leaked pictures from the Vanquish Pictures press office had caused a stir of longing for this new Mr Darcy in the collective psyche of women of a certain age. Benn liked how quickly he had managed to get back into shape but was grateful that Mr Darcy didn't require the same hard-toned physique as some of his more demanding wet-shirted roles. He didn't think he was physically or mentally up to recreating the bare-chested perfection of Henry Jones or Catcher Rothschild.

"Please can you sign it to Vicki?" the woman asked, as she passed him the pen and a copy of Pride and Prejudice.

He nodded, they had been standing here in full Regency wedding gear for the last three hours as they completed publicity shots and did a meet and greet with a few competition winners and the local press. He signed with a flourish, before giving Vicki a quick kiss on the cheek.

"Are you excited about playing Mr Darcy?" she was aware of the heat rising to her face.

"Well, as excited as you can be spending the hottest month of the year in a cravat."

He shot her the famous smile; the one perfected through years of public appearances and three weeks of painful dental work, and she visibly flushed.

"Can I get a selfie with you and Franklin?"

"Of course," he said, calling Mr Bingley over towards him. They all huddled in close together. "Smile!"

Vicki giggled as he kissed her on the cheek, she returned to her group of friends who all laughed with her before walking off triumphantly.

"Is it always like this, Benn?" Franklin said as they continued to pose together.

"Not always but enjoy it for now!"

"Oh, I intend to," he gulped at a bottle of water greedily.

Franklin had already been christened Bada-Bingley and as he walked off to speak to some more adoring fans, was clearly loving the attention. They had been on set since half six and it was now quarter to four and they weren't even a third of the way through today's busy schedule.

There had been the issues of aeroplanes; the location was under the flight path of Manchester airport and ten takes in a row had been ruined by the sound of Dreamliners ferrying holidaymakers overseas, secondly, Jenny could not remember her lines. She only had four and she fluffed them over and over. It made it hard for him to concentrate and he had snapped meanly at her, causing her to recoil like a kicked puppy. He got up and walked off the set, desperate for a drink and a puff on his e-cig. He grabbed a coffee from the catering truck and asked his assistant, Leanne, to get his bag from the trailer.

He wandered up past the Orangery and onto the top lawn, taking a moment to surround himself in a cloud of self-righteous pineapple vapour. Sitting on a bench at the top end of the garden, away from the tourists and the volunteers and all the popular bits that had been on the TV, you couldn't hear anything apart from the gentle chirrup of birdsong and your own heartbeat.

Benn wondered if Fitzwilliam had ever sat here to admire his mansion and gaze out on the land that belonged to him. He was nearly twenty years older than Darcy would have been when he inherited and didn't know how the gentleman had coped with it all, the thought of it made him feel anxious.

His phone buzzed. His wife's number still caused his heart to bounce, even if her text messages were never for nice reasons.

MADDY: You did it again last night.
BENN: I'm sorry.
MADDY: It's not good enough.
BENN: That's not fair.
MADDY: Neither is calling me in the middle of the night.

He was contemplating replying, but the indignant heat on his face meant that any reply would just be fuel to an already raging fire. The crunch of gravel underfoot caught Benn's attention; angrily walking past him was Lady Elizabeth, wearing a turquoise dress covered in swans and he was quite sure shoes with bees on them. She didn't acknowledge him but walked straight past, continuing her way with a forceful stomp and what he guessed was an inadvertent wiggle.

Benn sighed.

Yet another woman he had unintentionally annoyed, but at least he could try and make it up to her.

BENN: Can you send Lady Darcy some flowers?
LEANNE: Sure. What kind?
BENN: Something fancy...

LEANNE: Is this the 'I've Pissed Someone Off' bunch?
BENN: You know me so well... :)
LEANNE: You should get loyalty points looooooooool!

2001

The winter air was thick with cold and Lizzy felt the ice in her lungs as she climbed the steep hill from the car park and up to the house. The hill was steep, much steeper than she had remembered it being when dragging her sledge up it after careering down it during the winter, Mr Staughton calling to her from the top, promising hot chocolate and buttered seed cake whilst Winston watched from his study. The cold was taking her breath away and she struggled for a moment to reach the top, the icy wind blowing in from the peaks causing a chill in her bones. She pulled her coat in tightly around her, adjusting her mittens as she dragged three shopping bags up the deceptive incline.

The transition from a family home to tourist attraction was going smoothly for the house, which was enjoying a lavish and careful programme of restoration. There had been a serious repainting of the window frames, a thorough tending of the gardens and the deepest of spring cleans. Inside pictures were being restored and items rediscovered after a full cataloguing of the attics, including the rediscovery of a trunk of authentic and delicate gowns from the early 19th century, some of which, according to their labels, had belonged to Elizabeth Darcy herself.

She recognised a sparkly red gown with gold thread as one that she had dressed up in as a child, parading down the halls and posing for pictures that Maggie took with her new polaroid camera, before discarding the dress at the foot of the staircase and running upstairs to play skittles in the long gallery.

Lizzy had always thought herself slightly resilient to the cold of a Pemberley winter, but this year was particularly harsh; she blamed it on her hormones. The Doctor had confirmed the pregnancy early, there were benefits to being able to pay for a private consultation in Harley Street if you needed to, and she had spent the weekend holed up in the house on Upper Grosvenor Street pretending everything was okay.

Imogen had been bouncing around, giddy and dancing with glee singing Tiny Dancer in a decidedly Mediterranean accent; Carol was fussing and cussing about the nanny, Jacinta, who spoke too much Spanish; Hugh stormed about the house complaining about the noise whilst added to it in loud well enunciated tones; Charlie was home for a few days from Oxford with a few pals from the rowing team, and they hoo-haa'ed and drank.

Lizzy sat there in the middle of it all, feeling like the calm eye of the storm.

"*Tu Madre está loca*, Lady Lizzy."

Jacinta said, one lonely dark night as they sat in the kitchen together, both unable to sleep in the house where silence fell like lead after ten pm.

"*Ella no es mi Madre*," she frowned, stumbling with GCSE Spanish and a smile at the older woman, who passed her a small sweet biscuit wrapped in waxy paper.

"You must eat," she said softly. "The sickness will pass, but you must get stronger...."

Lizzy was apprehensive, unsure how the small woman with almond-shaped eyes and olive skin knew her secret.

"I have had many babies... I know the signs. You mustn't be worried, you are *fuerte*... strong...*y usted es* clever." Jacinta placed her hand gently on Lizzy's shoulder, "I am a firm believer in this, Lady Lizzy, *donde hay gana, hay maña...*"

Lizzy shook her head at Jacinta nonplussed.

"How you say..." she thought, "Where there is a *deseo*...desire...ummm... will, there is a way... always in my family, we say this."

"You do?"

She nodded, pouring a cup of hot, sweet coffee.

"My great-great-grandmother raised three sisters alone after their father was gone."

"What happened to him?"

"He was a gentleman. A Captain. They fell in love, but she was poor, and he was from a rich family, they would not have approved."

"Ooh, a secret love affair! Did he ever tell them?"

Jacinta fussed over the biscuit wrappers in her hand.

"That is the tragedy of it...his ship sank on the way back home to her. She never saw him again. He was lost to the ocean," the coffee was being stirred through with cream now, "but my ancestor, she pressed on always striving, always better. You are like this too, *pienso... Valiente.*"

"Brave?"

"*Sí, es usted* brave, very *valiente, muy, muy.*"

"She sounds very brave. I hope I can have half of her courage."

"I know that you do, Lady Lizzy."

Jacinta took her by the hand, the crinkly tanned fingers squeezing gently, before the older woman padded down the stairs to her little flat in the basement of the house, crooning a soft melody in Spanish, the words rolling off her tongue.

Lizzy pondered and sipped on her drink, taking the time to delicately dunk the small biscuits, watching as they soaked up the liquid, never faltering. She didn't know what kind of mother she was going to be, but she did know that she was going to do her best.

It was the Darcy way.

"Hello, I was wondering if you would be able to help me," Lizzy asked the kindly faced woman at the Student Advice desk on the second day of term.

"I will have a go."

The woman had a warm Mancunian accent, the badge on her lanyard said that her name was Barbara.

"I was told that I needed to register a name change to ensure that it's correct on my transcripts?"

Lizzy had been dreading this day, it felt so pretentious. She had loved being able to coast as Lizzy Darcy, getting the odd smirk from an English Lit undergrad or a glance of recognition from the occasional lecturer, but mostly she had been anonymous at Manchester.

Barbara took Lizzy's name and student ID and begin to tippity-tap into the keyboard; they had only recently moved over to a new computer system and she wasn't used to it yet, preferring the old-fashioned methods of cards and files.

"Right, so I will need your marriage certificate, have you brought it with you?"

"Marriage certificate?"

"Yes, your marriage certificate... for your change of name?" She glanced down at the protruding bump between them, a friendly smile spreading across her face.

"Oh," Lizzy wrapped her coat around her tightly, "no, I haven't got married ..."

"Have you changed it by deed-poll or been legally adopted?"

Barbara's tone was getting ever so slightly more official with each word she spoke.   Lizzy reached into her bag and pulled out the envelope that contained the letter and legal information from her uncle's office, which documented the change in her name from simply 'The Hon. Miss Elizabeth Darcy' to 'Lady Elizabeth Darcy'. Barbara scanned through the letter, before taking it to a colleague, who squinted over it before looking at Elizabeth as though she was bonkers. Barbara came back and placed the letter back on the desk, taking time to fold it flat.

"Did you get this for Christmas?" Barbara flicked through the documentation with a well-manicured fingernail. "Because I know it *says* you're a 'Lady', but those gift packs aren't legally binding, we couldn't update it on your degree certificate. Do you understand, love?"

"Yes, I do understand that, but this is…" she smiled politely at Barbara, who proceeded to look at her as if she was a simpleton. "Wait! I have the card for my Uncle's office, and you can speak to them and they will confirm it… I wouldn't usually have bothered, but apparently, it's a legal requirement."

"Well, yes," Barbara grumbled as she took the card and then retreated to her colleague, who phoned the number, both women stood looking at her from across the sea of office furniture.

The smaller woman glanced over at Barbara and nodded, Lizzy could see her visibly redress herself and she returned to the counter with an ingratiating smile.

"All of that seems to be in order, *Lady Elizabeth*, so I will get your records updated and we will reissue last semesters transcripts and send them out to your home address, which is…?"

She stared with squinting eyes through the thick lenses of her heavy brown spectacles.

"Pemberley."

"Oh, yes. I see."

Barbara wondered what had happened to the young woman with the frizzy hair and heavy eyeliner, that she was here now all alone with no husband and a baby on the way. Her face softened, and she glanced at Elizabeth with a thoughtful and kind look.

"Can I ask you a question, Lady Elizabeth?"

Lizzy wondered what this could possibly be.

"Yes, of course."

"Did Colin Firth walk about in that wet shirt *all* day?"

Lizzy reached the top of the hill and hurried towards the porch, desperate to get inside. Instinctively she turned left, before remembering and turning right to enter the house via the staff entrance. She went into the estate office – this had, thankfully, not changed – although Winston's office was now occupied by the House Manager. Carefully she placed a tin of posh biscuits on top of the staff sign-in sheets – the people who had led the Pemberley tours before were all kept on by the HHS and she was happy that there were still so many familiar faces, as well as lots of new ones.

Winston had always bought biscuits for the small team, always looked after the people who loved the house, small gestures like handwritten cards at Christmas, a picnic party in the Summer, and she knew that wherever he was, he would want her to carry on these traditions that made Pemberley feel less like a workplace and more like a family. It had always been the Darcy way, he said.

As she reached the door to her flat, she took a deep breath, fully aware that it would be freezing; dumping her shopping on the floor, she scurried quickly through to the bathroom, not noticing the figure sitting on the couch. The woman waited for her to return, eyed her up and down as she walked out of the icy bathroom wiping her hands on a similarly cold towel, watched as she removed her coat and turned on the kettle.

"Hello, Elizabeth."

The cut-glass boarding school tones seemed hideously out of place coming from the lofty, slender woman with pink dreadlocks and a nose ring. Lizzy was astonished to see the woman standing there, having only ever seen her on photographs at Maggie's, where she wrapped her arms around Matthew with Big Smiles and city landscapes. She was much taller than Lizzy had imagined and had a frostiness that was incongruous with her general appearance.

"Cara? So nice to meet you finally, I have heard so much about you."

She crossed over with her hand outstretched, the origins of Lady Liz beginning right now at this moment.

Cara Dalhousie did not take Lizzy's hand, nor did she smile or move, instead she stood as still as a stone statue.

"Was that before or after you fucked my boyfriend?" Cara stared with cold, dead eyes, her pupils massive like a great white shark getting ready to strike its prey. "Or was it during...did he tell you all about me when he was taking you roughly from behind?" She giggled, but there was nothing funny about this. Cara Dalhousie was not used to people playing with her toys, she trilled. "I mean, he wouldn't look at your face, would he? Little frizzy thing, aren't you?"

"I beg your pardon?"

"This bullshit might work on Matthew, but it sure as well won't with me," she hissed. "I know your kind, Elizabeth Darcy, pretending to be all innocent on the outside..."

"I have no idea what you mean."

She felt cornered, wanted to push this leggy stranger out of the way and run down the stairs.

"That."

Cara pointed at the small rounded bump slightly protruding from under the heavy jumper. Lizzy pulled her coat around her protectively and turned away slightly.

"My fiancé's baby, I'm guessing."

She spoke with a sneer, a condescending tone with a sadistic chord on the sharp edges of her sentences.

There was silence; it was filled with doubt and betrayal and rage. When Matthew had returned from Derbyshire after the funeral, he was different, and she knew that something had happened. It hadn't taken much to get the information from him, a weeping confession eked out over the course of three days. He was always rubbish at lying. She made him promise never to contact this Lizzy again and he agreed, not wanting to lose her.

Cara Dalhousie firmly believed that the best way to pretend something didn't happen is always to ignore it. She hadn't meant to read the email, but it was there in his inbox; an important message from his sister who felt that he should know. It was as if the weight of it dropped right through her because fucking someone else was something she could forgive – they were young, and love was fluid – but a baby? Well, that was something completely different. A baby gave the betrayal arms and legs and screams in the night.

"You really are ridiculous, aren't you?" Cara sniggered. "Were you going to keep this a secret? Do you have any idea what this will do to your father's reputation?"

"My father knows," Lizzy felt unshielded, but she wasn't going to show it. "He's happy to welcome a new Darcy into the world, and his opinion is the only one that matters to me."

"A new Wickham, you mean…that will be fun for the press." She raised an eyebrow, a sadistic chortle escaping her lips. "But what about your stepmother? Your little sister? Your brothers? Don't you care what your carelessness has done?" She circled her like a hungry hyena, waiting for her to fall, to show any sign of weakness. "I mean, it's *obvious* you engineered this whole shitstorm and conveniently left it too late to have it sucked out of you."

Lizzy digested the words. The truth was that she had thought about it, how much easier it would be to not do this; but when it came down to it, she hadn't been able to, because the thought of not going ahead with it was much scarier.

"You know, I never understood what he saw in you. You're mediocre at best, Darcy." She looked at Lizzy, tilting her head to one side. "He told me about that afternoon, how he felt sorry for you. He took pity on you and you practically *threw* yourself at him. Did your grandfather never tell you that it's very bad form to fuck the staff?"

Lizzy swallowed hard, bit her tongue; she had a whole barrage of weapons that she could fire at Cara Dalhousie, but there was no point; no need to cause any more pain. She softened slightly, knowing that for all her anger and insults, Cara was simply a girl whose boyfriend had hurt her.

"I know you are upset about this, but you are taking it out on the wrong person. I didn't cheat on you, *he* did!"

"You let him cheat on me!" she raised her voice, then composed herself. "You facilitated it, and now we have this," she pointed at the bump.

"We don't have anything," Lizzy said with resoluteness in her voice. "I have never asked for your involvement."

There was a moment of silence and the two women eyed each other up from across the room. Lizzy had always been taught to stand up for herself and she was not going to be bullied by a woman who was taking the moral high ground on behalf of her cheating boyfriend.

"Your issue is more to do with Matthew, and not with me. If he wants to be involved in this baby's life, then there is nothing I can do to stop it, and neither can you."

Cara Dalhousie was used to getting her own way. It had been the same since she was a small child and was a character flaw that had seeped like spilled ink into her adult personality. Matthew always did as he was told, always complied with her wants, needs, and desires. That was what made him such a perfect partner – she set out to get him and now she had him, but the stone in her bespoke leather shoe was Elizabeth Darcy and this unborn baby. She knew full well that Matthew longed to be involved, wanted to move back north and transfer his course credits to Manchester. Cara didn't want this, was already planning to actively object. Lizzy Darcy could stay in her mouldy old manor house in Derbyshire, but she wasn't going to be schlepping up here every other weekend to visit a brat.

"I'll tell you what is going to happen, Elizabeth," she intonated carefully. "You will go and see Matthew now and you will tell him that you don't want him to be part of the baby's life. I think that will be best for all parties concerned."

"I will do nothing of the sort," she swallowed hard.

Cara's features were hardened now, the veneer of spiritual assuredness failing as she realised that she was not going to get what she wanted. Lizzy turned on her heel and walked into the kitchen, shouting back over her shoulder.

"Now unless you have something nice to say, I would like you to leave. For future reference, this area of the house is out of bounds to the general public."

Cara's footprints were heavy on the oak floorboards, her exit signalled by a loud slam of the door. Lizzy took a moment to regain her composure before sitting on the floor of the kitchen, holding her belly tightly and feeling the baby kick sharply in protest.

"No, little one, I don't like her either," she whispered, before getting to her feet and putting her shopping away.

It was nearly eight o'clock when Maggie knocked on the door tentatively. She had helped her friend decorate in a warm yellow colour a few months before, but the colour did nothing to brighten up this dark evening. She knew that the letter she held in her hand probably didn't contain the words that Lizzy wanted, and she was reluctant to hand it over.

Matthew had already left a few hours before, chasing a stomping Cara as she headed towards her Range Rover. They were arguing; shrill expletives being scattered about, following by softer apologies, before escalating into shouts and screams on the driveway of the stables. Gary, the head ranger, had come out of the office and demanded in his bellowing northern tones that they take their disagreements elsewhere, and they had sped off towards the driveway and then back down the M6 towards London.

The room was freezing, and Maggie made two steaming mugs of coffee before lighting a fire in the large fireplace that dominated the room. Lizzy was cocooned in a blanket on the couch, her head resting on a pillow, her closed eyes puffy and red from where she had been crying.

She noticed that the mantel was covered in new pictures – photos of her friends from university, a picture of her little sister Imogen cuddling their even smaller brother Joe just after he was born in May, an old polaroid of Maggie and Lizzy cuddling on the grand staircase on Christmas Day, and a newer photograph of Winston from a few months before he died. Lizzy was trying to make the flat feel more like home, but she didn't have the time, the energy or the inclination. Between travelling back and forth to Manchester, working at Pemberley on the weekend and growing a baby, she was absolutely exhausted. Jean was worried, Maggie was concerned. There was still a while to go yet. She noticed a scan picture that she hadn't seen before, placed on top of a pile of books, the image was clear, and she could see arms and legs now, rather than the indecipherable blur that she always pretended she could identify as a baby.

"Did you find out what you're having?"

She plonked herself down on the couch and passed Lizzy her mug of coffee from the table. The room was beginning to warm up now, the condensation on the twelve-pane windows starting to dissipate, Lizzy leaned over, breathed on the glass and wrote 'girl' as she stared forlornly out of the window and out onto the lake.

"You're having a girl?"

Maggie had really wanted a niece, had already bought some little pink bootees and a tiny romper dotted with embroidered flowers.

"I am."

"Mum will be so happy. We haven't had a girl in the family since I was born!"

"I'm going to be able to do this, aren't I?"

"Yes. Of course, you are."

"I'm exhausted already, and she isn't even here!"

It had been an emotional day and she hadn't felt prepared to deal the onslaught from Cara who, quite frankly, was a lot worse than she imagined. She wasn't sure if it was the shouting or the horrible realisation that maybe it had meant more to her than it had to Matthew. Afterwards, there had been little time to talk about it, and the few conversations they had had before he went back to London were stilted and empty.

"You have to remember that your great-granny raised two children and ran this whole estate all by herself, and she didn't have me like you do."

Lizzy felt a smile on across her face, Maggie was right; she had a generous allowance each month from her inheritance from Winston, who had ensured that she would be well cared for. She knew that she could afford to comfortably look after herself and the baby, as well as continuing her studies – and she had Maggie and Jean over at the stables who would be there when she needed them.

She didn't need Matthew Wickham and his stupid face to help her; she understood why Cara was angry, but it was her boyfriend who was at fault here and if she was quite happy to let him into her bed every night, maybe she should try making him be accountable for his bullshit, maybe that would help her align her chakras or whatever crap it was that she needed to do.

Maggie could see the thoughts running through Lizzy's head as she formulated her plan, and then she saw her face as she noticed the letter from Matthew sitting on the table; she knew his writing immediately, the spindly but firm letters imprinted on the envelope – 'Lizard'. She had hated the nickname, given to her by Charlie and Matthew one early teenage summer as she spent almost a fortnight basking in the sunshine near the lake; the name had stuck and by the end of August even Winston was calling her it. Seeing it on the envelope she was cross that he dared to recall this earlier affection, annoyed that he dared to play on their history together. She picked up the envelope, felt the weight of the expensive paper in her hands, the inky scrawl of her name across the paper, and threw it onto the fire.

"Lizzy, what have you done that for?"

She jumped up and tried to pull the letter from the blaze with the poker, but the envelope was already ablaze, the final fragments disappearing into the flames.

"Don't bother with that! If he had anything of worth to say, he would be here saying it to my face rather than sending a letter. The only time your brother has ever sent me letters is when he either needs to lie about something or has bad news; I imagine that letter contained both."

Lizzy folded her arms defiantly. Maggie wasn't sure what was in the letter, wasn't sure what her brother felt about anything anymore, and now they would never know.

The atmosphere in the car was icy. Cara held onto the steering wheel firmly, her eyes locked on the road ahead. She hadn't spoken to him yet, she probably wouldn't for a few days now. He needed to learn his lesson.

Matthew stared out of the window. The world flashed by him as the landscape transformed from the built-up industrialised centres to the rolling pastures of the countryside, as the day began to fade, and everything dimmed, illuminated by streetlights, deep inside he felt something he hadn't felt in a long time. Happy and hopeful.

He had told Lizzy all of this in the letter he had written in his childhood bedroom, scribbling down his excitement and wonder and love with a smile on his face and an image in his head of how it would be.

He could feel the joy painted across his heart.

Eight

The bar at the top of the Beetham Tower was suitably glamorous, with tall sweeping views across the cityscape fading into the countryside beyond, the windows reached from floor to ceiling and small polished tables were dotted around the edges as all shapes and sizes of Mancunian society enjoyed the food and the fabulous cocktails.

It was on the twenty-third floor that this small intimate gathering was taking place and the four figures were perched awkwardly on stools at one of the large tables that edged the centre of the room. Lizzy, befittingly dressed in something demure teamed with red sparkly shoes, was trying hard to make conversation with Carol, who was more stretched and artificial every time she saw her. Hugh was murmuring softly to Matthew, who kept looking at his watch and then at his phone before smiling up at them apologetically. They walked over to the bar together and she grazed his hand with her fingertips, noticing immediately when he brushed them away before ordering their drinks.

"Is it something I've done?"

"Of course, it isn't anything you've done," he dismissed, "you're paranoid."

"There's obviously something."

"Sometimes it isn't always about you."

They stood in silence and she felt like a hollowed-out tree.

"Maybe you shouldn't stay at mine tonight, then."

"Who said I was?"

"You never say you are, it's usually a given."

"Well, tonight I'm not."

Matthew was acting strangely tonight, she thought, constantly checking his phone, ignoring her attempts to make conversation. It was as if he was ignorant of her presence. It was weird, and she didn't like it. He walked off in the direction of their table and she followed sullenly.

She hadn't wanted to come to this tonight, and she found that, once she sat down, she was swinging her legs petulantly like a spoiled child, banging her heels off the metal of the stool, and sipping her Old

Fashioned through the tiniest of straws. Matthew kept glancing at his phone and then up at her as they made small talk with her father and Carol, who had already annihilated a bottle of Merlot.

Hugh Darcy didn't want to be here tonight; he had better things to do than sit in a bar with his wife, who would get drunk and then pick an argument on the way home. Lizzy looked equally bored, and Matthew was scrolling through his phone. Wickham was an alright sort, he guessed, the pair of them muddled through with their unconventional set up, and Harriet was loved dearly, which was the most important thing. Hugh wanted to see his daughter settled though, wanted her to find someone with a good heart and a wicked sense of humour. Someone who was clever too, or who at least could hold his own in a conversation – she was too sharp sometimes and she needed someone to smooth her edges. Darcys were always ridiculously unlucky in love, it seemed; he was no exception.

He watched his wife start flirting with the cocktail waiter as she ordered her weight in gin and wondered where he had gone wrong. Benn Williams was forty minutes late now and they were all running out of things to talk about deemed suitable for polite conversation.

Benn parked the car near the Museum of Science and Industry, stumbling past a group of lads on the street who accosted him for selfies and bought him a beer, chatting jovially with him and then letting him continue on his way. He always found it important to take time to speak to fans, never being dismissive as he found some of his peers did. It was never his intention to be late, in fact, he hated being late for anything, and as he looked at his watch, he realised that he had kept the Duke of Derbyshire waiting now for over fifty minutes.

He was immediately recognised in the lift, the two women in the corner mumbling and giggling, before taking sly photos with their phones thinking that he wouldn't notice and slipping out of the lift laughing out loud and turning back to look at him, just to make sure. Matthew waved him over impatiently and he plastered on his smile, holding out his hand and greeting the Duchess with a kiss on the cheek, the Duke with a firm handshake and Lizzy with a semi-reticent smile.

"And how are you finding Derbyshire?"

Hugh tried to engage Benn in conversation as the starters were placed on the table. The service had been quick for this VIP group, the chefs in the kitchen advised that not only did they have Benn Williams in house, but also Lady Imogen's mum and dad, and Lady Liz, who always tipped well.

"I find it charming, although I am a northern boy by birth," he stabbed a juicy prawn and shoved it in his mouth. "Despite what my agent would have you believe, I'm not actually from the Home Counties."

"Oh, but you play the gentleman so very well. You were a brilliant Heathcliff – that was your big break, wasn't it?"

"It was actually 'Praise to the Skies'."

"I *love* that film," Carol exclaimed. "Steven Malis was a delightfully devilish cad," she purred at him, leaning over and placing her hand suggestively on his arm. "Whereabouts are you from? Cheshire? We have a lovely set of friends in Wilmslow, perhaps you know them…"

"I very much doubt that."

"Benn is rags to riches story all by himself," Matthew dragged his eyes away from his phone to participate in the conversation.

"That's right," he agreed. "I grew up as poor as a church mouse in a tiny council house. My mum still refuses to move."

"A council estate?" Carol enunciated snottily, retracting her hand quickly and sniffing her wine with unmitigated pretension.

"I do take some responsibility," Matthew interrupted, "if my little film hadn't plucked him from obscurity, then you would be all be running in very different circles."

"Really?" Carol said with a strangely haughty tone, that made Matthew and Lizzy look at each other knowingly. "But you always seem to be so… well-bred."

Lizzy guffawed before eating her bruschetta, crumbs falling over her dress. Benn glanced over, a smile crossing his lips as he addressed the Duchess directly.

"It's all a façade, I'm afraid." He flashed his charming smile, before whispering conspiratorially, "all cheap trickery and posh accents, but don't tell anyone, it can be our secret. Although I hear the slight hint of a Yorkshire twang there, Your Grace, are we both faking it?"

He watched as Carol visibly buffered, like a YouTube video failing to load, and he took a large swig of his water, before throwing Lizzy a wry smile which he was pleased to note she returned.

"You know, Matthew, I find your attitude a bit presumptuous," Lizzy said, the words bitter like lemon. "I'm fairly certain that Benn would have made it with or without you, to be fair."

"There is always some truth in everything," Benn tried to placate everyone on all sides.

"Although it's not like Matthew found you cleaning out the whippet cage, is it?" Lizzy smirked, looking pointedly at the man himself, who was glaring at her.

"Well no, but…"

"I mean, you did go to Cambridge, after all. You were in the Footlights with Tom O'Mara, for crying out loud."

Benn sensed the tension between Lizzy and Matthew, wasn't sure what was happening or even if he wanted to get involved. She was sparking with anger, he could see it written across her body as she postured herself in hard angles.

"Cambridge? An old boy like myself," Hugh, desperately wanting the night to end, poured himself another glass of wine, tried to prevent an awkward silence. "Oh yes, I remember Lizzy telling me earlier."

Benn's attention turned towards Lizzy and she swallowed hard. After their last encounter, she had pulled up his page on Wikipedia, read how he had graduated from Trinity, played Rugby, been an active member of the Footlights, and dated a society It Girl for three years before there was an awkward break-up just after graduation. He had moved to London and won a post-grad place at RADA, where he met Madeleine Tennant. And the rest? Well, that was tabloid gold.

"Lady Elizabeth seems to have done her research," he smiled at her genially, and she found that she smiled back despite herself.

The dinner passed in a haze of laughter and information, Matthew was charming and delightful as usual, and Benn did his best to charm Carol, who was decidedly less snobby now that he had discovered her secret. Hugh asked questions and was polite in the way that he had been brought up to be, being generally affable and polite as he waited for his turn to speak. She noticed a touch of iciness between Hugh and Carol – they were always weirdly distant, her stepmother having all the warmth of an ice pack, but this was more pointed than usual, and she wanted to get her dad alone. It was probably the stress of her sister, whose name alone caused eyes to roll and feathers to ruffle whenever it was mentioned.

Carol and Hugh were the first to leave. She tottered out on heels that were too high, he held her arm like the gentleman he was, and she grasped it tightly, denoting ownership and using him to balance. Benn followed them down in the lift as Carol's glacial fake laughter shattered against the granite walls. Matthew left next, his attention half-drawn for most of the night by a vibrating phone and excuses, followed by whispers on the outskirts of the conversation.

"Are you not taking me home tonight?" She questioned, as he stood to leave.

"No," there was a dismissive tone in his voice. "I'm not going back that way."

Lizzy was left at the bar, sipping on a Pellegrino and pondering whether to order an Uber or get the train home, and equal parts fuming and confused at the events of the evening. Pulling her phone out of her bag, she sent Matthew an angry, but passive-aggressive message. It single ticked.

"Pellegrino," came the voice. "Cleansing. Glad you decided to follow my advice."

She shoved her keys and her phone into her bag, a vintage-looking embroidered clutch that Harriet had made her use – even though it held nothing, designed for the days when women only carried cigarettes and lipstick - and jumped off the stool; the bag fell to the floor and the contents spilled out. He kneeled quickly, placing her belongings back into the bag.

"Do you make a habit of insulting people, or is this specially reserved for me?"

"Just you, I'm afraid," he handed the bag back to her and she accepted it with a small smile as Benn Williams kneeled at her feet.

"Well, thank you," she said with more than a dash of sarcasm and a roll of the eyes.

"I wanted to ask you something," he ordered a water. "Did you get the flowers?"

"Yes," she said begrudgingly. "I did, thank you, they are very beautiful. But flowers don't work with me, generally. Matthew sends far too many when he has done something dubious, so I'm fairly immune."

The massive hand-tied arrangement of roses, lilies, and hydrangeas had arrived at the office the previous afternoon, causing Deb to raise her eyebrow and Harris to begin sneezing and complaining about his hayfever. He stood next to her, and she shuffled uncomfortably as their arms touched at the busy bar.

"So, what would work with you," he enquired. "Just out of curiosity."

Elizabeth was suspicious, this felt as if he was flirting with her, but he wouldn't be. Maybe she was just terribly out of practice.

"Macarons maybe, or a bottle of fancy gin if you have done something terribly bad…and I mean an expensive batch one in a nice bottle, not Bombay Sapphire."

"Noted. So, have I *done* something terribly bad?"

"Aside from being rather rude, not really. I'm going to give you the benefit of the doubt and attribute it to method acting."

He was silent. She wondered why inside she was daring him to say something, wanting him to challenge her, but he didn't.

"I wondered when you would say thanks, I thought manners were rectally inserted into posh types like you at Cheltenham Ladies."

"I've been avoiding you because you're an arsehole," she said, "even if you do have an assistant with very expensive taste in flowers." She smiled slightly, "and I didn't go to Cheltenham Ladies."

"I can tell – you're not walking funny."

She viewed him curiously, took another mouthful of her water and wished she was somewhere else. She wasn't mentally prepared to verbally spar with Benn Williams and his Double First from Trinity.

"Didn't your ex go to Cheltenham Ladies?"

"Sarah?" He remembered that she had been cyberstalking him all week. "Yeah, she did."

"I've met her once or twice, she's fairly unpleasant."

"You're telling me."

There was a roar of screams and laughter from the doorway as a hen party entered from the lift, a perfect storm of snapping heels, Michael Kors perfume and hair extensions. Lizzy was jostled at the bar as the bride to be aimed straight for the barman and ordered tequila for the whole party.

"Would you like a lift home?"

She nodded yes frantically from the midst of the throng.

He drove her back to Pemberley in a dark blue 4x4 with cream leather seats and a Rocket Lolly air freshener hanging from the rear-view mirror. It was very tidy, if you ignored the backseat where jackets had been thrown and the footwell where two pairs of pink trainers and a Minecraft sling bag had been discarded. The world swished by with a gentle hum and the soft melodies of Smooth FM.

"Strange choice for a movie star," she said, voicing her dismay. "I expected a Range or some kind of Jaguar, I was looking forward to being driven home in something fast and stupid. I might not have accepted if I'd have known you drove a Volvo."

"It has all the bells and whistles," he said defensively. "Look!" He jabbed at the dashboard, the display flickering to life, the radio blaring offensively, "I can connect it to my phone. Watch this – it's *voice-activated* – Route to Pemberley House."

The panel flashed to life and the journey back home was plotted out in vibrant HD.

"Okay, it's a very fancy Volvo."

"I'm going to be honest with you, I do have something fast and stupid too, but it's not really suitable for country roads and doing the school run."

"You do the school run? Who knew Henry Jones was such a modern man! Let's hope Piers Morgan doesn't find out."

"Are you going to tell him?" He glanced over at her and grinned. "I've been off most of this week, and it was great to pick them up, hear about their day. Esther is eleven and she thinks she is far too old to be picked up, so complains constantly."

"What about your youngest?"

"Anya?" He looked over quickly, "she speaks French now, it's amazing, but I'm pretty sure she's always swearing at me and I have no idea."

"I bet you miss them."

"I do."

"Do they live in France full time now?"

"Mainly at weekends, but they're in London during the week… and holidays. I see them on the holidays."

That small wave of sadness passed over him again, and she caught it this time but didn't know what to say and they continued in silence for a while. He broke the quiet, unsure of what he was asking.

"What was going on with you and Matthew? Forgive me if I am being too nosey."

"Nothing is going on with Matthew and me. Why do you ask?"

He viewed her with a growing curiosity, could see the doubt running across her face.

"I'm nosey."

"Well, in that case, it's a very long, dull story that will bore you."

Benn knew that wasn't the case, he had witnessed the on-location visits, the phonecalls, the hidden messages pinging up on Matthew's phone between scenes. He always viewed any kind of infidelity as bad, but now after the breakdown of his own marriage, his opinions had changed somewhat.

"What happened with you two?"

"Life happened," her tone was sad. "It's like you have a time slot, and you missed it, and whatever you do you can't go back. However much you want to, but there's no real reason for it, it's just …gone."

"Sometimes there are no reasons and we have to just accept it."

"We do." There was a silence before she blurted out, "Benn, did you ever love someone so much that you would be happy if they were happy… even if it meant that they were happy without you."

"Yes, I have. I mean, I do… I *do* love someone like that."

"Madeleine…"

"Yes," he replied wistfully. "She is a truly extraordinary person. We have a connection that I can't explain; it was instant...unexplainable. She was married to someone else when we first met, you know."

"Yeah, I remember the stories in the paper. That must have been difficult."

"You can't help who you fall in love with, even if the timing is terribly inconvenient."

She studied his face under the yellow motorway lights, it was hard to think of someone who was so very famous having real feelings like this. It was as if she already expected him to have moved onto the next woman, to be comfortably attached to a random starlet. But he was a real man with real feelings, and she appreciated his honesty in sharing them with her.

"Will it always be her, do you think?"

"Always, until I convince myself that it's a bad idea. I don't think I will ever love anyone the way I love her. I don't think anyone would compare." he pulled a hard-boiled sweet out of the cup holder and handed her one. "But we're not talking about me. This is about you. You are in love with him, aren't you? Because surely that's the most important part."

"I have always been in love with the idea of him, but the reality isn't quite enough...and I don't know if that's because I can't have all of him, or if all of him isn't worth having," she paused. "I don't even know why I am telling you this... I'm sorry!"

"Stop apologising. It makes it easier I think if you get it out of your head."

"I don't even know you."

"Maybe that's why it's easier."

He turned and smiled at her, finding that she returned the gesture. The lights of the M60 flashed against her face until they turned off the motorway and onto the winding country lanes that led to Pemberley.

"Benn, can I ask you a question?"

"Of course."

"If you love Madeleine so much, then what on earth possessed you to cheat on her?"

His jaw immediately clenched, his eyes fixed on the road, a frostiness on his warm geniality, and she immediately wished to grab the question from the air and shove it back into her stupid mouth. Lizzy recalled the horrible headlines, the death throes of the marriage plastered all over the newspapers, the paparazzi shots of Benn emerging red-eyed and bedraggled from a hotel in Paris, the photos of the elfin blonde actress wearing large over-sized glasses holding a smoothie and walking from her house on Venice Beach, images of Madeleine and the girls marching stoically through the airport.

There was silence again.

"I'm sorry, I've spoken out of turn," she said.

"No," he tapped the indicator, "you haven't at all, but I don't have an answer to your question."

There was no way that she could even begin to imagine what the last year had been like for him, with the eyes of the world focused on the disintegration of his marriage. It was true that the Darcy family received press attention, but not at the same level as Benn Williams, whose every move it seemed was documented and reported and published. There had even been a story popping up on her phone this morning, an anonymous source commenting on how he was now so fat that he was having to be strapped in his breeches, alongside a picture of him shovelling red velvet cake into his mouth; the next story was about how fit he was now. No wonder people never knew what to believe.

"'Maybe the most important thing you should know about me is that I don't believe things I read in the paper, or on the sidebar of shame," her voice a comforting hit of summer air melting his wintry coolness.

"Me neither."

The car turned into the north gate and she tapped in the code before they curved down the driveway, juddering over the cattle grid, she noticed he strictly observed the 20mph speed limit, even though she would usually race up the winding road. The silhouette of the Cage dominated the view on the left-hand side, the moonlight catching the stately angles of the structure and making it appear not of this earth, as if in the morning it would be gone.

They pulled up in front of the north front gate and he got out of the car, opening the door and being generally quite gentlemanly as he walked her to the large, studded door that closed off Pemberley from the rest of the world.

"I am sorry that I was a dick at the party," he said. "I know you were trying to be friendly."

"I think we might just have got off on the wrong foot," she said. "I'm willing to start again if you are."

"I can do that."

The clock chimed midnight out across the courtyard, and she gestured for him to sit next to her on the stone seat in the porch. Reaching into the paper bag that she had brought from the restaurant, she pulled out a large tub of carrot cake with a dollop of cream and two plastic spoons.

"Now, I was saving this, and Harriet will never forgive me, but seeing as you have been so kind as to drop me off."

She passed him one of the spoons and offered up the bowl. Benn was ravenous for cake and dug into the moist sponge, savouring each mouthful of the frosted walnut and carrot confection. They sat in silence. The only noise in the great park, usually so alive with voices, was the sound of the occasional owl hooting out its lonely cry to the darkness.

"So," he licked the frosting from the spoon, "are we friends now?"

"We're either friends or I've secretly poisoned you with vanilla frosting."

She watched in part admiration and part disgust at the vehement way he was attacking the spoon.

"Are you happy being friends with an 'arsehole'"

"I think we agreed that you are a *complete* arsehole," she laughed, "and as long as you are happy to proceed on that basis…"

He smiled with his whole face and she noticed that his eyes lit up and actually sparkled, but maybe she was imagining it. It was strange seeing them up close and not displayed in giant size on the side of a bus. They were much nicer in real life. He was much nicer in real life. He was normal, and she liked hearing the northern inflections appearing in his voice when he dropped his guard and forgot who he was meant to be.

She shoved the last spoonful of cake into her mouth, and munched away happily, swinging her legs against the stone porch. Benn had presumed all ladies of the aristocracy were like his girlfriend from Cambridge – a privileged coolness tinged with a haughty arrogance all wrapped up in a beautifully manicured and coiffured package, smelling like Penhaligon's fragrances and the luxury of not having to work, but Lizzy didn't seem to be a typical Lady at all. Her nails were roughly painted, her hair loose and wild, and she smelled like a packet of ginger biscuits.

He had spent the whole night trying to work out what it was, the indistinct whiffs of it teasing his nostrils throughout the night. But now he realised it was the same smell from his childhood and he imagined Lizzy was very much like one of those little biscuits from the kitchen of his Nan's house in Salford, hard and unmoving until softened by the warmth of a cup of tea; because here she was, holding out the hand of friendship to him – a man who was in desperate need of a friend.

"Lady Elizabeth, I do not believe we have had the pleasure of being formally introduced" he proclaimed in his best Mr Darcy voice, gallantly holding out his hand, which she took gracefully and shook firmly. "I am Mr Williams of Thurleigh Road, Clapham, currently residing in Derbyshire at the home of Mr Fitzwilliam Darcy."

Laughing, she played along.

"Pleasure to meet you, Mr Williams!" She did a small curtsey. "I am Lady Elizabeth Georgiana Darcy," there was a pause as she thought about something, "but my *friends* call me Lizzy."

He wanted to eke out the last drops of the evening, enjoying feeling like a regular person rather than being dismissed back to his lonely hotel for room service and Netflix.

"Do you fancy going out for tea sometime, somewhere not poncey? I would like to say sorry properly, I am usually much better behaved… and I mean tea as in dinner," he laughed. "I think I have some coupons for the Toby Carvery."

"Ooh," she giggled. "I do love all you can eat meat buffets!"

"It was just an invitation to tea, Darcy, don't go getting all overexcited."

Lizzy flushed a little, she had no idea why she had said that, but she liked that he teased her about it. There was more to Benn Williams than she had initially thought, and she enjoyed the slightly irreverent flirt with the handsome gentleman who was currently spending his days dressed in a cravat or being forced to run up and down the Gritstone Trail in order to shed the pounds.

"Tea would be lovely," she grinned, already wondering what on earth they were going to talk about.

Pemberley

the Park and Gardens
home of the
Darcy Family
for over 600 years
and gifted by
Winston
Fitzwilliam
Darcy
to the
Historical House
Society
Opened on
15 July 2002
by the
Earl of Struthers
for the
Health, Education
and Delight
of the People

2002

Hugh Darcy thought that little Harriet was the cutest little button he had ever seen, he could see the family resemblance – the grey eyes, the sharp chin, the upturned nose - but he could also see that she had inherited her father's darker countenance too. She was now six months old, shrieking and laughing as he bounced her on his knee. His own youngest son, Joe, was not quite two and Hugh felt ancient as he chased the boy around, he hadn't remembered it being this hard when Charlie and Lizzy were younger.

"Are you alright with her, Dad?"

Lizzy was running around making sure everyone okay and she could sense that Harriet, trussed up in the family Christening gown, was getting a bit fractious.

"Yes, of course, I am," Hugh gestured towards the grand opulence of the dining room. "Have you made sure that everyone has a drink? I'm not bloody paying for the staff to flirt with Aunty Julia all day."

Guests mingled between the two rooms and out in the garden through the French door which stood open. The noise of shoes on the oak floorboards, the smells emanating from the kitchen, and the soft clink of crystal glasses being filled with champagne seemed to imbue the room with a magical feeling of life and excitement. It was as if Pemberley was putting on a well-rehearsed performance, one that it had enacted time and time again.

Aunty Julia, now bleached blonde and with skin like creosote, was taking advantage of the copious amounts of champagne which she drank in the corner with Aunt Sybil. Imogen, her blonde curls bigger than her head, was running wild around the room, bashing into things and twirling about under the sparkling chandelier, Lizzy ran over and picked her sister up, spinning her around and hearing her laughing louder than the elegant music.

"Elizabeth, please can you not do that with Lady Imogen."

Lizzy rolled her eyes at her sister who giggled and ran off in the direction of the cake, she turned, smiling brightly at her stepmother.

Carol Darcy, Duchess of Derbyshire, the former receptionist of the Premier Travelodge in Doncaster was a woman who, despite her middle-class upbringing, was snooty about everything and everyone. She sneered at Lizzy, looking down her newly adjusted nose which had come courtesy of a Harley Street plastic surgeon.

"I do apologise, Carol."

"You're not the one who has to deal with her later," Carol's accent reminded her of a school secretary. "Jacinta will be run-ragged with both of them. It's bad enough that we're having to stay at that grotty hotel rather than here."

"I did offer you my flat, Carol."

"Don't be ridiculous, Elizabeth," she snorted. "The HHS could have offered us one of the other rooms given the amount we have spent today. I am the bloody Duchess after all."

"As I said, I apologise most wholeheartedly."

"I don't even know why your father insisted on making such a fuss about this."

Carol looked around at the string quartet and the canapes, and through into the stag parlour, which had been decorated with twinkling lights and a table holding court to a very regal, iced cake that stood three tiers high.

"I am very grateful to you both, obviously for the effort."

"And the expense," she said dryly. "Don't forget who paid for it. I don't suppose the father contributed, did he?"

There was a particular emphasis on the word 'father', Carol had retracted her invite for Christmas when she learned that not only was her stepdaughter pregnant but that the 'seedy little film man' was responsible.

"No, Carol. He didn't."

"It really was a nasty business, Elizabeth. I know your father doesn't seem to care, but I do. Did you ever think how terrible it makes us all look with you having a love child? I know times are different now, but we're still meant to set an example!"

"Oh yes, I had forgotten about how bad it makes us all look," Lizzy said with more than a hint of sarcasm in her voice, as Carol obviously overlooked the fact that her late father-in-law was the product of a clandestine tryst. "You must excuse me, I've just seen Harold."

"Harold?"

"The reporter from the Matlock Chronicle? He's come all this way just to cover the story."

She caught the horrified look on the face of her father's wife and turned quickly on her heel. Uncle Jeremy was here, and he waved her over, gesturing for another glass of Moet.

"Elizabeth, motherhood is treating you very well it would appear."

Uncle Jeremy had the stately gait of old money, but his cut-glass tones hid a gentleman with a filthy sense of humour, a penchant for artisan ales and, until his recent marriage, cheap women.

"Why thank you, Uncle Jeremy! Although I have tried very hard today to not look completely exhausted."

"You always did scrub up well, Lizzy," he put his arm around her shoulder. "Your mother's genes though, they always were going to shine through, more than ours, and they did thankfully, all our bloody generations of marrying cousins and what-not!"

"Dad said you wanted to speak to me about something...?"

"Ah yes, he said you had nearly finished at Manchester – is that right?"

"Yes, I have finals next year."

"Bloody hell," he said incredulously. "It doesn't seem five minutes since I was standing up for you at one of these damned things." He gulped down his champagne, "any thought to what you are doing after? You're going to go into practice, surely?"

"Well, yes but..."

"Tell you what, come and complete your LPC with me at the firm. If we're lucky you might even be our next Darcy QC, eh?"

"I very much doubt that..."

"Nonsense, you can come and live at Longbourn with Victoria and me, we would love to have you... and the baby, of course. We have the nanny – Vilda, bloody scary Scandinavian type – she won't mind another. It's a bit of a blasted commute to town, but you can always use my driver if you need to."

"Are you sure Victoria wouldn't mind?"

Victoria was Uncle Jeremy's third wife, a twenty-seven-year-old career-minded partner from the firm; she had given birth to four babies in quick succession and hired a whole team of staff to help look after her young brood.

"God, no! We practically have a small primary school anyway, no bother to add one more. Oh, Sybil is calling me over... is she pissed?"

Lizzy nodded, "never one to turn down a free bar."

"Christ, wish me luck."

Jeremy wandered off towards Aunt Sybil, who was wearing a purple chiffon gown and an angry grimace. She had never quite forgiven her older brother for giving away her childhood home and she was usually very vocal about it. Lizzy watched as Jeremy embraced the Darcy matriarch and laughed to herself as she watched Sybil bat him away.

Maggie was over by the fireplace talking to Pete, Jean was posing for pictures with Harriet, Hugh had Imogen slung over his shoulder and was walking towards the gardens. Lizzy grabbed a glass of something fizzy from a passing bow-tied waiter and eyed the man with the canapes from across the room. Steve Carter, the ginger-haired employee of the HHS who had accompanied her to the hospital on the day of the birth was standing awkwardly in the corner, pulling at his new suit.

Steve felt out of place mixing with, as the rest of the staff put it, the upper crust. There had been much teasing in the staff room when he had received the fancy foiled Darcy crest embossed invitation, and the personal handwritten note from Lady Liz herself. The stiffness of his shirt made him feel uncomfortable, and he had felt completely gormless standing up at the altar holding a candle and promising to be Harriet's godfather. He didn't even believe in God.

"You look very handsome."

"Thank you, Lady Elizabeth, that's very kind."

He should have known it would have been Lady Liz, although he still didn't think he could look her in the eye after the events he had witnessed.

"You know you can call me Lizzy now, after all, you have seen my vagina."

The younger man flushed such a deep shade of red that Lizzy was reminded of a freshly cooked lobster.

"Don't say that, Lizzy."

"It's true, but I'm very grateful that you decided to spend your first overnight shift here being my birth partner. I couldn't ask for a better godfather for Harriet either."

"My mum says it's a massive honour even to be asked," he stammered. "She told all of her friends at the WI about it."

"Really? Well, we better find that photographer and give her pictures to stick in her scrapbook, hadn't we?"

Maggie played the role of godmother beautifully and she had looked at Peter wistfully, wondering when they would have a baby of their own. He had grumbled off and gone to get food as she walked around the room with Harriet, pointing out the portraits of King James II, Lady Mary of Derbyshire and Hortense Holland, the baby had wriggled and squirmed in her arms, and they ended up sitting on a bench outside in the summer sunshine, Maggie feeding her niece and cuddling her under the blanket.

MAGS: Everything went really well, mum cried x
MATTY: I wish I could be there.
MAGS: I know, but it will just cause a load of aggro. You don't want to piss off every woman in your life, do you?
MATTY: I manage it with alarming regularity these days.
MAGS: It will all sort itself out eventually.
MATTY: It will. Harriet looks so much like Lizzy.
MAGS: She looks like you!
MATTY: Don't wish that on her! How is it?
MAGS: Hugh has pulled out all of the stops, champagne, the works. Carol is mad about it.
MATTY: How's Lizzy?
MAGS: You should ask her yourself.
MATTY: You know as well as I do that it would be a terrible idea.

Jean Wickham posed for pictures with her granddaughter, who looked so much like her late husband that sometimes she became overwhelmed with the remembrance that he wasn't here to share these special moments with her. John had died when Matthew had been a similar age and this celebration had upset her more than she wanted to let on. Jean had always laughed with Winston about the Wickham and Darcy heritage, but now as her son's daughter was claimed as a Darcy, she found that the whole thing left her with a sour taste in her mouth, and a feeling that the old prejudices against her family were very much alive.

"I just don't think it's right that Matthew isn't here, Margaret."

"Mum, you have to realise that my brother wouldn't want to be here facing the full wrath of the Darcys."

"That baby should be a Wickham," she leaned over at the sleeping baby. "Look at her, Mag, she looks just like your dad."

"I know, Mum, she really does. I know that…"

Maggie had listened to this conversation nearly every night since Harriet was born, she understood why her mum was upset, but she also knew why Harriet was a Darcy, and it was it nothing to do with Lizzy. She knew that Lizzy had written to Matthew on numerous occasions, asking him to contact her to put his name on the birth certificate. But he hadn't. The baby was called Harriet Sophia Darcy because Lizzy didn't have another choice

"You're going to take Lizzy's side on this, I know you are, but… I don't think the Darcys have given Matthew a fair trial."

"He hasn't been here, Mum. He's in London with his fiancée, what was Lizzy meant to do?"

"She could have told him that she loved him, and then everything would have been as it should, and I wouldn't have to put up with Cara looking down her nose at me."

"Cara doesn't just look down her nose at you. She looks down her nose at everyone, even Lizzy!"

"I just don't think it's right that she hasn't even got our name, it's like she isn't even one of us."

"She isn't. She's a Darcy."

"Well, being a Darcy isn't as grand as everyone makes out."

Lizzy's bright yellow polka dot dress might have gained a few grass stains, her sister's pale pink skirt and expensive chiffon top might have gained a few more after they had spent at least half an hour rolling down the hills on the top lawn. As they walked back towards the garden entrance hand in hand, laughing and chatting, she could see Carol admonishing their father and pointing at them both. Turning around, they walked off towards the Orangery, deciding that smelling pretty flowers and playing in the fountain was much more fun than being told off by the grown-ups.

"Are you excited for school, Imo?" Lizzy asked, prising a crumpled flower from her sister's hand.

"No, I don't want to go to school," Imogen pouted, jutting out her chin in the same way that nearly every Darcy did.

"But it will be exciting, you will get to have fun and learn new things and then Mummy or Daddy or Jacinta will pick you up and you can tell them all about it."

"Mummy says that I will be sleeping at school and I don't want to."

Lizzy was confused; surely, they weren't sending her away to board…No, that couldn't be right, she had only just turned four in February, there must be some misunderstanding.

"I'm sure that's not what Mummy means," she soothed.

"It is!" Imogen sniffed. "She says I am a pest."

She pulled her little sister in close for a big hug, "well, I don't think you're a pest. I think you are wonderful."

"Can I come and live with you?"

Lizzy smoothed down the frizzy curl poking up from Imogen's plait.

"Of course you can," she pulled the smaller girl to her feet. "Do you know that you are Harriet's Aunty, Imogen?"

"I'm *Aunty* Imo?" This was a completely new revelation for her. "You are silly. I'm not an *Aunty*, I am too little."

"I think you are super big now! Look," she said picking her up and lifting her high, "you can reach the top of the fountain, only the biggest girls can do that!"

"I'm the biggest girl!!" She shrieked.

Lizzy swung her back down again, Imogen was beaming.

"Lizard, I promise that I will be the bestest Aunty ever to my Harriet and I will love her forever and ever. Pinky promise."

"Pinky promise," Lizzy curled her finger around her sister's. "Now, shall we go and get cake?"

Imogen ran off screaming in the direction of the house and Lizzy was surprised to see her dad emerge from the side of the Orangery, where he had obviously been having a cigarette, whilst hiding from the disapproving gaze of Carol. He walked over and placed his arm gently on her shoulder before kissing the top of her head.

"Thank you, Dad." They sat together on the bench outside the Orangery, the scent of the camelias within seeping into the air. "I'm really grateful."

"My pleasure, Lady Lizzy." He gave her a little nudge and she giggled.

"I don't think I will ever get used to that," she knew that she wouldn't. "Even though I knew it would always happen eventually, it just seems so strange."

"I went to Harrods last week and the man behind the counter kept calling me 'Your Grace', I find it fascinating."

"I find it fascinating that you go to Harrods for groceries," she rolled her eyes. She knew it was more about Carol trying to maintain a certain level of appearance rather than her dad wanting to do the weekly shop at Harrods.

"How is Charlie with the new title? Earl of Berks!" She started to laugh uncontrollably. "I can't think of anything more fitting."

"You know full well that it's Earl of *Bark*shire," he corrected with his serious face, before laughing too. "Although, Earl of *Berk*shire, is probably more apt for your brother... look at us, renting rooms by the hour in our house, what have we been reduced to?"

The summer months had produced another army of volunteers who swarmed upon the house daily; tidying, fixing, repairing, cleaning. Lizzy knew that they had made the right decision; Pemberley had to continue after they had gone, always had to be present and alive. It was always more than just a house.

"Somebody told me once that when the roots are deep, then you do not have to fear the wind," she placed her arm through his as they stepped down to the south front of the house, "Winston knew what he was doing, y'know. He knew this would be a breeze that lets us spread ourselves about a bit."

He gave her an unsure glance, "how much of my finest paid-for champagne have you had?"

"Not much," she grinned. "I'm serious. We're the Darcy family, and the very foundation of us is buried deep underneath the ground here. It always will be."

"So, in your special and rather elegant round-about way you are saying we did do the right thing."

"Yes, we did," she knew that they had. "Well apart from the curator who totally has it in for me. She's a complete harridan. Thinks I'm a horror, obviously, and keeps sending snooty letters because I keep smoking on the roof. Fire hazard, she says. I don't think she realises that it was Winston who used to go up there smoking to begin with. Bloody Joyce."

Hugh remembered a young woman called Joyce who used to work there when he was at Cambridge, she had been funny, battling him with her sharp wit and disregard for his position, treating him as a regular chap off the street. He had found it immensely refreshing and enjoyed their brief interludes, until the summer after graduation he had come home, and she wasn't there anymore, gotten married and popped out some sprogs probably.

"It's not Joyce Hutchinson, is it?"

"Yeah, I think that's it," she nodded with a curious expression on her face. "Do you know her?"

"Name rings a bell," he said, knowing full well who Joyce Hutchinson was.

They walked back to the party the long way around, chatting softly as they walked down the steps and ventured up familiar paths. On the lawn, a few visitors pointed and waved at the Duke, who they recognised from his portrait in the hallway, and he took his time to acknowledge them and welcome them to Pemberley.

From her vantage point in the library, Joyce Hutchinson saw Hugh Darcy for the first time in too long and she was disappointed to note that her heart still skipped a beat.

1816

The morning had been quiet. There had not been the sound of running up and down the halls, nor the frustrated shouts of the nursemaid, nor the general uproar that usually accompanied sunrise in the Darcy household. In fact, Elizabeth had been surprised when she had been able to rise at her own leisure, enjoy a bath before beginning her toilette, and enjoy a somewhat still and restful breakfast. It was a rare thing indeed, and something that she had enjoyed very much. Now as she finished her book and enjoyed tea with lemon biscuits, she gazed down onto the front lawn from her position in the library and could see Fitzwilliam and his younger, more adventurous brother, James, playing croquet with their father.

The older boy was more reserved, much more like his namesake – observing and calculating every outcome before committing to any action, whereas the younger threw himself all in and damned the consequences. Her husband was laughing, the loud deep sound falling out of him as he picked the boys up and swinging them around, until all hope of completing their game was abandoned and all three of her Darcys were racing each other up and down the grass in the early April sunshine, looking like a herd of deer being chased down from the hills.

The past few years had gone by in a whirlwind and before they had even settled into a daily routine of family life, the family had found themselves as the parents of two boys. Fitzwilliam had been not quite two when James was born, a wonderfully easy birth which she had rejoiced in, and they were the best of friends and partners in crime. Now five and three, they were about to welcome a new Darcy into the world and although she would have never said out loud, Elizabeth hoped that this new babe would be a girl, so she would, at last, have an ally in the household. That said, she was so large and unwieldy that Darcy was convinced there were about five babies in there.

"Is normal for your body to be so different with each babe, Jane?"

Mrs Bingley had been over visiting from her Cheshire estate, she had borne four children in quick succession and was the paragon of motherhood to all of the former Bennets.

"Very much so, I would think, Lizzy. After Peter was born, I decided that Charles was to be banished to his own chambers until I recovered from it all."

"There is a lot to be said for separate chambers, Jane." She took a plate of cake, "and how are my nieces and nephews?"

"Charlotte and Abigail are delightful, of course," she gestured to the maid for more tea, "Charles is a boisterous little tyke, I fear for his master's when he gets sent to school. I do worry about the smallest."

"Peter is still sickly?"

Jane nodded sadly, "four babies in five years is enough to take its toll on anyone, it seems unfair however that the child should suffer."

"I am sure all will be well, Jane," she took her sisters hand and squeezed it gently. "How does Mrs Hurst?"

"Spending her inheritance," the older lady laughed. "Although when she does, she spoils her nieces and nephews most heartily. Caroline… sorry, Lady Dalhousie is very much in good health too."

"Any children yet?"

"Not yet," there was a small sigh, "rumour has it that her husband believes her bloom to be quite gone."

Elizabeth pulled a face at this, "Caroline is but five-and-twenty, there is plenty of time for her to provide him with an heir."

"Hopefully it will happen before the season, as I would prefer not to have her company in town, having her at Dunmarleigh for Christmas is more than adequate."

The children had been taken to the nursery for the afternoon and Darcy had convinced her to take a turn with him around the grounds, he knew that light exercise was always good in the later stages of pregnancy, and he knew how much his wife loved to walk. Darcy held his wife's hand tightly in his own, who would have known seven years ago on his first visit to Hertfordshire that he would eventually return to Pemberley and Miss Elizabeth Bennet would be its mistress. He observed her closely, she had changed a great deal in those seven years, but all for the better.

They journeyed out of the south front of the house and walked up past the newly built Orangery. It was the route that they had taken on Elizabeth's first visit to Derbyshire when Darcy, filled with hope, longing, and anxiety, had taken it upon himself to show her how much of a gentleman he could be after her rebuke and rejection of his first proposal. She had not realised how much hurt that had caused him, throwing the words out, as she did, like arrows and not caring where they landed. But he had been grateful.

She had highlighted to him the error of his ways and had allowed him a second chance to prove to her that he was worthy of joining his life with hers. They trod their well-worn path up to the rose garden where once, newlywed and enamoured, they had foregone propriety and kissed fervently under the tiled roof of the pergola, before returning to their rooms quickly before all modicum of respectability was lost.

"Darcy, this life of ours makes me happier than I ever hoped I would be."

Elizabeth was leaning back on the wooden bench looking down onto the newly budding roses and the lake beyond. Darcy reached for her gloved hand and raising it to his lips, gently kissed it.

"Me too, Miss Elizabeth Bennet."

She laughed at him before kissing his hand in return and holding it tightly. Elizabeth felt as if she could conquer the whole world with one hand if Darcy was holding the other.

"I never thought that I would ever be the mistress of somewhere like Pemberley, I never wished it for myself, my only wish was for the deepest love and maybe a small household somewhere far enough from my mother that she would think twice about visiting every day."

"I hope, Mrs Darcy, that you did eventually marry for love."

"Mainly for love, partly for the big house."

"And my ten thousand a year!"

Even though he laughed, she could sense his fleeting but underlying insecurity that it was his wealth and not himself that had attracted her, it was something that not even nearly eight years of marriage and two children could fully abate. She gently cupped his face in her hands and kissed him gently on the nose.

"You know I would love you even if you were penniless," she reassured, "all of this means nothing to me."

He took a short moment to recover himself, gazing out into the distance at the grand south front façade of the hall, with its Palladian columns and ornate statues. He knew his self-doubt was a failing and he was constantly trying to resolve it; he gave his wife an appreciative look, which she returned, her eyes sparkling in the afternoon haze. Elizabeth was fully aware of the inner workings of his mind and the constant battle he had within himself to be both Mr Darcy of Derbyshire, and Fitzwilliam, the husband and father.

"But," he stated, "ten thousand a year always makes a man appear more attractive in the eyes of a woman."

"This is true, I mean if you had not a great estate in Derbyshire then I would not have been able to overlook your pointy chin."

"My chin is not pointy."

"It is, husband, something you cannot deny, but hopefully beards will be the fashion again in the not too distant future and you will be able to disguise it somewhat."

"Mrs Darcy, you take great pleasure in offending me I feel!"

He enjoyed the teasing and easy repartee that had become a fixture of their everyday lives.

"Why, of course! A wife must always tantalise their husband with wit and humour! Now Mr Darcy, if you would be so kind as to accompany me to the top lawn then I will be happy to oblige you with more offence than you are used to."

Darcy took his wife's hand as requested and tucked it under his own; every day she confirmed to him that he was, without doubt, the happiest and luckiest man in England.

Every Picture Tells A Story

The Darcy family, made globally famous by Jane Austen in her novel 'Pride and Prejudice', have overseen the sale of over thirty family portraits to Austenation, who purchased them on behalf of the Historical House Society, the current custodians of Pemberley. Sally Quince, head curator at Austenation, said "the portraits, including those of Fitzwilliam Darcy, his wife Elizabeth Bennet-Darcy, and Lady Sophia Darcy, the mistress of James II, are of national importance historically and should belong to the nation." The paintings, including two by Sir Peter Lely, and one by American society painter John Singer Sargent of Cecily Darcy, the Duchess who perished on the Lusitania, will remain at the country house in Derbyshire. Entrance is free for Society Members. Open Tuesday – Sunday 11 – 5 NB: please check website before visiting, due to location filming taking place, some areas of the house and garden may be closed to the public

Nine

Harriet slumped into the large couch which dominated the flat. She had been on set since 5am, trussed up in her maid's costume and performing the same action a hundred times. Her dad had been a complete idiot all day – she knew that it was what he did for a job, and he was really good at it, but he was so bossy and demanding that she had wished she had just gone to work at the souvenir shop in Lambton, where she could sell Mr Darcy magnets and Lady Catherine's Lemon Curd to foreign tourists. It would have been much easier. At least she could tell him to bog off, no-one else could.

"How did it go?"

Her mum's voice echoed from down the stairs, followed by the clomping of her footsteps on the wooden staircase.

Harriet grabbed a bottle of water from the fridge and took a long swig.

"Dad lost his shit with Jenny Graves and she ended up crying."

Lizzy fumbled about distractedly at the mirror with mascara, "he made her cry?"

"Yeah," she threw herself on the couch. "It wasn't even her fault, it was Benn bloody Williams."

"Really?"

"Kept messing up his lines and everything, it was really bad. Like he couldn't remember."

"What did your dad say?"

"He started shouting and screaming about unprofessionalism and demanded that everyone left the set apart from Benn and Jenny, but she was too upset and so she stormed off. I think she went home."

Lizzy peered down onto the courtyard below from the tall windows. Crew members were busy resetting for the 'Return to Pemberley' scene that Matthew was so excited about, she guessed that they would be having another go at it tomorrow.

"So, is Jenny okay now? Your dad shouldn't be making her cry."

"God knows," she sighed. "You look nice…where are you going?"

"Just out."

"With Aunty Mags?"

"No, just with a friend."

"Which friend?"

"Bloody hell, Harriet, nobody expects the Spanish inquisition!"

"Okay, well, have a nice time…and don't forget the code for the gate has changed."

"I will, and thank you, and be good!"

"Yeah, yeah… No prosecco, Mum, I'm warning you!!"

Lizzy slipped on her blue sparkly heels and disappeared out of the door, her laugh still loitering in the hallway.

Harriet wasn't sure what was going on, but she did know that her mum was smiling a lot more than usual and laughing a whole lot more too. She had also noticed that her dad was spending much less time at the flat. She wasn't stupid; she knew that they had been at it for ages, she just wished that they could decide what they both wanted and get on with it.

She wasn't sure what was happening with her dad either, she hadn't been able to get in touch with Cara, and the iMessages that she sent to Oleander remained unread. Her brother had been messaging her a lot before their dad arrived at Pemberley, he had been tired of the arguing, but now it had stopped and there remained an unnerving silence that he hated even more. She hasn't spoken to him for three weeks now, and it was a concern.

But for now, she had a glorious and unexpected night home alone; she had the big television all to herself and a spicy pizza in the freezer for later.

Harriet Sophia Darcy was truly living her best life.

"You look lovely," he said, kissing her on the cheek.

"Thank you. What's this?" she said, noticing the smooth black Jaguar and be-suited driver.

"*Movie Star Perks*," he said proudly. "And my driver, Robert."

The black-suited gentleman nodded his head and opened the door for her.

"This is much more impressive than the Volvo. I feel I must warn you that I could really get used to this."

She clambered into the back seat, he climbed in after her and wondered what the hell he had let himself in for.

The Toby Carvery in Kympton was packed full of parties and people; they ended up queuing for a table in awkward silence, neither knowing what to say. He could see a girl of about ten, with wide eyes and a large pink bow in her hair, looking over at him shyly, watching as she turned back quickly and pulled on her dad's arm. The man turned around, he was a large man with a tattoo of a dragon on his bare arm, the hint of musky aftershave and hard work surrounding him.

"Lady Liz?" He grunted in gruff, Derbyshire tones.

Lizzy squinted up at him. She knew that face.

"Martin!" She screeched and pulled him into an embrace.

Benn stood there awkwardly, wondering who this guy was.

"Oh, this is Benn," she explained. "Martin used to work in the café at Pemberley with me when we were at school."

Martin offered his hand, "nice to meet you, mate."

Benn offered his own, "same, y'alright?"

"It's me gran's birthday, so we're out celebrating," Martin told them, as the girl pulled on his t-shirt.

"It's Grandma Vi's birthday? How old is she?"

"She's eighty," said the little girl, who had been listening in.

"Eighty? That's amazing!" Lizzy kneeled down to the girl's height; she had on sparkly shoes and her hair was tightly pulled into braids.

"And what is your name, my new sparkly shoed friend?"

"Scarlett, your ladyship," she said with a little curtsey.

"She's a little nosey parker!" Martin laughed, as Scarlett stuck out her tongue at him, before smiling shyly at Lizzy.

"You must let me pick up your bar tab, Mart."

"Don't be daft, Liz, there's no need for that. We're over in the corner near the loos, pop over when you have your drinks – she would love to see you."

"We definitely will," she said, looking at Benn, who nodded his agreement.

"Y'know, I hope you don't mind me asking, Benn…" Martin began. Benn prepared himself for the questions and the obligatory autograph request. "Were you in Coronation Street?"

Lizzy guffawed, as Martin fumbled awkwardly.

"Was it Emmerdale? Sorry mate, I only watch them when the missus makes me, you just look familiar," and then to Lizzy, "come over for cake, yeah?" Swinging Scarlett up on his shoulders, he walked towards the table decorated with balloons as she waved happily.

Benn enjoyed watching his date for the evening being suitably feted. He hadn't realised how well-known she was, and as he watched her talk to the birthday girl and her friends, asking them about themselves, greeting them all like old friends, and paying for their drinks, he found he was mesmerised by her assumed aristocratic persona.

"Does that happen a lot?" He asked as they queued for Mega Plates with extra meat.

"Not really," she admitted. "Usually only with the card-carrying members of the HHS – the local ones. It's the Lady Darcy show they love, not me."

"They seemed to like you quite a lot!"

"That's not me though," she nudged him forward in the line as the chef gestured to Yorkshire Puddings and she filled her plate with a vast array of vegetables. "You must know that. It's a character"

"I know what you mean, I suppose I'm just a bit put out though."

"That nobody recognised you, you mean?"

"Yeah," he said, a little niggled. "I know I look different with dark hair, but not that different, surely? Those women in Manchester recognised me."

"People don't expect Benn Williams to be queuing up for roast potatoes at the Toby Carvery." She sat down at the table and started tucking into the cauliflower cheese, "you must enjoy that though, you must get recognised everywhere."

"I do, but never intentionally," he shook his head. "I suppose that's why this feels odd."

"I'd enjoy it if I were you, Violet keeps looking over and I bet she was a big fan of Wuthering Heights. She'll recognise you if you take your top off."

"Funny."

"Perhaps," she laughed. "Maybe I just want you to take your top off."

They were halfway through their sticky toffee puddings when Violet and her guests walked past waving goodbye, Scarlett bouncing happily being carried by her dad, brandishing a massive confetti filled balloon. There was a loud rush of noise and clamour as they exited, and then silence. The door suddenly opened, and Martin rushed back in looking agitated, he came straight over to their table.

"I've just realised! You're *Benn bloody Williams!*"

"Cover blown."

"You must think I'm a right idiot," he said, as he held out a beer mat for an autograph.

They posed for a few selfies before Martin gave Lizzy a massive hug, Benn a manly pat on the back and then left them to enjoy their desserts.

"Are you ready for home?"

He said, offering a discount coupon to the waitress who harrumphed at him and wandered off to retrieve a new receipt. Lizzy finished the rest of her drink.

"I'm not actually, are you?"

"Surprisingly, no. Do you know anywhere?"

"I might know a place. Do you trust me?"

"Indubitably."

The bar was small and dimly lit, one of the new pubs designed to feel like having a drink at a friend's house. It was cosy and very hipster – Kympton obviously a few steps ahead of Lambton in the trendiness stakes.

"Tell me about your divorce," she asked as she nonchalantly studied the drinks menu.

"Really?"

She noticed that he sat up straighter, adjusted his collar.

"You don't have to if you don't want to, I'm curious…nosey, I guess."

He studied her for a minute; she played with the foiled beermat, applied lip-gloss from a sparkly tube.

"There isn't much to tell you about," his face turned serious, wistful almost, "It's all nearly done with now, the first bit came through a while ago, now it's the last bit. The bit that makes it real. I have a great lawyer though, he's called Mark Goulding. Costs an utter fortune."

Her face flashed with recognition. "Oh, I know Mark! We did our LPC at the same time. He is bloody brilliant! Ruthless as they come though, he works for my Uncle Jeremy's firm."

"Should I ask him for Mates Rates?"

"You can if you want, but he will tell you to bugger off. You don't get to be a Senior Partner before you're forty without being a special breed of money-hungry bastard." She ordered a bottle of wine between them from an uninterested waiter, "we can share, right?"

"Yeah sure," he nodded as the bottle was opened at the table. "You're a lawyer though, right?"

"I suppose. I deal with wills and stuff, which is nowhere near as glamorous. I hate it," she fiddled with the olives on the table, "it's what is expected of Darcys though, we breed barristers and business people."

"And why are *you* not a barrister?" He raised an eyebrow, "you'd look pretty cute in one of those wigs."

"I didn't care enough to be barrister, which is a shame, because I *do* look cute in one of those wigs... but it's not me. Not anymore. Law never has been really, it just pays the bills, and despite what everyone at Pemberley thinks, I do have to do something for a living."

"Can you not give it up? Do something else?"

"Like what? Join the WI, or be a patron for a local charity? I've made my bed, I'm afraid. Still, not too many years until retirement!" She grimaced, "but sometimes you want to do something more than what you are born into, do you know what I mean?"

"Yeah, I totally get it. I wasn't exaggerating when I said we were poor when I was a kid, and I knew that I had to do something if I didn't want to stay there."

"Luckily, you were pretty smart."

He took a swig of his wine, "Luckily, I had my very own cheerleader."

"What do you mean?"

"My grandad was my biggest supporter. He was the one who paid for my piano lessons, took me to rugby practice, paid for the extra tuition for the grammar school exam. He was the one who told me to always aim higher."

"I expect he's very proud of you."

"He was, whatever I did. He was always very proud."

Lizzy didn't need to pry, she guessed that wherever in the grand scheme of things Benn's grandad was, that he would be insanely proud of his wildly successful grandson.

"My grandad was the same too." She raised her glass, "to *Family Patriarchs...*"

"...and all who sail in them," he said, clinking his glass against hers.

She finished her wine with undue haste, then thought better of it and ate a couple of the mauled olives. He watched as she concentrated on stabbing them with the wooden cocktail sticks.

"How has it been having Mr Wickham polluting the shades of Pemberley?"

"Matthew? Oh, it's as it always is. I heard you pissed him off today."

"It's very easy to piss him off," he admitted. "He wants everything done very particularly. Like he's Scorsese. I mean, he's good, but – not to namedrop - I have worked with Scorsese, and Matthew Wickham is no Scorsese."

"Alright, show off! But you remembered your lines?"

"Of course, I remembered my lines…" he said with a casual shrug.

Benn poured another glass of wine; he had forgotten his lines. It was embarrassing. They were falling out of his head, he couldn't quite grasp them and make them stick.

"Was your big break really 'Praise to the Skies'?"

"People like to think that, but it took years. Honestly, years! I did a few small films when I left RADA, terrible films" he groaned, recalling some of the shocking scripts he had accepted to be able to pay the rent. "Then there was a lot of regional theatre – I was the best Widow Twanky in Leicester for three seasons."

"You did panto?" she questioned, "I thought actors like you were made in labs somewhere in Hollywood."

"Actors like me? What's that supposed to mean?" He grabbed an olive.

"Are you kidding? Look at you, you're not *real*," she poked his now firm bicep across the table. "When they said you were going to be Darcy, I was hoping that you would be much shorter and fatter in real life, and not as…"

She noticed the way he was looking at her, listening carefully to everything she said and became immediately self-conscious.

"Not as *what?*"

"Not as Benn Williams in real life. I mean you're all *Hollywood* tonight, but you were still pretty hot when you got here all 'off duty' with your scowl and your pubey beard!"

He raised his eyebrows, so the beard was pubey.

"Well, I am flattered."

"By what?" She shrieked impertinently, throwing Pinot down her throat.

"You fancy me. Can't say I blame you, you're only human."

She laughed at him, possibly a little louder than she thought, judging by the tutting that emanated from the couple on the table next to them.

"I don't fancy you! But," she stopped herself to think, "do you remember that film with Amelia Hunt…? The one where you're topless for most of it…? I might have watched that more than was socially acceptable."

"Really?" he had more than a hint of surprise on his face.

"Had a bit of an inappropriate crush on you in that, if I'm being honest…" she said, taking a mouthful of wine.

He glanced at her as if waiting for an explanation, and she ploughed on.

"I don't know what it was, you were just so delicious in it."

"I don't think I have ever been called 'delicious' before."

"Don't expect me to say it again!"

"I won't. It's funny, you know. I was *convinced* that film was going to be my big break"

"I think it *was*! I mean, it was only a few years after that when you were in everything."

"A few years is a long time as an actor without a job."

Benn didn't want to go through telling her about the long spells working in minimum wage jobs and traipsing to auditions on his days off, how his family had been constantly anxious that he had chosen a life of uncertainty and borderline poverty, instead of the entry-level well-paid job in the City that had been offered. Sarah had freaked out about it as well, wanting a man who could give her the lifestyle she was used to and the Tiffany ring she expected. She had brutally dumped him via a friend of a friend. She had even kept his Madness t-shirt.

The conversation faded a little and she called for two bags of crisps, more wine.

"So which part of P and P is your favourite?"

"Favourite?"

"Yes, which bit?" She grabbed her compact from her bag, powdered her nose while she questioned him, "I mean the book, not the films, obviously."

"Erm... there are so many," he finished his glass of wine. "Probably the bit where Mr Darcy dives in the lake."

She finished her own wine and laughed at him loudly; he looked back at her confused and then she realised.

"You haven't read the book!"

"I haven't, is that bad?"

"Oh. My. God. I cannot believe that you haven't read the book! You are kidding me, aren't you?"

He shook his head.

"Mr Darcy – what an impertinence!"

"I know, it's bad."

"Bad? It's not just bad, it's *shocking*! You should be ashamed of yourself."

"Shush, shush," he was giggling now. "I'm sorry, I'm sorry..."

"You should be..." she was feeling a little tipsy now. "Please promise me that you will read the book or at least listen to the audiobook. Please please *please*!"

"Okay, I promise!" He laughed. "One please was enough, Lady Darcy!"

"Be quiet," she whispered in a theatrically loud voice, "I'm incognito."

"You're very giddy when you're drunk."

"I'm not drunk, I'm just giddy," she poured the dregs of the wine into her glass and knocked it back.

"You are a bit drunk."

"Maybe a bit."

"Shall I take you home?"

"Probably for the best," she started to put on her coat, "but, please don't be expecting anything untoward, acting is such a vulgar profession, and you, Mr Darcy, have no sense of propriety... I am a Lady, you know."   There was that laugh again, it felt strange coming out of his body; but he liked the way it felt, liked the way she made him feel. He dropped her off at the door of Pemberley, making sure she managed to get inside. He hadn't even reached the end of the driveway when his phone beeped in his pocket.

LIZZY: Thank you, Iamnot, drjunnk. I can still spell. Soz.
BENN: Soz? You are drunk.
LIZZY: Perhhpas.

2004

The days were long in London, and not as much as Lizzy had thought they would have been. Uncle Jeremy worked her hard, thinking that he could get the best out of her whilst she was still hungry for it, but she truly knew in her heart of hearts that she wasn't. It would have been different if she had been living in the city with friends, but she was commuting out each night back to Longbourn, her spare time filled with studying for the LPC, or tear-filled phone calls back to Derbyshire where she realised that she missed Harriet so much that her heart physically ached. Meanwhile, her daughter was having the time of her life, staying at the Stables with Aunt Maggie and Grammy, who doted on her; she was even learning how to ride on her small pony, Peanut, courtesy of Maggie's on-again-off-again boyfriend, Peter.

As Mark piled another binder of paperwork on top of her desk, Lizzy sighed loudly at him, and he rolled his eyes at her.

"We're all heading for a drink, fancy it?"

"You are a terrible influence, Mr Goulding."

"Your uncle owns the firm, Darcy. Surely you can spare a precious few hours on a Friday night to indulge me."

"Okay," she said grabbing her bag, "but you're buying the first round."

The bar was smoky and crowded, the dull thud of music vibrating underfoot – it was half nine on a Friday night in Soho, the room filled with every type of person you could imagine, and all pushing for attention at the bar. Catching the attention of the pierced friendly girl behind the bar, she ordered another large vodka and coke and retreated over to the cigarette machine. If Lizzy was getting drunk, then she was planning on smoking at least ten Marlboro Lights and making it worth her while; she took a large swig of her drink, feeling the delicious, familiar warmth of it rush down her throat. She hadn't had a proper drink like this since arriving in London and it was hitting the spot. In the corner stood the small group from work – including Mark, attempting to chat up a beautiful red-haired girl that was completely out of his league, at the edge of the room.

Lighting her cigarette, she stood there observing for a moment; the dancefloor was full of people, gyrating, dancing to the loud thump-thump of the bass, a blue haze of cigarette smoke floating over the crush of the crowd, the faint breeze of perfumes, the pungent waft of aftershave, the push of freshly washed shirts and shiny fabrics moving against each other, and above all else, ringing out in the corner, she heard his voice. She could recognise his laugh anywhere and it felt sad somehow to be on the outside looking in.

He had grown his hair out a bit longer than she was used to, had grown a stubbly beard, looking so different but so similar that she felt overwhelmed with it all. She hadn't expected to feel like this, hadn't expected to feel the prickle of anxiety run all over her back, hadn't expected that seeing him again – for the first time since they had spent the afternoon together in the Lantern, for the first time since she made him a father – would make her feel so helpless as her heart thudded in her chest, almost to the beat of the music.

Stubbing her cigarette out on the floor, she downed her drink and pushed her way out of the bar. The cool air of the early evening felt great against her face and she stood for a moment, before getting her bearings and walking towards the tube.

"Lizzy!"

Her name echoed on the street, causing a few people walking to turn around and look before carrying on with their Friday night plans. She didn't want to look back, taking a deep breath and carrying on walking.

"LIZZY!"

She stopped, nervous energy bursting along her spine like freshly popping corn. It would be weird to see him like this, and not as his friend either, but more like an outsider stealing him away from his inner circle.

"Hey. How have you been?"

It was midnight when they stumbled back into Matthew's flat, their inhibitions reduced by the copious number of cocktails they had drunk in the Chiquito's on Leicester Square before they were politely asked to leave by the bouncer for causing too much noise. From there they had gone to a karaoke bar in the depths of the West End, singing terrible songs and dancing on the stage, and they had fallen into each other's arms and kissed passionately on the street outside until a kindly WPC asked them to move along and hailed them a cab. They had fallen into the house, barely opening the doors before leaving a trail of clothes to the bedroom. The morning after was altogether different, she had tried to kiss him, and he hadn't responded, making her feel small and flat. She left, wondering what she had done wrong, thinking about it as the train rumbled toward Manchester, contemplating as she caught the connection to Lambton, and driving herself half-crazy with her thoughts as she walked the country lanes home.

The lights were all on at Pemberley, Maggie had been to tidy the flat and had put a shepherd's pie in the oven, waiting until she got back. Harriet was already fast asleep, and Lizzy went up, kissing her on the forehead and tucking the blanket up under her chin. Slumping on the sofa in her PJ's and watching some crap on the tv, she grabbed a pile of unopened post, a small stack of bills, junk mail, and then. A soft lilac envelope addressed to her and Harriet in a beautifully handwritten script.

Lord and Lady Andrew Dalhousie
cordially invite you to celebrate the
happy union of their daughter
The Hon. Cara Jayne Dalhousie
& Matthew Stuart Wickham

In the quietness of his flat just off Portobello Road, Matthew sat and stared at his phone. He needed to be wanted, and Cara wanted him with her whole heart, not just the part of it she deigned to share. He loved her in the way that he thought she wanted to be loved, and they had been fairly happy for the first few years before it slipped into something that felt like boredom. She had told him that she had forgiven him for Harriet, but he knew that his daughter would always be living, breathing proof of his transgression and he didn't know how much of his life he could devote to apologising.

The wedding had been her father's idea; Lord Dalhousie was a different breed of aristocrat to the ones he was used to, and he had been swept along with the idea of it. But now… Lizzy was always so closed off, always too reserved in her affections. He couldn't spend his life half waiting and half guessing when she would next decide she wanted him, that was if she even wanted him at all. But he needed to know. Needed to know once and for all if there was any chance of it. He tapped out a question, and then he pressed send.

@Royal_Babes   Topless Photos of Lady Imogen >>> CLICK HERE>>>> www.bit.lie/ladytitmuss

Ten

Deb clambered into Lizzy's car. There were papers and sandwich boxes tucked into the doors, CD cases littered the floor and the back seat was covered in a collection of coats, jackets, and shoes, with a blue-ribboned bonnet tucked onto the parcel shelf for good measure. Pervading the whole car was the vague smell of off vegetables where, on a client trip to Birmingham, Lizzy had managed to spill a whole cup-a-soup onto the passenger footwell, attempting to mask it with a jolly Rocket Lolly air freshener that dangled from the rear-view mirror. She held tight to her handbag, not wanting to place it on the floor of the car – she didn't know what might get stuck on it.

"Do you not earn enough money to buy a new car?"

Deb did the payroll and knew exactly how much Lizzy earned and she knew full well that she could afford something not as grim as this twenty-odd-year-old Mini. Lizzy rolled her eyes as they pulled out of the car parking space that had her name on.

"I like this car."

The journey was short, and they decamped to the store quickly, avoiding a quick shower of unseasonal rain for which neither of them was suitably dressed, stepping over puddles in the uneven tarmacked floor.

"So, what is he like," Deb said, whizzing paper bags full of granola squares and choc chip shortbread into the basket. "Is he like Iain in 'Still into You'?"

"The one where he played the narcissistic sociopath? Yeah, he's exactly like that," she snorted.

"All I'm saying is that since you went out for tea with him a week ago, he has been at your flat every night and you have barely said two words about him," she threw pitta chips and humous into the basket.

They surveyed the sandwiches on offer, reaching past elderly ladies with blue rinses to reach their favourites.

"We seem to have just clicked… and I'd rather have him over at my house with company than rattling around the Armitage by himself."

"I bet you do!"

"I do!" She protested, perhaps a little too adamantly. "He makes me laugh, I mean, he is genuinely really funny, not in the way he is in interviews either…he's funnier…"

"And fit as fuck! Stop pretending to me that you don't even find him slightly attractive."

"I'm not blind, of course, he is attractive, but it's not like that."

"Oh, come off it! I know a liar when I see one Elizabeth Darcy!"

"Literally he comes over and we have food and watch a film or something." She pulled a carrot cake off the shelf. "Although I did find out that he used to work in this record shop in Manchester that I used to go to."

"Really?" Debs rolled her eyes, "sounds fascinating."

Debs was the mum of two girls, both in primary school and as opinionated as their mother; they had moved from the small town outside Newcastle when the youngest was three – escaping an abusive marriage and looking for a new life somewhere green. Debs had chosen Lambton because she fell in love with Pemberley after watching Colin Firth walking across the lawn in his wet white shirt; it had been on television one night at the hostel she had run to with her children after her husband's behaviour had spiralled and she knew she needed to escape.

Derbyshire looked like a nice place on the small flicker of the 20" screen in the shared sitting room, and she began to look for a house, for a job, and for a new future. It had been hard, uprooting herself and her girls' miles from their support network; but she had found the job online, interviewing with relative ease and plopping herself down smoothly into a brand-new part of the world. It had helped that Lady Darcy was a single mum too, and they often discussed the perils of children and dating over a bottle of wine and frozen pizza in the flat at the top of the tower. Deb was always amused how Lizzy called the flat 'little' when it covered over three floors and was bigger than her house and the one next door put together.

Lizzy didn't think twice about throwing a twenty quid bottle of Sauvignon Blanc into the trolley or dropping fifty quid on a new set of towels that she simply must have, and Deb found that she was a little jealous of her lack of budget. It made working out the expenses claims a nightmare, and she was constantly pestering Lizzy to keep all her receipts in the little tin she had bought her off eBay. Lizzy might not have been bothered about claiming for petrol and hotel stays, but Harris was – wanting everything above board and accounted for – and Deb found herself spending the last few days of the month writing out receipts and checking Lizzy's card statements to make everything balance.

"Oh," she started, reaching into her bag, "I checked your receipts from last month, one of them was a bit off."

"Really," Lizzy was scanning the cake through the self-service checkout, "which one?"

"It's a place in Kympton...you remember," she raised an eyebrow, she had heard all about it.

"Oh, yes," she took the paper and scanned it. "That can't be right, surely..."

"What's the matter with it?"

She tried to remember the night at the bar where she had got drunk with Benn; he called it their first date and she told him to stop being silly.

"I can only remember ordering two bottles of wine, but there are four on here... and whiskey. I definitely didn't have whiskey, it makes me throw up."

"Maybe Benn drunk it?"

"Four whiskeys and at least two bottles of wine? On a Wednesday? Humm..."

"Maybe they messed up your bill," Deb surmised. "I need you to check it, that's all."

"I'll text him after lunch – have you got everything?"

Deb nodded and took her bag from the self-service till. The rest of their lunch break was filled with a conversation about Debs' new boyfriend, Gareth, who was blessed with both a large member and a voracious appetite.

It was a match made in heaven, Lizzy thought.

LIZZY: Afternoon!
BENN: Oh hi, you okay?

He was currently enduring his specially portioned ration of food from the black box, which Cheryl had shyly handed him from the catering truck. After lunch, there was a 5k up through Knightslow, over the fence, up a massive hill, along the park wall, up to the Cage and back to the house with Patrick, who was getting frustrated at his lack of commitment. Benn was looking forward to later when Harriet was making them all Falafel wraps and scones for tea, it was only the thought of clotted cream and jam that was making him want to run in the first place.

LIZZY: Just a quickie, receipt for bar is four bottles Pinot and Talisker?
BENN: That's not right.
LIZZY: No, thought not.

2006

Hugh Darcy had never really appreciated Pemberley when he lived here, it was always unbearably cold, especially in winter, and his memories of coming home from school for the holidays were of being freezing and coughing from the smoky fires, which were never cleaned often enough. His room, called the 'mahogany room' due to being panelled from floor to ceiling in the deep dark wood, had two windows which faced the lake, and both rattled when the wind rushed over the moorland.

During one particularly harsh winter, the roads out of the estate were unnavigable, and even though the ice on the lake was thick, the Darcy boys were banned from donning skates for their amusement – their Aunt Sybil sharing the story of Peter Darcy, her grandfather's brother, who fell through the ice at the age of eight and was lost for eternity.

Ever enterprising, Jeremy and Hugh opened every single window down the length of the long gallery, pushing up the creaking sashes as blasts of cold air whooshed into the room, then they tipped buckets of water all over the floor and waited for it to freeze. It didn't, of course, but the two brothers felt the icy wrath of Mrs Reynolds, who demanded that they clean up before their father discovered what had happened.

Hugh had secretly been hoping that Winston would find out and send them back to the warmth of school as punishment, but he didn't, and they spent an afternoon soaking up freezing cold water with rags before being sent to bed without supper, although Staughton did send up hot buttered toast and tea after Mrs Reynolds had retired for the evening.

Summer had always been wonderful at Pemberley; especially when their mother decamped to London to star in a show in the West End, or off to Pinewood to film the terrible comedies that she still regularly appeared in. Sylvia Pratchett had only been twenty-two when she married the dashing Duke of Derbyshire, a man who was twice her age, and even though he was still handsome they found that they had little in common. The new Duchess longed for parties and society, whereas Winston preferred country living, or rather his mother preferred him living in the country so that was where they remained. They divorced quickly the spring before Hugh was sent to Eton; the Darcy children mainly saw their mother at the cinema, her ghostly image flickering to life on the screen as she giggled and romanced her way through an illustrious career. When they saw her in the flesh, she never quite seemed as real.

The baton of motherhood passed to Aunt Sybil, who had returned from Boise when she discovered, after fifteen years of marriage, that her handsome GI husband was actually someone else's handsome GI husband too. Without any children of her own, the pouting, acerbic woman with the transatlantic accent and pointed fingernails, took the Darcy children under her wing and introduced them to Pemberley the best way she knew how – well-organised, well-planned adventures. There was boating on the lake, a mini-Olympics on the lawn, orienteering in the woods, climbing at the Lantern – a broken arm for Hugh, a broken ankle for Jeremy, tears and tantrums from Julia – and baking cakes and pies in the kitchens, much to the annoyance of Mrs Reynolds, who complained bitterly to Lady Millicent.

Joyce was walking up towards the Orangery when she spotted the Duke walking towards her. He must be here to see the girls, she thought, as she mentally worked out where she could walk to avoid him. But it was no use, she was halfway past the portico and couldn't turn back on herself, it would be too obvious.

No, she would have to walk past him and be courteous.

Pretend that she didn't recognise him.

She smoothed down her jacket as she walked, hoped that she looked presentable, surreptitiously glancing up under her fringe as she casually walked past.

He hadn't changed. His dark hair may be sprinkled with silver, his eyes a little crinkly, but he was the same man she had fallen in love with over the course of a summer. She had been working every hour as a house guide to help pay bills and he had been languishing about with nothing to do.

Hugh had joined her tour more than once, asking tricky questions that he knew she couldn't answer, purposely trying to annoy her; he apologised afterwards and pulled her up onto his horse, riding hard to the top of Cage Hill with her clinging onto his waist for dear life; there was swimming in the pond on the hottest day of the year and she had screamed at him when he had thrown a frog at her. He had wrapped his arms around her that day and they had retreated to the cottage on the edge of the woods where they lay together on the flat coolness of the stone floor and she knew she would never be the same again.

On their last night before he returned to Cambridge, they had taken the Duke's expensive telescope onto the roof to look at the stars, it had accidentally fallen down the stairs with an ominous thud as they shared kisses and sweet nothings. Joyce was fully aware that it could only be fleeting, could never be more than what it was, and she cherished her memories of that glorious Pemberley summer.

Now here he was again, standing in front of her, saying hello.

She found herself inadvertently doing a little bob, "Your Grace", before moving to walk past him.

"Joyce," he said hesitantly.

He would have recognised her anywhere; remembering her face in vague memories that were tinted with the heat of the sun, the sound of laughter and the smell of strawberry shampoo.

"Sir," she tucked her hair behind her ear, smiled brightly. "Nice to see again…after all these years."

"Yes," he nodded. "You haven't changed at all, you're the same as I remember."

"Thank you."

"This is a surprise, I turn up here for Harriet's first day at school and here you are. I knew you worked here, of course, but I have never seen you about when I've visited."

They began to walk together, inadvertently walking in step with each other down towards the west front of the house overlooking the Dutch garden.

"I've been here for five years now," she said, turning the bleeping radio down.

After the near-miss at the Christening, Joyce had scheduled her own rota to purposely avoid times when Hugh would be here. It was awkward, especially when the Duchess was here too, lording it over everyone as if she thought she truly was the lady of the manor, rather than a hotel receptionist who had caught Hugh's eye on a lonely work trip to Doncaster, which is what she was. Joyce wasn't a snob when it came to rank and titles, because there was a difference between class and breeding, but Carol Darcy, Duchess of Derbyshire, had neither.

"Five years, crikey! Does that qualify you for a special award or something?"

"No, unfortunately not, but I do get to work here every day and it's still my favourite place in the world."

"It always was, wasn't it?" he twisted on his signet ring, suddenly feeling slightly nervous as he fiddled with the cuffs on his shirt. "I never understood, not until recently, why you always loved this place so much."

"Pemberley is magic," she grinned. "It casts a spell on you, I think."

"Or gives you influenza!"

They reached the edge of the gardens and stood for a moment in silence before the radio made a racket that she couldn't ignore.

"I have to go, but it's been lovely seeing you again."

"Yes, it has been lovely."

He held her gaze a little longer than either of them felt comfortable with before Joyce walked away firmly in the direction of the house. Hugh watched for longer than was necessary before walking purposefully in the opposite direction and back upstairs where Lizzy and Harriet were waiting for him.

The playground of St David's Primary was the same as she remembered. The same gravelly finish underfoot, and the same oak tree languishing regally in the corner, its branches waving tall and proud above the classrooms. Harriet was beaming with excitement and eagerly ran over to the little friends she knew from pre-school – a short, stout girl with big blue eyes and massive blonde curls called Summer, who reminded her of Imogen, and a taller girl with two ginger plaits and a serious face called Caitlyn. They started to dance about on the grass, running and whooping with laughter, before stopping suddenly, grouping together and comparing their identical shoes, before setting off again with giggles and screams.

Moira, Summer's mum, came bounding over introducing herself; fawning over Hugh and calling him 'Your Highness' at every possible opportunity, which he found highly amusing. She eventually bounced back to the other mums in the corner of the playground, but not before she had pressed her business card into his hand.

Standing in the same place they had played as children, was Matthew. Married now, he looked tired, his hair artistically long, his beard gone, the chip in his tooth fixed with pearly white veneers. Standing next to him, creeping and congratulating was the headmistress, Mrs Sanderson, who had always been mean and angry, but who was now brightened by being so close to retirement age. He glanced over and caught her eye; Lizzy looked away too quickly for it to be unnoticeable.

The first time had been the trip to Disneyland; where they had shared a bottle of Merlot and a bed. The second time he had turned up at the flat after a long day filming in Manchester under the pretence of seeing Harriet, and they had quiet, giggly sex on the sofa whilst she slept in the room upstairs as a hurricane raged outside. The third, fourth and fifth times were tinged with guilt, and Lizzy had stopped it, said it wasn't fair, even though they both knew that Cara Wickham was currently sleeping with her personal trainer. Matthew wasn't even sure if the baby was his, could barely remember when the last time they had been intimate had been, but he owed it to his wife. He knew he did.

"We need to stop doing this," he grinned, as he pulled at her top and she fiddled with the buttons before pulling the shirt over his head.

"Yes," she breathed heavily, she could feel the heat of him on her cheek, the soft pressure of his lips on hers, his arms around her neck, she pulled him into her, the weight of him pushing her back against the wall.

"But we can't."

"But we should."

He sighed into her neck as he ran his hands over her hips, lifting her skirt, his hands on her thighs ensuring that the tingle ran through her like an electric current.

"It will always be you and me, Lizzy. You know that as well as I do."

She inhaled quickly, the breath catching on her lips as his mouth moved down her body. She ran her fingers through his hair, it was longer now, more like it had been when she had first realised that kissing could feel this good, how the push and the pull made you sparkle all over. Even now, she could still feel that familiar burn for him deep within her and they moved together in an unrehearsed performance.

Eleven

It was after six when the last of the staff left, their soft chatter and gentle footsteps echoing through the bright gallery and down the north stairs as they clocked off for the day, eager to get home and enjoy the last bursts of glorious sunshine. The gallery ran around the house on three sides and had been the perfect place to learn how to roller skate, despite the unevenness of the floorboards. People forgot when they walked around the house using hushed tones of reverence that Pemberley had always been a family home. Lizzy loved it on busy Summer holiday weekends when dozens of small visitors descended upon the grounds, dressed up in regency costumes borrowed from the dressing room and ran around the gardens laughing and shrieking as they did.

"My god, it's busy today," she exclaimed to Kate from the ticket desk, as she helped restock the shelves in the shop. "Did you see those little kids chasing each other with the croquet mallets?"

"Yes. Steve was panicking as it was his idea to grab it out of the storage cupboard, and now he has to fish the hoops out of the lake. You finished for the day?"

"I have indeed, it's Harriet's prom today so she has been out with her friends getting spray-tanned and manicured, and I've got to make myself presentable."

"Baby Harriet is going to Prom? Bloody hell, Lizzy, that's one way to make me feel old as Moses."

"You feel old? How do you think I feel?"

Lizzy stepped outside of the panelled oak door that was marked 'private' and led the way to the Wyatt tower and up to her flat, usually she didn't use this door, instead climbing her way up the three flights of steps in the south corner of the courtyard, and through corridors and passages that visitors didn't see, places that had allowed the servants of Pemberley to historically move about the house unnoticed and unseen. Sitting on the top step, she felt the thick, woollen carpet underneath her fingers, it was another thing that had never changed, although it was a lot cleaner now that when she had been younger.

She got to her feet and took a firm grip of the handles of the small jute bag decorated with bees, which contained the bottle of fizz and the two crystal champagne stirrup glasses that had belonged to her great granny. The great thing about a stirrup glass, she had always thought, was that to the untrained eye it looked like a bell but was so designed so you had to drink your full toast before you could put the glass down. She imagined Millicent got very drunk.

"Mum," Harriet gave her a gentle hug, "are you ready?"

Her daughter was dressed in a sparkly fitted turquoise dress that she had bought in Los Angeles at Easter, and super high red-bottomed Louboutins that her dad reluctantly purchased from Manchester the day before after lots of gentle persuasion. They were the same height now and Lizzy was convinced that her daughter was sure to grow another few inches and surpass her within the next few years.

She had the Darcy chin, but rather than jutting out, it was softer giving her a nice shape to her face. Her eyes were dark too, but the grey was softened by a hint of gold that made them look like gems. Harriet was very much like her mother, but there was something about her that was inherently Matthew and she sometimes saw it streaked across her in bright, bold colours.

"Yes," she smiled proudly. "Shall we retire to the saloon, Honourable Harriet?"

"Why yes, Lady Elizabeth, that would be most agreeable to myself," she tumbled over the words in a fake posh accent. They walked down the stairs, Harriet pondered for a moment and then frowned, "am I really an honourable or do you make that up?"

"I make it up. Sorry, Harry."

"It's not fair," she harrumphed. "Tom is like a Viscount or something and he's only *twelve*! I want to be a Viscount-*tess*."

"You can have a whole conversation with Sybil about the unfairness of primogeniture. She is still furious that she isn't a Duchess."

"Did she tell you that some guy from Utah emailed her and said he was her nephew?"

"No!" Lizzy was immediately put out, "she manages to phone me about her sodding subscription to The Lady, but not about this."

"She'll tell you all about it tomorrow I'm guessing, you need to take her some fruit cake from the shop too."

"She *is* a bloody fruit cake."

Grabbing her mum's hand with as much grace as she could muster, the two Darcy ladies promenaded down the grand sweep of the oak staircase, taking their time to do the customary salute to General George Darcy, whose portrait dominated the hallway, and taking a few selfies for posterity.

"Do you think he would approve of people tromping around his house, spending four quid on fudge and then having a cheese butty in the ale cellar?"

Harriet paused at the base of the painting, the ornate gilt frame catching the tiny shards of sunlight that were glinting through the protective blinds, looking at her ancestor with his stately face and stony gaze.

"The other alternative would have been Pemberley being converted into flats or a hotel, I think that would have been worse, don't you?"

There had been talk of it sometime in the forties when the family coalfields in Lancashire were requisitioned by the government, the once bountiful family income had reduced considerably, and they sold off pockets of land on the borders of the estate to builders, resulting in little fringes of curling Crescents and Closes edging the park like lace.

"They could never do that to Pemberley, you could easily find some Austen-obsessed foreign trillionaire who would buy it and turn it into-"

"-turn it into a theme park or transport it brick by brick to Dubai? Never say never, Harriet."

They walked through the main doors into the saloon, the room had been designed for Fitzwilliam Darcy and had been his masterpiece at the centre of the house – purposely intended to impress visiting guests and showcase his immense and increasing wealth. In the middle of the ceiling hung a magnificent chandelier; Harriet stood underneath it, staring up at the light as it glinted with crystal, illuminated with over twenty bulbs.

"How many people do you think it took to light all the candles, do you think?"

"I have no idea, but it took Aunty Sybil five minutes to change a bulb dressed in an evening gown and wearing heels at Winston's 70th birthday party."

"Really? Good old Sybil."

"She was quite a force to be reckoned with when she was younger, you know."

"Sybil is a force to be reckoned with now, and she's nearly a hundred!"

The smell of early August drifted into the room as Harriet opened the sash window. She was fully aware of her lineage, that being a Darcy was a responsibility, but she wasn't going to live her life in the shadow of anyone, and she was certain that Fitzwilliam wouldn't have wanted her to either. The room was filled with the stories of his daughter, but one information board showed a miniature of him looking young and excited about his future, before his dad had died, and he had been left in charge of the Darcy estates and his little sister. So much responsibility, the lives of hundreds of people held in his immature twenty-three-year-old hands – no wonder he ran off to Hertfordshire and fell in love with the first woman to tell him no.

"You alright, Harry?" Lizzy noticed her daughter looking wistfully up at the ceiling.

"Yeah, just thinking about Fitzwilliam. I hope that he's proud of me."

"I can't think of any reason why Fitzwilliam Darcy wouldn't be proud of you, Harriet. He always had a deep admiration for girls who knew their own mind and their own heart, as well as beautiful ones with great intelligence and a fiery temper." She pulled her in close as they both looked out over the lake. "I think you would make him very proud. You make *me* very proud."

Harriet smiled up at her mum; they had a fun life here together at Pemberley, but she knew that it was coming to an end.

"You need to find someone, Mum"

"Do I? Thanks for the advice, Oprah."

"I mean it! You're still young and pretty enough, you could find someone really nice. You could even have some more babies if you wanted, you're not too old!"

"Thanks for the vote of confidence!"

"You know what I mean," Harriet teased. "I don't want to end up visiting you in Kympton like Aunt Sybil"

"Don't be mean about Aunt Sybil, she dated Frank Sinatra!"

"Everybody dated Frank Sinatra."

"Sybil slept with him a bunch of times too, so that counts for something."

They stood on the balcony, enjoying the silence. The house and gardens were always so full of people that sometimes it was nice to be alone to appreciate it all.

"Oh god, Mum, I'm so nervous," she said, holding the stirrup glass firmly in her hand, the bubbles popping and fizzing in the crystal. "Things like this are so not my scene at all."

"Well luckily, these things are very much my scene indeed," Matthew strolled in from the hallway, brandishing a bouquet of flowers, which he handed to Lizzy. "How are my two Darcy girls?"

Harriet kissed her dad on the cheek, "I thought you were meeting me there?"

"Well, my darling girl," he said with a smile, "I wanted it to be a surprise."

"Definitely is a surprise!" She did a little twirl, "what do you think?"

"You look stunning, Harriet, how are you even mine?"

Matthew knew that he missed a lot of things in his daughter's life; and even though he had planned to meet her at the venue, he didn't want to miss this. Didn't want to miss the pictures and the excitement and the giggling.

"Are these for me?" Lizzy asked as she smelled the luxurious bunch of peonies.

"Your favourite."

"Dad, how do you know they're her favourite?"

Matthew laughed as Lizzy filled a plastic cup with fizz for him, "I know more about your mum than I tell you."

"Ugh, you two are gross," she groaned, walking off to check her dress in the huge mirror that dominated one end of the room.

"Thank you for these," Lizzy gave him a tenuous hug.

"I couldn't miss the big Pemberley send off now, could I?" He pulled her in closer. "It was bad enough that I missed ours," he whispered into her ear.

Lizzy had a look of confusion on her face, he had hardly spoken to her in the whole time he had been in Derbyshire; he hadn't been over, hadn't sent her any messages, had been at Pemberley nearly every day and hadn't seen her. Now here he was bringing her flowers. Men were weird, Matthew was infuriating.

"Dad, are you going to be embarrassing? And remember don't flirt with Summer's mum, she needs no encouragement as it is."

"Be nice to your dad," her mum chastised. "He bought you those very expensive shoes."

Kath, the purple shirted head of the house team, popped her head around the door, "Lizzy, the rest of the girls have arrived – they're in the Courtyard taking pictures."

"About time!!"

Harriet stomped off leaving her parents to gather up their things and follow her.

Summer, Caitlyn, their mums, dads, and the odd granny, were busy posing and uploading pictures as best they could with the dodgy internet access on this side of the house. Lizzy thought that they both looked amazing, particularly Caitlyn who was fully emerging now as the beautiful swan.

"Our girls," Summer's mum placed her arm roughly around Lizzy's waist, "Time for a selfie," she pouted, dipping her head down and holding the phone high up in the air.

"That better be my good angle, Moira…"

"Of course, it will be, you only have good angles. Have you seen my cupcakes?" She brandished a box full of pink iced cupcakes, each with a sugarcraft Colin Firth on top. "The girls voted on which Darcy they wanted on top, and Mr Firth won."

Moira didn't wait for a response, she was already out in the small throng doling out cupcakes and taking random pictures of anyone she could. Lizzy knew that within the next half an hour her phone would be buzzing saying she had been tagged in numerous triple-filtered images.

"Right, we are all going to get these pictures done," Moira announced loudly to her audience, "that means you, Lizzy," she pranced over in their direction, her Cath Kidston 'Darcy' scarf fluttering down her back, "and you too, Mr Wickham," she purred, threading her arm around his.

"Well, I would love to, Moira," he was charming her and she didn't even realise, "but I need to pop back to my car."

"Oh, well don't be long!"

"I won't," he flashed Lizzy a look and she held back a laugh.

"He is so gallant, isn't he?"

Despite her husband standing about three feet away from her, Moira was visibly flustered.

"Oh yes, he's a regular knight in shining armour."

Moira went walking off by herself, organising people as she did, leaving Lizzy to walk three steps behind her in her polka dot heels.

Matthew strode over to the car with purpose. He had another gift for Harriet tucked inside the glove compartment. It might not be as grand as all of the Darcy paraphernalia, but it was part of her heritage and had been willed to his daughter by his mother. He opened the box, the small silver locket sparkled in the light; this was something special and he placed it carefully in his pocket.

"Hey boss, what are you doing here?"

He looked up and Benn was walking towards him dressed in joggers and t-shirt, a backpack slung over his shoulder. What on earth was he doing here? He didn't mind Benn as a rule, they had worked together on so many projects now that he considered him a mate, but tonight was different. He wanted to share the evening with Harriet and Lizzy without work getting in the way.

"I could ask the same of you."

They fell in step together, walking towards the house, tramping over the circle of grass in the centre of the outer courtyard.

"Joyce said I could practice the dancing in the house," he said quickly. "Still haven't got the grasp of it, so I thought I would pop up and see when she wanted me."

"The cotillion? Didn't you go to the lessons in Manchester?"

"Yes, but... It's not going in," he admitted. "I was going to ask Lizzy if she was free this week, she said she would help."

"Lizzy? *My* Lizzy? You're on first-name terms now, even though you asked me to keep her away from you?"

"Yeah, about that... I apologised."

"Did it involve food or wine?"

"Carvery and copious amounts of Chardonnay."

"That usually works for her."

"I figured that out."

"Food usually works for you too, but..."

There was a pointed look, and there was a sharp second where something was understood.

"She's become a good friend."

Matthew didn't know how he felt about this information because neither Benn *nor* Lizzy had told him that they were even on speaking terms, let alone that they had become 'good friends' as he put it.

"Oh," he said. "Right."

They stopped under the cloisters at the steps that led to the Estate Office. It was a full stop to their conversation and their journey.

"Is it a problem?"

"No, I... No. Lizzy is always good at stuff like this. She used to try and rope me into dancing when we were kids."

"Did you ever do it?"

Benn sensed that Matthew wasn't as cool about this whole thing as he was letting on.

"Only once."

The shouts of Harriet echoed through the courtyard.

"COME ON, DAD!!"

"I'll get practicing then!"

"Alright mate, see you tomorrow." He began walking towards the shrieks of his daughter emanating from the lawn. "Your early call is like 5am I think."

"Oh, thanks for that!"

Matthew raised his hands in the air, "don't thank me, thank Evelyn, she does the schedules!"

Benn dropped the backpack to his side and wandered off towards the estate office to find Joyce, remembering what the laughter and shrieks were in aid of.

They were out on the lawn, taking glorious photographs in the gardens, posing in front of the grand place that Harriet called home.

Summer, Harriet, and Caitlyn all standing, poised and graceful, on the steps leading up to the house.

The Mums and the Girls all together huddled in close.

The Girls and their Dads, standing to attention like Victorian party goers.

Summer and her Mum.

Caitlyn and her Gran.

Caitlyn and Summer

Harriet and Caitlyn.

Harriet and Lizzy, posing underneath the Palladian columns, the grandeur of the house towering above them.

Matthew and Harriet.

Matthew and Harriet and Lizzy.

Matthew and Lizzy. For old times' sake. Taken by Harriet who begged them to smile.

As she stood at the edge of the lake with the house behind her, Lizzy felt her phone vibrate in her pocket, she opened the message.

BENN: Back from London, got you a surprise.

Harriet noticed the change in her mum's expression.

"Are you texting your fancy man?"

"He's not my fancy man."

LIZZY: Ooh, I'm excited!

"Okay, your 'friend'" She mimed the inverted commas with her fingers and laughed heartily at herself.

"Harriet!"

"It's cute," she laughed. "I hear you both up on the roof, with your plastic cups and your schoolgirl crush, all laughing and flirty."

"Harriet Darcy, can you please remember that you are speaking to your mother?"

"Yes, my mother who has a huge crush on the star of the film that my dad is directing."

Lizzy's phone buzzed again in her pocket, Harriet eyed it with humorous suspicion and then looked away, as her mum blushed reading the message.

BENN: So...tomorrow? Dancing? I'll even let you step on my toes :)

Harriet sighed, "see, there it is again – your happy face."

"I'm always happy."

LIZZY: Oi! I know how to dance – I'll bring my steel toe-capped boots in anticipation!! ;P

"Maybe, but you get happier when your phone beeps."

"What's all this," Matthew asked as he sneaked up behind them.

"Oh, nothing," Harriet said.

"Doesn't sound like nothing," he said. "Tell me."

"It's nothing," Lizzy said.

BENN: I look forward to it. Hope all goes well for Harriet tonight. Big night!

Moira started demanding attention and letting everyone know that the cars had arrived.

Matthew knew it was something because he saw the look on her face as she tapped into her phone, and he realised that he didn't like the thought of sharing her.

HARRIET: I'm going to be late back, Moira has organised karaoke at a place in town. Exciting! Love you xx
LIZZY: Have a good time xx

"Was that Harriet?"

Matthew was naked under the sheets. The smell of sex hung in the air, but Lizzy found that she was already annoyed by his presence. He tapped her on the hip with his foot.

"Yes," she said. "She's had a good time."

"Ah, good," he grinned. "although I'm sure it will cost me an utter fortune…"

"You can afford it."

She slipped over her dressing table, illuminated by the moonlight sneaking in through the arched window. She looked lovely, he thought, standing there naked apart from a t-shirt.

And then he remembered something.

"I heard that you've made friends with Mr Darcy?"

Lizzy continued to apply her face cream, "he brought me home that night, you remember, in Manchester? He gave me a lift," she pulled a lip balm from the drawer and applied it. "you know me, Matthew, I don't hold grudges for very long."

He studied her, watching as she went through her nightly ritual, "I know. I was just curious."

"He's still so in love with Madeleine Tennant," she turned, offering him a sip from her bottle of water. "I asked him why he cheated on her."

"He didn't cheat on her."

"Yeah, he did," she snorted. "It was all over the paper."

"She left him, but he was never unfaithful," Matthew always wondered why Benn Williams decided to take the fall. Maybe it was better to be the cheater than the cuckold.

"Oh, I wonder why he just didn't tell me that."

"She was seeing someone else, it was all convenient for her, I guess."

"Convenient? Why?"

He wasn't sure if he should reveal this information. It wasn't his secret to share. He took a deep breath.

"Benn likes to drink," he said firmly. "Sometimes too much."

"So, he gets a bit drunk occasionally… so what? We all do."

"No, it's more than that."

She sniggered, "are you trying to tell me that he's an alcoholic?"

He nodded. He didn't why he expected her to be shocked or repulsed or angry, because he knew – he always knew – that in fact, she would feel an overwhelming rush of care for Benn Williams and his hidden vice.

"It's why 'Shellstone' ran over last year – you know when I was taking the kids to Florida? We had to do reshoots because he went missing for three days. We found him holed up in a room at the Savoy."

"It explains how he still loves her. Poor Benn."

He came up behind her now, moving her hair out of the way and kissing her neck in the way he knew she couldn't resist.

"Explains why she left him, more like," he murmured, "but I'm not here to talk about Benn bloody Williams…"

His soft forceful kisses increased in pressure as his hands wrapped around her waist, under her breast, pulling her back into him, and she fell into it.

She always did.

2010

The train started rolling out of Manchester Piccadilly station as Lizzy Darcy ventured to London for the final time in what had been a frantic and tiring nine months. She was dealing with a difficult inheritance case; this trip should be the final visit to the beneficiary of a complicated lady's complicated estate and, though it had taken many hours of work, many gallons of coffee and fair amount of sleepless nights, she was content that she had done her best work and proved herself, finally, as the latest of the Darcy attorneys.

The first Darcy to take up Law was Francis, youngest son of Fitzwilliam and Elizabeth, his father approving of the career path and agreeing that it was most useful in the legal wrangling that was occurring behind the scenes at Pemberley. He had been a brilliant lawyer and a key member of the Law Society in its early days; there was an Italian marble bust of his likeness in the hallway of the headquarters on Chancery Lane and Uncle Jeremy always gave it a reverent nod when he walked past.

The youngest Darcy son had been known for his hideous fits of temper, which saw him screaming for servants to do his bidding and resulted in him being disliked by senior members of the household. Afterwards, he would ride into the woods for hours and only return after everyone was in bed, still demanding supper. Lizzy was often saddened by the story of the bachelor uncle who defined the career path of his Darcy descendants; he was buried in the graveyard of the small church next to the house at Longbourn after succumbing to pneumonia at the grand old age of ninety-five – born when the country was celebrating the victory of Waterloo and dying when the world was embroiled in what felt like an unending war.

Francis had never married, had lived the life of the Bachelor Lord, focusing on his career, and becoming a genial uncle, assisting his young nephew in running the estates when he inherited prematurely. It was in stark contrast to the bad-tempered youth who had shouted at housemaids and vexed Mr Staughton. In the letters to his dearest

Mama, Lizzy could read between the lines, understanding more than Elizabeth herself why the gentleman never took a wife.

"You look busy…"

The man sitting across from her smiled as the train pulled into Stockport station. Usually, she hated when strangers tried to speak to her on trains, preferring instead to hide behind the safety of a book, this was why she always paid the extra money for First Class. He looked friendly enough, was dressed in a smart suit and a pair of nice oxfords, Hugh had always told her to pay attention to a man's shoes.

"I am sorry, how terrible of me not to introduce myself," he said, in a way that was rather dashing, "I'm David Forsythe."

He held out his hand, and she returned a firm handshake which she could tell surprised him a little. It made her smile to herself.

"Elizabeth Darcy. Pleased to meet you," she had smiled back at him, as a thousand butterflies danced across her belly.

By the time the train arrived at Euston, they had exchanged numbers and planned to meet for dinner later that week. It was a whirlwind and one that she let herself be carried along on. He worked in the City and had a whole wardrobe of nice suits, expensive shoes and an apartment with a view of the Thames. David had been obviously impressed with the Grosvenor Square address, where she was staying with Charlie, Emma and the boys, and her ability to obtain tables at The Ivy. Their second date ended with crazy, drunken sex on his Conran sofa.

In the first few months of their romance, after copious amounts of wine, he proposed to her on the balcony overlooking the river with a Haribo ring and a massive grin on his face.

"Marry me, Lady Elizabeth Georgiana Darcy! Make me a very happy man!"

"Are you serious?" She giggled.

"Of course, I am," he said on one knee, struggling to get back up. "Who would not want to marry you, Lizzy. You rock my world!"

"Rock your world? You are drunk… and an idiot," she was kissing his face, pulling him towards her with each touch of her lips on his skin. "But I will marry you. We can be Mr and Mrs Idiot."

"That sounds absolutely bloody perfect," he gently pulled at the straps on her vest top, sliding it over her shoulder. "Although, we would be Mr and Lady Idiot, of course…"

The morning brought bacon sandwiches, coffee, and croissants. There was no mention of the proposal.

A year later, she had booked a fancy hotel room for their anniversary and travelled down to London with expectation in her head and a longing for more in her heart. This love felt different to how she expected, she thought, always believing that falling in love would be very much slowly and then all at once, but she found that she had fallen quickly into the deep end and was struggling to keep her head above the water.

"Lizzy…" he said, unable to look her in the eye. He hadn't removed his coat, which she thought was odd, but she ignored the voice at the back of her head.

"Is everything alright?" she said, unsure but doing her best to stop the echoes of disappointment crossing her face.

He nodded, as he looked down at his shoes.

"I picked the tickets up for the show, have you ever seen Les Mis?" she continued with a false enthusiasm that belied the waves of panic rising in her stomach.

"Lizzy, please stop…"

She stopped, her heart thumping hard in her chest. She noticed that he wasn't wearing his suit, wasn't dressed for the dinner at Le Gavroche that she had planned for them, on his feet were battered gym trainers.

"David," she said carefully. "What's going on?"

"It's Bianca…" he said flatly. "She's pregnant."

It wasn't as surprising as she suspected he thought it would be, but it still hurt. Still felt like a hard, heavy thump in the heart as she realised that this was the end of it all now.

"It's yours, isn't it?"

Sitting down on the edge of the bed, he explained in fits and starts that they had always wanted children, but nine failed rounds of IVF, with its invasive nature and disappointment, had made each time harder to get over. Each time it didn't take a part of them died and then it drove them apart.

"Lizzy, you made me realise what it was I wanted this whole time. You and Harriet, you're so close and you are both so great. I want a family," he paused, and then slowly, ashamedly, "but I don't want to insert myself into yours, I want my own family, my own children and the only person I can imagine being their mother is my wife."

"Well, I'm glad I could be of use to you, David," she said, "What was I in all of this?"

He paused, thought about it carefully and then he spoke.

"A distraction."

He reached out to put his hand on hers, but she moved away and walked over to the window. The sparkling city was illuminated below her, and she wished, more than anything, that Harriet was there to look at the view with her and get over-excited about the glittering lights of the capital. Suddenly the gentle touch of his hand on his shoulder felt like a personal attack.

"Don't touch me."

He looked across at her sadly, but she refused to look at him, didn't want him to see the angry tears running down her cheeks.

The door closed softly as he left.

Instinctively, she reached for her phone.

LIZZY: I need you.
MATTHEW: Where are you?
LIZZY: St Martins Lane.

He checked the time; Cara was out tonight, the boys supervised by Meena, the Polish nanny who had been chosen specifically for her unattractiveness. He waved them all goodnight and slowly clicked the door closed.

MATTHEW: I'll be half an hour.
LIZZY: Promise.
MATTHEW: Always.

It felt like forever as she watched the minutes tick away.

1912

"She is nearly twenty-one," Cecily sighed one evening to her husband. "She must be settled soon."

The famed society hostess was concerned about her youngest child. The last of three and the only girl, Millicent Augusta was a force to be reckoned with, even for her fiery American mother. Edward Darcy was unsure what his wife wanted him to do, it's not as if he could force his daughter to marry someone; this was the twentieth century, after all.

"I agree that she needs to find a decent chap, but there is no hurry, is there?" He removed his robe and climbed into the bed that they pretended they didn't share. "You were nearly twenty-five when I married you, practically an old maid!"

"And you're lucky that I had you!"

"I know, my love," he pulled her into an embrace and kissed the top of her head. "We will find a match for Millicent. I hardly expect her to look after us when we are old."

"Can you imagine," she said closing her book, "she would have us marching in protest for reform and paying to educate our servants."

"What about my cousin Henry's boy, Rupert? He's a decent sort."

"The dull gangly one who used to stay with us over summer? Do you think he is suitable … would he be able to keep up with her? I don't want her to be bored."

"They were always running about the place before he went to school. I imagine that he is much improved now. I think she taught him how to shoot!"

"Trust your daughter to be the one to teach a boy how to shoot," Cecily smiled softly. "I suppose it might be worth inviting him for a visit. I shall write to his mother."

"It would mean she would be a Countess eventually," Edward thought out loud. "Would that finally satisfy your father's inherent social climbing?"

"My father's social climbing means that you received a very good settlement with which to install electricity and indoor plumbing!"

"Your father's social climbing meant that I was very fortunate to have married such a wonderful woman who, coincidentally, had a very large fortune." He kissed her gently, "we will find a husband for her soon enough."

Cecily snuggled down into her husband's embrace. Daughters were always a worry.

Edward was reading his newspaper at his club on St James's Street when he heard that his daughter had been arrested for setting fire to a post box in the name of Women's Suffrage. This was the twelfth time that he had been summoned to the police station to bail her out and it was becoming tiresome.

"Are you sure it's her, Boothroyd?"

"Yes, Your Grace," the voice confirmed. "Lady Millicent is currently in custody, although the detective there said he can release her if you get someone there before noon."

Edward sighed, "alright, call Albert Armitage, pay what you need to. I will be there to collect her."

Despite his wife's disgust, and the cost to his own purse, the Duke of Derbyshire was secretly proud of Millicent's newfound infamy as one of the younger leaders of the suffragette movement in the north, along with the Pankhurst's, whom he funded with anonymous donations. He wasn't surprised, however, to find that instead of bailing out his daughter, he was faced with a working-class girl with red hair and a smattering of freckles.

"Don't you work for me?" He asked her quickly.

"Yes, sir," she curtseyed.

"And your name?"

"Kitty, sir," she said, with the hint of a tremor in her voice. "Kitty Blake."

"Well, Kitty Blake," he said rather sternly, "why are you standing before me and not my daughter?"

The girl shifted in the borrowed shoes; she was wearing Millicent's heavy purple wool coat and her dress too. The Duke was a nice man, she had heard Mrs Reynolds say so, but looming over her in the street he was quite intimidating.

"You need to speak up, Kitty." The tone of his voice changed, "I know my daughter can be very persuasive and I imagine it was Millicent who convinced you to accompany her." He noticed the look of fear on the girl's face. "Does Mrs Reynolds know that you are here?"

"She thinks I'm sick, and in my bed," Kitty's voice raised slightly. "Please don't sack me, Sir, I'll work ever so hard."

"Miss Blake, I have no intention of that," the girl was drowning in lilac, "you better get back."

Kitty curtseyed out of appreciation and relief.

"Oh, Kitty," he called after her. "If you are sneaking in, I always find that you are better going through the stables and up the back-south stairs."

Kitty smiled briefly before setting off down the street, Edward watched after her before looking up at the Police station. God only knew where his daughter was now, he should have known. Millicent would often switch identities with the poorer girls, knowing that her rank as a member of the aristocracy granted her a particular leniency not usually granted to women of a lower status. He quite admired her spirit, although he had no idea what he was going to tell his wife.

It would be three months before Lady Millicent was released, celebrated by the group of sisters outside the gates of Holloway, who cheered and celebrated. Furious and weak, but battle-hardened by the hunger strikes and force-feedings, she went straight to the WSPU headquarters in Kingsway, where she planned to attend the Derby. The plan was to pin rosettes to the Kings horse as it hammered past them; but the crowd was too busy, the horses too fast, and Millicent and the rest of the women dotted about the crowd watched as their friend was trampled to death, powerless to save her. Arrested once more, she was bailed and returned to her father like lost luggage. He promptly sent her back to Pemberley for recuperation and fresh air, despite her objections.

"We are fighting for revolution!" the younger woman screamed at the unflappable Cecily across the dining table, "why can you not understand that this is for all women, it's for you too!"

"You will forgive me for doubting your revolution, darling, when all of us are aware of how it all worked out for the aristocrats in France."

Cecily continued with her onion soup; she rolled her eyes. Edward, failing to notice the cue, took a mouthful of the meal before being verbally accosted by his daughter.

"And you, Father, do you not think that it is ridiculous that women don't have any rights or any say over what they do? A woman is her father's possession until she marries and then she is the property of her husband. What if she never marries...who does she belong to then? Does she finally belong to herself or does she get entailed away?"

"I'm not sure, Milly," he stammered, looking at his wife for assistance. "Do you really think this is –"

"You should know!" She threw her spoon into the decorated china, it clinked loudly, soup splashing over the tablecloth. "This is intolerable. You are keeping me a prisoner here."

Edward shot a knowing glance at his wife, who took a large mouthful of wine. She didn't know what she had done in a previous life to deserve such a boisterous and argumentative child, but she imagined it was the rebellious American half trying to burst through the dusty establishment. Although Millicent's behaviour may have been tolerated in New York or Chicago, even Boston at a push, Cecily knew that it would never be acceptable in the upper echelons of polite English society.

"I wish you would start behaving like the Lady that you are," Cecily gestured to James to pull out her chair. "The thought of this has given me rather a headache, please excuse me."

She disappeared into the drawing room, shooting a firm glance to her husband. Edward looked sternly at Millicent.

"What have I done now?"

"Could you, for once, at least put up the pretence of being a respectable young lady?"

"How very dull," she said with a wave of the hand.

Edward sighed. He would, at some point in the future, like to enjoy dinner in its entirety without either his wife or his daughter storming out between courses. They were so similar. He nodded at Mr Staughton who was standing by the door; the butler acknowledged this and dismissed his staff, leaving the Duke and his delinquent offspring alone.

Millicent rose from the table and walked to the window, the dining room looked out onto the Elizabethan knot gardens, the Orangery, and in the distance, Wyatt's folly still stood firm and proud in its place in Lantern wood. There had been a tree planted in front of it by one of Fitzwilliam Darcy's children, which had grown and blocked the view, and now the poor yew tree stood with the top left quarter cut out of it, vexing the gardeners whose job it was to keep it suitably trimmed.

"It's amazing, isn't it? How generations of Darcys have stood here in this spot and looked out on this view, and it doesn't alter. It's the same view that Piers D'Arcy saw when he arrived with his parchment, the same landscape that Sophia Darcy would have looked out upon when she was plotting in the stag parlour."

"Millicent, you know we don't talk about Sophia."

"No, we never have done. Nothing changes. We still don't talk about Sophia two hundred years after she, to all intents and purposes, vanished into thin air, we still cut a chunk out of the tree rather than simply chop it down, and there on the hill…the Lantern still looks the same as it did when I was a little girl, and yet here I am. So very much altered."

"I like to think that Pemberley is a constant. A perpetual sentinel in this tumultuous world."

"Maybe it is, but not you or I. We will be gone, and Pemberley will still be here, god willing." She looked at his face, a permanent frown now embedded on his forehead, "and the news from Europe. I don't like it, Papa."

He nodded, "terrible business. War is on the way, there is no avoiding it now."

"The world is changing, Papa. We need to make sure that we are not left behind."

She lit a cigarette and took a long drag, Edward frowned at his daughter's current vice, especially in the dining room.

"Maybe you are changing too fast for it, Millicent."

"Maybe it needs to catch up with me."

Rupert Fitzwilliam always thought that Millicent Darcy was the most spiffing girl that he had ever had the good luck to know. From childhood they had played together in the grounds at Pemberley, hiding in the ravine with the gardeners as Cecily demanded fresh flowers for her parties, or sneaking onto the top landing and looking down on the fancy ladies and handsome gentlemen in the saloon. It was a blissful golden era and every time Rupert returned to the big old house in Derbyshire, he fell a little bit more in love with his second cousin, who didn't care about fighting him on the lawn or falling about in the lake, splashing him in the sweltering heat of the summer sun, despite her mother's yells that it was decidedly unladylike. She taught him how to fire a shotgun, already knowing better than the boy who permanently lived in London where to aim and what to shoot.

When she was twenty-one and he was newly graduated from Oxford, he attended her coming out ball at Derbyshire House. They had danced on the marble floor of the ballroom, before escaping to the roof, drinking their stealthily procured champagne from the antique crystal stirrup glasses that Rupert had given her for her birthday. The house was alive with the sound of music and laughter, but it was the cool calmness of the skies of London that Millicent found the most comforting.

"You really are a terrible clod, Rup," she teased. "But I, for one, am so very glad that you are here."

"You are? I was beginning to suspect that after dinner you would rather I were not here at all!"

"Any man who stands up against my mother in matters of women's suffrage to defend me is definitely a man I want at my father's table," she poured another glass of the champagne. "Although I very much doubt she will have you back again. More than likely she is, this very instant, talking to your mama and demanding your sharp departure and return to Belgravia."

Rupert Fitzwilliam was much improved since their youth, she had been pleased to note that his dancing was much better than in the past when he had stomped on her feet. She offered him a cigarette, lighting it and passing it to him in a slow, exaggerated movement.

"Thank you," the smoke curled upwards into the air. "You must know that I have been sent here as a potential suitor, Millie. Our mothers have been conspiring against us."

"Oh, I am fully aware of the courtly machinations of dearest Cecily, no doubt spurred on by my grandfather who would love to add another peerage to his trophy cabinet. Buccaneers, darling!"

"Does he have many?"

"Aunt Isabella is married to a stuffy old Laird up in Scotland; Aunt Adeline managed to convince an Earl to propose after six weeks, which I think was a record even for the Drew girls; and my mother got the top prize, of course, Mr Darcy himself."

"I always forget that your mother is so exotic," he finished his champagne, turning. "Isn't your grandmother Cuban?"

"Yes, she is, although we don't mention that, we only talk about the fortune," she grinned with delight, "and the jewellery."

"Indubitably, how very vulgar!"

"You're the one with the German granny!" She teased, but things were getting serious in Europe now, a tinderbox ready to spark. "What has Lady Anna to say about the Prussian hysterics?"

"All she will say is '*Nein, nein, mein schatz...* this is all big fuss *über nichts*', I don't think she believes anything will come of it."

She leaned over and put her arm around his shoulder, teasing the combed and waxed hair at the nape of his neck into an unruly twirl.

"But it is coming, isn't it?" She was wistful, gazing up at the stars.

He could feel every hair on his body standing to attention, every nerve twitchy with expectation.

"Would you ever consider a proposal from a gentleman like me?"

He was so close now that she could smell the hint of his cologne, it smelled like leather and cognac mixed with his own earthy scent.

"If I were going to marry anyone, Rupert, I think you would have a very good chance."

"That's encouraging."

"But before you make the arrangements, I have to advise you that I do not plan to marry."

"Not at all?"

"This war is going to make everything different. You and I, we owe it to ourselves to see what the world will be like before we make any decisions."

She had never noticed before how blue his eyes were, or how his moustache curled at the ends, she caught him looking at her in the same way, as if he had never seen her before – people always look so different when you are inches away from them, your body tingling with anticipation and each breath taking a lifetime.

"Well," he said optimistically, "if I were to make any proposals at all, which I am not planning to do I must add, then I wouldn't go into it blindly."

"No one must," she said in a voice that was more than a touch suggestive. "One must go into these things with their eyes wide open. Don't you think?"

"I do."

She saw the little pout of his lip, the dip of his head before he looked back up at her. There would be no going back after this point, but she was fully aware of what she was doing.

"I would really rather like you to kiss me now."

"Penny, I can think of nothing else I would rather do."

Rupert tentatively leaned towards tracing his fingertips over the back of her hand, causing goosebumps to race up her arm.

Slowly and with great trepidation, he ran the flat of his palm up her arm and to her shoulder, into the crease of her blue taffeta gown, his fingers catching on the beaded embroidery, she watched still and silent, unsure what he would do next.

His fingers continued their slow journey up to her face and as he placed his hand on the back of her neck and brought her mouth slowly to his own.

Emboldened by a brazen disregard for society's rules and social etiquette, she took his hand and they walked the short journey to her room, where he proclaimed he loved her under badly embroidered sheets.

For Shame, Imogen.

Lady Imogen caused uproar last night at the Salamander Society Ball. The Darcy debutante, 21, who arrived in a sedan chair carried by four men in blackface, emerged wearing a full-length rabbit fur coat. Miranda Marsh of animal rights organisation SAMDA called the actions of the audacious aristocrat despicable and very irresponsible.

Twelve

Benn had planned to meet her in the entrance hall just after twelve. The house was closed today, silent apart from the faint sound of music in the distance, and the occasional whirr of a vacuum from the conservation stores. To call it an 'entrance hall' was unfair, Lizzy thought, because it was a huge decadent room complete with three huge columns and hung with seventeenth-century tapestries on three of the walls, one of which was dominated by the marble fireplace commissioned by Elizabeth Bennet-Darcy, and the huge portraits of Sir Piers D'Arcy and his wife, Matilda, the founders of the dynasty. The room dated from the day the house was built and used to form part of the medieval banqueting hall – it stood on a level all of its own, engineered by a fancy Italian architect in the 1700s, and was the grandest and most impressive room in the building. Fitzwilliam Darcy had redesigned this floor when he came of age too – creating an entertaining suite designed to simultaneously impress and intimidate, and as Benn looked up at the tapestries and the paintings and the gold-leaf covered plaster he felt both in equal measure.

Lizzy stepped tentatively down the smaller set of steps that led the way, she unhooked the velvet ropes with a subtle clink. Quietly, with all the lightness of a prima ballerina, she delicately stepped down the staircase. The music was louder now, the unmistakable rhythm and melody from her childhood echoing through the corridor, she was immediately taken back to being twelve years old and performing country dances in the courtyard with Winston and his mish-mash troop of dancers, led by Mrs Winifred Wharton, who he had obviously been very much in love with. She walked down the steps and directly towards the sweaty and dishevelled form of Benn Williams, his face scrunched up with concentration. He had been so engrossed in trying to remember the steps for the blasted dance that he hadn't even heard Lizzy itching her way towards him in polka dot heels.

"What are you doing?"

"Can't you see that I'm trying to dance?"

"I can see you're trying to do something, but it doesn't look like dancing to me."

She glanced over, a humorous expression on her face as she kicked off her heels, standing in her bare feet on the wooden floorboards and then she took a seat on one of the chairs as if waiting for his performance. He had been in rehearsals for this over the last few weeks and it was taking ages to sink in, even Jenny and Franklin had perfected it and he was clonking about like Frankenstein's monster, feeling huge and weighty.

"The dance instructor has almost given up on me," he puffed, red-faced and sweaty. "Jesus, this is like a bloody gym circuit."

"Don't say that too loudly or 'Mr Darcy's Regency Workout' will be available on shelves before you know it!"

He took a swig of water before returning the bottle to his bag on the far side of the room. Joyce had been very specific about not eating or drinking on the wrong side of the rope.

"Do you think you can help?"

"Definitely! You're not a lost cause to me, Williams!"

For the next hour, Benn listened to Lizzy explain to him the intricacies of Mr Beveridge's Maggot and how the choreography meant that Elizabeth and Darcy moved up and down the longways dance, constantly forced to face each other.

They walked through the dance, moving together and then apart – substituting a card table and a chair as the other couple. She might be a bit rusty, she thought, but surely dancing was like riding a bike, something you never forgot.

Sitting down flustered on the large yellow settee in the centre of the room it felt as if they had been dancing for what felt like an eternity. He remembered that Joyce had told him that he should definitely not sit on this piece of furniture.

"I always used to think it was called 'maggot' because of the way everyone moved up and down the dance," she confided, "like a maggot, yeah?'

"I'm guessing it's not because of that then," he took a moment to appreciate his surroundings and the enormous room that was taking on a hazy glow in the late summer afternoon sunshine.

"No," she sighed. "It means 'fancy', so really the dance and the song are called Mr Beveridge's Fancy.

"I imagine Mr Beveridge was very fancy, he sounds it."

He smirked at her, taking a large gulp from his water bottle. He caught a look pass across her face as she leaned back, she looked away quickly. Rising to his feet he did a bow and held out his hand in his most gentlemanly way.

"Lady Elizabeth, may I request your hand for the next two dances?"

He pulled her up from her seat, misstepping she fell into him, she was close, so close that he could smell her perfume and that sweet, warm scent that was all her. She breathed him in for quick, quiet instant before remembering herself and pushing him gently back into his starting position.

"Mr Williams, such a level of impropriety will not suffice! We have at least five years before the Waltz becomes fashionable and this level of dancefloor fondling is permitted. This kind of malarkey is just a threat to my virtue!"

"Do you make a habit of dancing with strange men you barely know?"

"Always," she grinned.

They moved together as the dance began, concentrating on the complicated movements, and she tried to ignore the fact that every time his hand touched hers it felt a little bit like lightning.

"Anyway, you said you had a surprise for me," she said later as they walked out into the warmth of the evening sunshine. "It had better be an actual gift!"

"Oh, yes."

He had been away for a few days, back to London to see Esther and Anya, and recording a small cameo for an animated film called 'Puffins in Space', which his youngest daughter was terribly excited about. He pulled the small bag from his holdall, she recognised the pink branding, the ribbon tied around the top, and inside a full box of rose and violet flavoured macarons. She was surprised that he had remembered her telling him about the little bakery on Portobello Road.

"Thank you," she said softly, with a grateful smile, before giving him an awkward hug.

"I couldn't resist," he admitted.

They walked up through the car park to the edge of the formal gardens; up the short but steep incline that lead to Lime Avenue, passing the Dutch gardens, with their formal planting and outrageous colours. The fountain splashed merrily away, and they continued up the hill, emerging directly opposite the Pemberley view.

"I always forget how impressive it is," he said as he plonked himself on the grass, admiring the Palladian columns, and noticing the classical features reflected in the lake, which was as still as a millpond on this warm night. The park was beginning to settle into dusk and the last of the guests were leaving for the day as the bell rang for closure.

She sat down on the grass next to him, a flurry of dandelion clocks scurrying up into the air.

"You owe that view to John William Darcy."

"Ah yes, the one with the rich wife," he remembered the story. "It must be mad to think of your ancestors tottering around here, I think you forget."

"I don't forget."

"I know you don't, but I do. It's just one of the places that you visit in the summer holidays when the kids are driving you mad, but for you –this is your history!"

"I don't see it like that at all," she shrugged. "Pemberley is just where I grew up."

"I can't even begin to imagine growing up in a place like this."

"I turned out okay, I think. Harriet too. It might have been different if we had boarded somewhere, but we're just normal people."

"Who happen to live in a massive country mansion!"

"In the servant's quarters!"

He observed her closely as she popped a rose-coloured macaron in her mouth, offering him a choice of one from the box. She was so unlike anyone he had ever met, and he wasn't sure if he would ever be able to figure her out.

"Do you ever feel the pressure of being a Darcy..." he asked carefully, "I mean, the legacy of Fitzwilliam and Elizabeth, that's massive."

"Yeah," she nodded. "It is massive, but there's no pressure with it...maybe a... maybe an expectation, I guess, but never any pressure."

"I just... I just wonder sometimes if it stops you from doing what you actually to do. That you're so focused on being a 'Darcy' that you forget to be Lizzy. Surely there are things that you want to do without the weight of Pemberley on your shoulders. I mean, I can choose to walk away from being 'Benn Williams', but you're always going to be Lady Liz."

Her face was beginning to sour, that crinkle above her brow turning into a frown and he immediately began to retreat.

"I don't mean that to offend you," he continued, "but I'm sure that Fitzwilliam would have wanted you to do what made you happy, from what I have learned about him he always followed his heart."

She softened slightly, but he realised that he had touched a nerve.

"You haven't offended me. One of the burdens of being part of this family is that there are certain codes to conform to, and people get mad if you don't act in a certain way."

Her gaze was focused on the grassy tufts now; she was fiddling with her nail, twisting the ring with the green stone on her finger, "But, Pemberley hasn't been around for so long as a result of us all doing what we wanted. It's bigger than me, bigger than all of us."

"I'm sorry I said that it was rather rude of me," he apologised

"You don't need to say sorry. It was a very Darcy thing to say."

"I am, of course, Mr Darcy," he pouted, looking extremely Darcy like. "I own half of Derbyshire – my ego is as large as my fortune and you, Lady Elizabeth, are only tolerable and not handsome enough to tempt me."

Lizzy watched as he closed his eyes and basked in the hazy golden glow. She knew she would be lying if she said she hadn't missed him.

It was dark when he finally left. Skirting down the driveway, Benn thought back to the first night he had been invited up to the flat in the tower, how it now felt like a second home to him. They had wandered through the cloisters of the courtyard, then up the winding staircase in the far-left corner, the entrance to which was concealed behind a large oak door, lit by a dim bulb in a glass and iron lantern. He wondered how he hadn't noticed this before; the hidden corners of Pemberley now being revealed to him. Lizzy's key had clanked in the lock and he felt as if he was being let in on the secret as he followed her down passages and through doors, he had never seen before and then up the narrow flights of stairs to her odd little apartment in the tower behind the famous Palladian facade. She told him that the flat comprised of the old Tower bedroom and the rooms above which had made up the female servants' quarters.

They slipped through the door, which had a sign screwed to it: PLEASE KEEP THIS DOOR SHUT, and then into the main room, which was large and airy, with a tall ceiling and three large windows that glanced down over the lake – at one end there was a large dining room table, covered in books; at the other a large sofa and a small, squat chair that stood next to a round table.

The room was painted in a deep, dark blue, with pictures and mirrors and photographs covering the walls. The centre was dominated by a wooden kitchen with dangling lights and large wooden topped island. She told him how it had been cobbled together by the Historical House Society after they inherited her and needed to find somewhere for her to live, but he found it was stylish, understated and a bit eclectic, with odd shabby pieces of furniture, which he assumed were family heirlooms, mixed with newer bits and bobs. There were also piles and piles of books, on the coffee table where she had temptingly placed a few biscuits on a plate, and over in the kitchen where one wall was home to a massive bookcase.

"Do you read?"

He realised that it was a stupid question, given that he was surrounded by books, but then thinking that maybe they were all for show. His own coffee table was filled with thick slabs of self-importance that were rarely touched unless Anya needed something to lean on when she was drawing.

"Yes, I do like to read, quite a lot actually," she crossed over and plonked herself on the large leather armchair. "It makes me sad to think that there is a massive library in the house down there and nobody ever reads the books in it anymore"

"Can you not go and read in the library downstairs," he questioned, intertwining his fingers around the hand of the coffee mug, "would that be against the rules?"

"Against the rules in the sense that I would get really told off, but also that it's not really my library anymore – not the one I grew up with," she mumbled. "My grandad bequeathed all of the books to the HHS, but they didn't want a lot of them, so the ones you see in here with the Darcy coat of arms on are the ones from the library. If you go in there and it hasn't got this gold bull on it," she pulled one of the books from the coffee table to show him, "then it's not from the Pemberley library. It's an imposter."

He took the book from her - 'The Mysteries of Udolpho' – noting the angry little bull with his whipping tail, embossed in gold on the spine

Back in his room at the Armitage Arms, his phone sounded out with a loud R2-D2 ringtone, especially downloaded by Esther who had recently discovered the wonder of 'Star Wars'. The name on the screen caused a smile to cross his face.

LIZZY: Darcy and Elizabeth actually danced our dance on the night of the Netherfield Ball.
BENN: Our dance?
LIZZY: Oh, shut up, you know what I mean.
BENN: I do. How do you know?
LIZZY: I'll show you next week.
BENN: Next week?

LIZZY: Yeah, I'm helping Maggie move this weekend.

He was only on set on Saturday afternoon for an hour and then had a radio interview on Monday. It wasn't enough time to go and see the girls, and he had left it too late to arrange anything with anyone else because he had planned on asking her if she fancied going out somewhere or just watching tv in the flat. He didn't want to be alone this weekend. He didn't know whether to offer to help Maggie move, would that be too desperate? Benn had met Maggie once, she had blushed for the first ten minutes before settling into a conversation tinged with nervous energy and frantic laughter. He decided not to. It would definitely be too desperate. He could take his mum out for lunch or something, offer to take his nephew to Legoland. That would be okay. Because he couldn't offer to help Maggie just so he could spend more time with Lizzy, could he? He needed to play it all very cool.

BENN: Ooh, tell her good luck with it! I'm intrigued anyway.
LIZZY: Don't get too excited.
BENN: I said intrigued, not excited.
LIZZY: Pfft.
BENN: That's not even a real word.
LIZZY: Benn, I need to ask you something.
BENN: Fire away.
LIZZY: Did you drink tonight?

He was typing and thinking and deleting and retyping. He needed to be honest, but he was ashamed. Ashamed of what he was letting happen. He was turning into his father and he hated himself for it. Tonight had been the first time in a long time that he hadn't felt the need to drink, apart from the short bitter espresso he had ordered from room service when he got back.

BENN: No. Why do you ask?
LIZZY: Matthew told me about Shellstone.

As soon as she sent the message, she wished that she hadn't.

So, the secret was out, he thought, it had only been a matter of time. Benn didn't understand Matthew's motivation, but he suspected that there was some underlying jealousy at work. The whole history with them was so complex and secretive that he should have known his friend would have been a little territorial. He would tell her. He would be honest. No point lying about it all now.

BENN: He shouldn't have told you that.
LIZZY: I'm sorry if I'm being too nosey, seriously you can tell me to fuck off.
BENN: You're not being nosey. I should have been honest with you.
LIZZY: Be honest with me now,
BENN: I never thought the shakes were a real thing. They are. Fuck me, they really are. They were awful when I got here. That night at the party was my second night without a drink and I wanted to punch someone. I knew I couldn't do the whole shoot without drinking something.
LIZZY: That sounds awful.
BENN: When we went out for tea, I was nervous.
LIZZY: Did I make you nervous?
BENN: No, I was nervous about going out. I had been drinking before I picked you up. It was the reason I brought the driver.
LIZZY: So, the bill was right?
BENN: The bill was right. I am so sorry for lying to you.
LIZZY: Are you okay?
BENN: I've been much worse. I've been better. It's exhausting fighting against yourself every day
LIZZY: I'm sorry if I am being overly familiar.
BENN: You're not. You're being my friend. I need one of those.
LIZZY: If drinking is your demon, then you need to do all you can to defeat it. It's hard to dance with the devil on your back, so shake him off.
BENN: You're so very wise.
LIZZY: It's Florence and the Machine.
BENN: Oh. So it is.

1756

Glittering with diamonds, smothered in satin and powdered to perfection, the beautiful mistress of Pemberley was bent over the wooden table in the quiet fragrance of the still room, being roughly taken from behind by one of her dinner guests; his wig was tilted to one side, his cravat loose and his breeches flapping around his ankles. Her husband watched for moment, unseen, before returning to the dining room, the dancing and their friends who were all waiting for the return of their illustrious hostess.

At twenty-two, John William Darcy he had inherited a near-bankrupt estate, a dilapidated house and was tied to paying a crippling annuity to the Royal Household. Pemberley had suffered greatly after the death of his grandfather, Cyril. His own father, Richard, had neither the aptitude for estate management or the desire to live in the country, especially when the pull of London society was so great, and he had taken the fortunes built by his ancestors and frittered them away at the gambling tables of St James Palace. As a respectable and somewhat god-fearing gentleman, John William realised that his responsibility was to restore the family fortunes in the only way currently open to him. Marrying rich.

Embarking on the hunt for a suitable bride, Darcy was feted by gentlemen of trade – newly monied and fashionable - who longed to see their daughters lauded in higher social circles and as mothers to heirs of venerable old family estates. One such gentleman was Roger De Stratton, a merchant from the far north, who had made his fortune in cotton. He had invested wisely in new processes and procedures, his wealth and new business empire continuing to grow. Mr De Stratton offered an attractive package in his oldest daughter, a somewhat opinionated, but very pleasant woman of five and twenty.

Isabella Stratton was beautiful and whilst John thought that he could have eventually found himself in love with her pretty features, smart retorts and ability to laugh heartily at herself, it was clear that her own ambitions and wishes for life were very far removed from his own. Their wedding was a grand and lavish affair, with her father footing the bill for the banquet and the wedding jewels, a fact that neither the bride or her father would let John forget.

The new Mrs Darcy was as smart as her father, and had times been different she may have eventually found herself in charge of Stratton Mills, rather than as mistress of Pemberley. Holding up her end of the bargain, she was predominantly faithful to John and bore him three children – two sons and a daughter – before promptly abandoning them to live in Paris with her French aristocratic lover, who had promised her the moon on a stick and a ribbon wrapped around it. It would have been most agreeable for this forthright woman of fortune to have lived a long and happy life on the continent, however, she was found dead in her bed seven years later, her jewels stolen, her purse emptied and her lover nowhere to be found. Her husband brought her back home to England, lovingly arranging for her to be placed in the family mausoleum at the little church on the outskirts of the estate.

John William Darcy raised his children as best he could – he taught them always that their duty was to Pemberley first and to their own wants and desires second. He hoped with all of his heart that they could find a path in life that would be a perfect blend of the two. John tried to fight the waves of depression and grief that washed over him with increasing regularity. He continued to repeat to himself, over and over, that he was not a romantic man, that he did not need the pull of a wife to distract him from his duty to his estate and his responsibilities as an MP for the local area.

The family coffers were now restored, and he boosted them by selling parcels of land from the far edges of the parkland and investing his money wisely. He pushed on with his parliamentary work, never inattentive, and focusing on anything other than looking for a new bride, but John William Darcy realised too late that a life without love is a miserable one indeed.

One late February morning, a few days before his fiftieth birthday, he walked into the oldest part of the woods and blew his brains out. It was classed as a 'hunting accident' for purposes of report, even though it was deemed peculiar – the shot being close range and hunting out of season.

Thirteen

Of all the talks Lizzy presented in the small chapel at Pemberley, her favourite was the one about John William Darcy, Fitzwilliam Darcy's grandfather. She thought he was such an interesting and tragic figure that it was pity his efforts and achievements were mainly overlooked by the fictional version of his grandson. As much as she loved telling people the real story of Darcy and Elizabeth, she wished that sometimes they would ask about some of the other characters who had walked down these halls and been married in this very chapel, rather than having to point them in the direction of Mr Darcy's Pond, which was over a mile away through the parkland and where only the most devoted fans travelled to.

Usually, the room was packed full of part-time historians and everyday visitors who were eager to learn more about this elusive gentleman, especially after 'The Guardian' ran an article on him a few months back, but today the white-washed chapel was mainly empty as the bulk of her usual crowd were outside watching the filming. The only audience members were the plump, eager girl who was here every weekend mouthing the words, two German tourists who were obviously very confused, and smiling at her from the back row was Harriet, dressed in full costume and looking every inch like a time-traveller from the early 19th century.

"That was really good, Mum."

"Yeah, did you learn anything?"

"I learned that *Wo sind die Toiletten?'* is German for 'where are the loos?'"

"I knew I was right. I was sure they were only here because they got lost!"

They walked along the corridor hidden in the cloisters of the house, which felt dark in the shadows caused by the summer sunshine, before walking out into the bright glare. The ground floor rooms at Pemberley were cool, and the heat of the afternoon sun hit them as if they were getting off a plane somewhere humid and hot. They walked to the rocks at the base of Cage Hill, taking shade under one of the multitudes of trees that dotted the landscape.

"How long have you got before you're back on set?"

"About twenty minutes now," Harriet grimaced. "Dad is being a massive arsehole today."

"More so than usual?"

"I'm serious, something is obviously bothering him. I spoke to Oleander before, but he was being weird, and Cara was shouting and being shrill in the background telling him to get off the phone. I don't even know where Brixton and Jude were."

"Cara is always shrill, what was it today? That her Aeolian Flow had been disrupted by the Shamanic Current? Did the housekeeper pick up the wrong kind of tofu?"

"Mum."

Lizzy checked herself.

"How was Ol?"

"Upset," Harriet said sadly. "He said that all Dad's stuff is gone from the house."

"How are the other two?"

"Brixton has been crying all the time, Jude's too little to know what's going on though. It's Oleander I feel sorry for."

Lizzy felt her heart drop to her feet. It had been something she had wanted to hear for a long time, but now it seemed like a very real possibility she didn't feel how she expected she would. She wasn't excited about the news, wasn't anticipating the future that had always danced at her fingertips.

"Harriet, how do you feel about it?"

"Let's be honest, Cara hates me – for obvious reasons, but she has always been fake nice to me and she is my brothers' mum, so… I feel bad about it, but it's not like I went over every weekend or have any kind of relationship with her, is it?"

Harriet was, for someone who was only just sixteen, remarkably wise.

"Is Benn over for tea tonight?"

She had been sceptical when Benn Williams first came over to the flat – he was so very tall, so very famous, and he had been so very rude to her mum to begin with that she didn't understand why he was even in their house. The Darcy good opinion once lost was usually lost forever, but the more she knew of him, the more she liked him. He took the time to ask her about her plans for college, told her to always aim big because if someone like him could be a raging success then there was hope for everyone. She had laughed, and he told her she looked like her mum.

"Yeah, but I can tell him not to bother if you want to talk about it."

"No," she said. "I like it when he comes over. It means that there's one parent I don't have to worry about!"

"What do you mean by that?"

"You fancy him, and he totally fancies you too."

"Don't be daft, Harriet."

"He messages you all of the time, he brings you gin and cake, he practically lives with us during the week. You should just ask him to move in and get right to the point!"

"He's my friend," she protested softly. "Just a friend. I'm allowed to have male friends, Harriet."

"Of course, you are...you keep telling yourself that."

She turned on her heel and walked off in the direction of the production tent, which had taken up residence behind the Orangery. Harriet really did talk utter nonsense sometimes, Lizzy thought, but as her phone beeped again, she felt her heart do a little flip when she saw his name.

Benn arrived at half-past six as promised, his Darcy hair pomade free and unruly, holding a box from the little bakery in Lambton. She had made chicken fajitas for tea, and they sat together on the couch, her legs casually swung over his as he nibbled on a tortilla dipped in salsa and flicked through the channels on the TV. She screamed out when she saw him on the screen, making him jump and knock the table, causing his drink to spill, small pools of coffee forming around the base of the cup.

"Fuckssake, Lizzy, what the shit!"

"It's *you!*"

It was a shrill tone that he suspected only dogs could hear. Giddy with excitement, she slapped him on the thigh, directing his attention to the television. Henry Jones was shooting up villains, jumping from rooftop to rooftop, getting the girl and doing it all whilst doling out suave one-liners and sipping whiskey on the rocks; he was currently driving a superfast, supercharged sports car down a winding, twisting Swiss road.

Benn groaned, he hated watching himself. 'Illusion of Fire' was something he had never expected to be offered and the iconic role had been amazing to film, but it had also been hard and exhausting. The remaining two parts, 'The Hustler's Door' and 'Dangerous Horizon' had been filmed back to back, resulting in him being away from home for nearly ten months. He had been paid well; enough to pay off the mortgage on their overpriced house ten times over, but he missed so much – his daughters had started school, learned how to ride bikes - and when he watched the films now, as exciting and fun as they were, he wasn't entirely convinced that it had been worth it.

Lizzy jumped and laughed throughout the film, even in the parts that weren't supposed to be funny, and he had cringed during the love scenes with Rosie Schaffer who was, as far as the public believed, the reason for his wife leaving him.

"I don't know how you manage to do it, y'know," she shouted later from the kitchen as the credits rolled. They had eaten the cheesecake and she was now busy decanting delicate pastel macarons onto a blue, patterned plate.

He got up from the couch and followed her to the centre of the room, where she stood at the kitchen island pouring out the coffee into their mugs.

"Manage to do what?"

He reached for a violet macaron as she handed him his cup.

"The romance stuff..." she busied herself washing a few pots in the sink and then continued casually, "I know you had the Darcy and Elizabeth kiss today and you have to make it seem really *real*. You've never worked with Jenny Graves before have you?"

"No, but she does make me feel like Mr Darcy should be on some kind of register."

"She's the right age to be Lizzy though. It's not her fault that you're old enough to be her dad."

"That's pretty rude!"

"True though."

"She is *so* young, isn't she?"

"Yeah, she's only four years older than Harriet, which makes me feel super old. She is an amazing actress though, I adored her in 'Soul Shine Blue'."

"Yeah, she was brilliant in that, has a really good eye for scripts, which reminds me..." he said quickly, reaching into his bag and pulling out a thick wodge of papers. "I decided on the next script."

Lizzy crossed her fingers, she had read four of the scripts he had brought over and fallen in love with 'Lilac', a small arthouse project from a young London writer who was now based in LA. It was very dialogue-heavy and she had fallen in love with it on the first read – imagining Benn playing the troubled, vulnerable Oscar. It was so different from his usual work, but she knew, without question, that he would be amazing. She hoped he had picked up on her vibes.

"Lilac was the best one, you were right!"

"I'm always right," she laughed, taking the pages from him. "It bodes well for you if you accept that sooner rather than later. Can we have a read of it?"

"Yeah sure," he passed her the script, "where do you want to start?"

She flicked through the manuscript and landed on a random page, "Okay, here we are. Sc 35: Venice Beach. Ext. Day. Janey stands with Oscar. Things are tense."

"So, *right now?*"

"You need the practice, from what I heard you were awful with your lines today!" She said it teasingly, but saw a look of doubt cross his face, "we're all entitled to off days, Benn. Even you."

Benn smiled, despite himself, tried to stop himself from laughing at her raised eyebrow and flirty tone of voice.

"Right Lizzy," he said firmly. "Let's do this. Scene 35."

He glanced over the script, pulling his glasses down from the top of his head and concentrated for a moment.

"You know it's basically a rip off of a Hemingway novel, right? 'A Farewell to Arms'...that's how I read it, anyway... I could be wrong."

"You're never wrong, Elizabeth."

He looked up at her over the rim of his glasses, and she did a quick nod in agreement.

"Okay. Scene 35," she paused for a moment. "You won't take the piss, will you?"

"Can't promise that I'm afraid! Just read it, I'm sure you're perfectly adequate."

"Perfectly adequate? Well, thank you for the vote of confidence!"

The first line was hers, but she felt overcome with a strange embarrassment, even as he stood there with an expectant look on his face, and she swallowed hard. In a laidback LA lilt, she said:

```
                    JANEY:
I always wondered what you would have said that day.
```

He noted her accent, it was good, but he wasn't going to tell her that.

```
                    OSCAR:
I would have said that you needed to get the fuck
out of my life because I was sick of dealing with
your bullshit
```

```
                         JANEY:
There was no bullshit, that was all in your head. You
-
```

"Hang on, Lizzy... You need to pull it back a bit."

"Alright, Mr Kubrick," she grinned.

This was fun. She composed herself, reined it in.

```
                         JANEY:
There was no bullshit, that was all in your head. You
never saw it, did you?

                         OSCAR:
Saw what? How you threw all of your problems and
trauma at me and expected me to deal with it for you
like I did every single fucking time before.
```

He looked up at caught her smiling at him.

"What?"

It was a tone of exasperation. Amateurs must annoy him, she thought.

"It's just really impressive. I forget that you're a real actor, forget how good you are. Look, I've got goosebumps!"

She brandished her arm out in front of him so he could see how dimpled the skin was.

"Lizzy. Stop it. Do your line."

She rolled her eyes and continued but noticed that he smiled a little bit too. He might not accept compliments graciously, but she was sure that he secretly appreciated them.

```
                         JANEY:
You love sorting things out, Oscar. You love being
the hero. You love riding in on your white horse and
saving me.
```

Benn noticed the little wobble on her accent as she stumbled over some of the lines, concentrating on her delivery. He thought it was adorable, but he most definitely wasn't going to tell her *that*.

```
                         OSCAR:
It was never about that.
                         JANEY:
What was it about?
                         OSCAR:
It was about you wanting me to save you
```

```
                              (beat)
When you knew that all I wanted you to do was save
yourself.
```

He leaned into her, close now pulling her towards him, putting his hands on her shoulders, gazing deeply into her eyes. Benn was in full-on actor mode now, and she sensed the difference in him; he was no longer Benn but a brand-new person she had not met before. She glanced down at the next line on the page.

```
                         JANEY:
I did save myself, and I did it without your help.
                         OSCAR:
I always knew you could.
                         JANEY:
So why are you back now? Do you want to break me
again, so you can watch me rebuild, over and over?
You sick fuck.
```

"Ooh," she squealed. "This is so good."

"It doesn't say 'sick fuck' in my script," he double-checked the page.

"I thought it needed it," she shrugged.

"It doesn't."

"Spoilsport," she jumped on the counter and took a mouthful of coffee.

"Do you want to finish the scene or not?"

She nodded, and he began again.

```
                         OSCAR:
I don't want to break you.
                         JANEY:
You can't break me anymore, I won't let you.
                         OSCAR:
Don't ever let anyone, promise me that at least.
```

He reached over and pushed a stray curl from her face, placed his hand on her cheek. Lizzy felt the blush spreading all over her body.

```
                         JANEY:
What are you doing?
                         OSCAR:
Kissing you goodbye.
```

He leaned in to kiss her, and then stopped suddenly and pulled back. She looked up at him expectantly, her eyes wide, and he suddenly realised that he *wanted* to kiss her, wanted to see if her pink lip balm actually tasted like cherries, felt that if he didn't do it now then he would never do it.

"Benn," she said, "this would be acting, right?"

"Yeah," he said, "all the romance stuff."

He took a deep breath, could see her gently tilt her chin, her lips parting to receive his mouth on hers. Focusing on the tiny details of her face, he could see the little flakes of mascara under her eye, the faint smear of gold on her eyelid.

"Don't let me interrupt anything!"

Harriet called out from the stairs, standing in her pyjamas, as she watched her mum and Benn Williams fluster about the kitchen like naughty schoolchildren.

"Shall I put the kettle on?" Benn grabbed a cup, and the moment was forgotten.

1914

The younger male servants were the first to leave, and they paraded to Lambton in their smart khaki uniforms after Mr Staughton took photographs on the courtyard steps of the Pemberley Pals. There were twenty-three footmen, under-butlers, gardeners, stable hands and the middle Darcy child, Albert, who had signed up to fight the Hun. Only two of them would return.

The Duchess was summoned back to her father's estate on Long Island in the early months of 1915. He was ill, frail; hoping to see an end to this silly British war before his time was up. The Duchess packed up her luggage and booked a passage to New York with Cunard.

"You will be home soon, won't you, Mama?"

"Not long, my darling," she said, trying to calm any fears her daughter might have. "Grandpa Drew is not going to be in this world much longer I believe, and it will be much emptier without him."

"Do you have to go?"

"Penny," she rarely used the pet name from the nursery, "if it were your Papa and this may be the last chance of your ever seeing him in this world, I know you would too."

"I know we have our differences in opinions," she took her mother's hand. "But I will miss you."

"I will miss you too, my darling girl."

Millicent held onto Cecily's hand tightly, embracing her gently before she climbed into the Daimler and waved them all goodbye with a joyous wave and a tinkling laugh.

She would never see her mother again.

Later, as the war continued longer than the world anticipated, more of the residents of the estate were conscripted, including George. The heir was not scared about what lay before him, he was determined to seek revenge on those who had blown up an ocean liner and murdered his dearest Mama.

"Please don't go, Georgie," Millicent pleaded one May afternoon when the sun was high in the sky. "You don't have to go to France, at least. Ask Papa to find you work in the War Office."

"Penny, you know I have to go."

"You do not."

"Yes, I do." His voice reverberated in her heart and they both knew her argument was futile. "You and I both know that one cannot be exempt for serving one's country simply because they are the future Duke of Derbyshire. What use is a peerage if we are all speaking German?"

"I know what you are saying," she stared out at the lake, knowing that if she looked at him, she would be unable to prevent the tears from flowing, "but Mama would not have wanted you to have gone."

"Mama would have wanted me to do what was right," he said firmly, "don't worry, everything will be alright, you'll see. We'll all be home and having tea on the lawn before you even realise."

If Millicent had known that she would only see her brother again one more time, she would have imprinted the smell of him and the sound of his voice more deeply into her heart. The eldest Darcy boy – the Earl of Berkshire - would lose his life during the Battle of the Amiens. Also lost that day was his cousin, the sixth and youngest Fitzwilliam boy, Thomas, not quite nineteen, who would die screaming for his mother under the cerulean summer sky.

Albert, now with his brother's birthright, returned at the start of 1919. He had been injured but approached this with his usual good humour, laughing and joking with his sister as she wheeled him up and down the ravine. The scars were deeper, more ferocious than the angry red stump where his arm used to be. The sights and sounds he had witnessed were emblazoned across his mind, and he couldn't close his eyes without seeing the masses of obliterated comrades, bleeding on the battlefield. Music caused his heart to race, laughter caused his body to shake with fear. He disappeared into the woods one freezing cold night, shuffling off during a dinner party held by his father to celebrate his return. Searches proved fruitless until Albert was found dead three days later by Arthur Wickham, the private who had served with him on the front, the last surviving Pemberley Pal.

There was never going to be a winner in a war such as this. There was a victory, but it was as hollow and empty as a drum. Nobody wanted to celebrate, they simply wanted to mourn.

Every family on the Pemberley estate lost somebody, but it seemed as if the Darcys lost most of all.

Fourteen

It had been the turn of summer when Matthew Wickham, all packed up for his return to London with clean clothes and Warburtons bread, had ventured up to the Lantern and found her there in the soft light of dusk. The evening air was still warm, the house silent, the grounds dark. She was drinking a can of lager and smoking a cigarette, until she coughed and spluttered, stubbing it out and placing it in the empty can. She was always very vigilant about the risks of forest fires, he remembered.

He walked over and pulled her under the blanket with him, and she nestled into the crook of his arm and snuggled into him in the same familiar way that she had for as long as he could remember; he knew it was a comfort, an escape from the grief and confusion still abound at Pemberley. They settled in the silence, gazing down at the dark building nestled in the land below.

"Come a little closer," he murmured.

"Closer?"

"Yes."

"This close?"

Her face was inches away from his now, he could see the traces of mascara in the corner of her eye, could smell the sunscreen she had applied earlier that day, the soft pinkness of her lips caused by that shiny lip balm she used. He moved closer, so he could feel the heat of her breath on his face, the smell of tobacco on her skin. He looked down at her mouth, she was biting her lip and he knew she was nervous. She pressed her head against his own, a giggle escaping and lingering in the air.

This was serious now though because they both knew that this would change everything, this one event would change their friendship irrevocably. He could see the reticence in her eyes, could see her reluctance, understood it, but he did it anyway, kissing her fully, feeling her yield to his embrace.

It had been nearly eighteen years, but every minute detail of that night, fuelled by cheap beer and adrenaline, was still branded on his memory.

Lizzy took her well-worn route up the Lantern, she needed to feel the cool morning air in her nostrils and shake the cobwebs out of her head. It was always good to get up onto the moorland before the fell runners and the mountain bikers and the dog walkers, just so she could feel completely alone.

After only five minutes of walking up Lime Avenue, the grand parade of lime trees that lined the old south drive, she could no longer hear the gardening team trimming the hedges, couldn't see anyone else on the dewy grass paths that led up and out of the estate. She plodded on up the small incline and through the gate that led into Knightslow, the medieval wood with its ancient arcing trees that hid secrets and spectres, and then out into the wide expanse of the parkland which lay before her, vast and indifferent.

There was no-one else this far into the park so early on a Sunday morning, the formal gardens of Pemberley were always so full of people that she found she basked in the isolation of the empty hills. She was halfway up her final ascent when the heavens opened, and the rain began to pour. Running the last stretch of the way, she heaved herself over the stile, and found relative shelter under the canopy of oaks and sycamores in Lantern Wood, sprinting awkwardly towards the shelter that would be found in George Darcy's folly.

"Oh, hello," she hadn't expected to see him.

"Lizzy," he was shocked, equally as surprised to see her there. "I didn't think you came up here anymore."

"Oh, I do," she rose to her feet, shifting nervously.

"Right," he sat down.

She stood awkwardly before taking a seat next to him on the smooth step that led the way into the stone structure. There was that feeling again, those words getting ready to burst out of her mouth, but she wasn't sure that she wanted to say them yet, wasn't sure if she needed to.

"Lizard, we need to talk."

She feigned surprise before realising it was pointless; he knew her like the back of his hand. This was going to be a hard conversation. They had been dancing this familiar dance for a long time now, but he knew that it had been for too long. Now they were just stepping on each other's toes, afraid to let go and spin off across the dancefloor in case the melody was just too different, the steps too cumbersome.

But they both knew it was time, and she nodded.

"We do."

"This place…being up here," he said, grasping at a memory he had hidden away. "It always reminds me of you. Everything here reminds me of you. I was up in the long gallery yesterday…" the words stuck in his throat, hard to say as he remembered, "…can you remember when we danced?"

It flashed into his head, like a scene from a film, a flashback sequence replaying in glorious technicolour. They were sitting there on her bed, watching the little portable black and white television flicker away in the darkness; the late-night film that neither of them was watching, the nervous thud of his heart as he waited for the right time, the time that never arrived, the heart that flickered and jumped as she leaned on him, her head on his shoulder, her face temptingly close.

She remembered it, the details faded around the edges, had already disappeared into the periphery, but the feeling, the anticipation… yes, she remembered that, all too well. How her fingers had felt against the soft wool of his jumper, how he had smelled like soap and washing powder, how she wanted him to make the first move, scared of the rejection in case she had misunderstood.

He had jumped up, turned off the television, putting on the Nina Simone record from Winston's collection, the voice crackling into life, the music echoing across into the long gallery. He had taken her by the hand and led her into the moonlight, pulling her into a dance, shuffling and turning on the wooden floorboards as the moonlight shone, casting the shadow of the sash window onto the floor like a checkerboard. It had felt surreal, and as sweet and heady as the lilac wine in the lyrics of the song.

They were treading water in the shared memory, the time when they were almost something bigger than what they were. If she thought about it, she could still smell the wax on the newly polished floor, could still hear the pounding of his heartbeat against his chest.

"You should have kissed me that night."

He eyed her curiously, swallowed hard. If he had known that she had wanted him to then he would have done it. But he hadn't, and she didn't, and they couldn't, and the time was gone now.

"I wanted to kiss you that night, the things I wanted to do to you that night. I had it planned in my head," he felt as if he was telling her a great secret, "but I couldn't quite get up the nerve."

"Maybe things would have been different if you had."

"Who knows, we are all of us only ever one decision away from a different life," he said, his words tinged with a faint hint of regret. "But that was the thing, you didn't really *want* me to kiss you."

"I really did, but I didn't want things to change."

"But things did change, Lizzy."

"I always wanted us. That never changed. But I couldn't have us. You would have resented me eventually, for holding you back. I had no intention of forcing a future on you that you didn't ask for."

"It wouldn't have been forced. Being with you, having a baby with you... the thought of it..."

"The thought of it sent you running back to London with your girlfriend."

He didn't understand this, because that wasn't the way he remembered it. He had gone back to London with Cara, but there had been the letter. He studied her face, he always thought she had known this and chosen to do it all without him anyway.

"The thought of it made me happier than I had ever been," he moved next to her. He felt her relax a little. "I was ready to do it all with you... ready to be a dad, be a husband if that was what you wanted. I was ready to do all of these things with you because the thought of doing them with someone else... well, that just didn't make sense to me."

"Matthew, you never told me this!"

"I did tell you," he said adamantly. "I wrote everything in the letter."

She hadn't read the letter, hadn't wanted to see his rejection written down in words on the page.

"I didn't..." she shook her head quickly.

"No response is still a response. When I messaged you before the wedding, I needed to know how you felt. I would have called it all off for you. It was still you, Lizzy, even then."

She was still the same girl that he loved for nearly his whole life. Different kinds of love – playful, angry, romantic, lustful, unrequited, jealous, empty – but love nonetheless in all its different forms. It was simply never the right love at the right time and their time had faded quietly into history now, never to be revisited. He had always believed that in some other glorious alternate reality their time streams had collided in perfect harmony – blazing across an imaginary universe with incandescent fire. But a relit cigarette never quite tasted the same as it did before, and they both knew it.

"They always say that it's a question of timing, don't they? That you meet the right person at the wrong time."

"They do," she said. "It was never that with us, was it…"

She had always felt that these little snippets of him, the half days and hours of frantic attention, the stolen kisses, the hidden relationship had been all she deserved, that this was all he wanted to give her, but she realised that all this time he had been holding back. He couldn't keep offering his heart on a plate to her time and time again and have her refuse it.

"No," he said gently. "You see if you meet the right person at the wrong time, it only means one thing."

"It means that they're not the right person."

"However much you might have wanted them to be."

There was a look, a single glance, and she knew that he understood. She grasped his hand; the one that used to be covered in mud as they scrabbled about in the woods as kids, she studied it – it was almost as familiar as her own; his little finger was slightly bent from where he broke it one summer learning archery, the odd nail on his thumb where she had closed the car door on it and it had swollen and cracked with infection, and finally the ridge on his finger where his wedding ring had been.

The band of gold had always been removed before his hands had touched her body as if he thought it was able to bear witness to his infidelity. All that was left now though was a faint indent in the skin as the reminder of fifteen years of marriage. She wondered how he felt about it now that it was over, she knew she would never ask. For Lizzy it felt as if the vast path of destiny had conspired to keep her at Pemberley, her roots firmly entrenched in the dark soil, her branches tangled and lashed, her leaves refusing to unfurl.

ARCHIVED: 'THE STAGE' 23/1/200-

Tennant/Wolff Split Shock

Madeline Tennant, the child star of 'Happily Ever Now', has left her husband of a few months for her 'Pursuit of Happiness' co-star, the relatively unknown bit-part player Benn Williams. Tennant, 28, daughter of the late Richard Tennant and actress Jessica Entwistle, walked out on BAFTA-winning actor Dominic Wolff, 44, after meeting Williams during rehearsals for the new play by Casey Muir, the writer who wrote last year's Oscar-winning short, 'Ubiquitous'. Madeleine moved out of the home she shared with Dominic in Bayswater last week and friends say that he is heartbroken. The couple had been together for six years. Tennant and Williams, 29, are said to have become very close and an insider at the theatre said it was only 'a matter of time' before a relationship began. A spokesman for Miss Tennant confirmed the split last night and said: 'Madeleine Tennant and Benn Williams attended RADA together, they renewed their friendship during the rehearsals for 'Pursuit of Happiness' and began a relationship a short time ago.'.

'Pursuit of Happiness' by Casey Muir, and starring Madeleine Tennant is on at the Old Vic Theatre until September.

1677

Lady Sophia Louisa Darcy was the only daughter of George, Duke of Derbyshire. Whilst most titled men with a considerable property longed for a brace of healthy sons to inherit, George longed for a girl. After a short wait, eleven years and three sons to be precise, the Darcys were blessed with a delicate, dark-haired bundle and they declared their family complete. As the first of their children to be born in England, she was rewarded by being sent away at the age of eight to be the companion of the second daughter of the Duke of York at the special request of Queen Catherine, who favoured the pretty girl with curls, whose laugh sounded like sunshine.

Anne was a clever, playful girl whose wit and down to earth humour was at odds with that of her stern, older sister. The Princess and Sophia, of the same temperament and mischievous nature, would often sneak away from the nursery and into Mary's chambers, moving her possessions to cause confusion. The two girls were inseparable and often found hiding in corridors, under tables, and in each other's beds, giggling and laughing away, something that would continue for the next few years, much to the exasperation of their governess. They grew up into well-refined ladies of court with all the pomp, finery and expectations that came with it.

Sophia was home for the Hunt and breaking her fast with eggs and sausage. It had been an early start that morning and already she had taken an illicit, solitary sojourn around the grounds before returning to the house. The surrounding countryside was entirely beautiful at this time of year and it was wonderful to be back at Pemberley because it was home. Home. What a strange notion! She had barely lived here during her childhood, but the house in Derbyshire cast a magical spell over her – it was and would always be the place where she was the happiest in the world.

King Henry VIII had ridden out with the Pemberley Hunt over one hundred and fifty years earlier, and to think that she was such a small part of a much bigger history overawed her much more than it probably should. There was a painting of the famous Tudor in the gallery at Richmond, and she would spend time looking at it. She wondered if the man himself had been as foreboding as his reputation. That was the problem with men, and husbands – they had all the power and the wives merely had to do their bidding. Marriage was something that Sophia was fully aware was looming in her future and she pretended with all of her heart that it wasn't.

"Is Hortense at home?" Sophia inquired, taking a bite of sausage.

Cyril looked up from the papers he was reading at the table and, taking a swig of his coffee, shrugged, "when is my wife ever at home?"

Sophia studied her older brother, dressed and proper as always, ready for another day of taking charge and making everything right. Since their father was always at court, it fell upon Cyril to look after the daily running of the estate. He did it remarkably well.

"I must admit to you, brother, that your wife being away from this house is not such an unfortunate event."

She suspected that Cyril was equally unhappy with his choice of bride as were the rest of the household, but she was waiting for his confirmation.

"Sister, this is not talk for the breakfast room," he stated, folding his papers and getting up from the table. "It will not do."

She wished that he could find some semblance of happiness in his marriage, even if that meant becoming a widower at a very early age. It was wrong to have such thoughts, but since her arrival, Hortense had managed to aggravate everyone in the house in Derbyshire, including her.

"I am so sorry that you have been saddled with such a dull wife, Cyril. If only dear Charles or poor Henry had lived, then surely you would have been spared such a terrible fate. Such is the responsibility of the heir to continue the line with a reputable and well-monied lady."

Sophia's voice was dripping with sarcasm and it was a tone not lost on her brother.

"My wife really is the most unconscionable bore, sister," he grimaced. "I would not want to wish her upon anyone."

"I try to engage her in any kind of conversation," she gestured to Staughton to take her plate, "I am a great conversationalist, anyone of my acquaintance would agree."

"It would be easier to get a sentence from a lump rock."

"I imagine a lump rock would make a warmer companion of the bedchamber too!"

She glanced over at her brother who had been married to Lady Hortense Holland now for nearly two years with no child forthcoming. It was not a problem with Cyril, who had a little family of bastards with his servant girl lover out hidden in the woods, so the issue was definitely with his wife.

"You need to entertain the oldest Fitzroy when he arrives, Father is most adamant about it."

"Father is always adamant about everything, but I'm not of the mind to risk my virtue so he can claim the King's illegitimate offspring as a relative."

"I'm glad to hear it," Cyril rose from his seat, walking the length of the long table to sit closer to his sister. "Rumour has it that there is a bigger prize for you if you are patient."

"You make it sound like I could snare the King himself."

"He certainly admires you."

"He can admire from afar, for I will not be swayed or tempted before I have a husband. His Majesty can be as enamoured as he likes, but he will never be invited into my bed," she said firmly, "unless he would like to arrange a suitable match with a vaguely handsome gentleman who has enough wit about him to keep me entertained and enough money in his purse to provide a suitable home in which to entertain me! The King will always get what he desires one way or another, and he can make a cuckold of my husband, but he will not make a whore out of me before I am wed and respectable."

"I always recall you saying, most adamantly, that you would never marry! That marriage was for fools!"

"Unfortunately for me, marriage is the only protection for a woman in this day and age," she sighed. "If I were a man it would be different."

"If you were a man you could have married my wife instead!"

"I would not claim that honour, my lord, your wife is all for you!"

"More is the pity for me."

The Pemberley Hunt was one of the most famous in the county and her father took pride in the fact that he had rebuilt the estate after the war from ruins to a court playground. The house was now a wondrous cavern of small rooms, large rooms, nooks, crannies and hiding places, with the impressive picture gallery being the crowning jewel of George Darcy's reconstruction works. He had pulled panelling and features from other houses owned by the family, creating a lengthy space for entertaining and business. The centrepiece of the room was a suitably ornate mantel, emblazoned with the Coat of Arms of the House of

Tudor, gifted to Sir Percival Darcy by Queen Elizabeth. It had been moved from the house during the war, saved by the Wickhams, who had squirrelled away treasures and valuables, hiding them from looters and raiders until the family returned.

It was in the grand long gallery that a young gentleman was paying suit to Sophia Darcy as she sat in the window seat, looking out over the lake. She was flushing pink as he read her a rather romantic sonnet, fawning over her and flattering in such a manner, that she was convinced she could fall half in love with him before the day was done. James Fitzroy was so dashing on his horse, so regal, so handsome. She couldn't describe what she felt when she looked at him, but it made her feel a bit funny.

Walking quickly through the house, Sophia passed through the drawing room. It was full of women entertaining each other with cards and showing off – they were all eager for new husbands or new lovers, she thought, as she pushed through them, the air heady with scent and powder. Sophia entered through the heavy door, which was opened by a footman in blue and silver livery. At the north of the house, this room caught the early glare of the new sun and was the inner sanctuary where her mother prepared for her day. It had acquired the gentile title of 'morning room' now, but Sophia knew that this was where her grandmother, Margaret of Woodbury, had cried over her prematurely deceased husband. This room had been the mourning room, she thought, standing under the portrait of the great lady whose grief was now all but forgotten.

Over by the window, her mother was sitting at the ornate dresser being attended by Jane, her scrawny, undersized maid. Mary Darcy had seen her husband's eye turned too frequently by a bonny servant girl and had no intention of losing yet another good maid to the actions of a disloyal husband. The Duchess of Derbyshire was beautiful, despite being close to her fiftieth year; as a close friend of the queen, she was also a powerful courtier in her own right, learning quickly during the court's time in exile how to make friends, influence people and protect those closest to her.

"Sophia."

Mary was a formidable opponent in any argument, and her daughter could sense that she was already losing before she had even opened her mouth.

"You must exercise a degree of caution," she warned. "You of all people must know that this flirtation with James Fitzroy cannot go anywhere."

"Mama, I do not expect anything from Lord Fitzroy."

"He is not a *Lord*!"

"Mama, he is! Despite your opinion of him, you cannot deny a gentleman the honour of his rank."

"He is the bastard son of the King and a whore, and you would do well to avoid him. You were seen together today; do you deny it?"

Mary was furious that Sophia had taken it upon herself to walk, unchaperoned, into Knight's Low with Fitzroy, who had good manners and a terrible reputation. There had been at least three girls at St James's dismissed from service after being caught out by the advances of Fitzroy, who was – she couldn't deny – very charming. It was what made him so very dangerous to young ladies like her daughter who had not seen enough of the world to know better.

Sophia had not realised that she had been sighted; holding his hand, kissing his mouth, feeling the weight of him against her as she cried out no, whilst her whole body was saying yes. Her eyes flashed black and she flew into a rage at the unjustness of it all, words shooting out of her mouth like arrows.

"It was my father who told me to entertain the Fitzroy brothers, Mama! I was simply doing as I was told by your *husband*!"

Mary moved quickly towards her daughter, "I do not know what sins your father may have asked you to commit on his behalf, but it would do you well, child, to seek your own counsel,"

"You think I would give up my virtue to the first boy who asks for it?" she questioned. "You do not know me at all, Mama."

"I am simply saying to look to your own heart before you do anything rash."

"I understand, but I am not playing my father's game."

"We all play his game in the end, my child."

"Not I! I do not like the way he plays with others!"

"Be careful, Sophia, that's all I ask," the older woman had softened now, "as Darcys we have to be careful, we are easy targets for those who wish to hurt our family. Your father has made many enemies at court and we need to exercise great care. It is always our responsibility to save our menfolk from themselves."

"I will, you need not concern yourself with that!"

Walking out to join the remaining ladies she stepped hurriedly through the yellow bedroom, the rustle of her skirts felt loud, and she felt her face flush, could feel the flutter of her heart underneath her corsetry, the weight of the necklaces felt like a noose, and she had to stop, hiding out of sight. In the quiet and almost claustrophobic coolness of the wig room, she pressed her face against the glass of the small window. Underneath her the voices of men rose up from the courtyard, she could hear the brag and braw of men flattering themselves and conversing as if no-one could hear. Even out in the Derbyshire countryside, the conceit and vanity of the courtiers was still prevalent.

"Are you alright in here, m'lady?"

"Thank you, yes," she said to the son of her father's steward. "I am simply taking a moment to wonder." He looked up at her expectantly, she knew that he was curious. "You can ask me what I am wondering about if you like. We have known each other all of our lives, there is not a need for you to stand on ceremony with me."

"What do you wonder, Lady Sophia?"

"I wonder if all men are like that gathering of swaggering rakes down there."

Silas Wickham leaned past his mistress to peer down onto the courtyard, there was but six-inch between them. He could hear each indignant breath she took.

"I cannot claim that we are all exempt from occasional displays of bravado, m'lady, but if you don't mind me speaking out of turn…"

"You can always speak the absolute truth to me, you know that."

"Lord Fitzroy has a good voice to beg bacon, but I very much doubt he has it in him to slaughter a pig."

He leaned over, closer than propriety allowed, placing her father's second-best wig on its stand. She edged under his arm, smiling back at him as she passed through the dressing room and onto the north staircase. Sophia knew that there was a game in progress, but she had decided that she was going to change the rules, and they could all learn to play by them. Or they would lose.

Fifteen

The summer moon was high in the sky, the brightness glazing the countryside with its soft hues, illuminating the structure of Pemberley against the darkness of the Derbyshire moorland, and on top of the Wyatt tower, two figures were looking up at the stars above.

"Look," he pointed up at the sky, "that's Ursa Major."

"Where?"

She moved her head an inch closer, fully aware that there was now only a hairline between them. He leaned his arm over, directing her eye to the sky, and she saw the stars pitted in the darkness.

"There, can you see it?"

He didn't know how they had ended up climbing on top of the tower roof, navigating the creaky spiral staircase and lying behind the iconic Pemberley portico, but he was glad he was here sharing this night with her.

"How do I know that it is Ursa Major and you're not just making it up?"

"You'll just have to trust me," he declared, as they sat on a scratchy blanket drinking coffee from mugs. He pierced a soft, chocolate-covered pastry with a fork, passing it over to her. She took it from him with a small smile.

"I used to come up here when I was younger," she began, nibbling on the profiterole in a very unladylike manner. "My grandad had this amazing telescope which was a million years old and we always thought we could get it focused and see galaxies, but we never did and ended up dragging it back downstairs. I think it was broken, but he never believed me."

"Your grandad sounds cool."

"He could be a lot of fun. I miss him a lot on nights like this."

Benn saw a little wave of sadness wash over her, then it was gone, and the brightness returned, the crest of sunshine on the horizon. She must be so used to putting a brave face on everything that it was second nature now, he thought.

"Now let me get this right, your grandad was Winston...and, Harriet told me that your great-granny was Millicent Darcy. That's amazing! I remember girls at uni wearing badges with her face on."

"Yes, I had one of those badges," she took a mouthful of coffee.

He munched a profiterole. "Is it true that they want to build a statue of her?"

Lizzy nodded. "Yes! Although when they do, I imagine that some junior news editor will headline it 'Votes for Mr Darcy' alongside a picture of Colin Firth!"

"Does that happen a lot?"

"All of the time! Winston used to get really cross about it, but my dad thinks it's hilarious. I'm pretty sure that Millicent would find the idea of it all completely ridiculous."

"Why?"

"Because she's only a *famous* suffragette because of who her father was, and that kind of defeated the point."

She crunched on another biscuit, pulled her cardigan around her shoulders a little bit closer.

"She sounds like a remarkable woman."

"I think she probably was, I never knew her. Apparently, though, she made the best cheese pie. My grandad used to rave on about it all of the time. You can buy it in the tearoom, or there is a recipe for it in one of the cookbooks in the bookshop."

"Maybe you could make it for me, perhaps."

"Perhaps, as long as you're not allergic to cheese."

She bit into another profiterole, the contents escaping to her lip.

"I'm not allergic to cheese." He leaned over and wiped the cream off with the smooth firmness of his thumb. "I love cheese."

It was a slow, intimate act. He felt a little shiver run through him, certain she felt it too.

"Am I on a pie-based promise now, Lady Darcy?"

"Maybe."

She was teasing him, trying to pretend that goosebumps hadn't appeared on her arm.

"I'd like that,"

She felt the soft pressure of his hand on hers, saw him look away as if it were simply a happy accident. It was a level of intimacy that she wasn't sure she was comfortable with because friendship and flirting were fine, but this? This was something different. She wanted to move her hand, but there was something quite wonderful about the coolness of his palm on her skin.

"You would?"

"Why would you think I wouldn't?"

"Because you're *you*. You're *Benn Williams*, international man of movies, and I'm just..."

"*You're* Lady Elizabeth Darcy. You're *you*," he emphasised, "why would I not want to?"

"Don't say things like that to me, Benn."

"You're glorious," he half-whispered, not sure if he wanted her to hear, he looked into her eyes wondering if he would ever be able to accurately describe the way traces of moonlight were flecked across their silvery warmth. "I could get lost in your eyes."

If she had questioned the electric twitches surging through her veins before then she was left with absolutely no doubt now.

"My pondwater eyes?"

"Stop it," he said firmly, "none of that shit with me. You know I think you're incredible."

"I'm not incredible."

"Yes, you are."

She looked down at his hand on hers, trying to find something to say, *anything*, because moments like this did not happen to her. This was like a scene from a Hollywood film.

"You have big hands."

She looked down, hers seemed tiny compared to his.

"Not too different," he pressed his palm against hers, his fingertips like electricity. "I have quite small hands, really."

"They are much bigger than my dumpling hands."

Sitting on the floor with fingertips touching, neither wanting to move them.

"Good pilgrim," he did his best Olivier impression, "you do wrong your hand too much..."

She looked up at him, a smile of recognition at the line.

"...which mannerly devotion shows in this," she was showing off now, the passage she learned for GCSE Drama falling out of her, "for saints have hands that pilgrims' hands do touch—"

"And palm to palm is holy palmer's kiss."

She quickly pulled her hand away, aware that he was watching her intently.

"I didn't think you did Shakespeare."

"I was always the Nurse," he reached for his coffee mug, "but it doesn't mean that I didn't know the lines. I bet you were a great Juliet."

"I was never Juliet, I have always been the comedic relief and never the leading lady."

"I find that hard to believe."

The park was pitch black now, the moon distant in the inky sky. Looking out from the rooftop she could see the faint outline of Manchester twinkling on the horizon, like moonlight hitting the ocean. He moved closer, but it was hesitant, cautious. He had fallen into this with his eyes wide open, with no expectation, and over the last few weeks, he had slowly felt himself tumbling into something that he knew could be bigger than them both. But he held himself back.

"Do you feel it too, or am I going crazy?"

"Feel what?"

She knew exactly what he meant.

"I don't have friends like you, Lizzy. I thought that's all this was. But this isn't just friendship, is it?"

She sat down on the balustrade, could feel the rough stone under her fingertips, the gentle cool rush of a summer breeze dancing around her shoulders. This *wasn't* just friendship, but how could this ever have any chance of going anywhere?

"Can you remember what you said to me on one of your first nights here? You probably don't remember, but I remember... I asked you if you knew what it was like to love someone so much -"

" - that I would want them to be happy even if they weren't with me. I remember that."

Of course, he remembered that.

"Yes, and you told me that was how you loved Madeleine. Love like that can't disappear overnight, however much you're convincing yourself otherwise."

"You think this is all an act?"

"What else is it?"

"It's not acting, Lizzy. I'm not that good."

"It can't be love though,' she reasoned, 'please don't try and pretend it is."

He didn't know how she wanted him to answer that question, because he thought it could possibly *be* love eventually, or something a lot like it. She was right. It wasn't love now, but it *was* serious like.

"It could be," he said, taking her hand.

He shyly moved towards her, slowly, unsure, until she could feel the heat of his breath against her face. She was breathing in the smell of his woody, masculine cologne and the smell that was inherently him. It stayed on her clothes, her skin, lingered around her flat long after he had gone. His stubble grazed her top lip, but she pulled away quickly, not wanting to start something that she knew she couldn't finish.

"What's wrong?"

His eyes searched hers, found them confused, she shook her head gently and pulled away.

"Nothing is wrong."

She started to place the coffee cups on the tray, wanting to distract her heart from what her head was saying.

"Don't lie to me."

"I'm not ready for this. Neither are you."

Swallowing hard, she buried everything deep within her because she wanted to wrap her arms around him and feel the firm push of his kiss, wanted the heat and the weight of him against her on the roof under the stars over Pemberley, but she couldn't do this. Not now. Maybe not ever.

"Are you so scared of this?"

"No."

"Well, I can't think of any other explanation for this…"

She stopped him sharply because she *did* have an explanation.

"When I like someone, it burns within me like a fire, a *furious* fire. But I'm not prepared to light a match for someone who is clearly still burning a candle somewhere else. I'm sorry."

"It's not like that."

He wanted her to understand that what he felt for her was different and new. He didn't know what it was, couldn't explain it, but he wanted to find out.

"It's exactly like that."

He knew that she had her legal head on now, noted the change in tone, the preparation for an argument, the points all lining up in her head as they did when they had heated discussions in the flat, but this wasn't as if they were arguing about something trivial. This was something that could be serious, but he felt it slipping through his fingers, could feel her closing herself away again, retreating under her armour.

"You don't even want to give me a chance, do you?"

She sighed because deep down she wanted to take this chance and run with it. But she was a Darcy, it wasn't how she was made.

"The trouble with fires is that without care and attention, they burn out. This is all fine now when you're here at Pemberley, but it's like a holiday romance… don't set me on fire and then leave me with ashes."

"Why do you think I would leave you in ashes?"

"Have you ever had a relationship where you haven't been left with the remnants of that furious fire?"

"Well no, but," he spluttered.

"Me neither," she said sharply, but then in a small reluctant voice, "we have *this*. Too many friendships get ruined with a kiss, and I've done that before. I know how it works out in the end."

"With Matthew?" He saw her nod, and then he was angry. "This is you telling me that you don't feel anything for me then? That I'm not what you want? Lizzy, I'm not like that."

"I'm not saying that you are. I'm just saying that, for now, until we know what we want, then we should be friends. Best friends"

"This is more than that! I don't *want* you as my best friend!"

"Why not? What would be so different?"

"It's not what I want! It's not what *you* want!"

"Don't tell me what I want! Don't be so fucking arrogant!"

"Oh, so I'm *arrogant* now as well as not being good enough?"

"Did I ever say that you weren't good enough?"

"I can read between the lines, Lizzy."

She paused for what felt like a lifetime, saw him fizzing with frustration and felt herself soften.

"I would rather have you as my friend forever, and always have this, rather than jump into something that neither of us is ready for, and lose you. There is no need for us to rush. I wish you could see that this isn't a rejection."

"It sure as hell feels like one!"

"If that's what you want to take away from this then I don't know what else I can say."

He knew that he was acting like a child, knew that even though he wanted to be more than her friend if friendship was all she could offer right now then he was happy to accept it. He just wanted her in his life because her presence made it that much more tolerable, but as he moved to say something, she turned to walk down the spiral staircase, and he realised that it was the end of the conversation. The wooden door to flat clunked gently in the frame and he crept out of Pemberley slowly. When Benn had followed her up the spiral staircase to the roof, he was certain that it would have been the beginning of something, had never expected that it would be the end instead. Walking to his car he looked up at the stars, still sparkling above him, and felt like a complete idiot.

1816

The baby did not cry.

Darcy saw the small body covered over in the white sheet and the look of fear and anguish on his wife's face, Dr Jeffries shouted for him to be removed from the room, but he refused to go. Ellen was trying to push him away, but he had heard a cry. A small cry. Was he going mad?

He turned around to see Dr Jeffries holding another small body; that of a pink shrieking baby, writhing and kicking and very much alive. Ellen looked at him, the relief revealing itself on her face as she swaddled the tot in cotton and muslin.

"It's a girl," she said, handing the precious newborn to her father.

Darcy looked down at his daughter. She had his wife's eyes and his dark hair, and he was immediately and overwhelmingly in love with her. He took her over to his wife and presented the baby. Elizabeth, shaking with cold, exhausted and in pain, turned away and buried her head in the pillow.

Elizabeth looked around at the grandeur of her room, the printed paper on the walls, the wool rugs, the gilt dresser, the canopy – stitched with gold and silver thread - that stretched all the way to the ceiling. But all she could see everywhere she looked was the small body, wrapped up in a sheet as if to be thrown away. She had heard Dr Jeffries asking a maid to dispose of the bloodied sheet and she had howled, a low frantic moan, pulling at the covers, begging to see him, hoping and wishing that her love alone would be enough to bring him back to life.

Reluctantly they allowed it, despite Darcy's objections, and brought him to her wrapped in a pale blue blanket. He had the longest eyelashes she had ever seen, the same long tapered fingers shared by his oldest brother and the Darcy chin. He was perfect. Stroking his face, so soft and so cold, she held him close to try and warm him up. She sat there for a long time, softly whispering lullabies and kissing the top of his head until they came and took him away.

"Where are you taking him? I demand you tell me now, have you forgotten who your Mistress is??"

She pulled at the arm of the footman who had been tasked with removing the body of the child.

"Where is Mr Darcy?" She screamed so loudly that he winced, "Peter, where is your Master??"

Darcy was in the Chapel. He only prayed when he felt absolutely powerless. He heard the screams, the shouts, but there was nothing left in him today. No fight. He fell to his knees and asked God, whoever or whatever that was, to help him make everything better, because if Fitzwilliam Darcy couldn't do that then he didn't even know what he was good for anymore.

"You are doing the right thing here, Mr Darcy, sir," Mrs Reynolds busied herself making him tea as he sat in her parlour. "It has been very fortunate to not lose both children."

Darcy acknowledged this with a wan nod of the head.

"I think about dearest Princess Charlotte. How terrible for Leopold to have lost her and the baby."

"It can happen to anyone, even the Prince Regent's daughter; we are none of us safe when our time has been decided."

"That is a well-spoken truth, Mrs Reynolds," he agreed, "but I cannot bring myself to understand why this happened to us."

He glanced up at the older woman, not wanting her to see his face properly, not wanting her to see look at him in case a sympathetic glance made him collapse entirely. He was barely holding this all together, crushed by the weight of a world that he had placed upon his own shoulders.

She handed him a bowl full of soup from her own tray; he had not been eating properly, was not as tidy as usual. His face was not cleanly shaven, and he looked empty, she thought. In usual circumstance, Mrs Reynolds would never deign to speak to the gentleman she had known since boyhood in such a manner, but this was not a usual circumstance, it was a strange and uneasy time, and she had to resist the urge to gather up the man in her arms and comfort him as she had once done the child in the nursery.

"Fitzwilliam," she said tentatively, "the baby is nearly a month old, and she hasn't been given a name yet. Rather than wondering why something terrible happened, you have to focus on the babe you still have."

Darcy nodded. He knew what needed to be done now, he simply didn't know if he has the strength in him to carry it out. He arranged for

Samuel Joshua Darcy, named by his mother, to be placed in the family mausoleum at St Peter's Church in Lambton. It was something not usually done in cases such as these, but he felt that it was the proper resting place for his son, and he arranged for an appropriate service and a marker to signify the existence of the child they had lost. Elizabeth screamed at him, scolded him, held him, sobbed, but it was as if his own feelings and emotions were disregarded, his wife consumed by all-encompassing grief that was devouring her and he did not know how he was going to get her back.

Mrs Reynolds had employed the services of a wet nurse for nursing the baby as Mrs Darcy, still unwell with nerves, was unable to herself. It was a peculiar time, the lady thought as she swaddled the youngest Darcy in cotton blankets and held her as she once did Miss Georgiana, who had been left similarly, but more permanently motherless. Yes, she thought, these were peculiar times indeed.

"Do you think the mistress will recover," Betsy asked Ellen as they were finishing supper one evening.

The maid was concerned; she had been unable to rouse her mistress in any way, had tried to speak to her but been rudely dismissed on each occasion she had deigned to raise the issue of the baby, however subtly she had tried. She had Mr Darcy's ear on this matter, and she knew how worried he was too, but nothing she attempted was helping. Ellen had only seen this happen once before to a woman in the village who had lost three babies one after another, and she was unwilling to share the desperately unhappy outcome of that tale, scared that her mistress was slipping on the same treacherous path.

"Who knows," Ellen said. "She sees no joy in anything."

"She hasn't been out of her rooms in a week," Tilly added. "She doesn't want her sheets changed, she tells me to go away."

"I reckon that she would be best off in town with parties and balls to entertain her, divert her attention from it all," Betsy wondered out loud. "I think she would forget it all if she had a few new gowns."

The girls fell silent as the ominous figure of the Darcy housekeeper loomed behind the youngest housemaid, who was still talking oblivious.

"Do you not agree? I think a new gown and a dance at the Assembly Rooms would make *me* the happiest woman in Christendom, I'm sure Mrs Darcy would agree."

"We do not pay for your opinions, Betsy Harrop, and you would be best off keeping them to yourself," Mrs Reynolds scolded, clipping her over the head with a cloth, "any more talk like that and it will be Mr Staughton who boxes your ears."

"I was only saying Mrs Reynolds, that..."

"You need to shut your rattle, girl," the housekeeper said sternly. "Now prepare my tray before you go up, and no more talk like this from any of you. Do you think the master would want to hear it? It's bad enough that Mrs Darcy is unwell, he doesn't need to worry about idle gossip from idle housemaids!"

The older lady stomped off into her parlour and the girls looked at Betsy, who was still completely unaware of any offence she may have caused.

"Maybe they should just hold a ball," she said.

"You're lucky she only clipped your ear," Tilly said grimly.

Elizabeth kept to her rooms, which were stifling hot and unaired, and was rarely seen outside in the grounds. Darcy had held her, cradled her, wrapped his arms around her and caressed her face, but nothing could fill the hollow emptiness inside of her as she wept for the loss of her child. She stood by the window of her rooms, hiding in between the long, heavy curtains and the condensation that had built up on the rectangular panes of glass. Pressing her forehead to the cleansing coolness, she prayed silently for a release from this pain which seemed unending. This was the worst of times.

The following morning the household woke to the shouts of Ellen sounding out around the bright gallery, her voice carrying to the opposite end of the corridor, the crystal ringing.

Darcy woke suddenly and knew that something was very wrong.

Elizabeth was gone.

Sixteen

It was a crisp October morning at the top of Cage Hill, the countryside below was turning from soft green to burnished orange, the change of the seasons cascading throughout the landscape. Harriet had been there since before six taking pictures of the hunting lodge for her college project. She loved the way that it stood on the skyline, sometimes looking gigantic, and other times minuscule, and she had walked around the edges of the park taking photographs from different angles trying to capture the grand majesty of the ancient building that had reigned over the skyline in one form or another since Henry VIII was King.

Walking past Mr Darcy's horse chestnut tree, she noticed some conkers lying on the floor, snatching at them she peeled off the spiky shell to reveal the beautiful soft seed inside. Darcy conkers had always been the best ones, even better than the ones from the massive old horse chestnut tree in Lambton. Harriet smoothed the conkers in her hand until they were like polished gems, satisfied with their prettiness she began her descent towards the house. At the edge of the hill there was a large protruding rock which came up to her shoulder; when Harriet had been younger Lizzy had lifted her up to it and swung her down to the ground, it felt like flying as she had been spun round and round, the horizon fading to a blur before they fell about giggling on the hillside. It had also been in this spot on a cold, cruel December night that Fitzwilliam Darcy had died. His body had been found by servants from the house who had been sent up the hill to look for him in the waist-deep snow.

She looked at the tributes written on the rock – there were quotes from Pride and Prejudice, drawings of the various actors who had played the role, and, not unusually, a random flowery bra. Harriet thought it was crazy how people were so in love with the fictional version of him when the real man was much more interesting. He had travelled far and wide, adventuring across continents and raiding tombs – although she was undecided if he was a plunderer or a protector – bringing back countless numbers of objects that had been displayed in the rattling glass cabinets of Pemberley for longer than anyone could remember.

After his father died, he had become the MP for Lambton, overseeing the changes that were rapidly occurring as the people protested for democracy – even publicly vilifying the behaviour of the officials involved in the Peterloo Massacre, much to the outrage of his peers – and always pushing forward for change. In the distance, she could hear the train to Manchester rattling along the railway line that Fitzwilliam Darcy, with all his ambition and foresight, had petitioned for and which had been built, completed and then extended in the years following his death. Most people didn't know that he did these things, only saw him as a one-dimensional romantic hero. Personally, she blamed Colin Firth and his wet shirt.

Harriet realised that Mr Darcy would never have been happy with a meek and obliging society lady; that when he travelled to Hertfordshire, he had resigned himself to a lifetime of solitude, not knowing that he was about to meet the woman who would change his world forever. She pulled the two conkers from her pocket and gently placed them next to the rock, taking a moment to wish him a very happy birthday.

Loitering at the north front gate, she observed the dozens of people milling about like ants over the grounds, before walking down the hill to the car park, which was overrun with production trucks and catering vans, where she knocked on the door of her dad's trailer. There was no answer, so she stepped up and popped her head in.

"Dad?"

Looking left and right, she wandered through the trailer absentmindedly, but could not see him. Filming this time had been much more fun than usual as she had been able to do something; usually, it was about as much fun as sitting in the offices of Winchester, Sparrow and Jones, playing with the photocopier and waiting for her mum to finish with a client. Her friends from school didn't understand how visiting a film set could be so boring, but most summers her dad's filming schedule dominated holiday plans. Last year she ended up spending three whole weeks playing Minecraft with Oleander at some grotty little industrial estate in Kent rather than going to Florida like they had been promised.

She found it strange because her dad was usually on set by now, especially on days like this when his full control freak mode set in and everybody walked on eggshells until he was happy. Somewhere she could hear his distinctive text tone – his own voice at his Oscar acceptance speech – sounding somewhere in the trailer. She decided to ring; the theme music from Ubiquitous sounded out loudly, emanating from the bathroom, the deep bass vibrating against the wall and the pitchy violins sounding sharp and shrill.

"Dad, are you on the loo?"

There was a loud shuffle as something fell against the interior wall of the trailer.

"Harriet, can I meet you up at the house in about ten minutes?"

He sounded strange and she felt that she must question it.

"Are you alright in there?" She pushed, "is this like when we went to Mexico and you were wee-pooing for three days?"

There was a noise that she thought was someone stifling a laugh. There was someone here.

"No, H, it's okay... I'll see you up there, okay?"

The forced joviality in his voice was an obvious sign that he was trying to get rid of her now. There was definitely someone else here. She quickly scouted around the room looking for clues, but there was nothing obvious, which simply meant that he was getting much cleverer at hiding his various infidelities.

Harriet wasn't one to judge her father, but she wished that he tried a little bit. It made sense now that he had been away on location since June, and that neither Cara or the boys would answer her FaceTime calls, she had probably already caught him and was busy working out her next move, not needing the hassle of his other random child to confuse things.

"Okay, I'll meet you at the shop, but you will need to buy me something."

"Yeah, course!" She was convinced his voice had moved up several octaves. "See you in a bit!"

Harriet grabbed her bag, stomped over to the door, opened it and then closed it again before sitting on the sofa, just hidden from the view of the bathroom. It only took a minute or two before her father emerged, dishevelled and post-coital, followed by Tamsin McLeod, who was smiling until she saw the frowning face of Harriet Darcy in the corner of the room.

"Oh, Dad," she sighed, "what are you doing?"

"Harriet, I... uhm... you said you were... uhm," his eyes darted from Harriet to Tamsin. "I can explain this, please don't tell Cara... or your mother..."

"You know he's married, right?" she addressed Tamsin directly, the tiny blonde looking incredibly young without her professional make-up. "He's like twenty years older than you, you could do much better... what happened to Rowan? He's gorgeous! Please don't tell me you sacked off Rowan Morris for my dad because you would need your head checking if you have. Look at him, he's dead old!"

She pointed at Matthew, seeing a man who was nearly forty and, in her eyes, super ancient. Tamsin didn't see what Harriet saw, instead, she saw a deeply attractive man in his late thirties who was in a bad marriage, and she knew that she could put all of his broken pieces back together, even if he was fifteen years older than her. The role of Lydia should prove to be her breakout one, finally she would get away from playing studious nerds and could finally aim for the Manic Pixie Dream Girl roles that had so far eluded her, and if she managed to make Matthew Wickham super happy along the way then that would be the icing on the cake.

Tamsin, her hair rumpled and her eyes like saucers looked from Harriet to Matthew, then grabbed her shoes and bag, which she had hidden in a cupboard, before quietly exiting the trailer. Harriet stood looking at the father with her hand on her hips, a judgmental glare on her face.

"You look exactly like your mother when you do that."

"I expected better of you – she's twelve!"

"She's twenty-three, Harry, I think you're being slightly judgmental."

"Slightly judgmental? Are you not slightly married?"

He stood there, limp, saying nothing.

"And what about Mum?"

"I wouldn't expect you to understand adult relationships. They're more complicated than changing your Facebook status, you know."

"That's not patronizing at all, is it?" She picked up her bag and began to walk towards the door of the trailer, "and nobody under forty uses Facebook anymore."

"Don't come in here and speak to me like that," he protested. "Things haven't been great with your step mum and me for ages now, she barely tolerates me being there…and your mother…well…"

"What about her? You've been sleeping with her for the past ten years! It's like you think I'm stupid!"

"Don't speak to me like -"

"I'll speak to you how I damn well want to!" Harriet was livid, and she wasn't stopping now. "I'm not arsed about you sleeping with Tamsin McLeod. I. Do. Not. Care. But I do care that your sons are upset and worried, and you're ignoring it like you always do!"

"Harriet, please don't talk about things that you know nothing about…"

"You need to make this right for the boys," she said. "Stop thinking about yourself for once. Stop being so selfish!"

Harriet slammed out of the trailer.

Matthew sat on the sofa, threw his head back and exhaled every last breath in his body.

His daughter was definitely a Darcy.

1816

Dressing in a simple gown, jacket, and her sturdiest boots, Elizabeth Darcy had risen before the crow and ventured outside. She was surprised to see that the world around her was still the same when she was so different; all her emotions somehow deadened by the loss she had experienced and the grief that still overcame her when she was least expecting it. She had pretended to be asleep when her husband, he himself still grieving, had come to her rooms the night before and sat gently on her bed, pouring out his heart and soul to her, not aware that she was listening to every word he said.

He felt the pain too, he said. He did not ever think that they would lose a child, but that they had been given a great gift and had another baby to look after and cherish, and this baby and their sons needed their mother, and he needed his wife. She had wanted to speak up and tell him that he could not experience the loss in the same way she had, had not carried the babe in his belly for nine months and felt him move and grow, and now there was nothing. No life and no future for the dead child, the lost son, the missing Darcy.

Elizabeth planned to walk to the Cage, which she managed in a reasonable time, looking back towards her home which was still as beautiful today as the first time she ever saw it.

Onward and onwards, she walked further, through the deer park and into the moorland beyond. The early summer months had hardened the ground and she found it strong and easy to stride across.

Onwards and onwards, she pushed on until she could no longer see the outline of the three-hundred-year-old hunting lodge dominating the skyline.

Onwards and onwards, keeping the momentum of one foot in front of the other, over stiles and past cottages on the furthest expanses of the estate, whose tenants she visited in the winter, bringing them gifts from the house.

Onwards and onwards, until it was mid-afternoon, and she decided to stop; her feet aching and her mouth dry. She was unsure of how many miles she had walked, and she was aware of the impropriety of it all. But Elizabeth knew where she was going, and she trudged ahead, onwards and onwards.

Gallagher didn't expect to see Mrs Darcy of Pemberley, sunburned and dehydrated, walking down the driveway towards Dunmarleigh, he had thought the bedraggled and scruffy looking woman was perhaps a wandering gypsy looking for work. It was only when he spotted the expensive looking necklace under her spencer, the heavy fine embroidery to her mud-soaked hem that he realised he was mistaken. He jumped from his horse and pulled her under his arm, lifting her onto the chestnut mare and striding purposefully up to the house.

"Madame, are you alright there?"

She was pale, her bonnet falling down her back, the ribbon around her neck.

"I feel sick."

"Have you walked all the way from Pemberley, miss?"

He kept his eyes forward, not wanting to look at her.

"I think so."

"That's near enough twenty miles."

"I believe so."

"Pardon, Mrs Darcy, but why have you taken it upon yourself to walk twenty miles when, beg pardon m'lady, you have a fine carriage."

"Sometimes you need to walk away from your life, I think," she studied him. He was older than she expected now she could see him properly, strong as well, given the way he lifted her onto the horse.

"What is your name, good man?"

She meant it, he was a good man. She could see his goodness etched across his face.

"Gallagher, Mrs Darcy. Francis Gallagher."

"Nice to meet you, Mr Gallagher," she nodded her head, he responded with a nod in response.

"Mrs Darcy," he pulled the horse onwards. "It won't be long until we're at the house."

Mrs Bingley came running through the corridor, her bonnet coming loose and falling to the ground as she reached her sister and gathered her up, calling for small ale and ice. Elizabeth pulled herself into Jane's arms and was held there on the floor of the house for a long time, crying and sobbing until there was nothing left inside her.

Gallagher carried the lady upstairs to the Blue Bedroom, there was no weight to her; she looked up at him with scared brown eyes and pulled herself closer to him as he climbed the flight of stairs. He placed her on the soft coverlet, and she reached for his hand as he turned to leave.

"Thank you for the kindness you have shown me today, Mr Gallagher."

"You're very welcome, Mrs Darcy," he said in his rough, country brogue.

She smiled weakly at him and he wondered where her husband was and why he had been so negligent in letting such a wonderful creature wander about the country by herself. He left the room, glancing back at the grand lady who looked so tiny and small in the huge bed. If she had been his wife, he was sure he would never let her out of his sight.

"Thank you, Gallagher." Mrs Bingley said, in the soft, gentle manner he was used to. "Please, can you fetch Mr Bingley at once."

Jane gently stroked her sister's forehead until she fell asleep. Charles had ridden over to Pemberley to let Darcy know that his wife was safe and well. He had never seen a crack in the stern countenance of his friend but, on that night, Charles Bingley pulled Darcy into his arms and held him close as he wept tears of relief.

"Jane," Elizabeth said weakly. "I am so happy to see your face." Mrs Bingley placed some ice to her sister's lips, which were dry and chapped from the summer sun.

"Sister, how I have missed you. We have all been so worried."

"Oh Jane, it has been so hard, and I have been so lonely."

"Lonely, why? Surely you can speak with Fitzwilliam…"

"There are some things men do not understand, Jane, and I fear this is one of them."

"What do you mean?" She searched her face for an answer, finding nothing but pain there. "Lizzy…"

"Everyone keeps saying that I should feel happy that we are so fortunate that I survived, and she lived…." She held back a sob. "All I can think about is how he did not live and how unfortunate that is."

Jane pulled her sister close to her and embraced her gently.

"It was very unfortunate. I know that Darcy feels the loss keenly, but he is grateful that you and your daughter did not suffer the same fate, for it is very common to lose everyone. You cannot judge your husband, Lizzy, for taking comfort in the fact that you survived and that your daughter lived."

Elizabeth knew that Jane always spoke the absolute truth, there was nothing bad about her and no reason to lie or contrive a situation. It was only through speaking to her dearest sister that she began to feel the tremendous burden of surviving begin to leave her.

She took long strolls in the grounds at Dunmarleigh, walking to the edge of the park, where she could be alone with her thoughts and her grief. Looking up at the blue sky overhead, she came to understand that Samuel would always be a part of her that she carried around inside her heart, but that the loss of him should not prevent her from living.

"Do you have children, Mr Gallagher?"

Gallagher was Bingley's steward, trusted with the running of the estate in his master's absence, and he was accompanying her out for a ride into the grounds, leading the way on his chestnut mare. He was an authoritative man who instilled equal amounts of fear and respect in the estate staff. Elizabeth had discovered that he was also well-educated, and she eagerly anticipated their outings, away from the screams and giggles of the Bingley children.

"The Lord did not see fit to bless me with children."

"There is still time for you though yet, I shouldn't wonder."

Gallagher looked down, "no, there will be no time for that."

"Indeed? Why not?"

"I have already had my turn at it and, as I said, the Lord did not see fit to bless me."

"You are married?"

She had not heard speak of a Mrs Gallagher.

"I was," he said gently. It was a tone of voice she had never heard from him before. "But the good Lord did see fit to take my wife from me. My blessed Hannah died trying to give me a son. Gone now for good and naught to be done."

"I am very sorry to hear it."

She glanced over at him, his eyes were glazed as he stared purposefully ahead.

"It was the worst day I have ever had to endure, watching as they put everything most dear to me in the ground."

"I am so sorry to hear of your misfortune," she said softly. "How did you recover from such a loss?"

Gallagher didn't want to tell her the truth, because what would it help a woman to know the secrets that lie within a man.

"The truth is, Mrs Darcy, you never recover from it. Men always must be strong. There are many compartments to the heart of a man, and we are prone to keep all that fear and hurt and sadness wrapped up inside us. Because if we don't, then what good are we? What good are we to a woman?"

"A woman does not always expect the man to be the strong one."

"No, Mrs Darcy, but it's what we expect of ourselves. Do not think that we do not feel the loss as much as you, for we do."

They pulled up to fork in the road, onward into the parkland or back towards the house.

"I'm going onward now, Mrs Darcy."

"I will be going back now."

"Yes, m'lady, I think it is time for you to return."

She made sure that she was a safe distance away before she turned around to look over her shoulder, but he was already gone.

Elizabeth was at the furthest point from the house, dismounting quickly as Darcy had shown her one glorious summer when he was determined she would learn how to ride. She leaned back against the pony, who jostled slightly. Closing her eyes, she presented her face to the warmth of the afternoon sun.

"Mrs Darcy."

It sounded different from the voice she knew so well.

"Elizabeth."

It was not the voice that had proclaimed love and made vows.

It was not the voice that ran the world she lived in with a firm, authoritative hand.

"Lizzy."

It was a small, unsure voice in the silence.

It echoed in her heart.

Elizabeth opened her eyes to see her husband standing before her, she stood in front of him hesitantly, as if she had betrayed him in the worst possible way. Tentatively she moved closer towards him before falling into his arms. He held her tight, his arms around her waist, his forehead pressed against hers and they looked at each other deeply as if seeing each other for the first time.

There was not a need for anything else.

Elizabeth returned to Pemberley three days later, when her heart cried out to be home and see the faces of her children again. As she alighted from the coach and stepped out onto the cobbled courtyard, she heard the squeals and shouts coming from the far side of the house as the boys ran down the stairs.

"Mama!! Mama!!!"

They embraced her with such force that she was sure she was going to fall over. She knelt, kissing and embracing them before rising to her feet to see Darcy holding a bundle of wool and lace. Walking over slowly as if being introduced to a stranger, she peeked at the little face hidden in the embroidered shawl and found herself looking into eyes that were exactly like her own.

"Lizzy," Darcy murmured softly. "This is Mabel."

"From the Latin...?"

"I thought you would approve," he said, now hesitating a little over his choice. "Do you approve? *Amabilis*. Lovable."

"I do, I approve completely," she whispered. "It's an honour to meet you, Mabel Darcy."

She took the little hand in her own, the chubby miniature fingers a match to hers; the baby immediately grasped back, cooing and looking up at her mother.

"Oh! You are strong, Mabel! What larks we will have together."

Darcy gently placed his arm on her shoulder and kissed the top of her head.

"Fitzwilliam, how much I have missed."

"Hush now," he said tenderly, "there is all the time yet to come and thousands of moments to be filled with happy memories."

Elizabeth was grateful to be back home with her children, back at Pemberley where she belonged. He took her hand and led her out onto the front lawn, the boys already running ahead, screaming and laughing and throwing themselves on the grass, as the rest of the family followed behind them.

Madeleine

Madeleine Tennant was loved by the nation. As the only child of two very famous actors, she had grown up in the public eye and appeared in several feature films, television movies, and fishfinger commercials before she graduated from the over-priced theatre school she had been sent to. It seemed predestined that Madeleine Tennant would live a charmed life, and she did for the most part. She married her long-term boyfriend in a quick ceremony at Chelsea Register Office and everything was okay, everything was... fine.

It was when she met an old RADA friend during rehearsals for a new play, that Madeleine Tennant realised that everything was not okay. She left her nice apartment building in Kensington and moved into his not-so-nice flat south of the river. He was still doing regional stuff, still shuffling along with bit-parts and voiceover work, so she supported them both. She was happy to do it because he made her ridiculously happy.

It was when she took the role of the snooty Lady Rebecca Ferrara on ITV's 'Haringey Place', that he had bought her a massive bunch of what she called 'tissue paper roses', not realising that they were out of season and ridiculously expensive. In that instant, she knew that this was something very special indeed. They had married not long after, cementing their family with two daughters in quick succession and a house they could barely afford in one of the more affluent suburbs.

Benn Williams was thirty-five when he won the part of Steven Malis. It was a breakout role that saw him catapulted into stardom and award ceremonies. 'Praise to the Skies' earned him an Oscar nomination and a BAFTA, but the success that followed started the downward spiral that led to the ending of his marriage.

For the most part Madeleine had seemed immune to her husband's newfound fame, celebrating his success and happily holding his hand at award ceremonies, but he knew that as his fame grew she felt insecure about their relationship – little tremors of anxiety – and when the rumours had circulated about his friendships with various on-screen love interests, or when Star Goss had published pictures of her on holiday in Spain calling her old and frumpy, he could feel the palpable tension every time he walked through the front door. Filming took him away from home for longer and longer periods of time, culminating in a disastrous month where he missed Anya's birthday and his eighth wedding anniversary.

Antoine was someone she had known in a previous life, and he paid attention to her, laughed with her, listened. She found that in the empty hours in the middle of the night, he was stuck in her mind as waited for a reply to the message she sent to Canada hours and hours ago. When the reply never arrived, she thought about the future, and it wasn't Benn who was standing next to her, it was the loving, carefree Frenchman who made her feel all new and shiny and fresh out of the box.

Walking into the cold, empty kitchen she sat for a moment at the gigantic wooden table that they had bought in Camden. He had said it would be ruined by the children within days and he had been right. She ran her finger over the gouge in the wood that Esther had created slicing pizza. Pizza they had eaten watching a movie before falling asleep on the couch. There had been so much love, so much laughter and she felt her stomach turn as she realised that none of this would ever matter in the same way again, that all the happy memories they shared would be somehow tainted by her betrayal.

Her head ached under the weight of a decision she had already made, the choice that she had actively made a month ago when she started to slowly disconnect her life from his. She now realised that the tiny rifts in relationships can develop into vast, gaping canyons – deep, scarring and entrenched across our hearts – unsurmountable and impossible to fill. It was as if the dainty platinum circle was aware, fighting the inevitable, embedding itself into her skin so she had to twist and fight to remove it. She sealed her wedding ring in an envelope and placed it on the kitchen counter.

Two days before he arrived home, she left.

@HollywoodGoss @BennOfficial spotted smooching on Venice with @LittleMissRosie PICS HERE >>>> http://bit.lies/hotgoss @DailyMail RT @HollywoodGoss Cheating @BennOfficial causes heartbreak for @MadTee83 over #RosieSchaffer snaps.   @RoundhouseMgt Official Statement regarding Tennant/Williams split.   @DailyStar Secrets of Maddie and Benn's Marriage – EXCLUSIVE   @StarGoss Henry Jones Star Divorces Wife of 10 Years – Affair with Leading Lady @miss_thang52816 #TeamMadeleine Keep strng swtheart, we all love you! @BennOfficial is a loser @LovingAngelsInstead Oh @BennOfficial what a disappointment   you   are   #cheating   #infidelity   #thrownitallaway @Mr3_6_red @LittleMissRosie is young enough to be your daughter @BennOfficial #perv @BennOfficialFans We believe in you @BennOfficial   #staystrong   #TeamWilliams   #BelieveinBenn @RealLizzieBennet @BennOfficial as #MrDarcy in new #PrideandPrejudice ?

#NotMyDarcy

1685

Lady Sophia Darcy had no intention of simply marrying for love. She knew that in her position the best she could hope for was a husband that was mostly faithful and did not expect her to raise his bastards. William Clarendon was a young peer from Northumberland, and he amused her greatly, wooing her with poetry and dancing. He was rich and handsome but, and she had found this with a lot of the gentlemen in their set, he also suffered from stupidity and had a raging temper when his needs were not met. Luckily, her marriage was short-lived. Lord Clarendon was dead within the year from an unseasonable bout of smallpox, and his widow packed up her trunks and her jewels and departed for London.

Lady Clarendon-Darcy's return was much heralded by James Stuart. He was now His Majesty King James II of England, but to Sophia, he would always be her friend Anne's father - the generous man, who laughed a lot and taught her how to play cards one winter when they were all snowed in at Richmond. She appreciated his rugged handsomeness and forthright manner, but she was also fully aware that he was a decided womaniser and had a whole stable of bastard children wandering about the country with a decidedly misplaced sense of power.

There had been lovers, of course, all of whom proved to Sophia that men of certain rank and privilege believed that they were due more than their allocation. There was James Fitzroy, now the Earl of Wentworth; he was fine-looking, of course, but he also suffered from an unswerving arrogance of entitlement that meant whilst he was adequate for a friendly flirtation and the occasional visit after hours, he would never be a partner for her in the sense that she longed for. When he pressed a proposal upon her, no doubt encouraged by her fortune and legitimacy, she refused. Sophia was holding out for someone better, someone who she liked, and someone whom she would never feel obliged to marry.

The days at Pemberley were long that summer. Her mother was ill, and Sophia had promised to spend each day with her until she was well enough to ride up to the Cage and make fun of Cyril's terrible shooting aim, but both Mary and her daughter knew that she wouldn't ride anywhere ever again. The sickness inside her was as enveloping as the ocean and she felt as if she were drowning in the watery depths, unable to summon the energy to rise again to the surface. Mary knew that God had blessed her with the greatest of gifts, and if this was the price she had to pay for the fortunate life she had led, then she was happy to settle her debt.

Sophia didn't notice the difference in her mama at first, but once it began it was an onslaught, constantly battered by unknown forces and unable to retaliate, beaten into submission. George had ensured that his wife had the best care, of course, but he expended so much of his time at court now that he relied upon his daughter to attend to her. Sophia knew why her father was away. He would say that he did not want to see his wife wasting away into nothing, that it was too hard for him to see her, that he was unable to provide the care she needed, but the truth was that George was in town with his mistress, Lady Scargill, and he would rather utilise his hours in the company of a two-bit actress than sit by his dying wife's bedside.

It was the turn of the season, a glorious summer slipping into autumn, the tips of the first trees on the cusp of turning amber. It was very dark now and the torches had been lit in the grounds, the smell of the beacons drifting in, the harvest moon reflecting off the deep waters of the lake.

Cyril dropped his fishing gear at the door with Staughton and ran to the long gallery, the clatter of boots on the oak floor echoing through the hall. His sister was sitting there holding their mother's hand, her eyes red with tears.

"I cannot bear this, brother, how will we ever get over this loss"

"There is still hope, sister," he poured himself a glass of ale and sipped slowly. "Always hope."

The Darcy children held close to each other until the moon was high in the sky and the torches were embers. Sophia rested her head on her brother's shoulder as they sat with their mother, reading stories and sonnets until the morning sun appeared over the horizon.

The door opened slowly, George Darcy walked into the room, looking like a repentant man standing before God on the day of judgement. He removed his wig, something he very rarely did, and he knelt next to his wife's bed, took her hand softly and gently kissed it. Mary's eyes fluttered and opened, sparkling with recognition.

"My dearest love," she whispered. "I have waited for you."

George's voice faltered, "how could I let you go without kissing you goodbye?"

He kissed his wife gently on the lips and then on the forehead, lingering, smelling her scent, the comforting warmth of her.

"Mary, you have been my greatest love."

She slowly placed her hand on his face, looking at the man who had brought her comfort and pain in equal measure. Sophia could hear the rattle on her mother's breath, knew that it was nearly the end.

"We had a good time, didn't we, George?"

"We had the best of times," he soothed, a man haunted by his actions as he faced the woman who had loved him hardest and longest, who had protected and saved him during the worst of times.

"Do you remember this jewel, my dearest," the ring was on her finger, as he held her hand, "this little ruby was all we ran away with but look what we built again. What a marvellous time we have had. Thank you, my darlings, for the greatest of adventures."

Mary Darcy was dead, and the light in Sophia's heart went out.

It was a year later when the King noticed how Lady Clarendon-Darcy laughed with the gentlemen of the card table, how she flirted equally with the ladies – flattering and charming everyone sitting there. She was a formidable woman, he thought; the curve of her bosom and the sparkle in her eye caused a burn of lust in him that he had not felt in a while, and he was determined that he would have her. Sophia could see him eyeing her from across the room, but she was equally determined to ignore it, determined to pretend that she couldn't see the way he looked at her with desire in his eyes.

The touch of the King's hand under her skirts had made Sophia feel more alive than she had ever done. She had spent the evening flirting with him, pandering to his vanity and looking up at him knowing that he was completed enamoured. She was fully aware of the effect that she was having on this man who was old enough to be her father, this man with the soft fingers that touched and stroked her in places that made her shudder with desire and anticipation.

She surrendered herself to him that cold, unfeeling winter evening, as the ladies of the court were retiring, and the gentlemen roamed the halls looking for sport; as she felt him move inside her for the first time, pushing harder than she had felt before, she grasped for something to hold onto, afraid that she was going to fall off the earth.

Seventeen

The plate landed smoothly on the linen tablecloth, the dull sound of chatter and murmurs, the gentle hum of well-trained waiters going about their business, the familiar smell of her perfume hung faintly in the air.

"I'm sorry it had to be like this."

"Things like this happen," he said dismissively.

She was dressed differently, he noticed. No longer the tightly tailored trousers and fitted shirts, but softer linens, gentler fabrics that clung to the curve of her body. On her finger was a ring that he hadn't seen before – a diamond and rose gold usurper proclaiming victory. He hadn't expected that she would plan to marry Antoine. Hadn't expected that their engagement would be announced and official before he had even recovered from the shock of it all. But it had been, and he had to be happy for her, had to be glad that she was moving on.

He knew full well that he was sulking about it, he didn't want to be here, but his agent had pushed for it, and he was aware of the surreptitious glances over in their direction, the odd tell-tale click-whirr of a camera phone taking a snap. Her hair was different, he noticed; he had never paid much attention to the length or colour of her hair, never made a fuss when she returned home with a new cut, a new colour. The business they were in called for constant changes, constant reinventions. He wondered if this was a fault, maybe he should have, maybe it was the little things that he overlooked that caused the most damage.

"Your hair looks nice," he said, gesturing to the copper waves.

"Oh," she sounded surprised. "Thank you."

The starter was some kind of cheese, whipped to beyond recognition, and a gravelly crushed walnut on the side. She had the salmon, pushed it around her plate. He noticed that she wasn't actually eating anything.

"How's work?" She placed her fork down and laced her fingers together.

"Oh, fine." He placed a forkful of the whipped cheese in his mouth. It was strangely bitter.

"Fine?" She exclaimed with a laugh he knew wasn't because she was amused. "You're doing more than fine, Benn. Back playing with the big boys now that you've paid your penance."

There were hardly any secrets in this industry, his fuck-ups and disappearing acts on Shellstone and Insanity Circle had caused feathers to ruffle, his stock to plummet. He took a deep breath in. He didn't seriously think that he had a chance of being selected as Gainsma Quince – the male lead in a new fantasy film franchise that looked set to rival Star Wars – but he had no objections to two-week expenses paid trip to California. He needed some sunshine and to get away from this country. He didn't answer immediately, and she pointedly sipped her wine whilst rolling her eyes at him.

"Yes," he sighed.

"What about the girls?"

"I can take them with me if you want?"

A laugh escaped from her lips in a huff and she shook her head with what he knew was disappointment.

"Take them to America for two weeks at the start of the school term? Are you mad?"

"Okay then, my mum can come and stay at the house for a few weeks if you need me to have them."

"Your mother?" She put the fork down on the plate as if it were a loaded gun.

"Yes, my mother. She loves spending time with them…"

"You want to palm them off on your mother? Nice parenting from a man who is hardly in the country enough to see his children as it is."

"Do you want me to stop working, Maddy? Is that what it is? What do you want me to do?" He said through gritted teeth, aware that other diners on the top of the Gherkin knew who they were, eagerly anticipating one of the blazing public rows that they had been famous for. "Because I keep giving you solutions and you keep throwing them back in my face."

He sat back in his chair, crossed his arms. For all he had hoped, he knew that they had fallen into their familiar ritual. That this was how his marriage had ended; with passive-aggressive comments from Madeleine and petulant defiance from him.

"I have a career as well you know," she matched his tone with saccharine sweetness. "Perhaps you could consider someone else for a change."

"Maybe if you hadn't fucked off with a Frenchman," his eyes narrowed, but the smile was still plastered on his face, even as the words shot out of him with a stutter. He could feel the tension in every muscle.

"Maybe if you weren't a fucking alcoholic."

The sentence landed heavily on the white expanse of linen before them, and then silence. The waiter came, taking away their plates with a slow carefulness as if each piece of crockery were an unexploded bomb. Madeleine smiled amiably at him as he piled the dishes up carefully.

"Don't you fucking dare," he found he hissed the words, but more for discretion than dramatic effect.

"You don't even realise, do you?"

She eyed him from across the table, challenging, pushing him, she had always done this.

"Realise what? That my wife was having an affair? Or that she would blame it all on me?"

"You didn't need to take the fall for it, you know that."

"No," he looked up at her slowly, "but you let me."

"I think I wanted to punish you."

"It worked."

She was still staring at him, and he saw the look of pity in her eyes. The sparkles of anxiety shot down his spine, and immediately he reached for his glass, before changing his mind as her words ran through his head.

"You drink too much," she said. "Far too much now, after your dad…"

"No," he shook his head stubbornly.

"Benn," her voice was firm. "You've been drunk for the last three years."

There was something about being told a hard truth by someone who knew your softness. It always hurt that little bit more. She reached her hand out across the table; tentative, creeping, meeting him halfway.

"It was hard for me…walking away from us."

She knew how hard it would have been for him; coming home to an empty house and empty cupboards, that the sight of the girl's bedrooms devoid of trinkets and memories would have ripped him in half. But she knew that she couldn't've stayed, couldn't keep plodding on with no end to it in sight. He searched her eyes, he deserved some kind of explanation. They had never really spoken about this before. It felt that he went away as a happily married man with two gorgeous girls and a wonderful home, but he returned to a cold, lonely house, with a bottle of whiskey calling him from the drinks cabinet.

She took a mouthful of wine, he realised that she was still wearing the bracelet he bought her for their last wedding anniversary. He always thought she hated it, but maybe when he remembered it was how he had pulled it from the box and thrown it at her from across the room.

When he remembered, maybe it was how he had passed out on the couch and woke up hours later to find her cleaning up a shattered vase, glass scattered across the kitchen. When he remembered, perhaps it was how he tried to apologise, and she had lashed out, screaming expletives at him with hot, frantic tears running down her face. When he remembered, it might have been how they had argued in loud, projected voices until Esther came downstairs and begged them to stop. When he remembered, he knew it was how Anya was scared and crying in her bed, and when he tried to comfort her, she had cowered away from him. When he remembered how it was, he remembered why he had forgotten.

"I know you thought it was very heartless of me, Benjy," she fidgeted with the napkin between her fingers, the use of his pet name hit right in his heart. "If I could go back and change how I did it. I would."

They stared at each other, two pairs of blue eyes locked together. He turned away, couldn't stand the tidal wave of memories that washed over him. Those were the ones that hurt the most. The remembrances of how it used to be.

"I wouldn't want you to, Mads," he said, concentrating on the little scrap of skin that he was picking next to his thumb. "I deserved it all"

"No," she said in the soft voice that he hadn't heard in a long time. "You deserved honesty. You didn't deserve me running away in the night."

"I think I did. Can you ever forgive me?" He couldn't look at her, didn't want her to see the regret smeared across his face.

She took a deep breath, "when you drink, Benn, you turn into someone else. When you're you, you're wonderful and I love- I *loved* you. So very much. But the person you are when you drink, I didn't love him. We never knew who was going to be waiting for us when we got home, I never knew who would come back from location and I couldn't live like that anymore."

"I am sorry."

"Don't be sorry," she reached across for his hand and held it tightly. "Just get better and find someone to laugh with, someone who makes you happy. We laughed so much, Benn, it was the best of us."

He would always love her, would always want her to be happy – she had shared his life for more than a decade, she was the mother of his children, but he knew that this was goodbye. It was strange because he thought it would feel as if his heart was being wrenched out, but it was different; more like a wobbly tooth finally falling out. There was pain, but also a relief.

"Do you love him, Mads?"

"Yes," she nodded. "Very much."

"He had better be good enough for you."

"He is."

It had hurt, it was still hurting, it was mourning someone who was still alive, the grief felt so very real. She was the woman who had taught him what love really was.

"I love you, Madeleine."

"I know, but we both know that it wasn't the same way anymore," she said, "it hadn't been for a long time."

"I know," he agreed, "it doesn't make this any easier."

He was referring to the meeting they were waiting for. The meeting that would make the end of their marriage official. The meeting that would separate them for good.

It was the end of everything he once held so dear.

"We hold so tight to the wrong things, we forget that there are better things waiting for us," she had read it that morning on Pinterest. It seemed fitting for this moment.

"It doesn't mean I'll love you less."

"No, but there will be someone who you love more."

On the table next to them, an overly perfumed tanned man was clinking glasses with a woman shrieking with excitement over the ring placed on her finger. The room began to cheer for the happy couple who rose to the attention; as they sat back down in newly engaged glee, Benn realised that they had been the only ones not clapping.

1820

It was June when the news arrived of the death of Lieutenant George Wickham, who had sadly perished at the battle of Waterloo – the Newcastle regiments had suffered the highest casualties of any British troops, with nearly all Officers belonging to it being lost on the day. Darcy was handed the letter by his steward, Willis, absorbed the details of his brother in law's demise and then mounted his horse to travel to the Wickham household on the far reaches of the estate.

Old Mr Wickham had been a good and honourable man and Darcy's father, George, had trusted him implicitly – the role of steward was a venerated position in the household, responsible for the estate in the absence of the master. Wickham's son may have had ideas above his station and attempted to ingratiate himself into the higher reaches of society, but his wife, Eleanor, and remaining children were hard-working and devoted members of the Pemberley estate and continued to be well looked after and favoured by the Darcy family. Peter, the second eldest Wickham, worked as an under-butler, whilst his brother David was second coachman. Bridget, the only daughter, had been skilled in sugarcraft and had been utilised by Mrs Reynolds and the chef, Mr Artaud, in the kitchens, before marrying a local cousin and raising a family of her own.

Darcy was dreading telling Eleanor that George was not coming home from Waterloo. She had cried something dreadful when he had bought the commission to the Newcastle regiment and now this would destroy her. She was a soft, welcoming woman who had held him as a young man after his father had passed away and he had run away to Paddock Cottage on the edge of the woods to escape his family responsibilities. He had no secrets from Eleanor Wickham. Travelling through Knight's Low, he felt a small shiver of regret that his last words to George Wickham had been ones of anger, and he wished that things could have been different between them.

Raised almost as brothers, he had been closer to Wickham than anyone else in the world, and they had grown together, firstly as boys, and then as young men. It had been George Wickham who had travelled with him to Cambridge as they studied together, he was always more daring – always wanting to drink a glass more, ride a little harder, study a little less – at the end of their second year it was clear that his friend was not destined for the Church as their fathers had decided. Darcy would have assisted Wickham in any profession that he desired. He knew that his own fortuitous situation in life was based upon the luck of his birth and wanted to do anything he could to help his friend and brother find success.

Darcy had an easy-going and loyal nature, it was true that he could be obtuse and distant with those he did not know, and he was quick to judge people based on initial impressions, but he was fiercely devoted to those he loved. It was this that made the continual betrayals by George Wickham especially difficult to bear. Firstly, he ran up debts in Darcy's name with local innkeepers and merchants – resulting in Darcy receiving a beating one evening when returning home to his lodgings. Wickham had laughed jovially upon seeing his friends bloodied face and ripped coat, before flouncing out of the door with a young lady of questionable reputation on his arm.

But it was after the death of George Darcy that Wickham's behaviour escalated. Darcy - grieving, scared, drowning under the weight of the responsibility of the huge Darcy estates and the guardianship of his sister – gave in to his friend, lending him large sums of money and paying for his lodgings and bills. Wickham genuinely cared for Darcy, but he cared for himself more. He knew that old Mr Darcy had bequeathed him the living of Kympton – a clergyman! There were a lot of roles that George Wickham could assume, but he was most definitely not a man of the cloth, could not bear the thought of preaching about a non-existent God to a dreary bunch of worshippers before returning home to a less than comely wife and dull children. No, the Darcys had shown Wickham life outside of his social sphere and he knew that he was charming enough, handsome enough and a good enough lover to snare himself a reasonably wealthy widow who could offer him a good life in a more respectable society; if not he was sure he could convince an heiress that he was half in love and whisk her off for a wedding in Scotland before she was any the wiser. His was not to be a life left languishing in mediocrity.

Darcy had been expecting the announcement of Wickham's arrival at the house in Grosvenor Square since nine. He had risen early and dressed suitably, his countenance dominated by grief, his demeanour carrying the weight of his heritage. Wickham believed that being a Darcy was about parties, balls, women, and wine – but he forgot that the true inheritance of Fitzwilliam Darcy was being responsible for hundreds of people and a massive estate that encompassed thousands of acres. George Wickham did not understand this because on the days when he had been taken by his father fishing on the river, or swimming in the lake, Darcy had been in the schoolroom on the second floor of the house, learning how to maximise the profits of his estates, how to run a household, manage staff and maintain the general level of comfort and respectability that his family were used to.

Wickham entered the oak-panelled room and took a seat without being asked. Darcy visibly rumpled at the polished gentleman before him. He was the same height as Darcy but carried himself with a different air – one of arrogant, but undeserved, superiority. His clothes were always of the finest cloth and he had an aura of one who was comfortably affluent. Darcy himself did not, as a rule. He was shaven and clean, but he had not purchased a new suit since his graduation from Cambridge, and he failed to keep up with the latest fashionable trends, more focused on keeping his affairs in order.

"Fitzwilliam," Wickham stated with a forced geniality. "How the devil are you?"

He placed his hat on the desk, Darcy noticed that it was made from finest beaver pelt and looked relatively new, he wondered how much this fashion would eventually cost his own purse, given as it was that he was currently subsidising Wickham's lifestyle to an alarming degree.

"As well as can be expected," he stated solemnly. He had no desire to reveal anything of his heart to George Wickham.

"Death of a father is a terrible thing," he said shaking his head. "Why it has been but three years since my own passed on. It has been hard for my mother, of course. One suspected that Peter would have inherited the position of Steward, but I can see that it was not meant to be."

Everything Wickham said was pointed. Every remark made designed to inflict hurt. He did nothing without fully thinking it through.

"Peter was offered the chance to train to be a steward, George," Darcy corrected. "But he declined it as he felt much more comfortable in the stables, you understand that. Have you been to see your mother recently?"

"She has been ill with a fever these last few weeks and I have stayed in town in order to prevent the spread of it."

"Mrs Wickham was in perfectly good health last Thursday week when I visited her."

George visibly wavered. He was all for the appearance of outward respectability but did not like being questioned or contradicted in his assurances.

"Aye, I admit I have been away longer than anticipated. It is not as easy to travel back to Derbyshire when one has to travel by post, I would not expect you to understand as you always have the luxury of the coach."

"Actually, I have been travelling back and forth on horseback. I find it takes less time and costs a lot less money than the coach. Besides which, my sister Georgiana is currently visiting Ramsgate with her companion, and I thought it better for her to have exclusive use of it for the season."

"Why, yes," Wickham agreed. "What a splendid idea. The seaside will do her a great deal of good after the last few months of sadness. Losing a parent when one is so young will obviously have an impact."

"Well, quite," Darcy snapped.

Both men knew why Wickham was here, it was not to make pleasant small talk or exchange niceties. He was here to receive what was coming to him under the wishes of Mr Darcy's will. There had already been an exchange of correspondence between Wickham and the Darcy attorneys in Lambton and Darcy had already granted his former friend a sum of three thousand pounds instead of the living at Kympton, in addition to the thousand pounds that he had already been granted as Mr Darcy's godson. Taking the envelope from Darcy, which he promptly placed in his inside coat pocket, Wickham offering his hand and Darcy reluctantly shook it. He sincerely hoped that this would be the last he would see of George Wickham.

Eleanor had howled, long low moans of grief at the death of her firstborn son. Peter and David had been told the news up at the main house and travelled back to the cottage as soon as they could, Bridget lived in Lambton and Darcy had sent a man there to fetch her before he had left for the cottage. The Wickhams were like a second family to him and he shared in their grief, holding Bridget in his arms like a sister as she wept.

"What about Lydia, Fitzwilliam," Eleanor asked. "What will happen to Lydia?"

Darcy had not thought about his wife's sister, but it stood to reason that he would send the coach to Newcastle for her.

"She will come and stay at Pemberley with us and I will send her to you once she has settled."

"You know that she is with child, Fitzwilliam?"

If Darcy visibly blanched then he did well to hide it, he had not been aware that Lydia was pregnant, and he wasn't too enthusiastic about a child of George Wickham's being raised at Pemberley.

"I did not know, but this is remarkably good news on this sad day, Eleanor."

"Aye, but I cannot bring myself to be happy about it today."

Darcy left the family to their grief, promising to make all the suitable arrangements for the service and to ensure that Lydia would be safely at Pemberley within the next week. Mounting his horse, he rode back to the house the long way around, it was dusk, and he had been at the cottage for longer than he had intended.

Lydia Wickham arrived ten days later with three trunks and a list of creditors. She was large with child and her usual frivolous and self-centred self. Dressed in a black velvet gown and with her hair curled high upon her head, she had the appearance and demeanour of a very demanding duchess and summoned her sister as if calling for a maid. Darcy did not understand how Elizabeth could stand deferring to her sister in such a way, and he had Lydia and her various possessions placed in one of the less impressive bedrooms in an act of rebellion against her. She had ordered three mourning dresses and charged them to the Darcy account, as well as several bonnets and hats. Darcy trusted that her stay would be short, hopeful that the Bingleys would be willing to receive her at Dunmarleigh for the duration of her confinement.

The funeral passed with little drama, even from Lydia whose emotions were muted on the unseasonably overcast day. Darcy himself felt hollow as the empty symbolic walnut coffin was lowered into the Wickham plot at the church in Lambton, and he held onto his wife's hand as if trying to make sense of it all. It was Elizabeth who encouraged her husband to grieve for George Wickham in the days that followed, to remember the past with as much pleasure as he could.

Despite the incident at Ramsgate and his dastardly elopement with her own sister, Elizabeth was fully aware that Wickham had been a charming and affable man, and after conversing with Darcy about his childhood and his life before her, she knew that some of his positive qualities were as a direct result of knowing him. It was because of having to pay off his friend's debts at the tailors and hatters in fashionable parts town that Darcy had begun to invest in himself; paying for newly tailored suits more befitting his status, buying himself beaver pelt top hats and spending time at the theatre and recitals.

It was because of Wickham that Darcy had a sense of adventure – usually young men would travel to the continent after finishing their studies, but due to Napoleon's dominance of Europe, the two men had travelled to the Far East with a friend from Norfolk, returning to Pemberley with tales of their exploits and the sights they had seen, and artefacts from the holy lands that were on display around the house, as well as lengths of exotic silks and satins. It was talking about these escapades and remembering the aspects of his youth that Wickham had positively enhanced, which forced Darcy to remember George with fondness. It was only then that he truly mourned the loss of a brother and friend.

FIVE QUESTION FIRING:
BENN WILLIAMS – OOH, MR DARCY!

Production has nearly finished on Matthew Wickham's new production of Pride and Prejudice, currently being filmed on location at Pemberley, the historic home of the Darcy family. Benn Williams, currently donning breeches again in the role made famous by Colin Firth faces the Five-Question Firing this week. **How does the role of Darcy differ from Henry Jones?** Well, I haven't had to do as much training, although there were a few touch and go moments with the tightness of the pants and I did end up half-naked in a lake. **Has it been interesting filming the scenes at Mr Darcy's famous house itself?** It's such a wonderful location, you can see why Elizabeth Bennet was so enamoured by it. It was also great to be back up North too. **Everyone knows that you love cake. Tell me, which is your favourite?** That's the most interesting question... I used to be all for red velvet, but I have a new-found penchant for macarons. **Has Lady Imogen popped by to show you around her family home?** I haven't had the pleasure of meeting Lady Imogen yet, but I hear that she is a lot of fun. **Speaking of fun, you're currently footloose and fancy-free... any romance on the horizon?** Not at the minute, but my daughter keeps saying she will put me on Tinder! I don't even know how it works! **There you have it ladies, SWIPE RIGHT!**

Eighteen

Lizzy sat in the chair feeling every one of her thirty-seven years as she was primped and preened and prodded by the make-up artists of 'Pride and Prejudice' next to the gaggle of twenty-something actresses who were playing the Bennet sisters. She felt out of place, being the only 'supporting artist' to be in the same area as the actual stars of the film, and even though she knew it had been arranged to make her feel a bit special and important, it just made her feel awkward. Her mad curls had already been tamed and pinned up into an authentically intricate Regency 'do' and then been wrapped in a hairnet and pinned again to stop any movement whilst she was taken to costume.

"You know the design for this dress was based on one that Elizabeth Darcy wore, Lady Darcy," said an overeager wardrobe assistant called Ruth, who had fantastic eyebrows and wore glittery, purple Converse.

"It's beautiful," she smoothed down the royal blue silk, noticing how the sleeves and hem were trimmed in a gold brocade that twinkled under the dressing room lights. "You can call me Lizzy, y'know. You have just hoisted my boobs into stays, so I think we can be on first name terms."

Ruth blushed as she continued to lace her into the gown, "she wore it – Elizabeth Darcy, I mean – she wore it for her first Lady Anne Ball... The dress – I mean, not this dress, this is one we've had made - I mean that...Oh," she fumbled over a lacing and caught her finger.

"Ruth," she said. "There's no need to be nervous."

"I've never... I mean," Ruth fumbled over her words. "I've never met an actual Lady before. Like, you're the real deal, and this...this is Pemberley!"

"It is! Big Pride and Prejudice fan, are you?"

"I really am! Well, a big Colin Firth fan anyway..."

"Me too, you should have seen what I was like when they filmed here."

Ruth stopped lacing suddenly, "you mean you were here when Colin Firth dived in the lake?"

"I mean it was the pond and not the lake, but yeah, I totally did. I was still at school," she confided, "convinced my grandad to ask the director to let me meet some of the cast, but when I actually did, I just blushed and couldn't say a word to either of them!"

"That sounds exactly like something I would do. Is Colin Firth as handsome in real life?"

"Can I tell you a secret?"

Ruth nodded furtively.

"He was even handsomer...and his shirt wasn't the only thing that was see-through!"

Ruth did a massive snort, and then flushed, but Lizzy could see her visibly relax, before strutting off in the direction of the herd of shimmering starlets whose laughter filled the room.

Lizzy walked across the courtyard, the dress crinkling and the underlying petticoats noisily rubbing against her legs, eager to see the preparations taking place inside. The finale of the Ball ended with a long sweeping shot throughout the rooms where the action took place and Matthew was currently walking through the action with the Steadicam operator as they planned the complicated series of shots and sequences that were all detailed minutely.

For all his many faults, Matthew really was a tremendously good at what he did, totally passionate about any project that he embarked upon and she was glad that he was here, filming the story of Elizabeth and Darcy in the house they had lived in. She stood at the edge of the action; self-consciously looking around the room that she had known all her life, now transformed into the majestic ballroom of Netherfield Hall.

"Lizard! You look amazing!"

Matthew strode over to her with a notebook in his hand and smile on his face.

"Hey, you," she fended off the air kiss, so he didn't disturb her make-up. "You're looking very responsible tonight – how was Shepperton?"

"Hard work," he groaned. "Only two more weeks to go. I can tell I'm getting older, I'm absolutely jiggered."

She could tell he was tired now as the Derbyshire in him came flooding out through exhaustion. It always did.

"When are you going back to LA?

"I don't know if I am," he sighed. "Need to wait to see how much of my money the lawyers are going to take."

"Are you okay?" She slurped on her cup of tea through a straw carefully, trying not to smudge her perfectly applied regency lip colour.

"I am," he said with a considered smile. "It was always going to happen eventually."

"It's still a big deal," she took his hand. "If you need me, you know where I am."

"I appreciate it," he genuinely did.

"How are things with your little twinkie?"

"Brilliant," he grinned. "But she isn't a twinkie, she's amazing."

Lizzy noticed how his attention was drawn to where Tamsin stood laughing at the craft table, and she saw the look on his face, recognised it from all the times she had seen him glancing at her out of the corner of her eye.

"I really like seeing you happy, Matthew"

She loved how he had started smiling with his whole face again.

"It's a nice feeling. I like seeing it on myself."

Matthew watched Tamsin from across the room, she was dancing with Sam Gallagher, who was playing Captain Denny, and he felt a small pang of jealousy as she laughed and teased the young actor, pressing herself against his redcoat uniform and taking a whole host of selfies that would inevitably appear on her Instagram at some point that evening.

He had never expected to fall for the quirky, determined Tamsin, who had a funny smile and an odd accent. She was from a small village outside Huddersfield and he found that, even though the initial attraction had been physical, he loved the way that she took the time to understand him, how she genuinely cared about him, and he found that over the last few months she had become the first person he wanted to speak to in the morning and the last person he wanted to speak to at night. Looking at her now, all strapped into stays and petticoats, he couldn't wait until they had finished for the day so that he could pull her out of it and feel the warmth of her skin under his own.

Taking a seat in a quiet corner of the hall, Lizzy pulled out a random book that she had picked up at the airport on the way back from France and hadn't got around to starting. It wasn't holding her interest and she blamed the awkward week in France with Carol and Hugh for being distracted and choosing something with a pretty cover and little substance. They had barely walked through the door of the villa when Carol announced rather bluntly that they were separating, with Hugh nodding quietly and confirming that it was true. The week had passed with strained conversations and awkward outings as they performed a well-rehearsed charade in public. They had told her that the split was amicable, but now when she picked up the floppy paperback with the pink cover, all she could see were her father's sad brown eyes as he looked at her over breakfast on the terrace.

Benn hadn't expected to see Lizzy at the shoot, didn't understand why when he walked on set, she was sitting there reading a book and dressed in full regency regalia. The blue gown brought out the colour of her eyes, sending them spiralling from a dark grey to seemingly being infused with stardust; he couldn't help but notice how the corsetry had pushed up her bosom, even though he would never admit to it. He watched her out of the corner of his eye, wondering what she was thinking, wondering if she had thought about him.

Lizzy tried not to notice him as he walked on set; although she was fairly sure that her heart did a little flip. He was already fully costumed in one of the early, stiff Darcy outfits, his curls tousled to perfection and his cravat devilishly high. Casually she looked up at him and caught him looking at her, he blinked slowly and then looked away, turning his attention to the woman with bright red hair who was standing next to him, laughing at something she had said. Lizzy felt a prickle of anxiety sweep down her body, manifesting itself on her arm in goosebumps. It had been over a month now since she had seen him last, since that awful night on the roof when she had shouted at him. When she thought back to it now, she was mortified, and it was this embarrassment that had stopped her from sending him a message, or even a vaguely humorous meme, over the last few weeks.

Mr Darcy was laughing with Elizabeth, they had built a great working relationship over the last few months, and she made him laugh with the random snapchats she sent him, and the sense of humour that they shared over stupid things that happened on set. She even once provided him with a live commentary via text of one of his old films – a teen comedy from the nineties that he did straight out of drama school - where he played the best friend to the leading lady. Jenny's over attentiveness would have been annoying if it hadn't filled a terrible void of loneliness and made him laugh rather than think about drinking.

"I told him that I had a poster of him on the back of my door all the way through high school and he didn't believe me," Jenny laughed, as she spoke to her on-screen mother.

Benn was sipping on a Coke, blushing under his layers of make-up. "She's joking, obviously,"

"No," Jenny protested. "I actually think you were responsible for my sexual awakening, even if you are old enough to be my dad!"

He started to fight his corner but found himself interrupted by his former Henry Jones love interest, Mariella Jones.

"Only *just* old enough!" Mariella exclaimed in a soft voice, tinged with her native Edinburgh accent, very different to the shrill histrionics of Mrs Bennet.

"Listen, all I'm saying is the pair of you were both getting it on in 'Praise to the Skies' when I was in high school."

Jenny Graves' real voice had a gnarly Mancunian twang, Benn thought it was very reminiscent of Liam Gallagher. It always impressed him how effortlessly she switched from RP to Salfordeese between takes.

"Like that is it?" Benn grabbed her around the waist and picked her up, "you are being very, very impertinent, Miss Bennet."

"She is right though," Mariella laughed, "when we were doing the scene yesterday and Tamsin kept *corpsing*, all I could think of was when we did the big shag scene in 'Praise' and that shitty beard you had kept tickling my thigh."

"I had forgotten about that! You couldn't stop laughing!"

Jenny, her face a mix of horror and humour, passed her a Kit-Kat, "oh my god, really?"

"Yes, really," she said, taking the chocolate, "and I was petrified that I was going to break wind or something."

"She wasn't bothered about farting in front of me, just in front of the crew," Benn said with uncharacteristic nonchalance, a cheeky grin whipping across his face.

"Benn Williams, I have never been so insulted in all of my life,"

"Well, I've obviously not been trying hard enough."

"How many things have you two actually been in together now?" Jenny munched on her Kit-Kat. Mr Darcy and Mrs Bennet looked at each other, concentrating.

"Too many!" Mariella announced dramatically. "He is a very good kisser though."

"I am?"

"Yes," Jenny agreed, "you really are. My mum is really jealous that I get to fake snog you."

"Your mum? I don't know if that is a compliment or not, but I suppose it means a lot coming from the tantalising Jenny Graves and, of course, the marvellous Mariella." Benn said, pulling her under his shoulder for a hug, "who has always been easy on the eye and easy on the tongue."

"Eww," Jenny laughed, a smile teasing her lips. "You two are so disgusting, but cute I guess. I hope I'm this cute when I'm so old!"

"Hey!" Mariella's Scottish tones bouncing through, "it's easy to go off folk!"

"Drinks, ladies?"

Benn wandered off to the craft table in search of refreshment. He had spent the last six weeks at Shepperton throwing himself into sorting out his life. He had joined AA, visiting a small meeting in Ealing each week. He had spent wonderful precious time with Esther and Anya, he had embraced 'self-care'. He had thought about things, he had played his guitar badly, he had watched films, he had gone for dinners with friends, he had taken his nephew to the zoo. He had done lots of things to fill the gaps in his time, but whenever he saw something he loved, something that made him laugh, a silly article in the paper, all he had wanted to do was message Lizzy, speak to her, share it with her, but he felt he couldn't, that his urgency, those frantic feelings had burned the bridge and perhaps there was never any going back. So, he filled the gaps in his time, but he couldn't fill the Lizzy shaped hole in his heart.

Lizzy was partnered with one of the officers, a lovely young whippersnapper called Rhys, who didn't have any lines, but looked good in a uniform and had spent three weeks learning the dance. He was nervous as the first bars of the song played, but easily found his pace and they bounded through the cotillion with the other three couples in their set. Laughing with Rhys, albeit silently, she noticed that Benn would quickly glance in her direction as he observed the dancing from the outskirts of the room with a glass of Ribena masquerading as port. Even though the music played intermittently, the main noise coming from the room was the soft shuffle and stomp of dancing shoes as they moved across the wooden floor. As they moved into Mr Beveridge's Maggot, the dance which she had practised so hard with Benn, Lizzy was excited to see how well he had rehearsed.

All standing in position, Rhys and Lizzy found themselves adjacent to Benn and Jenny for the start of the dance. Runners and crew were positioning markers and adjusting lighting, whilst the Steadicam operator would move throughout the dance with the couples as if he was part of it. Lizzy saw Rhys glance at Benn standing next to him, he looked at him with an awe and reverence that she hadn't seen someone do before, but she imagined that this was, for the newly graduated drama student, of great importance.

He watched her intently. She turned to look at him, giving him that unassuming little smile that he realised still had the same effect on him. His heart gave a tiny stir, started beating a little faster and he was suddenly very aware of the heat rising to his face. As they stepped into the first movement, Lizzy watched as Darcy and Elizabeth stepped together silently, moving together and then apart; then it was her turn to repeat the movement, with a gloved hand she felt his fingers around hers a little tighter than expected.

As they moved apart again and back into the first position, she saw him look at her, his face saying nothing and his eyes saying everything, and it was as if they were having an almost clandestine affair on the set of the movie. She felt something that she knew she could not ignore any longer, and she knew he did too.

SC. 28. NETHERFIELD. BALLROOM. EVENING. INT.

The room is decadently decorated and bursting with life and people. DARCY and ELIZABETH are dancing to Mr Beveridge's Maggot, we see them pull towards each other and away.

> ELIZABETH:
> It is your turn to say something now, Mr. Darcy.
> (Beat.)
> I've talked about the dance and now you should make a remark on the size of the room or the number of couples.

> DARCY:
> And what would you have me say, Miss Elizabeth?

> ELIZABETH:
> Well, perhaps I may observe that private balls are much pleasanter than public ones.
> (Beat.)
> Or we could remain silent.

DARCY observes ELIZABETH for a moment as the dance continues. He dances with the other lady in the group, watching ELIZABETH.

> DARCY:
> Do you talk by rule, then, while you are dancing?

> ELIZABETH:
> Sometimes.

```
                      (Beat.)
       One must speak a little, you know.
                      (Beat.)
       It would be odd for us to be entirely silent for
       half an hour together.
```

```
ELIZABETH watches as DARCY dances with the other lady in
the group before she repeats the movement with the
gentleman as DARCY observes. This isn't a dance, this is
a duel.
```

It was the end of the section and everyone braced themselves for the command.

"Cut!"

The shot was over from this angle – the digital technicians immediately jumped on the footage, moving the files from the card and into the edit, syncing and backing up files so none of the precious footage was lost. Henry Gibbons – a stalwart of the British film industry, who was playing Mr Bennet - demanded that they checked the gate, and Matthew led him away gently, trying to explain that this wasn't needed anymore.

The scene was reset, a break of thirty minutes announced, and there was an immediate rush of people, a regency deluge reaching for bags and phones and cups of tea. Lizzy glanced up at the gilded plasterwork on the ceiling, the three tall columns designed to look like plaster and each containing the trunk of a tree from the estate, and the amazing chandelier in the centre of room – fully illuminated now with real candles and looking, quite accurately, like something out of a Hollywood production, even if there were several panicking HHS staff members hovering about, ensuring that nothing was damaged or accidentally set on fire. She could see Benn standing over by make-up being fussed and attended to by a throng of women, taking a deep breath she took out her phone.

LIZZY: How are the breeches working for you?

She saw him reach into his pocket and then turn around to look for her, but she dodged his gaze and disappeared. There was a reply when she reached the Servants Hall.

BENN: I'm remarkably trim this week, don't even need my fat pants on.

She barely had time to smile before the phone buzzed again.

BENN: How's your corset?
LIZZY: Booby

She was aware now that he was over by the craft services table, helping himself to a cupcake because he thought no-one was watching.

BENN: I was going to pretend I hadn't noticed, but I am a red-blooded man.
LIZZY: That's not very gentlemanly.
BENN: Who said I was a gentleman? Not me!
LIZZY: Are you going to eat ALL of that cake?
BENN: It would be rude not to.

She was surprised at how easily they fell back into it. How easy it was to pick up the pieces. He was looking at her from across the room, talking to one of the Bennets, his phone in his hand. She saw him excuse himself from the conversation and start to walk over.

"Elizabeth Darcy," shrieked a woman in a yellow ballgown, "how on earth are you?"

Immediately she was engaged in an unwanted conversation with a girl called Corrine who she hadn't seen since school, for very good reasons. She caught his eye as he walked past her, Corrine raising her eyebrows at the close proximity of Mr Darcy, pretending to fan her face.

"Oh, he is dreamy, isn't he?" Corrine glanced over at Benn, who was pouring himself a coffee. "I was worried when they said he was going to be Darcy, he's probably a bit too old, but he really scrubs up well."

"I'm sure he'll appreciate that," she said. "If you will just -"

Lizzy tried to excuse herself, but Corrine was here for the long-haul and there was no escaping this conversation. She stood there being talked at for the next fifteen minutes, as Benn walked around and occasionally shot her a look, paired with a knowing smile. She stood there and nodded politely, engaging in the conversation as much as she could as her phone vibrated in her hand.

BENN: Too old? How rude!
BENN: Do you want me to rescue you?

She caught his eye, a slight nod of the head, a small gesture. He appeared quickly at her side, a knight in shining armour, placing his hand gently on her arm, keeping it there a tiny bit too long. There was that fizz again.

"Lady Elizabeth," he said in his Darcy voice, "would you do me the great honour of introducing me to your friend?"

Corrine, slightly awestruck, was temporarily silent.

"Mr Williams, of course." She gestured to Corrine, who looked as if she might burst with excitement. "This is my friend from school, Corrine Hepburn. Corrine, this is Benn Williams."

"Well, I know who you are, of course," she trilled like an early morning alarm and as equally annoying.

"Would you like to come with me?" He proffered his arm, "it would be a great pleasure to introduce you to some of the cast. Any friend of Lady Darcy's is a friend of mine."

Simpering and giggling, Corrine threaded her arm through Benn's, walking off looking very smug as they went to talk to the Bennets and the Bingleys.

LIZZY: Thank you.
BENN: Anytime.

It was 10pm before filming was completed, amidst the hubbub and the noise of the cast of fifty all being defrocked and dewigged, their costumes and wigs placed in named boxes for the completion of filming tomorrow. Lizzy saw Benn standing at the doorway of the servant's hall, wrapped up in his North Face jacket and a tartan scarf. She felt a little bubble of happiness burst in her stomach at the sight of his face, he was surprised to see her dressed in her normal clothes and made a quick gesture of his head. Giddy, she jumped up from the make-up chair, wrapped herself up in her coat and walked towards the door. Without drawing attention to it, he shyly slipped his hand into hers and felt her squeeze it gently. Holding on to each other tightly they disappeared into the crowd of people dispersing for the night.

"Are we meant to come in this way?" He asked, as she pushed open the large wooden door and led him into the walled garden.

The south front of the house was in darkness, and he could only make out the lake because of the reflection from the moon. It was cold, and he could see his breath fading into vapour in the still air.

"Well, *you're* not meant to come this way," she said in a low voice.

Her hair had been curled and was still pinned up, although some was curling around her shoulder, disappearing into the Gryffindor scarf that he noticed her wearing before. Funny, he thought, he always had her tagged as a Ravenclaw. He was a Hufflepuff, but he would never admit it.

"Is this the scenic route?"

"It is," she grinned. "I wanted to say thank you for before."

"No need to say thank you," he shrugged. "We all know a Corrine."

They walked on into the rose garden, on the right the shadows of Pemberley loomed large. It was beautiful at night, she often wished that more people could see it like this, she pulled ahead of him and he found that he stepped more quickly to catch up.

"Where are you racing off to?"

Stopping sharply at the top of the steps that lead down the Lake, she planted herself down, gesturing for him to join her. They sat together in silence. There was still a gentle hum in the background, the noise of the crew packing things up, the HHS staff checking that everything was as it was before, the faint shouts of gaffers demanding that something be put away.

"I missed you," she said, meaning it entirely. "The more I tried not to think of you, the more I did."

"I'm glad that you did," he admitted. "It almost makes how much I missed *you* not feel quite as tragic. You see…"

She felt her breathing feather a little bit, suddenly aware of the pounding of her heart in her chest and suddenly she was utterly terrified of what he was going to say next.

"…what I said, how I felt. That hasn't changed, but I understand what you meant now about candles."

"It was never me saying no, Benn," she reached for his un-gloved hand and he held onto her tightly. "It was me saying, let's wait."

"And this is me saying that," he reached over with his other hand, moved a stray curl from her face, tucking it behind her ear. "This is me saying that I'll wait until you're ready… if you want me to."

"I think I do. I think I would like that very much."

They grinned at each other in the coldness and the anticipation of what was to come crackled. As she gazed up at him, he realised that he wanted to savour this moment, to enjoy every single second of this, wanted to look at her, shining up at him in the moonlight, the delicate wisp of her eyelash, the rosy flush of her cheek, and the look that she gave him made him feel as if everything was new and the world was to play for.

"Mum!"

There was a shout, a noise in the distance, rattling off the walls of the garden, echoing across the manicured lawn. She looked away, recognising the tone, drawn to the sound, before falling back into the bubble of happiness that she found herself in until the voice was clearer, louder and she pulled away, her eyes drawn to the oncoming figure in the distance.

"Harriet?"

"Mum!" Harriet's shout echoed across the empty rose garden. "Why aren't you answering your phone? They've been trying to call you!" She blurted out angrily. "They've been trying to call everyone, but none of you were answering the phone! They phoned the estate office, Joyce is going mad! She can't get hold of Grandad either..." She grabbed hold of her mum, relief and anger shaking out of her.

"Calm down, what's happened, who has been phoning?"

"The hospital."

"What? Which hospital? What's happened? What did they say?"

"They think Imogen took some pills, they don't know, but no-one was answering the phone and I've been waiting for you to get back." Lizzy hugged Harriet tightly, "Mum, you need to go there now... There needs to be someone there in case she -"

Lizzy looked at Benn, he didn't know what to do or what to say, but he wrapped his arms around them both before trying to take command of the situation.

"I'll drive you down there now," he said quickly. "I have my car."

"No, you have a film to finish, and you need sleep. Matthew will go mad if this film runs over budget..."

She put her head in her hands, running her fingers through her hair; thinking, concentrating, trying to work out everything in her head. He took her hands, made her focus on him, her eyes frantically searching for some reassurance; she looked terrified and all he wanted to do was hold her and tell her that everything was going to be alright. But there was no time for that, he had to be practical about it all.

"Lizzy, I'm going to take you. We'll go now, okay? You're in no state to drive and there is no way your car will make it to London," he grabbed her coat.

She started to protest.

"Look," he said rationally, "I'm not on set until tomorrow afternoon, I have plenty of time to drop you off and get back. It's London, not the moon. I'll text Matthew and ask him to come and collect Harriet. You'll be okay until your dad gets here, won't you?" Harriet nodded "Okay, Lizzy, listen to me. Go and pack some things in a bag, we don't know how long you'll be there, okay?"

"Okay."

"I'll go and speak to Joyce, see if she has managed to get hold of your dad."

"Okay."

Sometimes it was nice not to have to make decisions. He held her hand tightly in the car as they drove away. Looking forward into the darkness, she focused on the rocket lolly air freshener dancing jovially from the rear-view mirror and tried not to think of what misery lay ahead.

1922

The house was now closed and shuttered, looking as if it was falling asleep and drifting away into history. The family had kept a few rooms open, but with a skeleton staff and a severely reduced income, they had to make decisions about the future of their country estate. Millicent viewed the family home from her sanctuary in the folly at Lantern Wood. There were tough choices to be made; ones that she would make on behalf of the family, on behalf of all of the Darcys that came before her and those that would follow. She would be judged on this decision forever.

Pemberley was a huge undertaking. It wasn't simply the house, there were the gardens, and the park, and the tenants, and the farmland. There were hundreds of people who relied on the land to feed their families. The Darcys were no different to the Bramwells, who farmed the north end with rugged sheep in the winter and tiny lambs in the spring, or the Goddards, with their regal Highland cows lording over the rest of the cattle, or even the Wickhams at Paddock Cottage, who drove the deer down from the hills and provided the estate with venison. They all needed this massive behemoth to provide them with a living, the means to make a life, and Millicent was petrified of making the wrong choice.

The obvious solution would be to demolish the house – it was in a state of disrepair, a constant job to be done, a leaking roof, and so very cold – they could sell some of the land for housing and live in one of their other properties permanently. The house would be lost, but the park would be safe, and the estate would survive.

"Demolish Pemberley?" Kitty clattered her teacup in the saucer in an act of protest. "Have you lost your mind?"

"I most certainly have not, and I will kindly ask you to watch your tongue."

The two women were drinking tea in the housekeeper's room, waiting for Mrs Reynolds to return, as they polished the silver. There were only four members of staff now – Mrs Reynolds, Mr Staughton,

Kitty, and James, the footman. Her father was convinced that they were living like paupers, but what use was it having an army of servants for the two of them she told him one evening, as she listened to him plonk about on the piano.

"There will be another way," the younger woman said, swilling the last dregs from the pot before she started to buff the soup tureen.

The Darcy crested silver centrepieces lay before them, sparkling and shining and ready to be sent off to auction. Millicent ran her finger over the intertwined 'F & E'. These were the pieces of the collection that adorned the dinner table of Fitzwilliam and Elizabeth; she wondered if the most famous Darcy would judge her for selling it to fix the hole in the roof over the long gallery, plugging the constant drip that was causing the wood above the windows to fracture and crack. She couldn't help but think he would view her as a complete failure.

"If there is, I cannot find it," Millicent lit a cigarette. "God knows I've bloody well looked."

Kitty reached over and took a drag, "you will though, Penny, I have every faith in you. You always solve everything."

"I always like a *challenge*, Kitty, it's not quite the same thing."

"It is! You said it would be the *easiest* thing to have the house demolished, but in all the time I have known you, I have *never* known you to choose the easiest thing."

The answer came to her one fretful sleepless night. Who knew that Kitty Blake would be so wise? It occurred to Millicent, as she sat with a glass of brandy in the drawing room, that the house on Grosvenor Square was grand and opulent, but also empty and deserted for almost eleven months of the year. A discreet advertisement was placed in one of the more upmarket newspapers, and she received an offer from an American hotel magnate who remembered her mother with fondness. She negotiated hard, and in the end, the gentleman offered the family a grace and favour penthouse in perpetuity once Derbyshire House was transformed into the city's newest and plushest hotel. Furniture from the house was auctioned off, with people from across the world eager to own a piece of Mr Darcy and Elizabeth Bennet, even if the pieces they bought were refurbished, reupholstered fragments of what was once there.

She only kept a few items from the house that had been Isabella Stratton's inheritance. It had once played host to princes and archdukes, but now there were just so many things for her box up or get rid of. Portraits, old trunks full of gowns and other pieces of nonsense were sent back to Pemberley and put in the Wyatt tower, which was now devoid of giggling chambermaids and lay empty. Egyptian artefacts that had been brought back by Fitzwilliam Darcy were donated to the British Museum and boxes full of books from the library were packed up and ready to be shipped to Derbyshire. It seemed endless, but it had to end.

"You have twenty boxes to be removed to Pemberley, Lady Darcy, Ma'am," said the efficient removals man, brandishing a clipboard and asking her to sign. Millicent walked around the empty ballroom, a room that would soon be filled once more with noise and laughter and music. She gestured to a portrait on the wall. Dressed in yellow, her hair in ringlets, a pearl and diamond necklace around her throat, Elizabeth Bennet-Darcy smiled down at her from above the fireplace.

"That too," she said, as she signed the paperwork, before closing the front door with a firm clunk for the final time.

Edward never knew how his daughter had managed to keep her son a secret for so long, but he was pleased to meet the young boy who stood before him. He was five years old and had the light colouring of his mother and the furrowed brow of the Darcy men.

"Are you my grandpa?"

"Yes," he said firmly, with a quick nod of the head. "I am."

"You have a very big moustache."

"I suppose I do."

The two Darcys continued to study each other, Millicent stood at the edge of the room, watching them. The boy looked to her for cues.

"Mama says that I will live here with you."

"Yes, if you like," he gestured for the boy to follow him. "Come with me, young man, you can choose a bedroom."

Millicent watched as her son and her father disappeared up the grand staircase together. Edward had never asked her who the boy's father was, but she knew that he had his suspicions. Even though her son wasn't legitimate, there were enough husbandless wives up and down the country that she could easily pretend she was a grieving widow. It wasn't too far from the truth.

Edward Darcy walked down the long gallery watching as the boy ran ahead of him to the north end of the house and then back to him.

"Can we play billiards now, grandpapa? I am big enough to reach the table."

"Of course, we can, dear sweet boy," he said, ruffling the boy's blonde curls.

The war may have taken his wife and sons, but Edward knew now that there was a little flicker of hope, and his name was Winston Fitzwilliam Darcy.

Nineteen

Lizzy opened her eyes somewhere past Birmingham, the lights of the city flashing across their faces as they hurtled down the M6 and onwards to London. She reached over and placed her hand on his knee, wanting to feel something real, The Beatles were playing on the radio, and she tried not to think about what was waiting in the private wing of the Chelsea and Westminster hospital.

He knew how she felt – midnight calls and being summoned to distant hospital wards - it had been the night after Madeleine's thirty-eighth birthday party when he received a similar call. His dad had finally succeeded in drinking himself to the point of no return and his brother was on the phone, begging him to go to Manchester to make his peace with him, but he never had, would never be able to now.

"You make me dizzy, Miss Lizzy!" he sang badly, trying to glean a smile from her face. He was trying hard to maintain a level of seriousness about the situation, but also trying to keep her upbeat.

She turned the radio up – the smallest hint of a smile crossing her face as she remembered the tune, she thought she had forgotten it, but the lyrics were all there at the edge of her memory.

"My Nan was called Lizzy," he turned the heating up slightly after he noticed her shiver, sharing a memory that had been pushed to the back of his mind "I remember this song. We used to dance with her when we were kids."

They sat in silence again as the music turned to a song that Lizzy instantly recognised; she turned it up, basking in the husky, youthful tones.

"Please don't tell me that you like this," he laughed, reaching to search for another station. "I bloody hate Joni Mitchell"

"Don't turn it over."

He deep sighed and turned his eyes back to the road, "do you actually like this?"

"My mum…" tears unexpectedly and strangely forming behind her eyes. "She loved Joni Mitchell. So weird this song is on the radio." She wiped her eyes with the sleeve of her jumper, "This was her favourite...I think."

"You think?"

"I can't really remember much about her. Just that, she liked this song... strange what you do remember, isn't it?"

There another silence, but not a comfortable one; one that felt like a balloon being blown up to bursting point, waiting for the bang, the release, the noise. Lizzy inhaled deeply, gulping for air in the car which smelled like lemons and rosemary, she opened the window slightly, wanting to feel the cold rush of quickly moving motorway air pounding against her face, the resistant current push against her fingertips as they danced together.

"Do you miss her?"

"No."

It was matter of fact; as if she was ordering food in a restaurant. Benn was unsure how to react and she saw the momentary hesitation glance across his face.

"I didn't know her, so I don't know who I would be missing," she reassured him, trying to assuage any awkwardness. "I don't remember much about her. Coco Pops, the smell of acrylic paint – she was an artist you know, a really good one; some of her pictures are in the flat – custard creams, and George Michael, and she had a pink fluffy jumper, and she had me one made exactly like it, and I loved that jumper. This song reminds me of her a lot though, but I don't know why."

They listened for a moment before he felt he needed to lighten the mood.

"Oh, I could drink a case of yoooooou, darrrlllliiiiiing..."

"Good job you can act, because you really can't sing..."

Benn returned her smiled and reached for her hand in the darkness, finding that she instinctively grasped it, holding on tightly.

The services outside Oxford were half-closed, patronised by long-distance lorry drivers and a few other travellers on their way to Dover for the early morning ferries. Lizzy always recognised them by the proud stickers on their people carriers; the small tired-looking children plodding through the brightly-lit arcade to use the loo and buy magazines with garish toys taped to the front, the mums shrill and fractious as they tried to keep one step ahead of the itinerary, the dads scrolling through their phones.

She was sitting by the window, tucked into the corner, looking out at the past midnight nightlife, she had been checking her phone constantly – her call to the hospital had confirmed that there had been no change – she thought about her little sister who had felt so unhappy about her life on this earth that she had tried to remove herself from it, and she couldn't comprehend how the vivacious, bubbly girl with the long legs and the big smile had ever felt so alone.

Benn – currently being accosted by the barista, who was convinced he was off the telly – was buying coffee and cake as requested, and it seemed to take ages before he wandered over with a tray, balancing two large lattes and a slice of carrot cake. He slid into the booth next to her and handed her the drink, which she took greedily from his hands, slurping the caffeine into her veins.

"Did you get recognised?" She wondered how often it must happen for him; outside of Derbyshire nobody knew who she was really, and she was grateful for that.

"No," he took a gulp of his own coffee, needing to feel more awake than he currently did. "She thought I was off Coronation Street – asked me if I was married to Gail!"

"Everyone has been married to Gail, you should have said yes! We might have got free cake."

"Lizzy, I was nominated for an *Oscar*," he said with mock consternation

"Yes," she said cheekily, "but you didn't win."

"I was a close second," he said sternly, taking a forkful of the cake and offering it to her, she took it gladly.

They had been on set most of the day, and even though production catering was good, the cake made her realise how hungry she was.

"I'll have to watch out for this – first profiteroles, now carrot cake – you'll make me fat!"

They drank their lattes, Lizzy's phone bleeped several times: messages from her dad who was probably only about fifty miles behind them now, and a message from Matthew who had collected Harriet and taken her to the Armitage.

"He said that he can move your scenes to later on," she said, as they walked back to the car with coffees and cake to go. "So, you can sleep when we get there, can't you?"

"He doesn't want me to look like shit for the close-ups, that's all!" He opened the door for her, and she clambered in. "Don't think that he's developed a duty of care or anything!"

"He did say that you would need extra time in make-up and said…that he wouldn't be shooting your close-ups in 8k? Does that make sense to you?"

"Yeah, it does. The cheeky bastard!"

They began their journey again, the sleepy romantic songs of the middle of the night moving to more upbeat early morning ones and they found themselves dancing along to Meat Loaf as they hit the M25, before turning off the radio and driving into central London in a hushed silence, both preoccupied with their own thoughts and worries, but one thought lingered, kept pushing forward and he knew he had to ask.

"Do you know why she did it?"

"I have no idea. I'll never understand how anyone would feel so hopeless that they would want to do that."

"But sometimes people do feel like that."

"They do, but even when the world is really dark, there is always a little chink of light to be found somewhere."

She looked quickly at him, as if wanting a reassuring answer and found it lacking. He was clenching his jaw; his eyes were glassy and focused intently on the road.

"That day when we first met…"

"The day when you were a complete arse…"

She joked, but the look on his face made her realise that this wasn't funny.

"Yes."

He swallowed hard. She noticed the crack in his voice, the creases on his forehead, the way he was blinking as he did when he was nervous.

"What is it? Tell me…"

"I was in a bad place when I got to Derbyshire."

"I remember, you said that."

Her voice softened, and she placed her hand on his, wrapping her fingers around his.

"Last year was awful. The worst year of my life, and I was drinking a lot. I am a selfish, horrible drunk. I don't care about anything apart from where the next drink is coming from. I'm no good to anyone when I'm like that."

His voice was low, scratchy and he grabbed her hand, holding tightly, feeling as if he was holding on during a storm and letting go would send him falling beneath the waves.

"I had been drinking since eight that morning, not quite whiskey on my cornflakes, but not far off… the day was so empty, nothing in it… just thoughts running around my head. It was rush hour when I decided I needed more booze. My brother had been to all of the shops within walking distance, told them not to serve me, and they wouldn't."

He recalled that night, how he felt, how it hurt, "but London is a big place."

He was telling her was something that he kept hidden in the secret parts of himself, this had been buried somewhere deep inside where he never let any light in and he had never told anyone about it, scared that they would view him differently, that it would change their opinion of him. But now, driving to the capital in the middle of the night with her, he knew that he wanted to let her see all the hidden corners, allow her access to the darkest parts of his heart.

"There was a shop in Balham that would have happily sold me enough whiskey to drown in…"

His face was wistful, haunted almost as he tried to pull the events of that night from the dark, deep dungeons of his mind.

"I stood on the edge of the platform, waiting for the tube. Only one stop, get the booze, then home for Netflix and trying to forget the utter clusterfuck that was my life."

He swallowed deeply again, trying to centre himself. He knew he couldn't stop now, couldn't end the story, would need to carry on until everything was spread out before her, so she could see, so she could know that his confidence and charm was an act. That really, he was broken and bent and bruised.

"I stand right at the edge, feeling as if I could touch the other side and I know how easy it would be to let go of it all. I can feel my toes on the curve of the platform, that gust of air that you get before the train comes, that warm air, that smell's so familiar. All I could think that this would be my last breath and I breathed it in, wanting that comfort, that smell coating me inside…and then I hear that annoying song, that one off the advert with the dancing bear. Someone is playing it through a phone – the last thing on my mind would be that shit song being played shittily, and it annoyed me.

I hear the screech of the train and feel myself lean forward. I'm ready to go now, I've made my peace, and it's time. I know it's my time to go. I fall forwards, close my eyes, wait for the dark. But then there is a yell and then it hurts. It hurts so fucking much, and the train siren is blaring away. I can hear laughing. When I open my eyes, I see the train racing through the station, and I realise that the laughter I can hear is mine. This man with red braces and a stupid moustache who stopped me, who is glaring at me, who doesn't even know who I am, saved me. I came so close. I can understand the temptation."

He could feel the tears running down his face, hoped that she wasn't thinking less of him, or worse, that she pitied him. Lizzy reached over, pulling her sweater over her hand, gently dabbing the tears away as he drove on into the city itself and then she held his hand, feeling as if she could never let go.

As they passed the main entrance of the hospital, she could see that there were photographers already gathered, accosting anyone who came out, asking for news of Lady Imogen and she felt her stomach turn. The car pulled up outside the imposing structure of the hospital and as soon as it had stopped, she unbuckled her seatbelt and wrapped her arms around him, holding him in the tightest of hugs, the firmest of embraces.

"If you ever feel like that again, you tell me," she whispered into his ear, inhaling him deeply, gently pressing her lips to his cheek.

"I am so sorry to burden you with all of this."

It was shameful, he thought, laying this at her door knowing how difficult the next few hours would be for her.

"It's never the answer, you know, but I understand that it can sometimes be the question."

"Oh god, Lizzy, I'm so broken," he said softly.

"No, you're not," reaching out she placed her hand on the back of his neck, twisted his curl inadvertently. "But you have to promise me that you will do all you can to conquer this. You can't fuck it up."

"I promise I will do my best."

"I mean it," her voice took on an urgent tone that he had not heard before, "you have to promise me because I don't want to wake up in the world and you not be in it."

"Lizzy… I *promise.*"

She seemed reassured. He knew enough of Elizabeth Georgiana Darcy to know that this was as near enough to an admission of actual proper feelings he was going to get.

"Every day I think I have you figured out, think that I know who you are," he cupped her face in his hands, "but every day you surprise me."

"I try my best," she said in a small, honest voice free from joking and humour.

He leaned back, stretching out against the soft leather seats which creaked as he moved to face her fully, twisting his body around awkwardly so he could see the outline of her face in the pale light of the early morning. Benn had wondered what it would feel like to tell someone, but now as he saw the tender expression on her face, he realised that he shouldn't have been worried at all.

He didn't know quite what this was, but the name coursing through his veins, echoing around his brain, resounding within him like a big bass drum was Lizzy. She flowed through him in tiny sparks of gold and silver and he knew that she was why the universe had given him a second chance. It seemed as if she was standing there now before him, stripped down and raw and ready to be primed and painted.

He leaned towards her, kissing her gently on the forehead, the touch of his lips to her temple sending a little shiver through her; it was slow and unrehearsed. This was Benn Williams now, not the actor, not the professional kisser, but the man who might perhaps be part of her future.

There was a split second when she felt that this was the start of their story, that this was the way they would begin.

"C'mon then," he grabbed her bag and coat and got out of the car, before opening her door and taking her firmly by the hand. "Let's get this over and done with."

He guided her across the road, walking with her towards the photographers, protecting her from the questions, shielding her from the furore and the flashbulbs and the noise, before leading her through the revolving doors and inside.

1822

The marriage of Georgiana Margaret Darcy and Henry Montague Armitage was the most joyous of affairs, the happy couple exchanging vows at the small church in Lambton, before returning to Pemberley for their Wedding Breakfast. Elizabeth had arranged with Mrs Reynolds for a delightful summer feast, and the ladies of the kitchen had excelled themselves in the preparation of such. The centrepiece was a rich, fruit cake, covered in sugared icing and decorated with flowers.

The new Mrs Armitage and her husband were to travel firstly to Kent, and then onwards to visit relations in Scotland. Darcy thought that he might burst with pride upon seeing his sister so deliriously happy and he knew that this marriage with Armitage was more than he could have ever wished for her – the two were so in love and he was anticipating great things for their future, especially as he hoped to see them both at Pemberley very frequently.

"Elizabeth!" The shrill tone echoed from the entrance hall, "Mrs Darcy, I must demand your attention at once!"

Turning on her heel, Elizabeth made her way back down the stairs and towards Lady Catherine De Bourgh. Once so intimidating, Darcy's aunt had begun to shrink in her old age, both in size and demeanour. Eleven years had passed since she had refused to attend their wedding, stubborn to the core and with a ruthless snobbery that affected all of her close personal relationships, it had taken effort on Elizabeth's part to alleviate the animosity between her new relations. It had not been easy, and Lady Catherine had been a hard taskmaster

Anne De Bourgh had now been married to her cousin Richard Fitzwilliam for these past ten years, and they had one son and a smattering of daughters. Lady Fitzwilliam, once dominated by her strong-willed mother, but now strengthened by the love she never thought she would find, had enforced a move to the simpler dower house for her mother a few months after her wedding, which had caused ructions in their relationship.

Lady Catherine, reduced to the living on her widow's allowance, which was still a generous two thousand a year, found herself travelling the length of the country in the barouche box that her daughter still permitted her to use, residing with any relatives gracious enough to permit her to stay. She was usually in residence at Pemberley from the last week in July until the second of August – a three-week stay being the limit for the Darcys and their household.

Sitting in a large satin upholstered chair, she was scrutinising the new and imposing fireplace which had recently been installed, staring at it with a curious expression through the eyeglass that hung on a chain around her neck.

"Was this your idea, Elizabeth?"

"Lady Catherine, do you approve?" Elizabeth always found the best way to counteract her Aunt by marriage was to ask her another question, the Lady always enjoying advising others of her opinion, whether they asked for it or not. In this, Lady Catherine was not altered.

"I do approve," she nodded. "I find that it always benefits a house such as this to install new fancies and fireplaces to keep abreast of fashion. People scoffed when I commissioned the new chimneypiece at Rosings, the cost alone – eight hundred pounds, which is a vast amount of money – was a source of ridicule and dismay amongst many in our circle."

"It is a very impressive chimneypiece, Lady Catherine, I can testify to its superiority."

"Why of course it is, Elizabeth. My taste and fine eye for fashionable accoutrements are incomparable, I have often been told this by the greatest people of our acquaintance."

"I am glad that you approve of the fireplace, Aunt," she said in an affectionate tone, she had grown to hold this crotchety woman in high regard and whilst she would probably never say that she loved her, she appreciated her visits. Lady Catherine reached over and took Elizabeth's hand in her own, holding it tight.

"Mrs Darcy, since you have joined our family, I have been astonished at how amicably a woman of low-born connections such as yourself can assimilate so satisfactorily into the role of mistress of Pemberley."

She held back a laugh and smiled genially, "thank you for your compliment, Lady Catherine, it makes the toil worthwhile to know that you hold me in such regard."

"Indeed, it must be a daily struggle for you. Now, where is my niece?"

Elizabeth knew, with relief felt in every bone of her body, that she had been dismissed and went to look for Georgiana, who had escaped into the gardens away from her forever disapproving aunt.

Darcy was sitting in the grand chair in his study at the front of the house. From here he could see out onto the driveway, down the hill towards the gatehouse, and then onto the gardens of the west front, where the ornamental gardens – laid out only the summer before - were now fully in bloom, the scent of camellias drifting in through the open window on the warm, summer breeze.

This was his domain. On one side there was a row of bookcases from floor to ceiling – it was here that he kept items from his own private collections, volumes that he had collected on his grand tour, and manuscripts and books that had been given to him by his father-in-law on the occasion of his marriage from the gentleman's own admirable library at Longbourn. In the centre was the large oak desk that had belonged to George Darcy – the portrait of the gentleman hanging above the fireplace opposite. How he wished his mother and father were alive to see this day; to see Georgiana so agreeably matched and beginning her married life from their ancestral home, and how delighted they would have been to see his own young family.

There was a knock on the door. Henry Armitage was a well-rounded gentleman of nearly thirty; he was solid and smooth, never moving without cause, never saying more than needed to be said. He reminded Darcy very much of a Greek statue. Educated at Cambridge, as had Darcy, he was the second son of the Earl of Struthers and both families were pleased with such a fortunate match. Georgiana, with her dowry of thirty thousand pounds and newly-found confidence, had already decided that they would live in Derbyshire House for the first few years of their marriage. She had enjoyed the company of society in town and had made a strong circle of friends with whom she was regularly seen at countless parties, balls, and the theatre. Nurtured by the sisters she had acquired through her brother's marriage, she had flourished and grown into a desirable, accomplished and well-liked young lady of the Ton.

"Darcy," Henry's voice was firm and confident, the tutelage of the Old Bailey lending it an authoritative air. "I know that you initially had concerns about my fortune. When one is a second son, one has to make one's own way in the world somewhat."

"I did have reservations, Henry, but my wife reminded me that some things are more important than the size of a gentleman's fortune."

"Such as?"

"Such as the size of a man's heart."

"I want you to know that I love Georgiana, most fervidly. She is the most vibrant, clever, challenging woman I have ever had the pleasure to know."

"I know how it feels to love such a woman in such a way."

"Georgiana often mentions that she could not have settled for a man she did not love, she believes that yourself and Mrs Darcy set the bar very high in that respect."

"Did she indeed. I am of the belief that we are, all of us, so very fortunate."

"I believe we are, Darcy."

He looked at Armitage, who was full of nerves and yet so cheerful. He reminded him of himself on his own wedding day and he was taken back to that joyful day when he knew that Elizabeth would be his and his alone until death parted them. Walking over to Henry, he placed his hand on his shoulder and gave it a firm squeeze. The two men acknowledged an unspoken understanding – outside on the west front lawn, their wives were talking and laughing with a crowd of small children who were running about in the summer sunshine. Georgiana, dressed in a simple yellow wedding gown that belied her ancestry, had flowers in her hair and an immoveable smile on her face; Elizabeth was dressed in a pale lilac muslin and skipping along to the tune that was playing in her head, dancing with her children, immensely happy.

Twenty

Imogen Penelope Darcy had hair the colour of wheat and eyes as blue as the July sky she was born under. She was of such a pleasant temperament that she delighted everyone she met, dancing across the staterooms at Pemberley during the Duke's Christmas visit, her little voice singing a song by Elton John as she twirled next to the ten-foot-tall Christmas tree. Her mother watched proudly, and various members of staff clapped and took photos of Lady Imogen beaming widely and curtseying on their disposable cameras.

As she grew older, family members commented on how much she reminded them of her great-grandma Millicent in the painting that hung underneath the grand staircase. At just eleven and a gangly, tall, girl, Imogen could not see how she even resembled the magnificent creature in the portrait before her. Painted when Millicent had been in her late twenties and done by a respected society artist, she could not see how her own lip pouted in the same way – the gentle crease of the cupids bow on her top lip – her hands, long and tapered were almost the same, she could see that, but it was only when she squinted her eyes and tilted her head that she saw a face that resembled her own.

It was the eyes, she thought, they had the same eyes. Most of the Darcys had slate grey eyes, but Imogen had eyes like sapphires that sparkled even when she was sad, and everyone commented on how she was the least Darcy-like of all of Winston's grandchildren.

"Can you see it now, Imo?"

"Yes. Do you think I will be as beautiful when I am a grown-up?"

"I think you are that beautiful now."

The younger girl blushed; Lizzy unwrapped a packet of Cherry Drops and the two Darcy girls sat on the carpet in front of the painting, blocking the pathway for any paying guests. Imogen was mesmerised by the image of the Lady Darcy dressed in soft blue satin and posing against a table. Her hair was the colour of a harvest field, a glittering tiara of diamonds pinned through her curls; her lips painted red, her hands long and tapered, the embroidered sheer of her dress clinging gently to the curve of her back.

"This is for you, we thought you would like it."

Imogen opened the soft velvet pouch to find a delicate silver band with a pearl in the centre, two small diamonds on either side. She tipped it out of the bag and held it up to look at it in greater detail, slipping it on her finger she found that it fit perfectly.

"It belonged to her, it was one of her most precious pieces of jewellery. She wore it all the time, and Dad thought it was time it had a new owner. Look!"

Lizzy pointed up at the oil-painted Lady, watching her younger sister recognise that the ring on her own finger was the same one gracing the hand of Millicent in the ninety-year-old portrait. Imogen beamed and hugged her sister tightly, maybe she was more Darcy than everyone thought.

Lizzy sat by her sister's bedside in the private room of the Chelsea and Westminster hospital. Benn had walked her to the ward, holding her tight as if trying to fill her with courage and she had pulled him in close, not wanting to let go because letting go would mean that she would need to accept that this was real. That her little sister, the curly-haired diva, was lying silently in a hospital bed attached to tubes and monitors.

"It will be okay," he said, holding her hand as they sat outside the room waiting for the consultant.

"You can't know that."

He didn't really know what to say because she was right. He didn't know what was going to happen. Imogen had taken a dubious narcotic party cocktail, followed with a chaser of sleeping pills.

"I don't know what will happen," he said. "But I will be here whatever does. You don't have to do this by yourself, Lizzy."

She held him tighter and the tears came once more. It had been easy to watch Imogen go off the rails, especially when she seemed to have so much fun doing it, but now as she saw the pale face of the young girl, she wondered that if maybe all the times Imogen looked as if she was enjoying the rollercoaster ride that was her life, she was merely white-knuckled, clinging onto the safety bar, petrified of falling out.

His phone buzzed in his pocket, Matthew was calling, he declined the call, which was followed by a text message.

MATT: Can give you until 6pm, but no later. Hope Lizzy ok.

It was nearly 11am and he knew he would have to leave her, even if the thought of travelling back to Derbyshire without her was making him worry.

"Are you going to be alright?"

She nodded, holding onto him tightly as they said their goodbyes inside the building.

"My phone will be on and Leanne will have it," he reassured. "If anything changes, if you need me, anything at all, you call me."

"I will."

He held her for the longest time before disappearing outside, escorted by a security guard who helped him to avoid the press.

Lizzy sat next to the lifeless body of her little sister. Her hair was a ratty bleached blonde and even though her face had been cleaned, traces of eyeliner remained in the corner of her eyes. There was a tattoo of a bee on her wrist, which was new. On the bedside table in a plastic bag were the items she had been wearing; the Olivia Burton watch dad had bought her, a Tiffany heart necklace, and the small pearl ring that had belonged to Millicent. She found herself studying Imogen as she waited for any sign of movement, any sign of normalcy that would signal to her that this was all going to be okay, but she had been there for nearly twelve hours now and there had been no change. Hugh had been in and out of the room all day, Carol hysterical; it was all a waiting game now, wishing and hoping and praying that everything was going to be alright because if it wasn't, it would be the end.

Imogen was in a white room, she felt weightless and free. Ahead of her was a bright light, but there was a noise behind her. It sounded like music, a tune that she could recognise but couldn't quite remember... there was the faint sound of piano keys being hit and she followed it, as she did the room became grey, became black and there was darkness.

She could hear the words, could hear them ever so softly...

'Count the headlights on the highway...'

They became louder now.

'Lay me down in sheets of linen...'

She recognised the voice.

'You had a busy day today...'

As she fell into the voice, there was a rush of weight and heaviness and she coughed loudly, choking now...*struggling*...couldn't breathe... noises, voices, beeps, shouts, light, alive, sounds, smells... air – breath – gasp!

Tiny Dancer.

1693

Lady Sophia Clarendon-Darcy, the Countess of Dortmund, was silent in the stag parlour; raging in the hearth, a large fire was filling the room with overpowering heat. Seething with anger, the lady tapped her foot on the edge of the window seat in the corner of the room where she had been placed to prevent her from causing trouble. At the table her brother Cyril, her father George and the Cheshire Gentlemen, a small group of local landowners loyal to the former King James II, were gathered amidst smoke and ale, discussing their plan to restore the deposed Monarch to the throne in loud, bellowing voices which belied the secrecy of their very treasonous plotting.

As the mother of two Royal bastards, Sophia was a key part of this plan – but it had never been her idea to force action on behalf of the rightful King and legitimise her own children as his successors. Edmund and Richard, strong healthy boys, resided in the country – too precious to be kept close to the park at Pemberley, or even at her house in town. Even though they had been officially recognised as sons of the King, being given the name Fitzroy and the titles of Earls of Bentinck and Struthers, their position under the rule of William of Orange was tenuous, especially given his wife's own inability to provide the country with a Protestant heir. The Darcys themselves were staunch Catholics, but also staunch Royalists, and this most recent of developments had caused problems.

Sophia understood the risks that were being taken on behalf of her children, but she didn't have to agree with them. She knew that any hint of conspiracy or intrigue could result in the children simply disappearing. These silly men were prattling on about their plans to raise armies, about their plans to smuggle the King into the country and march down to London to reclaim the throne, but it was all so foolish. If they were going to be successful then they would have to be a little be cleverer with their plotting, or all of them would end up in the Tower, with nothing but a swift, merciless death ahead of them. She sat in the corner, her mother's Darcy Pearls pendant sparkling at her neck, her grey eyes incandescent with rage.

She coughed; loudly enough to be heard, but not loudly enough to command the room, and the chatter of twelve raucous gentlemen used to ignoring the voices of their wives continued to dominate the walls of the small parlour. Marching over to the fireplace, she banged on the floor three times with the heavy metal poker.

"Gentlemen, Gentlemen, Gentlemen! I beg your attention, please do not do the mother of the focus of your misguided endeavour such an injustice."

The men in the room began to quieten until Percival Warner, the lord of the manor that abutted their own to the north, began to gripe about her even being included in the meeting.

"We are the Cheshire Gentlemen, not the Cheshire Gentlemen and the Errant Daughter of George Darcy! This is simply the point which I am trying to make, albeit not as eloquently as I would like."

He leaned over to Henry Danvers, who was sitting next to him and began to laugh. The laughter began to spread around the room like wildfire until Sophia, furious and red-faced, screamed for them to be silent.

"How *dare* you have the presumption that you can use my children as figureheads for your futile exercise, whilst at the same time demeaning anything that I may have to say." She spat out the sentence, the room falling silent as the assembly now attended to her every word. "I may not be a gentleman, but the King created me a Countess in my own right—"

"If I remember correctly, Lady Clarendon, most of your fellow courtiers were rightly indignant at your elevation, the furore at the palace caused you to flee to Ireland for a year," Henry Danvers turned to his group of cronies, as they laughed with him.

"Sir Henry," she said, "do not be outraged because the King took a particular fancy to me and not your own daughter. If she had more wit and fewer lice maybe she would be standing here now. I outrank most of you here, and I am not flying under the flag of a flatulent and flaccid husband, for you all know that I do not have one, and do not wish for one either! I stand here as a woman alone, and I am warning you all that the arrogance of your sex will eventually be your downfall."

"We are here to discuss the action we are going to take, Lady Clarendon, and not sentimentalise your love affair with the King," quipped Robert Piers, a local landowner who would have been quite handsome, excepting the large scar on his right cheek which he had received in a less than honourable duel.

"As you know, Sir Robert, I was the accepted Mistress of the King at court, holding a position that you probably wouldn't recognise if it slashed your other cheek!"

Men like Piers forgot that she could hold her own at court, that she wouldn't be bullied and subjugated like their own wives.

"As far as I am aware, Lady Clarendon, we are all fully aware of the 'position' that you held in the palace and your ability to sire Royal bastards does not make your attendance here necessary."

George Darcy, the most senior man in the room rose to his feet and walked over to his daughter.

"Madame, you need to leave this room now, you are doing none of us any good."

He roughly grabbed his daughter's arm and pulled her out of the room and into the narrow hallway; to the left, she could hear the rumblings of the gentlemen, to the right the faint sound of a lyre being played; the gentle hum of gentlewoman behaving as they ought.

He was an old man now, but still fighting inside for what he believed to be right. George firmly believed that James was the rightful King of England, as he had believed that Charles was for all those years of fighting in the War or struggling in exile. There were risks in what he was doing, he was aware of that, but he did not contend with the idea that a god-anointed King could be usurped or replaced.

"Father, I know you," she pleaded with his face, now cast in stone against her, "and you of all people understand that we cannot raise an army against the King without endangering Pemberley; if you must -"

"Sophia, you embarrass me," he snarled. "You are a liability today, you have no idea of what you speak."

"I speak the truth, Father, and you damn well know it! His Majesty will have your head, and my brother's, and if you anger him, if you try and pin your banner of treason to my children, he will find them, he will murder them, and then he will destroy us."

"You have a quite a flavour for the dramatics, daughter," he smirked, "no wonder James sought you out. He did always love an actress."

"You pretend that you are above all of this, Your Grace," she derided. "However, if I were a man you would be congratulating me on the titles and riches that have been the reward for my indiscretions."

"If you were a man, there would be no such dishonour in you siring bastards, my child."

"But here we are, and as a woman who has known King William, who has seen the cruel mistreatment that he bestows upon his own wife, then I am begging you. Please do not do this. It will see the ruin of us all."

"Maybe, Lady Clarendon, but that is a risk and a gamble I am willing to take. We did not reach our current rank by always playing by the rules. I decide what course of action we take."

"Father, you need to realise that the game you are playing is not one that you will win. There will be only one victor here, and it will not be you."

"It will not be you either, my Lady."

"That may be so, but I do not intend to lose anything, especially not my head," her voice dropped, "if you proceed, you will lose, and you will lose everything."

"I never lose, Sophia," he sneered. "Now, go and sit with the ladies and talk of fripperies and fancy. There is nothing to concern you in here."

She curtseyed before stomping through to the drawing room where the rest of the ladies were in attendance. She could feel the flush of her cheek, the rage building up inside of her. Taking a seat by the window, looking out onto the north front range of Pemberley, the beacons were lit, illuminating the circular driveway and the men below, who were busily preparing the coaches for departure.

A year later she would watch helplessly from the same spot as four messengers and twenty-one Dutch troopers marched into the house to arrest her father for High Treason.

George Darcy was escorted to the Tower of London where he would await trial; as he was taken over London Bridge, he could see the spiked heads of Henry Danvers, Robert Piers and Percival Warner looking down on him with ominous, grisly faces.

"I'm leaving tonight," she told him in hushed tones, "it's not safe here anymore."

"I'll come with you."

They had been lovers for a while now, but they both knew that it had grown into something more than that.

"Silas, you would *never* be able to return to Pemberley."

"If *you* run, *I* run."

They packed what they needed, and they ran.

Twenty-One

Imogen was discharged back to the house in Upper Grosvenor Street a few days later, but it had been decided that she should travel to Pemberley to stay with Lizzy for a few weeks. She never quite remembered the journey to Derbyshire taking as long as it did today. They were in her father's Range Rover and not the hideous little yellow car that Lizzy always drove, and she struggled to keep her eyes open as they skirted off the M25 towards the north.

When they stopped at the services at Newport Pagnell, she requested a hot chocolate, but it remained untouched and resting in the cupholder. Her sister was sitting in the front, talking to their dad in quietened tones, occasionally leaning over her shoulder and looking at her with a look of concern that she found slightly comforting. She was being taken to Derbyshire to recover – well, that was what they said, but it felt like she was being exiled to the countryside to pay penance for her sins.

Out of the window of the car, the world got hillier and she only woke again when they juddered over the cattle grid and crossed the bridge over the railway line that Fitzwilliam Darcy paid for. As they pulled up to the north front gate, she was bundled out of the car and up the backstairs to the small flat at the top of the house, where she would live with her sister and her niece until she was better.

'Better' – what a strange concept, she thought, lying on the bed in Lizzy's spare room, which had been hastily made up for her. She couldn't explain to anyone why she had done what she did, didn't even want to talk about it in case it brought back those feelings of loneliness and despair. Imogen was not quite twenty-two, but she felt as if she had led so many lives now that she wasn't sure who she was anymore, but she knew that it had been the voice of her sister that had reminded her that life wasn't quite done with her yet and she was curious to see what fate had in store.

For the first few days, she had felt self-conscious in the flat with her niece, who was not much younger than she was, who eyed her with awkward suspicion one minute and a strange pitying look the next. They had bonded over a teen-based foreign-language series on Netflix that they found one night when neither could sleep, and now infuriated Lizzy by swearing at each other in Norwegian and leaving foundation all over the bathroom sink.

Bundled up in hats and gloves, and with cups of hot chocolate from the café, they were walking around the grounds – blowing off the winter cobwebs, as Lizzy called it – and getting to know each other properly. Imogen had had never realised that actual things of importance had happened at Pemberley, apart from Fitzwilliam and Elizabeth, obviously.

"So, what happened to Sophia Darcy?" Imogen asked as they walked down into the Killtime Ravine, "I have never heard about her before."

"No-one really talks about her because of what happens next..." Harriet paused for dramatic effect, pleased to have the attention of a captive audience.

"What happens next?"

"George gets arrested, goes to the Tower, and they don't let anyone visit him, even though Lady Scargill stands under his window singing to him until they nearly arrest her too, but then... they simply let him go."

"Just like that? I thought you were going to say that they cut his head off or something."

She pulled a funny face and then laughed. Harriet thought it was nice to hear her laugh.

"It was much worse than that, at least if they had done that, he would have been a martyr for the cause."

"Why? What did they do?"

Imogen was genuinely interested in what Harriet was telling her and, secretly, she couldn't wait until the house was open, so she could look at all these rooms that she kept mentioning, could immerse herself in the history, could stand where Sophia stood.

"Sophia was like a sister to Princess Mary and Princess Anne, they wrote to each other all the time and loved each other a lot. When Mary became Queen –

"Mary was married to," she tried to remember, "...*William?*"

"Yes, but when William and Mary became King and Queen, they kinda fall out with Anne and send her to her own court out of town, where they let her get on with it. Mary died young with no children, so when William got ill, he recognised Anne as his heir, and it all went tits. For Sophia and her children, anyway."

"What has this got to do with Sophia?"

"Sophia had two children by Anne's dad," Harriet pulled a face. "Firstly, her best friend's kids are her half-brothers – which is pretty gross – but secondly, they are boys and they can inherit the throne, regardless of how illegitimate they are. Worst still, lots of people think that *they* are the rightful heirs, along with their other brother, and not Anne."

"No wonder she got pissed off."

"Anne summoned Sophia to Court and took her children into her own protective custody."

"She took her children? You can't do that!"

"They can and they did. Have you ever wondered why Mr Darcy in 'Pride and Prejudice' is just Mr Darcy and not the Duke of Derbyshire like Grandad is?"

"No. Should I have?"

The air was cold around Pemberley today, with slippery patches of ice underfoot, and Imogen was freezing despite the expensive and fashionable coat. They were walking back up the ravine now, heading towards the gardens and their elegant symmetry.

"Anne didn't punish the family by having George executed or doing anything so obvious, but she did take away the title from them. No more Duke of Derbyshire, merely plain old Mr George Darcy."

"Poor George!"

"They also had an attainder to pay, a huge amount of money - the estate was virtually bankrupt, and we nearly lost Pemberley. It took ages before it was secure again."

"But what happened to Sophia?" Imogen had a face of genuine concern for this once lost but now found relative that she felt oddly akin to.

"Nobody knows," Harriet said with a grand finality. "She vanished."

"Vanished? Just like that?"

"Yes, no-one heard of her again."

"But then, she turned up?"

"Erm... I don't know, no-one does."

"Oh, well that's a shit ending," Imogen said indignantly. "Can you tell me a story with a better one next time?"

"You can find them out for yourself! You can't walk into a room without stepping into some kind of historical drama."

They walked under the garden arches and into the courtyard, where the cloisters gave them the merest hint of protection from the cold.

"Dad never really shares stories from here. I never knew half of this stuff even happened."

"They leave you to discover it yourself – it's much more fun that way. My mum is a bit obsessed with Mabel Darcy, but I love Sophia. She's my favourite because we all know what happened to Mabel, but Sophia is a real mystery. "

Harriet wrapped her arm around Imogen's shoulder, she noticed that she was still painfully thin under the goose feather coat, and whilst she had a superficial appearance of being 'okay' if you saw her from a distance, it was only when you were close that you could see the dry patches on her skin, the bags under her eyes and the scars on her arms that she tried to hide with bracelets.

"Who was Mabel Darcy again?"

"You'll have to go and find out!"

"All of these women, all of these lives… I didn't realise that being Lady Darcy meant there were big shoes to fill."

"We come from a very long line of amazing women – visitors always want to know about Elizabeth and Darcy, but that's just where they start their story. If you look closely, you will see that Darcy women are all made of much stronger stuff."

"If you say so."

"I know so," she said. "See if Paul is working today, he's really good with all of the history stuff. He would love to help you."

"Are you leaving now?"

"Yeah," she said with a curl of the lip, "two hours of A-Level Sociology."

"Could I come with you?"

"To college?"

"To Lambton? I could drive…?"

Imogen looked up at her with hopeful eyes, she was bored at Pemberley. Her life had gone from being at eleven to constantly being at two, and she needed something to fill up the days.

She gave her aunt a meaningful hug, "not today, but college might be a good idea. You should speak to my mum."

"I might do."

"You should. See you later."

Harriet walked off in the direction of the north stairs, leaving Imogen alone in the courtyard. It was eleven o'clock and the house was opening for the day, the large doors at the top of the stone steps being pushed open as the sound of the centuries-old bolts clanged around the walls. Imogen tentatively walked up the stairs, feeling in so many ways like she was walking in the footsteps of history. Was it these steps that

Sophia Darcy had run down in her crackling satin gown, chasing the soldiers as they took her father away? Did Elizabeth Bennet-Darcy, with her fine eyes and rich husband, ever walk up these steps with her head in a book?

She didn't know right now, but she was determined to find out.

Graeme opened the door for her, ushering her in. It was always a privilege to see one of the London Darcys.

"Lady Imogen! Welcome home."

"Home?"

"Darcys always come home to Pemberley, m'lady."

She was sure she remembered his lovely warm voice and friendly face somewhere deep in her memory, but as Imogen walked through the door of the house, she immediately knew that she was where she belonged.

"Yes, I suppose we do."

Benn Williams held the small velvet pouch in his hand, tucked inside the pocket of his shorts. It was something that he had bought that afternoon from a small artisan store on the boardwalk at Venice Beach. November in California was something altogether different, he stood out like a sore thumb in his summer sandals and board shorts whilst the natives were wrapped up in sweaters and Uggs.

There had been a few paparazzi hanging about trying to get pictures, but they got bored once they realised that he wasn't playing their game. He walked up to the small beach house, just off the main drag, which they had rented for the 'views' and which turned out to be a small glimpse of the 'Hollywood' sign if you leaned to the side and squinted.

Rosie was already in the kitchen, blending a mixture of kale, matcha, and spinach and proclaiming it the healthiest thing ever. He liked Rosie Schaffer a lot, she was fun and so Cali that it made him laugh at her pretentiousness. They had first worked together on a film a few years ago called 'Jackson's Bane', which had been terrible and filmed in the worst conditions ever. She had protested to her agent about the lack of Vegan options and was laughed at every day by the Polish catering team, who gave her piles of sauerkraut and beetroot.

"Hey you, where ya been?"

She poured him out a glass of green into a tall glass, he took a slurp and grimaced. It was on the set of 'Jackson's Bane' that Rosie had met Yvette, Benn's younger sister, and they had fallen madly and head over heels in love.

"I went shopping. What do you think of this?"

He tipped the contents of the pouch onto the counter, Rosie picked up the necklace and held it up to the light. The copper pineapple glittered in the bright winter sunshine, it was smooth under her fingers, the chain slippery.

"Is this for Miss Lizzy?" she said conspiratorially.

On his first night in LA, they had all gone out for dinner and she had seen the sparkle return to his eyes, the way his face lit up when he spoke about the crazy aristocrat with the bumblebee shoes who made him laugh at himself. It had been so long since they had heard Benn, who had been so shaken and insecure after his divorce, laughing and joking, and Yvette had shot her a look across the table that she knew meant this was someone special.

"Yeah, do you think she will like it? I wasn't sure, but I remember she told me this story about Mr Darcy and a pineapple – I thought it would be funny."

He was so unsure and nervous about his choice of gift that she walked over and gave him a reassuring hug. Her head rested just under his six-foot frame and, superficially, they made an attractive couple.

"I am certain that she will adore it, why wouldn't she?!"

"Women are strange creatures, Schaffer, you know this better than I do."

Benn was flying home in four days. He was excited to see her, practically counting down the hours, sending voice messages and videos and pictures and words… there were a few hours each night when she was awake and not at work, and he was free from meetings and rehearsals and lunches.

"Is it weird that I'm nervous to see you?"

"Look at that, Henry Jones is nervous to see me." He could hear her smiling down the phone. "Me too, but it's *exciting*."

On the other side of the Atlantic, Benn grinned. It *was* exciting and scary, and wonderful all at the same time.

"You're right, it is. God, Lizzy, I can't wait to see you."

Cuddled up in her pyjamas on the couch, she felt a sudden pang of longing for his face.

"Will you laugh if I tell you I'm counting down the days with eager anticipation?"

"No, not at all, I've been doing the same!" California had lost its charm for him now, and he wanted a bacon butty with HP sauce, a proper cup of tea and Lizzy Darcy snuggling into him. "Have you drawn the sign yet?"

"I've been colouring-in all day, you had better appreciate my efforts."

"And do you think your car will get us all the way to Stow-on-the-Wold?"

"Can't promise that I'm afraid!"

He could feel the bubbles of anticipation dancing across his stomach in waves, couldn't wait to whisk her away to the picture-postcard cottage he owned in the Cotswolds, spending the weekend listening to her laugh, and kissing every inch of her.

1830

Lydia Wickham was never known for her subtlety, in fact it was one of the many reasons why her esteemed brother Charles Bingley very rarely invited her to stay with his family in Dunmarleigh, preferring instead to refer her to Pemberley, which had more rooms and bigger park with which to escape from her and her raucous brood. It had only been two years after the death of Lieutenant George Wickham that his widow had remarried a highly eligible, if older, gentleman of fashion called William Hart.

Darcy had not been sure if Lydia had been motivated by love or by the Hart family fortune, but he approved of the match and did much to secure it for his sister. The family of five, consisting of the posthumously born George Wickham-Hart who was now eight, the three-year-old twins Emma and Eliza, and their parents, were visiting Pemberley for Easter, along with Mr and Mrs Bennet, who were travelling up from Hertfordshire, and the Bingley brood. The visit was planned for three weeks and Elizabeth was delighted that she would be surrounded by her family for this happy time.

William Hart was a good man from a good family, they owned a portion of the Lancashire coalfields on which their fortune was built. He had a handsome and refined air, enjoying the pleasures which music and literature provided, but he was also an overly tall man with a stocky frame and he sometimes felt awkward stomping around the ballrooms of Bath trying fruitlessly to keep up with his beloved, who adored dancing.

He knew that Lydia, desperate and living with any members of her family who would take her, didn't love him when he first proposed, even though he was completely enamoured with her. The many qualities of the former Miss Bennet which frustrated her sisters were ones that he was drawn to, and he loved her lightness and silliness. Even though he knew that she didn't love him, he did all he could to make her want him as a real, true husband – he never wanted to force her or make her feel obliged to him - and it was only after they were wed that William courted his wife and wooed her with ardent desire, treating her as if she were the most precious thing in his life, which she was.

Elizabeth noticed the difference in her sister immediately; she had only seen her fleetingly at family events since her second marriage, but she became aware that rather than being silly, Lydia's vivacious personality was now tempered into sometimes more beatific. She still sparkled, of course, still demanded the attention of everyone in the room, but now it was only for good. During her time as Mrs Hart, Lydia had learned how to play the harp and now delighted everyone with beautiful recitals in the drawing room, playing on the instrument that Darcy had bought Georgiana as a wedding gift. Mrs Bennet, always the biggest supporter of her youngest daughter, now had genuine reason to rave about her talents and advantageous marriage. Darcy would shoot a knowing look at William during these reveries of their mother-in-law and the gentlemen would politely retire to the cosy comfort of the stag parlour for port and cigars and about an hour's peace from Mrs Bennet before she demanded attention.

With the Darcy and Hart children firmly tucked away in the nursery, Elizabeth and Lydia were sitting alone in the grand saloon. The waning sun of early spring was catching the opulent gilded woodwork, seemingly causing the room to glow. The doors to the balcony had been opened to allow fresh air into the room before supper, which was being taken at London time due to their visiting guests. Elizabeth viewed her sister with new eyes. Motherhood suited her, and it was obvious that she revelled in being so adored by her youngsters. Lydia was standing on the balcony, looking over the calm, still lake.

"I want to apologise to you, Lizzy, for being such a vile sister when I was younger," she blurted out.

"Vile?" Elizabeth was confused, "Silly and ridiculous sometimes, but never vile, my dearest Lydia"

Lydia scrunched up her face and shook her head, before taking a seat on the yellow velvet sofa next to her sister.

"I did a terrible thing by running off with Wickham," she whispered. "I was so determined to have him."

"Lydia, nobody blames you for that. You were but fifteen years old and Wickham…"

"Wickham had a terrible reputation. Yes, I know."

"What can you have done that was so terrible? It was foolish and unthinking, but you were taken advantage of."

Lydia looked up at her sister, half petrified to reveal the truth about her trip to Brighton and the ensuing elopement that caused so much aggravation and nearly ruined the reputation of the whole Bennet family.

"It wasn't like that, Lizzy."

"Pray, tell me what happened."

She had never really known the details of what had happened, despite asking Darcy to reveal the secrets of the marriage negotiations that she had taken on the family's behalf. She saw Lydia visibly take a gulp.

"Now Lizzy, if I tell you, you must promise to never reveal this to another soul."

"Lydia, I promise."

"I seduced George," she stated bluntly. "I seduced him one evening when he was drunk on wine and we had been dancing and I went outside with him and we were alone. Then I kissed him."

"A kiss is one thing, Lydia, but that is not a seduction. I think you are blaming yourself for something that Wickham, a man who was thirteen years older than you, could have avoided."

"No! He could not have avoided it, because I made sure that people saw us! Despite his dubious character being known to most of Derbyshire, you must remember how half of us, including Mama, were half in love with Wickham when he was in Meryton, and it was the same in Brighton – everyone loved him, and he was eager to maintain this newfound admiration. He certainly would not have thought about risking it for a poor country girl with no fortune, would he?"

" I do not think that for one minute you should take responsibility for this. You were a child!"

"Oh, la! Lizzy, I think that being Mrs Darcy had taken away some of your cynicism – you are becoming rather like Jane in seeing the good in everyone."

"I simply do not want you to feel remorse over this."

"I feel remorse that dear Wickham, God rest his soul, would have rather signed up for war than spend another day in my household."

"That cannot be true."

"You have always been adored by every man you meet – clever and handsome Elizabeth Bennet. I never had such a luxury, I have always been pointless Lydia, the youngest Bennet who gets drunk on wine and makes every laugh at parties. When I saw how Wickham admired you, I wanted him for myself."

"But, Lydia, that is completely understandable, George was a very charming, very amenable gentleman. But why the subterfuge?"

"I knew he could never marry any one of us, of course, so I decided to force his hand. Mrs Forster knew what my plan was, she told

Wickham that he would have to take me away to Gretna to wed and so we set off that night. I was so scared," she admitted shyly, before rallying, "but thinking about the look on all of your faces when I returned to Longbourn as Mrs George Wickham soon alleviated any fears that I might have had."

Lydia poured them both a cup of tea from the stand at the corner of the room and returned to the sofa, the cups clattering in their saucers.

"So, my plan was working, however, Wickham decided halfway to Scotland that he wasn't sure, that surely some negotiation could be made as no severe improprieties had occurred. He knew that we had nothing, could offer nothing and you know that for George, after growing up here in the splendour of Pemberley, he would never settle for that. We went to London and he contacted a lady of his acquaintance called Mrs Younge who, as you know…"

"Was Georgiana's companion… that's how Darcy found you!"

"They were trying to figure out a way of getting me home with no mention of any scandal, but by this point, it was already too late and half of London already knew that I was living with George Wickham as his wife and there was naught that could be done."

Lydia glanced at the room around her, and then at her sister who was now nearly thirty-four years of age and getting more beautiful each time she saw her. The younger was always jealous of Lizzy, who commandeered the attention of their father and had boundless energy that could be rarely matched. Lydia truly believed that her sister was fearless and when she made the decision to make George Wickham her own, she truly believed that it was something that Lizzy might have done if she had her own gumption and disregard for society's rules.

"What happened at the wedding?"

"Darcy stood up with Wickham, as you know, and Aunt and Uncle Gardiner were there. Even though he didn't want to marry me, and by this point, I didn't want to marry him either, we were too embroiled in the situation to escape it and we had to go ahead." Lydia's voice dipped into a penitent whisper, "he married me to save my reputation and to save yours. For all the damage that Wickham tried to inflict on Darcy by attempting to elope with Georgiana, he truly saw him as his brother. He married me because he knew that Darcy was in love with you and any taint on our family reputation would have severely hindered his being able to make a proposal of marriage, or of you being accepted in Derbyshire society."

Elizabeth took a sip of her tea, it was cold. It was taking her a moment to process this new information about Wickham; she wished that he could have decided on what type of character he had wanted to be.

"Anyway, after we moved to Newcastle it was different. I wasn't clever enough, or funny enough, or witty enough and he was bored of me very quickly. I tried to distract myself with balls and dances and, you will not believe this Lizzy, practising my needlework."

"Practicing your needlework? My, Lydia, you must have needed the distraction."

"I did," she said softly. "He had a mean temper and he lost at the card tables a great deal. When I wrote to you and Jane asking for money, it was mainly to buy food rather than new gowns or anything of merit. We had very little. I know that Darcy gave him a fortune to wed me, at least eight thousand pounds, but it was all gone within the year with nothing to show for it. When they told me that he wasn't coming back, I... I was glad that he was gone. I was sorry that he was dead, but... I was glad that I was free of him."

Elizabeth pulled her sister into a firm embrace and the Bennet sisters sat there for a moment, listening to the soft birdsong traveling across the lake. Outside the smell of magnolia drifted in and Lydia hugged her sister even tighter, feeling as if a massive weight had finally been lifted from her shoulders,

"Look how things turned out," Elizabeth said brightly.

"Yes, I never knew what love would feel like when it finally hit me. I thought it would be like in books – all immediate and sparkling – but this love is so very tangible, so very safe. Friendship, I think, is always a very firm foundation on which to build a marriage and I am so very fortunate to have been given a second chance."

"Well it is clear to me that William loves you a great deal"

"He does," Lydia grinned, "and I love him dearly. Hopefully, this next babe will give him an heir."

"Truly?"

"Yes, truly," she nodded.

"What fantastic news," Elizabeth hugged her sister again and they sat silently for a moment.

"The thing that troubles me though, Lizzy, is this," Lydia said with a mischievous grin. "If I had known that Darcy had already laid his heart at your door, I could have seduced him instead, and of all this I could have been mistress!"

Elizabeth laughed at her sister, who was now dancing about in the grandeur of the saloon, admiring herself in the massive full-length mirror that dominated one wall. She was happy to see that her sister was now settled and saddened that she had not known the full extent of

Lydia's suffering at the hands of Wickham. Even though he had been gone for nearly nine years now, George Wickham would always cast a shadow over Pemberley, because even if his marriage to her sister was to protect her own reputation, she was, unlike Lydia, not convinced that he would have been acting truly altruistically.

When Darcy returned to the room, stinking of cigars and slightly merry, she held him close in a way that she usually only did when they were alone. He was unsure of what was happening or if he was in trouble for something that he wasn't aware of, looking up at him with eyes the colour of cocoa beans, she held his hand in hers and firmly kissed it before leading him through to the dining room where supper was being served.

BENN WILLIAMS AND FAMILY ENJOY DERBYSHIRE COUNTRYSIDE

Shooting for Matthew Wickham's production of Pride and Prejudice wrapped this weekend and Benn Williams took his two daughters with ex-wife, Madeleine Tennant, for a walk around the country estate of Pemberley, which features heavily in the new film. The threesome looked happy and content as they enjoyed a sunset saunter, with Williams sharing a happy family snap on his Instagram page @officialbenn

BOOZY BENN WILLIAMS PARTIES HARD IN LOS ANGELES.

Benn Williams, 42, currently starring as Mr Darcy in the new Jane Austen movie was seen dishing out shots and tacos last night at Barney's Beanery in downtown LA. Williams, in California for talks with Josh Hardman, producer of the Henry Jones series, started the year with divorce proceedings and ended it canoodling with a mysterious redhead.

Tanya: Benn Broke My Heart!

Glamour model, Tanya Banning, got a Tinder surprise when she swiped right on Hollywood hottie, Benn Williams. After talking on the online dating site for a few months, Banning claims that Williams, 42, wined and dined her in the capital after the breakdown of his marriage to Haringey Place star, Madeleine Tennant. Tanya, 23, says 'he took me to the best clubs, and we partied hard before making love in his London penthouse.' But Banning said that Benn binned her off after she asked for him to make a commitment. 'I suppose it would have been too soon, but I really thought he loved me," says the beautiful brunette, 'I only swiped right for heartbreak."

Ooh, Mr Darcy

Dashing Mr Darcy, Benn Williams, was OUT out last night in Las Vegas. Seen at the MGM Grand, Benn was at the tables with fellow Austen alumni, Paxton Marshall-Smith, as they drank and gambled the night away. Looking hot hot hot, DILF Williams was spotted leaving the casino at around 2am slightly worse for wear with his current squeeze, Debra Malone, the flame-haired temptress from hit US show, Afficionados.

War with soon-to-be ex-wife for Williams, as he flaunts new relationship with sexy co-star, Schaffer

It's no secret that former Henry Jones star, Benn Williams adores women – especially his younger co-stars. Recently spotted out in LA with Rosie Schaffer, the cutie who caused his split from actress wife, Madeleine Tennant, it looks as though Benn, 42, has been trying to rekindle the extra-marital flame with his co-star from 'Jackson's Bane' – the raunchy romance that saw the pair indulge in X-rated scenes, that had to be heavily cut before the film was granted a UK release. Could it be that Williams, currently slated as the leading name to star as Gainsma Quince in Jimin Jampol's 'Galaxy of Empires', has fallen for Schaffer? If so, we would love to be a fly on the wall as the battle with ex-wife, Tennant, continues in the divorce courts.

Twenty-Two

Click. Her name flashed up on the screen, accompanied by a picture had taken in the summer. It was his favourite of her. Her hair pulled back, a stupid smile on her face, him in the forefront as he took the selfie next to Mr Darcy's Pond.

"Hello you! Only one day to go!"

There was a silence, followed by the sound of his heart starting to drop to his feet.

"Lizzy? Is everything okay?"

Quiet again, except for the thud of his heart pounding against his chest, pulsing in his fingertips, popping along his skin. She spoke, her voice crackling on the line. It was a bad connection.

"I can't hear you, is everything alright?"
"No, it's really not!"

Her voice was harder than he had ever heard it.

"Tell me, what? I feel like I have done something wrong here."

There was a silence again and then in cold, cutting tones, she sliced through him.
"You said you would stop."
"But... Lizzy..."
"I'm sorry, I can't do this."
The phone clicked off.
Benn was left with silence.
There was already a drink in his hand.

"It's not like he was your boyfriend, I don't understand why you are so bothered," Imogen peeled a glow in the dark star off the sticky sheet of paper and placed it awkwardly on the ceiling. "He was just some guy you were shagging, it doesn't matter how rich and famous they are, they all do it the same way."

"I wasn't...*sleeping* with him."

"Don't worry about it then, it will all be crap anyway, the stuff they write about me in the papers is always utter shit. You have to let it go."

Benn Williams might not have been her boyfriend, but they both had known that something extraordinary was beginning. Now it was gone, fallen through her fingers like the rounders ball she had always failed to catch, and she was staring at empty hands, standing at the far end of the field.

"It's not that easy, Imogen."

"Did you actually like him? Let someone in for once..."

"Imogen, can you shut up for once, *please!*"

"Or was it the fact that he was divorced what really did it for you? I forget that you only tend to sleep with married men." As soon as the words escaped her lips Imogen regretted them

"Don't you *dare* make snide little comments about me or my private life! I have been covering up for you for years!"

Imogen recoiled, back on the defensive, retreating towards the couch; her heartbeat had risen to her throat, pulsing hard, visible to anyone who looked.

"That's what sisters are meant to do... it was alright for you," she sneered. "Being sent away to live in the idyllic English countryside with grandad, who adored you and treated you like a princess." Words were falling out of Imogen's mouth now, a waterfall of hidden resentment. "Everyone loved you and you got to be normal!"

"Normal? There was nothing normal about it all!" Lizzy screeched. "You got to live in France with your mum and dad, being brought up in a -"

"Have you even met my mother? Ever spent more than a few days with her? She has the maternal instincts of a velociraptor," she laughed hysterically. "Sending me away to school when I was four years old – do you know what that's like?" She walked to the window and glanced down at the courtyard below.

"I'm sorry that your-"

"I was so little, Lizzy," her voice was tiny, "so alone."

"I know what that feels like…"

"No," she said, the frustration evident on her face, "You were here tucked up in your special bed that we never hear the end of."

"Imogen, you don't know anything about it."

The younger woman stopped. There was no point in starting a war with her sister. It would be easy to blame her shitty childhood on Lizzy who had been sent to Pemberley to live with Grandad Duke, where she was looked after, and loved. But it wasn't her fault, wasn't anyone's fault really. She had no reason to argue, no axe to grind. Lizzy had always done her best to make her feel cared for, tried hard to make her feel special, but Imogen knew that she was just a lost soul, flailing about and looking for something, anything to grasp onto, and that wasn't anybody's fault except her own.

"You're right," she said, "I'm sorry."

Imogen thought carefully about what she was going to say, she had never seen her sister like this. Usually she was so calm, so unruffled.

"It's okay," she slumped down on the bed. "Carol did a really shitty thing sending you away, you should have come and lived here with me, gone to St David's with Harry, worn a blue polo shirt and your hair in pigtails."

"I liked wearing my hair in pigtails," Imogen admitted, "but it was always regulation French plaits at St Margaret's."

"You were very cute in your little red blazer and straw hat. Harriet was always very jealous of your uniform."

Imogen lay down on the bed next to her sister, and they settled comfortably onto the feather duvet, snuggled against the plump pillows. She was always the strong one, always the one to make things right. She wondered what she could say to make her feel better, she wondered what the words would be.

"Does he know?"

Lizzy turned, "does who know what?"

"Benn," she began, "does Benn know about your mum?"

Lizzy turned sharply, focused on the sticky, plastic star stuck to her finger.

"Lizzy…"

She shook her head, "of course not, what would that achieve?"

"Lots, of course," Imogen cuddled into her sister, stroking her hair, the curls knotted and tangled. "It's okay to let people in, Lizzy. You can tell him why things scare you or make you hurt."

"There would be no point to it."

"I think you're wrong in this instance, I think if he knew he would do all he could to make it better," Imogen pondered the thought in her mind, "and you're in love with him."

"I'm not in with love him," she dismissed.

"Liar."

Imogen turned to look at the synthetic stars too. She could see that her sister's eyes were red and puffy, that her skin was paler than usual, her hair unbrushed, her lips dry.

"Do Darcy fathers always pack their daughters back off to Pemberley when they become too much trouble?"

Lizzy glanced up, her arms folded over her waist. She remembered the conversation in the hallways of the hospital, where Hugh wanted Imogen away from the bad influences and drugs and the partying, where he wanted her safe and cared for. It had never been about sending them away, she knew that it was about sending them home.

"You're never too much trouble, Imo."

"Oh, I am," she rested her chin on Lizzy's shoulder. "Not like you, you always do everything right."

"Well, having a baby at twenty understandably made everyone very proud...especially your mum, if I remember rightly."

Imogen tried to imagine Carol's face when she had heard the news and it made her smile to herself, "but it didn't stop you from doing what you wanted though, did it? You still became a lawyer—"

"A solicitor, and it's not what I wanted to do. I wanted to be an English teacher."

"Still something though, isn't it? I haven't done anything apart from getting my name in the papers for the wrong reasons and become very good at shopping and social media."

The words faded into something that sounded like regret. Lizzy pulled her into the crook of her arm.

"It wasn't your fault, Imogen. We all should have taken more care of you. Especially me."

"You always did. Imagine what it would have been like if I have lived here with you, we would have been like the Three Musketeers, walking home from school for fishfingers and CBBC. Think how much fun my life would have been if I had grown up at Pemberley."

"You have strange ideas of fun. It's five miles to Lambton, so I don't think you would have liked the walk very much. Although I must say I don't envy your life in London at all. I am definitely not a society girl."

Lizzy was always Lady Darcy in Derbyshire, and that was fine. She could pop on her fake pearls, her Cath Kidston scarf – the aristocratic armour that allowed her to play the role in the way that people expected. But in London, at the important black-tie events with the daughters of the friends of her father's where she had to wear a tiara and an evening gown, she always felt inadequate and out of her depth, because they were all fully aware that she was faking it.

She knew that they sniggered as she walked away, mocking her in derisive, well-enunciated tones; their delicate but barbed laughter chiming against their crystal champagne glasses as their expensive heels click-clacked on the marble dancefloor. Lizzy had always been the odd woman with last year's dress and weird accent; a square peg desperately trying to wedge herself into a round hole.

"No-one should ever envy my life. It wasn't how it looked on Instagram," Imogen said. "I was very lonely."

"You always seemed to be having so much fun."

"The internet lies. Newspapers lie. Photos lie," she stated. "I lied. I always told you what a wonderful time I was having."

Lizzy faced her sister, sitting cross-legged on the bed now, holding her hand. She had never wanted to ask this question, but she knew that she wanted to know that answer, however much it might hurt.

"Did you mean to do it?" They both knew what the 'it' was. "Or was it an accident."

Imogen swallowed hard, tried to remember that night, tried to think back to what happened, tried to pull the memories out of her head and into her mouth. But she couldn't. He had been there because she could see him flitting across her mind, and they had gone to Beaufort House because she had seen Percy Wallace and his new girlfriend. She remembered that. And then they had gone back to her flat in Soho, catching an Uber. She fell out of the taxi. There was nothing else. But she knew he had been there because he had phoned the ambulance and occasionally, she saw vivid flashbacks of him bent over her with a worried look on his face.

"I didn't want to die, Lizzy," she said with a tremble in her voice, "I just wanted to feel safe. I suppose I've never felt like I really belonged anywhere."

"Well, you're home now."

"Do you mean it? Can I stay here with you?"

"For as long as you like. You have as much right as I do to be here."

"I do?"

"You're Lady Imogen Darcy," her sister said, "I think you need to remember that."

Imogen had returned to the flat that afternoon after being pandered and flattered and generally made to feel very special indeed. The ladies in the tearoom had presented her with three tiers of cakes and sandwiches, and she could hear the whispers from behind the counter about 'Little Lady Imogen', who used to sing Crocodile Rock and twirl about the tables.   Imogen liked the way that people remembered her, how they had fixed her in their minds as a happy, dancing girl who laughed and sang and span around. She hoped that being back at Pemberley would make her feel like that girl again, would allow her to discover who she was trapped behind this façade of who people expected her to be.

"Is dinner nearly ready?"

"*Tea* will be ready in about ten minutes, you're in the north now, Lady Imogen!"

The flat was warm and toasty, the smoky smell of chipotle pepper exuding from the slow cooker where the chilli con carne for dinner – *tea* - was simmering gently. She started to leaf through some papers in a cardboard box on the coffee table – there was half a box of macarons, and she quietly stole one thinking it wouldn't be missed, and a letter folded up tucked away in the myriad of tissue paper. Curiosity always got the better of Imogen; she was the kind of girl who would purposely seek out hidden Christmas presents, would always slow down on the motorway to look at accident scenes. The writing was loose and flowing, the letter addressed to 'my lovely Lizzy'. Oh, she thought, it was a love letter.

She had never known her sister to date, apart from the on-off extramarital with Matthew who had been an *ever-fix'd mark* upon the Darcy household for as long as she could remember. And then there had been David, who she had met twice in London – her sister gleefully clinging onto the arm of the man who had a haunted look in his eye and a faint mark on his finger where his wedding ring should be. Lizzy had been so happy with him – feasting on the scraps of attention he had thrown her way. Imogen always found it very sad that her sister kept her feelings so close. She guessed it was due to an inherited stiff upper lip.

"Did you steal a macaron?" Lizzy placed a mug of hot tea down on the table.

Imogen grinned guiltily, "I did, they are my favourites." She observed her sister, "he sent these, didn't he?"

Lizzy nodded. She had been so excited to receive the parcel, which had also contained a tiny bee pin that was currently attached to her coat.

It had meant a lot, she had told him, that he remembered these little things. He said that he had missed so much, that he wished he hadn't been going back to LA, but that he would make it up to her when he got back.

"Will you be standing at the gate waiting for me with a sign?" He said it jokingly, but seriously would have loved for her to be standing there with her bee shoes and mischievous smile.

"Only if you promise not to judge my terrible sign-making skills and poor lettering!"

"Of course not, as long as you're there I won't have any issue with your bubble writing. I have to warn you though, Miss Lizzy," he said with mock sternness, "I will be removing my sideburns."

"Oh, no!!" She laughed for the first time in a week, "I might have to rethink this whole thing."

Benn had laughed too, happy to hear the lightness return to her voice, and then in a low growl he said, "you had better not, you cannot even begin to imagine the things I want to do to you."

She had felt herself blush and was glad that he was two hundred miles away, so he couldn't see her face turn pink. "Surely it all depends on the effects of the sideburn removal on whether or not I permit you to do such things," she teased him, matching his low voice with one of her own.

"Do you even know what you are doing to me right now?"

"I could tell you what I want to do to you," she murmured, hiding her face from Kate from the ticket office, who was casually eavesdropping, "but I don't think it would be appropriate, do you?"

She could still hear his laugh.

1858

The paper was slippery, the ink thickened by the cold weather of the winter months and he found that it flowed slowly from the nib of his pen. The office at the front of the house was warm, heated by the fire that spat and crackled, throwing out the scent of woodsmoke and covering the books on the shelves closest to it in a fine layer of dust that was swept away once a day by one of their many housemaids. Over the mantelpiece hung the portrait of his wife that was painted a few months after they wed. He could remember the day so vividly, she had worn a simple yellow dress made from a daintily embroidered muslin that had been part of her wedding trousseau, posing for the Italian artist in the drawing room of their house in Grosvenor Square. He would have gladly paid for a grander selection of gowns but found that his new bride had chosen a modest selection of fabrics and dresses, all of which she looked beautiful in, and all of which he loved taking her out of.

Thinking back to those first heady days of marriage, he could remember the scent of violet and bergamot – it was a fragrance that could immediately take him back to dancing with her on the front lawn, falling about laughing on the soft grass, lying there with her nestled in the crook of his arm looking up at the stars over Pemberley as they twinkled and shone in the night sky. A soft chuckle escaped from him as he continued to write his letter, thinking of those summer afternoons where they drank their fill and danced the dances of their youth on the lawn, much to the hilarity of their children who would watch, laughing and teasing from the balcony.

Fitzwilliam Darcy was an old man now, nearly seventy-eight, and his hands – once firm and full of strength – were mottled with spots of age and wrinkled more than his vanity liked. Even though his fingers were still agile enough to complete the letter, they ached with the fatigue of holding the quill so tightly.

Elizabeth was always waiting for him in the drawing room, reading, or perhaps teaching their granddaughter how to play her instrument most ill, and then they took supper together in the intimacy of the stag parlour as they did every night when not entertaining. He had always been amazed at how much a look from her across the room thrilled him, how he loved to argue and debate with her on issues, still trusted her more than anyone else in the world and those fine eyes still shone brighter than any star in the sky. The Darcys had grown up holding each other's hands – he had been the proud, arrogant gentleman, still fumbling around with insecurity and the weight of the greatest of expectations; she had been the impertinent Hertfordshire Miss whose main defect was to wilfully misunderstand everyone, but together they were an unstoppable force; an ideal match of love and intellect.

There had been many triumphs in their marriage; his foresight to invest in the railway line that now ran across the northern edge of his estate had meant that the family coffers had continued to grow and, more importantly, had resulted in the family Dukedom being reinstated by the young Queen in a simple ceremony that took place with very little pomp at St James's Palace. Darcy smiled when he thought of how his Aunt would have reacted at having to call his wife 'Your Grace'. Lady Catherine De Bourgh was long gone now, but he suspected that the thought of it alone was enough to make her turn in her grave.

Charles and Jane had been gone a while now, passing out of this world within a few months of each other, leaving a family of seven children and twenty grandchildren at the last count; Georgiana, his wonderful sister joined their parents shortly after her fiftieth birthday, she had lived a joy-filled life with Henry, adding five children to their family, including her youngest son, who was named Darcy after his Uncle. Mr Collins had predeceased Mr Bennet, dropping down dead in the middle of a sermon during the Sunday service. His widow Charlotte went on to marry a gentleman recently returned from the navy, kept a happy home in Surrey, and gave birth to three healthy boys. With no other male heirs, the Longbourn entail was nullified, and the house bequeathed to the youngest Darcy boy, Francis, who had always been his grandfather's favourite, reminding him as he did of his second eldest daughter.

Sitting in his leather chair, he found it harder to see the words that he had already written on the paper; he hated how his body was failing him now, his mind was as sharp and alert as it had always been, but he found that he ached more, struggled to walk and drag his old bones around the house that he loved. Outside the snow was getting deeper, covering the circle of lawn in the centre of the forecourt with its obliterating whiteness. Mainly driven by the coldness that was pervading the room as the fire died down to embers, he finished his letter, folded it, sealed it with wax and placed it carefully in his drawer with a grand finality.

He took out his pocket watch, the rounded gold timepiece had been in the family for years; broken and worn, Elizabeth had seen to it that it was repaired as a birthday gift over twenty years ago now. Engraved with the family motto, it now ticked away in the pocket of his waistcoat; measuring its own heartbeat in time with his. Time would allow him a chance to ride up to Cage Hill before dinner despite the weather; the power of his horse enabling him to forget the frailty of his own wretched human condition as it thundered to the summit.

Darcy slowly began his ascent up the north stairs; the cold wind penetrating the draughty house and spiralling up the staircase behind him and he felt icy to his core, unable to shake the chill which was enveloping his body and taking his breath away. He took a moment to admire the portraits, the artefacts and the objects they had lovingly collected in their home; each item on display held a special memory, each portrait was of someone who was loved or had been loved by them. He crossed the landing, the welcoming sight of the grand staircase with the hand-carved balustrade and the ornate plasterwork ceiling with the Darcy family escutcheon dominating the centre. He was taking it all in as if he were viewing Pemberley for the first time; he walked towards the entrance hall, and felt lighter almost weightless, as he bounded down the small staircase and past the picture of Mary Darcy, which was hung there once more.

There was the first fleeting memory of his mother dancing in the hallway as she skipped along, holding his hands in her own, he could hear her gentle tinkling laughter and hear the noisy clack-clack of her pearl necklaces as they bounced up and down around her neck. He could hear his father's voice, quiet but authoritative, teaching him how to play billiards and the gentle thud of the cue ball hitting the red, and in the distance, the sweet trill of his sister Georgiana singing and playing joyfully, loudly for all to hear.

Amidst the music was the joyous sound of children's giggles, Fitzwilliam, James, the loud thumps of youngsters running towards him.

His memories were becoming cloudy in his mind now as if he was desperately trying to remember a dream, but he couldn't quite grasp it in his hands.

A flash of red and gold,
a laugh,
echoing around him now,
twisting past him,

running away,
slipping through his fingers

Elizabeth.

Elizabeth.

Elizabeth.

"I have waited for you, my love," she said, weaving around him, a voice in the air.

"I apologise, Madame, for taking an age to get here."

She was there before him now, her dress was red, her hair twisted and curled as it had been the first time, he ever saw her in a crowded Assembly Hall. If he knew then what he knew now, he would have danced with her all of that night and married her the next.

"It is time for us to dance now, Mr Darcy," she said, taking him by the hand, "are you ready?"

He moved close enough to smell violets and bergamot, in the far distance he could hear music again, a gentle waltz and he pulled her into him and began to lead her around the room until all he could hear was her laughter... and then there was a light... brighter than anything he had ever seen before, and a warmth that filled him from his boots up.

Mabel was waiting in the library for news of her father when Staughton entered, a sad look on his face and Darcy's watch in his hand. They couldn't know that the horse would slip and fall, throwing him from his seat; that as he landed, his skull cracked against the large rock on Cage Hill. The only daughter of Fitzwilliam Darcy would never know that as he took his last breath, he whispered her mother's name.

A Truth Universally Acknowledged...

With her famous family and her gorgeous looks, Lady Imogen Darcy, heiress of Pemberley – the country estate immortalised by Jane Austen – has an active social life, and Instagram account, and doesn't stick to any posh protocol. Imogen – youngest daughter of the Duke of Derbyshire – shares her glamorous lifestyle online, giving us all a taste of how the other half lives. Last month she was pictured at the premiere of the new Henry Jones film, accompanying dishy Marcus Stansfield, who plays Head of MI6 Gilderoy Manwaring, and only last week broke all the rules by posing topless on the balcony of the family villa in France. If we had Lady Imo's lifestyle and bank balance, we would be showing off about it too!

1985

The house was cold, but the little girl with curly hair was too busy playing with her new doll to notice. She was pleased that Grandad Duke had remembered she liked dolls with yellow hair. He had bought her this for her birthday. She was four now. The new dolly was called Jane. The rain was loud outside. Her room was at the very top of the house and sometimes it was scary. She was wearing a pink jumper that was fluffy. The carpet in her bedroom was blue.

Mummy was in the bathroom. She could hear her talking to herself. Mummy did this a lot. Sometimes she was very sad and would cry lots, but today she had been very happy and made Coco Pops for breakfast. She was never usually allowed Coco Pops, but Mummy had danced around the kitchen singing 'wake me up and pour me Coco Pops' to the song on the radio and she had laughed lots. They had leftover birthday cake with cups of sweet, milky tea.

Daddy had gone to work when it was still very dark. She had been sleeping in the middle of them, cuddling up to Mummy who had pulled her close under the heavy duvet. She had wrapped her little finger around Mummy's yellow curl and twisted it. Daddy had kissed her on the head and told her to be good. His beard was scratchy on her head. He smelled like aftershave. The one from the green bottle. Brut. He was wearing his purple tie. She was always good for Mummy, but Mummy sometimes forgot to tell Daddy. Sometimes Mummy forgot lots of things.

She went downstairs in her princess shoes – the best ones with the diamonds on them – they clomped loudly on the wooden steps. Mummy would be cross at the noise. She sat down and took them off. Her socks were pink and had lace around the top. Mummy's favourite record was playing, the one with the blue lady on the front. The carpet was wet in front of the bathroom door and she could hear the water running over the side of the bath.

"Mummy, you have left the water on again, silly."
"Mummy."
"Mummy?"
"Mummy?"

Her feet were wet now.
Something was wrong.
She ran into Mummy's room and climbed back into the bed. She took her socks off and hid under the covers until she felt warm.
The music stopped.

It was dark outside when she woke up, but she could not hear Mummy. Her tummy was rumbling. She slipped out of the bed.
There was water on the bedroom floor now.

Daddy came home with chips, she could smell the vinegar.
Then shouting and noise and blue lights.
Mrs Burrows tucked her Care Bears blanket over her legs, and they sat on the couch watching television.
There were custard creams and hot chocolate, but they didn't taste the same.

There was no Mummy.

Lady Darcy found dead in London home.

The Countess of Berkshire was found dead at the family home in Central London yesterday. Whilst the cause of death is still unknown, it is believed that Patricia Darcy, 29, drowned in the bath, although police confirmed that there were sleeping tablets and vodka at the scene. Elizabeth, the Countess's four-year-old daughter, was in the house alone with the body of her mother until her father, Hugh Darcy, Earl of Berkshire, arrived home around 7pm. Patricia, the granddaughter of Sir Percy Montague and former winner of the prestigious Holstein Prize for Art, married the Earl in 1975. They also have a son, Charles, 8. A spokesperson for the Darcy family said, 'we ask for privacy at this time, understandably the family are devastated by the loss of a wonderful wife and mother

DEBS: I'm so sorry. It's all my fault.

LIZZY: It's okay.

DEBS: It's not okay.

LIZZY: They need someone to make an example of, who better than Lady Darcy?

DEBS: Lizzy…

LIZZY: You need this job. You're good at this job.

DEBS: You do know that it's all a mistake, don't you?

LIZZY: Yes, I don't think for one minute that you're a master embezzler.

DEBS: Thank you, I will speak to them. This is stupid.

LIZZY: It will be alright.

DEBS: I know, everything always is in the end.

LIZZY: Always.

DEBS: Thank you, Lizzy. I don't know how I will ever repay you.

LIZZY: Deb, it's okay.

DEBS: I'll see you afterwards?"

LIZZY: Definitely, you can buy me a caramel latte!

Winchester, Sparrow & Jones   ESTABLISHED 1782

235 HIGH STREET
LAMBTON
DERBYSHIRE
DE42 8PX

STRICTLY PRIVATE & CONFIDENTIAL
To be opened by the Addressee only

Lady E.G. Darcy
c/o Estate Office
Pemberley
Lambton
Derbyshire
DE42 7JG

By recorded delivery and by email: e.g.darcy@pemberleyestates.org.uk

Dear Elizabeth

SUMMARY DISMISSAL FOR GROSS MISCONDUCT

I am writing to you to confirm the outcome of the disciplinary hearing held at the offices of Winchester, Sparrow and Jones on the 22nd April.

Having considered the situation in detail, including representations made by yourself during the hearing, I have reached the conclusion that you are guilty of gross misconduct and consequently I confirm that your employment is terminated without notice and with immediate effect.

According to our records, you have taken 6 days less than your accrued holiday entitlement to the date of termination. Therefore, the Company will pay you a sum in lieu of your holiday together with your final salary payment in accordance with your contract of employment.

Your P45 will be forwarded to you in due course.

Yours sincerely

Harris Jones
Managing Partner
On behalf of Winchester, Sparrow and Jones

1939

Millicent Darcy stood on the roof of the Wyatt tower. It had once housed the senior female servants and the occasional small child belonging to visitors, but now it was mainly used for storage and she had pushed her way past boxes and trunks to reach the highest point of the house, clambering up the spiral staircase in her velvet shoes with the diamante buckle which were once for dancing, but which were now for housework.

The moon was bright, the sky above Pemberley bluer than she had ever remembered it being in September, but it felt bittersweet. War was in the air and the rampage of Adolf Hitler throughout Europe had resulted in an announcement, the tinny reverberation of which had sent shivers down her spine as if each word was full of electricity, charging through her.

They had perched around the wireless in the drawing room, holding hands and smoking cigarettes, before Sybil started crying hysterically and Winston, fully aware of the obligations ahead of him, stared at his mother looking stoic, determined and frightened as hell. He had grown into an overly tall and lumbering man of twenty-two with a crease in his brow that had deepened after years of concentrating on being good enough. His blonde wavy hair tended to frizz out unless carefully attended, and he had a little curl at his forehead which he could never smooth down with Brylcreem no matter how hard he tried.

His mother knew that as a peer of the realm he was far too valuable an asset to be allowed on the frontline and risk capture, but she was also aware of her son's overwhelming need to prove himself. Even though he had been legitimised by an act of Parliament, there was still a feeling of inferiority that ran through Winston and she saw it manifesting itself in an urgent need to overachieve. He had to be the best, the cleverest, the most accomplished; and whilst she knew it for what it was, it appeared to others to be a very unbecoming aristocratic arrogance.

"You don't need to go, Winston," she stared at him from across the room. "I can speak to a number of people to ensure that you don't have to go."

"What? Have me as a pointless figurehead, tramping about in a costume pretending I'm doing something?"

"That's not what I meant, and you know it."

"If they will take me, I will go."

"I was afraid of that."

"Please don't go and leave me here, Winston," Sybil whined. "What if you never come home?"

"You are so dramatic," he pulled her in close and held her tightly. "Look, this might be all over and done within a few months – we don't know, but we have to set an example. People will look to us and we have to be seen to be doing what is right."

Winston reminded her so much of his father sometimes; the vivid memories illuminated with every familiar gesture, each little characteristic a remembrance of the brilliantly bright boy who lay silent in the lonely blood-soaked soil.

Lord Fitzwilliam felt duty-bound to send for Millicent Darcy after the telegram had been received informing him that his eldest son and heir had been killed in action. She had driven the Daimler, twisting and curving on the country roads, to the house near Wakefield that the Fitzwilliam family called home.

Inside the rooms were dark and cavernous, the faded grandeur of a family who had been hit hard by death duties and bad business investments obvious in each decaying, opulent room. Over the marble fireplace, hung a portrait of Mabel – delicate and beautiful in her wedding gown, wearing the Lady Anne necklace that Millicent's mother had remodelled into various pins, brooches, necklaces, and rings; the diamonds and sapphires scattered across the family-like stardust.

On the console table, there was a photograph of the same lady taken in 1907 when Lady Mabel was a shrivelled but proud old woman of eighty-nine, still firmly holding onto life. Millicent had only met her famous great-aunt once when she had been a very young girl, but she remembered how she had jutted out her chin with haughty arrogance, dismissing death as a mere inconvenience. She had done so many great things but was now simply a portrait on the wall, a forgotten face lost to history.

She wondered how the Fitzwilliam family matriarch would have felt about this time, and she was glad she was not alive to see her descendants clad in black - for David, for Henry, and for Rupert – three boys lost to the battlefields of France, three more still out fighting somewhere in the great big nowhere of the trenches. They sat for a moment, drinking tea, talking about Rupert as if he was merely out on the hunt, or simply in town for a visit. Catriona Fitzwilliam, the gentle red-haired Countess of Matlock took a seat beside her. She was sitting closer to her than was socially acceptable, but Millicent appreciated the proximity. There was an envelope. It was buff-coloured and regulation-sized. Millicent immediately recognised the hand.

"This came for you," she said, "it arrived the day after we... It arrived the day after we heard."

Millicent felt the smooth edges of the letter pressed against her palm.

"Have you read it, Aunt Fitzwilliam?"

Catriona shook her head, "it is not addressed to me, so I have not. But... can you let me know if he was alright? There are no more letters waiting for us, this is his very last one."

They both looked down at the ill-written hand, the little doodle of a bird on the reverse. He would not have drawn it seriously, she thought, probably distracted on the line, and now this little absent-minded bird had turned into something especially poignant.

Escaping into the untamed wilderness of the once formal gardens, Millicent hid near the river. She remembered sitting underneath this bridge before, it was where she had once played with Rupert. They had whipped off their tough leather boots and thick woollen stockings and dipped their feet into the water, feeling the current underneath tickling their toes, before they ran back to the house, arriving breathless, barefoot and filthy. It was always worth getting scolded, she thought, as she slipped off her shoes and dipped her stockinged feet in the water. Tentatively she ran her finger under the seal, thinking of how his lips had once touched the paper.

My dearest darling,

How I miss you, how I long to have you next to me once more scolding my terrible penmanship and bad turn of phrase. Your last letter gave me so much joy. I thought my heart would burst with love, my world has become a little brighter, my days over here not as arduous knowing that there will be you and our babe to come home to. I remember when we spoke about marriage and you said that you would not, but this war has made me think that maybe I should ask you again. Say yes, Millicent Darcy, be my wife. Find this ring as a symbol of my unending and complete love for you and for our child, who will be loved beyond measure.

Be safe, my sweet Penny, I love you.

Until we meet again,
Rupert

P.S: we have just heard that the Germans are retreating. We think it's all over.

It is now, she thought sadly as she tipped the ring out from its velvet pouch. It was a silver band with a round, luxurious pearl as the centrepiece. She wondered how it would have looked next to her wedding ring on the wedding day that would never be now, how would it feel as he slipped the platinum band on to her hand in the little church in Lambton, would the lace of her veil have been scratchy, the heady perfume of the lilacs cascading down the aisle. His uniform would be starched and proper and the sunlight would glint off the trim of his epaulette, the hair at the nape of his neck turning into a curl.

Millicent knew that she wasn't the only woman in England with a missing sweetheart, but it didn't stop her heart from shattering into pieces as she sat on the riverbank with his ring on her finger and every dream of them drifting away on the current. She removed the ring gently, tucking it safely back into the soft pouch and then tightly into the pocket of her bag. He had bought her the bag somewhere in France, sending it over with a gentleman called Fothergill-McHeath, who had called on her in London. Rupert had seen the bright blue lining and it had reminded him of dancing with her in the ballroom of Derbyshire House when she had worn the aquamarine dress that matched the colour of his waistcoat. He could still feel them twirling around, he had written, how he had been unaware of anyone but her.

She fell out of her daydream and jolted back to earth, where it took all her strength to maintain a quiet dignity on the riverbank. She wondered how long it would take before her heart realised that he was gone for good.

It was days later when the tears finally came; she had huddled under the covers of the bed in the room that had been his, feeling the world was ending and nothing would ever make sense again. The Countess knocked on the door gently, directing the servant girl with a tea tray to place it on the table, walking over to the bed she gathered the girl into her arms and held her until the dusky blanket of night fell upon the estate.

Catriona noticed the rounding of the belly under the cotton nightgown, the fullness of her bosom; she had birthed eight children and recognised the early signs. She realised that though fate and gunfire had taken three of her sons, God had given them a great gift. She pulled Millicent in closer and whispered to her that everything would be alright, everything was always going to be alright, and they both cried for the loss of Rupert, David, Henry and the millions of other boys who would never make it home.

The last war had been all about loss, but she sensed that this one would be about survival and she needed to do all she could to protect Pemberley and her family's legacy. They volunteered to take in evacuees from the local industrial towns, and the long gallery was filled with lines of small trundle beds ready to be occupied by frightened children who had never seen sheep before, let alone the herds of deer that still roamed over the ancient hunting land. Looking out at the horizon towards the city lights of Manchester, Millicent took a long, hard drag of her cigarette. All they could do now was wait for it to be over; wait to see if they all made it through alive.

She twirled the small pearl ring around on her finger, still wore it as a remembrance of him, a sad memento of a future that never was. She had loved again; the handsome American who had delighted in her for a year before travelling back to Utah and marrying his childhood sweetheart; she had been left with a beautiful daughter who had emerald green eyes and perfect teeth. And there had been other lovers, who had come and gone, passing through life, touching their footprints upon her heart for a short time.

But it would always be Rupert she chose in every lifetime, in every eventuality; and sometimes when the nights were cold, and the moon was high, she could still feel the rough scratch of his moustache on her breast, the smell of leather and cognac ricocheting around the room.

Imogen

Imogen knew that the stories in the papers were always rubbish, and she knew because they had been writing them about her since she was sixteen years old. She was tired of it all now, it was exhausting always trying to be what people expected of you. At first, the attention has been fun. People knew her name, thousands of likes on Instagram, retweets on Twitter, the 'friends', the freebies.

But then people thought they knew you, owned a piece of you. She had found out the hard way that freebies were never free. She had told him no. She had told him no over and over. But he had done it anyway. And no-one had believed her.

I: I need to speak to you
I: I need to know what happened…
I: Please call me
I: This is important
I: I don't understand why you are ignoring me, I don't even know what I have done wrong.
I: Fine.

The sky above Pemberley was never usually this blue, she thought, it was the colour of sapphires, the stars sparkling like encrusted diamonds. Underneath her feet, the sandstone felt cold and rough, like a pumice stone she thought as she delicately tiptoed along the narrow bannister, her years of ballet classes paying off. Lifting her arms high above her head, Imogen felt the cold night breeze flow over her like a baptism of ice. It felt dreamy, almost ethereal; she was a spectral goddess dancing across the rooftops – her sheer floaty gown lifting gently with each gasp of air, before falling in waves across the sky like a parachute squadron.

Imogen stood at the corner of the balustrade – a foot on each side - on the left the pointing Verdigris encrusted figure of Neptune furiously stabbed the heavens with his trident, his lead face incensed and raging for eternity. She laughed out loud at his metallic wrath, the wine she had drunk earlier to numb her emotions finally serving its purpose.

And then she fell.

1649

General George Darcy, a short, stout man with a friendly face, had earned himself a formidable reputation during the tumultuous years of the Civil War as a fierce General and a brave warrior. His courage, valour and sheer determination to succeed had marked him out to the Duke of Newcastle, who had required his support during many key battles in the attempt to defeat the Roundhead army. Oliver Cromwell himself had singled Darcy out and focused some of his attentions to the medieval manor house, which had been targeted during the last few months when it was obvious to all involved that the Royalists were not going to be triumphant.

The family had left England in the first few days of 1649 when it became clear that Charles, the proud uneasy man who tried to force his divine rule upon a tired and bankrupt country would not live long into it. As a man of twenty-two with a young bride, he had sailed from Scarborough to Hamburg, where they were lucky enough to find sanctuary with their fellow exiled natives. He was unsure if he would ever be able to return to the country of his birth or the green hills that he called home.

Mary Darcy, nineteen and two months wed, was hysterical for the most part of the journey. She had married George for the security he had offered, but now she found herself running away with her small dowry of jewels - her mother's ruby ring, a sapphire locket and necklace with a silver clasp, made from three strands of pearls given to a relative by Mary, the Scottish queen, a long time ago.

Her father, Henry Wharton, had fought with Prince Rupert at Marston Moor and died on the battlefield not knowing that his two sons had already suffered a similar fate. Mary's mother, a favourite of the Queen, had sailed for France and safety, leaving her daughter to decide her own destiny. She didn't know this man she called husband, but she did know that he was her only hope of survival in a world that was changing around her and so long as God had joined them together, she would do His bidding.

Maybe it was the cruel whip of the wind against her face that was making her eyes water, or perhaps it was the sheer helplessness she felt, but Mary sat down on the deck – not caring for rank or cold – and began to sob. She sobbed for the situation, for the freezing wind that was making her shiver under her bodice, for everything that had happened. Mary knew that these were selfish sobs because, despite her loss and her grief, she was alive and escaping from the confusion and anger that was now rife in her country.

The war had been brutal for everyone. At Morevale she had seen the worst of times; had seen people die in front of her, from their wounds, from sickness, from the terrible crush of people being thrown together in such horrendous circumstance. Mary had been but a child when the rebellions had begun; her father and brothers off to fight for their King – and continuing to fight even when it became obvious that they were not on the winning side.

They had never recovered the body of her father, that tall, dark-haired man with the hearty laugh and easy charm, but his watch had been returned to her months later by a man who had worked their land in the summers and fought by his side in the battle that had claimed his life. The watch was in her pocket now, keeping time, still constant. She instinctively reached for it and turned it over in her hand, feeling the soft rounded metal, the tremor of each second as it ticked away in time with her own heartbeat.

Sitting here on the deck of a sloop ship, running away to safety was not how she imagined spending her first few months as a newlywed. The ship was called 'Mercurial'. It was smaller than she had imagined it to be, she thought that if she stretched out as wide as she could she would reach both sides, and she didn't know how it would manage to convey them across the vast sea. Mary Darcy had never seen the sea before, except in books and on paintings, it was much colder than she had imagined.

They were travelling to Hamburg, and suddenly she was struck with regret that she did not pay more attention in her classes at the modest manor house where she had grown up. The rounded, brown-haired girl was unsure how life had managed to conspire against her in such a way that she was on a boat in the middle of the North Sea with a man she barely knew, dressed in clothes that she had borrowed from a servant girl. The garments were itchy, her stomach rumbled with hunger and the wind was icy. She had moved onto the deck to try and abate the nausea that had overcome her, but it was no use. Nothing was helping, she feared nothing would again.

'Mistress Darcy?'

Mary raised her head from her knees and looked up. It was George, he looked tired – she supposed he would be, they had ridden through the night after the call came from the neighbouring estate that Parliamentary forces were gathering up their opponents for questioning and almost certain execution.

'Mary, are you alright? I did not know where...where you had...had gone,' he stammered.

For the most part, George managed to keep this childhood habit under control and defeat it, but when he was nervous or worried or scared, it would remerge. He walked over to her, offered his hand and then pulled her up to her feet. His eyes searched for hers and he found them tired and red.

'Have you been weeping?'

He reached inside his jacket – the garment of his steward, Wickham – and handed her a handkerchief. She held the cloth between her fingers – she noticed that it was her own embroidery, one of the few things that she had stitched for him before their engagement. It was their interwoven initials in a bright blue thread.

'You kept it,' she said warmly, a small smile brightened her face.

He nodded, gently taking the handkerchief from her.

'Of course, one always finds a handkerchief most useful for wiping away tears and blotting the noses of beautiful young ladies on the decks of ships."

He pressed the cloth gently to her face and wiped her tears.

'I know you are scared, my love,' he said. 'I know that you are unsure about what the future holds for us, but please know that I will do everything I can to protect you'.

Mary looked at her husband. He was shorter than she remembered – maybe even the same height when she was in her cotton feet, however, he was broad; solid and reliable. She was not sure if she loved him yet, but she trusted him and believed that he would do everything he said he would, he was so wise for such a young man.

It came over her quickly, the sickness, before she even knew, and she vomited on his shoes. George stood silent for a moment, then looked at his wife with a kindly look in his eye and laughed. Despite herself and her embarrassment, she laughed too.

'I think you need something to eat, Mistress Darcy,' he said, as he let the seawater wash the sick from his shoes.

'Will you give me the honour of accompanying you downstairs for supper?'

And with that, they retired into the cramped warmth of the lower deck. As she nursed her aching belly and wiped away the tears from her eyes, Mary Darcy didn't know that it would be eleven years before she would set foot again on English soil, that the regard and gratitude she felt for George Darcy would develop into a deep, respectful love that would envelop her body and soul. Mary would return to England as the mother of three children – with one more yet to arrive in the years following – the house would be rebuilt, brick by brick, stone by stone, George's fervent promise to rebuild resulting in a grand country seat of which she would be the mistress.

With her husband's title restored she would be received in court as the Duchess of Derbyshire, be a close personal friend of Queen Catherine, and treated with more deference and respect than this country girl would have ever hoped. But these things were in the future, and for now, she felt more scared and alone than she had ever felt in her life.

The sky was getting darker now, around her there were shouts of noise in a language she did not understand. Mary Darcy vowed to herself that if she were fortunate enough to survive this and tell her children about it, then she would embellish it as the greatest of adventures. At the end of the storm, just about as far as her eye could see was a clear sky, and she knew that her life would be perfectly wonderful if she could have to courage to chase that small patch of blue.

Twenty-Three

It was February when the roof in the west wing started to leak, the water trickling down the interior walls and causing the wood in the mahogany room to swell and crack. The offices of the HHS also suffered, with three rooms being off-limits due to plaster falling from the ceiling; superficial symptoms of a larger and more dangerous hole in the leaded roof that was threatening the very structure of Pemberley itself.

Joyce had blamed herself for what she saw as a terrible failing, but it was more due to the huge budget required to keep the house in tip-top condition. Matthew Wickham's 'Pride and Prejudice' was slated for a Christmas release, which meant that all the promotional material that they were relying on to drive visitors to the house couldn't be used until at least July. Even though the west wing wasn't as strategically important as other areas of the house, it still housed some keys parts on the visitor trail and was currently closed off to all but the most senior of HHS staff.

She sat in the leather chair in her office at the front of the house with her eyes focused on the spreadsheet on her computer screen. Whatever she thought of, wherever she clicked, there was just simply not enough money to fix this right now, she looked at the small portrait of the formidable family matriarch Mary which hung in the corner of the room.

What would she do? Joyce thought to herself, as the stress of the last few months bubbled to the surface. There was a small knock on the door, she took a breath – inhaling deeply, before dabbing at her eyes with a tissue and then throwing it away quickly.

"Come in," she took a large mouthful of tea from the mug on her desk, it had gone cold and she grimaced as she swallowed.

"Joyce, can I have a word?"

Lizzy Darcy stood at the doorway, dressed in muted tones, her hair scraped back into a tighter than usual bun, and Joyce had noticed that in the last few months she had been a lot flatter than usual. She had been going through the motions, but there had been nothing extra from her. Joyce had watched her walking up into the moorlands every lunchtime, returning a few hours later just before darkness fell. She wondered what was wrong and gestured for her to come in and take a seat.

"Would you like a drink?" Joyce got up from her desk and walked over to the kettle next to the fireplace.

Lizzy took a seat on one of the blue upholstered chairs that she knew used to live in the bright gallery. It was always a strange experience coming into Joyce's office, which had once been Winston's inner sanctuary – where he had prepped her for GCSE's and her A-Levels; where she had found him one evening keeled over and suffering and unable to breathe, the place where the paramedics had rushed in and connected him to machines, where they had lifted him onto a stretcher and taken him away in the ambulance, a feeling of panic in her as she followed the blue lights, racing behind with Staughton in the ancient maroon Jaguar. It was also the room where she had listened to Uncle Jeremy's partner from the firm read out the last will and testament of her beloved grandfather a few months later.

It was always strange to come back in here and see the room looking so different – filled with all the accoutrements required to run a massive estate – but so similar. The walls were still the same colour, the windows still letting in draughts and, if she closed her eyes, she could still smell sugared almonds and cigar smoke.

"I've come in a more official capacity. I think I have something that could help us with the roof."

"Is it half a million pounds in used banknotes fresh from the vault?"

Lizzy had never known how to approach this woman who had poked and prodded and challenged her in every aspect of her life over the past seventeen years. She eyed her caramel highlights, the soft creases around her eyes, the subtly expensive jacket; and then she spoke firmly.

"I know that you don't have the money to fix the roof, and I know we need to fix it. If water is coming in like that, then we need serious repairs..."

"Lady Elizabeth," Joyce started. "I don't need you to tell me how to do my job. The amount of paperwork I had to fill in when your sister fell off the roof was ridiculous, that's time I won't get back."

"She fell a metre and broke her ankle, I'm pretty sure that the only thing really wounded was her pride. This isn't about that though," Lizzy countered, "you need me to help you."

She reached into her bag and pulled out a folder, then another folder inside that folder and then a plastic wallet. In it was a piece of old paper, it was a letter written in faded ink.

"Are you suggesting a treasure hunt again, because last time Steve got sick of pulling kids out of the lake?"

Joyce shot Lizzy a withering look, whilst she appreciated her attempts to help with Pemberley, Lizzy really had no idea what it was like to run a visitor attraction with all the red tape, ramifications and wrangling it entailed.

"Joyce."

She pushed the letter towards her, the script was small but tight; elegant cursive regimentally written across the page. There had always been rumour of the last letter that Darcy had written to his wife, and despite the archivists from Austenation searching the house it had never been found. For once Joyce was silent eyeing the paper on the table, she looked up at Lizzy hesitantly.

"It's the last letter. You found it?"

Lizzy nodded, as Joyce's eyes scoured the letter, speed reading at first and then her eyes going back up the page, absorbing the words that he had written. She had found the letter hidden between the pages of a musty atlas, its seal had been opened but it was still intact.

"Do you know how precious this is?"

Joyce placed the letter down respectfully in the centre of the desk that belonged to the man himself; in all likelihood, this was the room where the letter was written.

"I do know," she nodded. "I have more letters."

"You do? How many?"

"All of them."

"But why did you not tell me?"

"I was saving them for myself," she knew Joyce Hutchinson would never understand her reasons, "I wanted to keep Elizabeth and Darcy and Georgiana and Jane and Lydia all for myself."

"I can understand that," Joyce did, with all of her heart.

"You can?"

"Of course, I can," she passed her a cup of tea. "You're a Darcy. Your family is part of one of the world's most famous love stories. It's completely understandable that you would want to keep some part of it just for yourselves."

Lizzy took a mouthful of the hot, sweet tea, it was exactly the way she liked it. So, Joyce *did* understand.

"But don't you think we owe it to people to tell them that even though Darcy was amazing, he was still flawed... that any man can be a

Mr Darcy if he's the right man for you. Their love was hard and scary, and there are some parts that will break your heart. Love is like that, and I think people forget."

Joyce knew the history of Darcy and Elizabeth, knew the historical evidence, but she didn't feel as if she knew them as people. It was very easy to think of Darcy as a perfect romantic hero, because that was the way he had been written, but there was always much more to him, and Elizabeth was always perfect on the page, but she knew that there had been tragedy too and she wondered how Austen's heroine coped with it.

"Well maybe you should tell people," Joyce said, "show them that no love, no matter how great, is ever perfect. Love isn't perfect, it's about finding someone who sees your flaws and imperfections and loves you anyway."

Lizzy sat down on the chair and picked up Darcy's letter, stared at it carefully for a moment.

"Darcy loved Elizabeth for so many reasons, and he loved her through so much."

She laid the letters out on the table; short notes on pale paper written by Elizabeth, long winding epitaphs from Darcy, giddy ramblings from Lydia, graceful and restrained missives signed by Jane, the beautiful hand of Georgiana, the tight cursive of Mr Bennet. It was the untold story of Elizabeth and Darcy – more than a love story, but the story of a life together.

"I am going to tell people their story – the real story. I've been editing the letters and putting them in some kind of order," Lizzy said, suddenly embarrassed by it all. "Maggie has spoken to Astrid Mulhoon at Austenation, and they are really excited about it. They want to publish it."

Joyce smiled, this was a little ray of hope on a dismal day.

"But what about now? It will take ages for any money from a book to reach us."

Lizzy had never understood why this woman disliked her so much, how she always rejected every suggestion, always dismissed her, possibly thinking that she was silly and frivolous.

"There is this," she took an envelope out of her folder. "It should help with any immediate costs."

Lizzy had never cared for the necklace that had been given to her mother on the birth of Charles, and she knew that whilst the Darcy family traditions and customs were special, Pemberley itself was far more valuable. She sold her Darcy Pearls pendant to a fanatical Austen fan in Utah, who had paid her a ridiculous amount of money for this unique piece of family history.

Joyce opened the thick envelope with steady hands and pulled out a cheque, she looked at it incredulously before walking over to Lizzy and giving her the biggest hug.

"I don't know how you have managed this, Lizzy. How have you managed this??"

"I'm a Darcy. It doesn't matter who owns it, or who lives here, Pemberley runs through my veins."

"Pemberley is magic."

"Yes. It really is."

An understanding passed between them, for now, they were on the same side, fighting the battle against rotting roofs and failing timbers and light damage to protect the place they both loved. "

"Whatever you need us to do, we will do. We're the Darcys of Pemberley, that doesn't ever change."

Joyce spent the rest of the afternoon contacting the HHS Head Office and the engineer, started putting into action the plans that she had arranged in her head when she was praying for a miracle. Lizzy stayed in the office and started to arrange the precious letters on the large round table. Looking over at Joyce, efficient and passionate, she realised what her dad saw in her as she arranged and organised and planned.

"You should call him, you know," she said as nonchalantly as she could whilst making a pot of tea. Joyce turned around sharply from the whiteboard, where she was plotting her schedule.

Joyce shook her head, pushed her glasses up her nose. Lizzy eyed the older woman out of the corner of her vision, as she poured the tea and walked over to hand her a cup. The teacup clinked in the saucer.

"Do you love him?"

"Lizzy, what I feel for your father is of no concern really. Nothing is going to happen from it, we are merely two old friends who spent some time together."

Lizzy sipped her tea, quietly observing the slight flush on Joyce's face, the way she distractedly fiddled with the silver ring on her finger, the way she picked at the skin around her thumb trying to release nervous energy. She noticed it because it was exactly what she did, and she wondered if she had more in common with Joyce than she thought.

"I think you could make each other very happy," she put down her cup in the saucer and placed it on the table. "Don't let your animosity towards me prevent you from having your own happily ever after."

Joyce glanced up quizzically at the younger woman.

"Do you think I don't like you?"

"It's obvious that you don't like me. There's no need to pretend."

Joyce recalled the occasions in the past where she had severely reprimanded Lizzy for her behaviour; the stern, official letters that she had written about her tenancy in the house; the rejection of her offers for help when they were busy, and she suddenly felt a tremendous wave of guilt pass over her.

"I do like you, Lizzy, I admire you a great deal."

"Oh, come off it."

"Seriously, I remember when you first arrived here. You were so small, so scared and so alone." She remembered preparing the room at the end of the corridor for the new resident, hoping that the Elizabethan tester bed with the badly embroidered curtains wouldn't be too scary. "My heart cried out to run over and hug you, this little mass of curls with a sulky lip and a suitcase bigger than she was."

The room was softly lit now, the fire was crackling in the hearth, outside the first snowflakes of the year began to fall on the ground. There was comfortable silence and they took deep gulps of tea and warmed their toes by the fire.

"That day was so scary; I had only ever spent Christmas and Easter here. Winston was so angry-looking, that first night," she glanced at Joyce quickly, before looking away, "I don't even remember going to sleep, I just remember wanting to go home."

"Mrs Reynolds sent me to Lambton the next day to buy some fairy lights to wrap around your bed, and then spent the next three months complaining about them."

They both remembered the very firm and not very fair housekeeper who had worked there since the sixties. Her name wasn't Mrs Reynolds, of course; her real name was Janet Lewis and as far as anyone could imagine she had been born fully formed as an angry, short woman with beady eyes and yielding bosom. She had a heart of gold, tightly hidden in musty layers of starched linen, tied up tightly with cooking string. Her death a few years earlier had left a gaping hole in the heart of the Pemberley family.

"I think I was jealous a little bit. I spent my childhood coming here, and then when I was older, I spent ages cleaning out the plaster in the dining room with a paintbrush at the top of a scaffold or hoovering the tapestries."

"I can remember you doing that. I always thought you were so brave."

"You ran riot throughout the place. Winston always used to say that you shook us all up in a paper bag...and you did, I guess. You're still doing that."

Joyce remembered the ten-year-old running through the halls, barging through the doors, slamming up the stairs – loud, noisy, incorrigible Lizzy. She took her hand, noticing that her normally polished nails were bitten and chipped, and gave it a reassuring squeeze.

"If I was ever mean, or horrible to you, I want you to know that I didn't mean it. Not in the way you think, anyway. You Darcys have a stiff upper lip and when you shout at someone, you mean it. When I shout or scold it's my way of showing affection, ask my boys! I was always trying to protect you; you never really had a mum, not really, and I always wondered what it would be like to have a girl."

Lizzy realised that maybe she had misjudged Joyce Hutchinson and her rules and her guidance and her disapproving glances; that everything she had seen as an affront was actually just kindness and care. Joyce loved Pemberley as much as Lizzy did, they were on the same side.

"Please phone my dad," she said. "He might be Mr Darcy, but I am fairly convinced that he will have no objections to your family or your social standing, despite what you might think. I also think he can look a lot like Colin Firth if he combs his hair the right way..."

Joyce looked hesitant, she had been scared to contact Hugh, everything had started to move so fast and so furiously, but then Imogen had been ill, and it all felt too awkward and she had left it too long.

"Do you think I should?"

"I do."

She studied Lizzy's face; she was tired, saddened by the events of the last few months, exhausted by the drama. She didn't know all the particulars, but there was something do with receipts and expenses claims, Lizzy had been asked to leave the job at the solicitors' firm in Lambton. There had been visits from the Geordie woman who had been tearful, and Lizzy had comforted and hugged; it had been alright in the end, but it had taken a while for it to get there.

And then there had been Benn Williams.

Joyce had got on well with 'Mr Darcy' and he often popped into her office in between takes, stealing Kit-Kats and being friendly and casually flirtatious in a way that would have made her blush if she had been twenty years younger. She had seen the friendship between Benn and Lizzy develop into something she couldn't quite pinpoint, but for a while now there had been nothing and she wondered why.

"What about you," Joyce asked, trying to change the subject.

Lizzy wasn't sure if she was ready to talk to anyone about Benn Williams. Because that feeling… that feeling hadn't gone away. When she thought about the way he looked at her, it sent shivers up and down her spine; remembering the gentle rub of his stubble against her chin, the gentleness of his kiss, the way his body felt when he was laughing and she was holding him close; then there was the way he had comforted her over the phone when she was convinced that her sister wasn't going to make it, how he had stayed up all night listening to her sob never once faltering in his steadfastness, but she had been the one who had ended it and she had done it to protect herself, without thinking that maybe she was the one who needed to save Benn Williams from himself.

"Oh, I'm fine."

They both knew that she wasn't.

1832

Thanks to years of practice, Mabel Anne Darcy was accomplished in a lot of things deemed suitable for a girl of her rank and age. Her singing was delectable, her drawing and painting refined; she could play both the pianoforte and the harp, spoke French and Italian to a high degree of fluency, but she could never quite perfect needlework or anything to do with hats. It was more lack of interest, rather than lack of skill. Ribbons were a curse, and she was happy to leave trimming bonnets to her plump, jovial Bingley cousins, who were frequent visitors to the house in Derbyshire; each visit engineered by Aunt Jane to encourage her in some of the more delicate pursuits.

On the days when the house was packed with giggling girls, Mabel loved to hide away; hidden from view behind the pile of trunks that would loiter at the bottom of the grand staircase as servants hurried about fetching refreshment for the visiting guests. It was here that she would sit with a pile of books – the special kidskin bound tomes of Shakespeare that had come from her grandfather's library at Longbourn, or the smooth leather hardbacks filled with history and science. Later when the house was silent, she would carry the sensually gothic novels of Mrs Radcliffe up to her rooms and read in secret during the dark, deep hours of the night.

She ran her finger up and down the lines of regimented books in the library, each ordered by size and then alphabetically, each book rebound to her father's exacting standards, each manuscript stamped with a tiny golden bull on the spine before it was admitted entry. She picked up a thin, tightly bound novel and flicked through its pages quickly before tucking it into her pocket; with the red leather-bound book carefully stowed away, Mabel danced up the grand staircase, lightly stepping on each of the wide, shallow steps, twirling past the aspidistra that dangled over the edge of the bannisters and saluting General George as she had always done. The deep bellowing tones of Mr Staughton were already echoing around the courtyard as he directed the hordes of servants that were scuttling about the corridors and staircases, and she did her best to keep out of his way and avoid being a nuisance.

Pemberley was busy with people – it was the week of preparation before Lady Anne's Ball, and everywhere there was hustle and bustle and noise. Her father had already ridden out early this morning, pretending that he had urgent business to attend to, when really, he was hiding up in the woods until the cacophony had abated, and her brothers were all away at school leaving Mabel to entertain herself for the most part. It was always so lonely when they were away, and she missed them a great deal.

Fitzwilliam had an easy-going nature and reminded her of their mother. He delighted in anything fun and loved balls, dancing and the company of ladies. He was in his last year at Cambridge, although everyone knew that his real education would come from papa as he learned to run the Darcy estates in their entirety once his formal education was completed.

Francis had been sent to Eton for Michaelmas Half and then returned at least six inches taller than he went. He had always been serious, but school had made him more so, and he stomped around the house with a frown on his face – only deigning to speak to her through gritted teeth, as though her very presence grieved him a great deal. She was grateful when the carriage carried him back from whence he came, and she did not have to avoid his foul moods which settled over Pemberley like a storm cloud.

James had gone to sea as soon as he was old enough and sent her letters from all four corners of the world. She was always thrilled by each missive that she received from him and devoured them immediately, absorbing the tales of faraway lands, lost cities, new cultures, and strange foods. He had left Oxford after only a year of study, and her father had purchased him a commission in the Navy, where he was under the command of a Captain Jenkins from Lyme Regis. Her brother was currently in the East Indies and for her last birthday she had received from him a sparkling hair clip dotted with flowers made from tiny rubies, wrapped up in a thin muslin cloth that smelled deeply of exotic spices and adventure.

Mabel eventually stowed away in her favourite place at the far end of the long gallery, where she could see the smoky haze of Manchester in the distance – the gargantuan Stratton-Darcy cotton mills of Ancoats pumping soot and steam into the atmosphere. Taking out the half-inch wide book, she didn't have to read too far into it to realise that this story was something very close to home. It had begun with the names –

Elizabeth, Jane, Kitty – common names, aye, but Bennet? And then the places – Meryton, Rosings, *Pemberley*… how odd.

Mabel closed the book quickly, her hands holding the red bound novel tightly shut. She flicked back through the smooth paper pages to the front of the novel, then closed it again, then opened it again. She had been enjoying the story very much, and even though she was almost certain that she knew how the narrative would end, she wanted to see how the author arrived at the conclusion.

Elizabeth Darcy was getting ready for dinner when there was a loud knock and her door opened. Mabel was standing in the doorway, her curls half falling out of her ribbons and the green gown crumpled, an expression of confusion upon her face. For the most part, she was the epitome of Fitzwilliam Darcy in the form of a sixteen-year-old girl and was usually a fearsome thing to behold. But tonight, she was softer, understanding, looking at her mother with an almost dreamy expression.

Elizabeth wondered; if her daughter has been a child of Hertfordshire, she has no doubts at all that she would be found roaming the fields each and every day wandering back and forth to Meryton or running down the country lanes; but she was Miss Darcy and the same restrictions which had confined Georgiana were also placed upon Mabel. She was very much a bird in a gilded cage, frantically trying to escape via any means necessary.

She threw herself onto the bed, causing the wood to creak, and Ellen to exit the room with undue haste and a knowing look to her mistress. Elizabeth remained perched at her dresser, continuing her toilette and eyeing the figure lying on the bed.

"Mama," came the sigh. "I need to question you about a novel I came across today in the library."

She removed the book from the pocket of her dress, before placing it on the embroidered coverlet. Elizabeth picked the leather-bound volume up and eyed the spine, she inadvertently raised an eyebrow and an amused smile crossed her lips.

"Why are you smiling?" Mabel folded her arms, looking at her mother questioningly, "this book is all about you! And Papa, of course," her voice dropped to a whisper as if she had discovered a great secret, "and Aunt and Uncle Bingley."

She had read all about how her father had tried to stop the marriage of her favourite Aunt, how he had arranged the marriage of her third favourite Aunt, and how he had loved her mother most ardently, so much in fact that he proposed twice. Elizabeth flicked through the pages of the book, swiftly reading a passage and looking amused as she did so.

"If you have read all of this novel," her eyes questioning her, "tell me, Miss Mabel, which is your favourite part?"

"I like all of the parts, Mama." She picked up the book and flicked through the pages, pulling at her hair, before finding the page she was looking for. "I think Elizabeth Bennet is the most wonderful character in all of English literature."

"I find that I must agree with you on this point," Elizabeth said as she finished pinning her hair. "My favourite part is when she tells Mr Darcy he is the last man on earth that she could ever possibly marry."

Mabel deep sighed again, "ever be *prevailed* upon to marry, Mama." She grabbed the book and turned the pages vigorously until she reached the correct chapter.

"Oh yes," she smiled, "how very foolish of me."

The dinner tonight was particularly important as her father planned to charm the owners of the neighbouring estates, determined to see the building of a railway line for locomotives across the edge of the Darcy lands, needing their consent for it to cross theirs too. Mama was determined to flatter the gentlemen with her wit and impress their wives with her vast array of decadent jewels. She studied her mother, watched as she slid the sapphires onto her to fingers, as she clasped the diamond bracelet around her wrist, as she placed the glinting emerald clip into her hair.

"Mama," the younger woman prodded, "*are* you the Miss Bennet of this story?"

"What is your own opinion of this? Do you believe it to be true?"

"Aye. There are far too many similarities for it to be purely coincidental, and she talks like you do. She has the same *manner*."

"My same *impertinent* manner," she said wryly. "Remember we are not the first obstinate, headstrong girls to live at Pemberley."

"We won't be the last either."

"Indeed! But you see, Mabel, if I were the Miss Bennet of the story, then it may be a very foolish thing indeed to have the story of one's own courtship – hindered by pride and prejudice – lying about for their offspring to read, do you not agree?" Elizabeth rose to her feet, smoothing the soft satin of her gown, "that is if I *were* the Miss Bennet of your story."

She eyed her daughter mischievously before walking out into the bright gallery, the fashionable red walls illuminated by the oil lit chandeliers at each corner, the polished painted faces of their loved ones lining the corridor, the artefacts that her husband had brought back from the Holy Land carefully displayed in glass cabinets that sparkled in the light. Mabel held the book close to her heart and fell back on the bed in her mother's chambers, fully believing herself to have been let into the confidence of a great secret.

The lights were low after dinner when she heard the distant sound of the piano being played less than adequately by her mother, followed by the sound of her father singing and then laughter, so much laughter. She softly stepped down the staircase, peeping into the drawing room, where her mother was sitting at the pianoforte; her father stood to one side turning the page as she fudged and slurred through the hard passages of the work, and he looked at her adoringly, a sparkle in his eyes as she laughed at his off-key singing and forgetting of the words.

Mabel slipped along past the edge of the staircase, and through into the library, placing the book back in its spot on the shelf, ensuring that it was perfectly aligned with the rest of her father's collection. She then returned to the gilt room where her mother stopped playing and called her over with a warm smile, and her father beckoned her towards him, pulling her into the firmest of embraces.

As she stood with the hero and heroine of her story, the daughter of Fitzwilliam Darcy and Elizabeth Bennet realised that, along with her brothers, she was the epilogue to a beautiful tale, one that was still being written.

Hugh

She followed him into the darkness.

"Where are we going?"

"Stop being impatient."

"I'm only being impatient because I'm cold!"

"Well, we're here now," he murmured. "Let me warm you up."

He pulled her in for a kiss, softly at first and then firmer, with more potency. She let him wrap his arms around her, feeling the same tingles from when he had first kissed her that night on the rooftop of the Wyatt tower when the stars had burned in the sky and they had given in to their summer-long flirtation.

Joyce knew that she might get burned by Hugh this time, but at least she would have tried, at least she would have known that what she felt years ago was justified.

"Are you warmer now?" He pushed her fringe away from her face so that he could see her blue eyes in the moonlight.

"Yes."

For the first time in a long time, Joyce felt like she was home as if she had found her missing jigsaw piece. She placed her hand on his cheek, running her thumb along his cheekbone.

"You look the same."

A small smile caused his cheeks to dimple and she was taken immediately back to the hot July afternoon when, hot and sweating, he had recklessly dived into the pond and then pulled her in after him, her shoes sliding down the dry earth of the embankment. She had fallen into the water with a splash, tumbling, frowning, emerging gasping for breath, and he had enfolded her in the warm dampness of his arms, before kissing her slowly and passionately in the cool water.

"Shall we go inside," he said taking her by the hand, "so you can perhaps see me without this flattering glow?"

They were standing outside of a lone cottage on the furthest reaches of the estate, below them, the illuminated outline of Pemberley stood like a beacon in the blackness of the parkland. Inside Paddock

Cottage, the fire was already burning, the comforting smell of pine alight infused the room and the humble stone interior was gently lit with candles.

"I should tell you off for leaving candles burning unattended, you are at serious risk of damaging the property of the Historical House Society."

He looked at her earnestly, looking like the boy she had admired so much, "do you like it?"

"The cottage…"

"You remember?"

"Of course, I do."

She had been in this room a hundred times since then, but at this moment, it was as if she had stepped back in time.

"I never forgot."

"Me neither."

"When I came back from Cambridge, you were gone. I thought I had done something wrong, that you hated me…"

"Hated you? No, that wasn't it."

"Then what?"

"You were the Earl of Berkshire, you needed someone who would know how to be a Duchess. I knew that person wasn't me."

"I think I would have done a better job of matrimony if I had married someone like you."

"You know that wouldn't have worked. There were bigger expectations of the heir to Pemberley. You couldn't have married me. You needed a society heiress with a private school education and a trust fund or a title."

"I found one."

"I know. Your wife was lovely."

"Did you meet her?"

"Only once, she came to Dunmarleigh when she was pregnant with Charles. She was very sweet."

"She was. Lizzy reminds me of her a great deal. They have the same laugh. Patricia was always laughing, I often wonder what I did to make her so unhappy."

"I don't think it was anything you did, I hope you haven't spent all of these years blaming yourself."

Hugh sat down on the stone floor, staring into the fire.

"I truly believe that she did mean to do it, you know. I would never tell the children that, but I think it was intentional. That morning she was so happy, she phoned me at work to tell me that she had been painting with Lizzy. She told me she loved me. The last thing she said to me. I wanted to believe she was getting better, but now I think she was happier because she knew it was nearly all over."

Joyce reached out to him, her fingertips on his arm. She knew loss too, the immediate and devastating loss of a partner, a husband, a friend. It was something she tried not to think about, but the knock on the door just after midnight and the sad-looking couple of WPCs who let her know that Stephen wouldn't be coming home; not just that night but ever, and the two sleeping, unknowing boys in their bunk beds who would go through their lives without a father. She knew what it was like to always wonder.

"We make choices in this life based on what we know right now, we can't possibly know what fate has in store for us."

"But I do know what fate has in store for me," he turned, looking at her, "fate brought me back to you, and I don't want to bugger it up again."

"Hugh…"

"I let you decide for us once, I won't let you do it again."

"What are you saying?"

"Joyce. I'm saying that I love you. I've always loved you, and if you'll have me, I want to love you for a lot longer."

"Well," she said, "that sounds like a brilliant idea."

Hugh grinned, pulling her towards him and kissing her until the candles extinguished one by one.

Sometimes love can become lost, can become hidden, can be love forsaken; but love always has a way of seeping into our bones, finding its way back to us, seeking us out and drawing us back into its orbit.

Twenty-Four

Nearly twelve months after the principal photography on 'Pride and Prejudice' had completed, Matthew Wickham contacted the CEO of Vanquish Pictures and let him know that the final cut was ready for approval. Even though he had accolades and awards, he was always unsure about having to submit the print to the studio – to letting himself be so openly judged by his peers; there was always an underlying insecurity there that he hid with a layer of bravado and noise, attempting to shield the ever-present nervousness that he wasn't quite good enough. He needn't have worried.

Benn Williams was perfect as Darcy, any concerns about his age completely unfounded, and Jenny Graves shone, sparkled and stole every scene she was in as Elizabeth. Pemberley itself looked magnificent – if this doesn't increase visitor numbers for Joyce, then I don't know what will, he thought – and as the rough credits ran Matthew smiled to himself, content that he had done the story and his childhood home justice. As he had worked with his editing team, Matthew had fallen in love with Pemberley all over again, seeing it through new eyes.

"Matthew!"

Linda hovered at the glass door of the corner office suite.

"Cara is on line one for you, are you taking the call?"

He sighed, leaning back in the plush leather chair, waving his hand and rolling his eyes towards Linda who nodded in agreement before returning to her desk in the cubicle outside. They had worked together for eight years and she could anticipate his needs, remind him to take his echinacea, book appointments with his dental hygienist, and bat away soon-to-be ex-wives with a simple click of the telephone switchboard. It was all done with the utmost professionalism, of course, and as a result, Linda Sobreski was one of the highest-paid assistants in Hollywood.

"What do you mean 'he's busy'? Don't bullshit me, Linda, because having lunch at Sugarfish with Benn Williams and his latest conquest is not what I call busy."

Linda stood firm, genuinely fatigued by the almost hourly rants.

"I apologise, Mrs Wickham, would you like to leave a message?"

There was a saccharine tone to her Brooklyn accent that she knew would cause Cara to get even more aggravated than she already was, and it was intentional. For all his demanding ways, fuelled in part by his ego, Linda was irrevocably and totally on Matthew's side and would defend him to the death in any battle, especially when his foe was someone as obnoxiously condescending as Cara Wickham.

"Fuck you, Linda," the voice shrieked in jarring, clipped British tones, before the slamming of the phone down harshly signalled the end of the call.

Linda smiled with the merest hint of smugness, anything she could do to make Cara Wickham's day ever so slightly more unpleasant was worth it.

"What time is the flight to Heathrow?"

He flicked through a pile of post on his desk, the sun was warm despite it being nearly November and he was glad that he would be back in England to feel the change in the seasons. As much as he loved living in LA, the constant heat and unwavering joviality of the natives caused him to long for the content silence of the tube or the pleasantness of unseasonal rainfall where you ended up soaked to the skin.

"Eight o'clock, but there were no transfers to Manchester, so I've booked a car to take you up to Pemberley," Linda confirmed as she handed him a wedge of travel documents. "Tamsin's tickets are in there too."

She raised her eyebrows at him, he looked at her aghast with mock chagrin. Linda hadn't seen Matthew happy in a long time, and whatever this girl was doing for him then she wanted her to keep on doing it. They would be away for a few months now; there was the promotional tour of the film that would be planned by the studio and Linda was looking to her vacation in Hawaii as she handed over the reins to her British counterpart. Matthew threw a few items in his bag, kissed Linda on the cheek and waved her farewell. It was going to be a long few weeks.

Lizzy watched as he hurried across the courtyard in the cold night air and tapped in the code which gave him access to the north staircase. Harriet was already waiting for him at the top of the staircase, eager to see her dad after the long separation. He bowled through the door of the apartment as he always did and plonked himself on the sofa, with

Harriet following behind carrying a bag of doughnuts that he had picked up from the motorway services.

She was always so amazed at how similar they were, the same mannerisms manifesting themselves so clearly now that she saw them both together, the way they both spoke with their mouths full – eager to eat and tell the world a story, how they crossed their legs in the same direction, or placed one arm behind the head and onto the opposite shoulder as they concentrated.

The television was on a low murmur, the lights lowered apart from the gentle glow of the reading lamp that hovered over the couch where she was sitting. He padded softly down the winding wooden staircase, his fingers grazing the rough finish of the wall as it curled into the living room. He had wandered down this staircase so many times; back when they had been children, sneaking up into the forbidden storage area and onto the roof, finding treasures and secrets, and then when they were teenagers; drinking and smoking, hanging over the balustrade laughing. And then on a dark, stormy night, when the wind was howling against the sash windows, rattling through the house like a freight train, he had knocked on her door, could hear Harriet through the wood, scared by the weather and the rumble of the thunder seething ominously across the peaks, and they had sat with her until she slept, before wrapping their arms around each other.

That had been the beginning of part two of their story, the tale that they had been writing since they were small. A story that had now ended.

"Do you wanna brew?"

She nodded, closing her book and following him into the kitchen. He boiled the kettle, warming the pot as she put two slices of bread in the toaster.

"Toast is always a brilliant idea," he agreed, his arm gently grazing the base of her back as he reached into the fridge for the milk and passed her the butter.

"Are you sure you're okay having full-fat butter and not avocado spread," she joked, as he grinned at her pouring the tea.

They walked back into the front room, taking seats on opposite couches, munching on toast and slurping on tea.

"Harriet tells me that the book is doing well," he stated as he brushed toast crumbs from his jumper, crossing his legs as he sat up on the couch.

"Yes," she enthused. "I can't quite believe it…it was a little project, who would have thought it really."

The book of letters – *'Most Ardently – the true story of Darcy and Elizabeth'*- had immediately become a bestseller, remaining at the top of the charts for three months – Lizzy had crafted an amazing narrative out of their letters and the result was a story that was heartbreaking, uplifting, inspiring and ultimately true. Together with Maggie, Joyce had convinced the big bosses at the HHS to allow rare pictures and portraits from the archives to be reproduced within it and the book was filled with images of the Darcy family, including a photograph of elderly Mabel Darcy, which they had found in an auction on eBay and bid on ferociously. There were even rumours that it was going to be turned into a film.

The sales of the book had raised enough money to repair the roof and allowed Paddock Cottage – childhood home of the dastardly George Wickham – to be restored and re-opened on the visitors' trail. The letters from Elizabeth to Jane had somewhat vindicated Wickham, and Maggie had cried happy tears when she read them.

"Proud of you, Lizard," he uttered, draining the last dregs of tea from his mug. "You were always wasted in a law office."

"I'm glad you approve. Maybe it can be your sequel!"

"Let me get this one out of the way first…are you coming to the premiere?"

"I wouldn't miss it for the world," she grabbed her cup and his, gestured that she was making a drink and walked back into the kitchen. "Linda has managed to get me an amazing dress – Stella McCartney!"

There was a rattle of the front door and Imogen walked in, followed by Sam – one of the estate under-gardeners – it was late, and they hadn't been expecting an audience, Sam fumbled a kiss as Imogen turned around quickly, distracted by the noise, and his kiss ended up on her shoulder.

"Erm… hello… didn't expect you to be still here" She walked over to Matthew who rose to greet her, planting an air kiss on her cheek, "thought jet lag would have got you."

"No, but your sister has been plying me with carbs, so my personal trainer will be pissed once I get back home," he looked at Lizzy, who had come back through with more tea, with a cheeky glint in his eye.

"I'll get off now," Sam stammered from the doorway, where he had stood awkward and silent. Imogen walked back to him, ushering him out of the door so that they could say their goodbyes.

Matthew took a seat next to Lizzy on the old red sofa where they had made so many memories and mistakes.

"That seems to be going well," he laughed as he dunked a Rich Tea into his mug.

"She seems happier in Derbyshire, I think. She enrolled herself in college."

"Doing what?"

"Estate Management. I think she's angling for Joyce's job"

"And Farmer Giles?"

"He doesn't have a trust fund or a drug problem, so he isn't her usual type."

"That's not a bad thing."

"Exactly."

Almost on cue, Imogen entered again and looked at them both sheepishly before announcing that she was going to bed.

Matthew watched as Lizzy pottered around the front room; she was happy enough, he thought, but he felt that maybe she had lost a little bit of her sparkle. He thought he knew the reason why. He had seen how devastated Benn had been when Lizzy had called him in LA, had seen how he had thrown himself into dating anyone, everyone; but each woman he had dated, slept with, who knew what with, hadn't made him happy. Not even this one now.

"I had lunch with Benn a few days ago."

He watched her, trying to gauge her reaction. He knew her better than he knew himself sometimes, had spent years reading and judging and trying to second guess what she was feeling. He knew that Benn had contacted Lizzy a lot during the last few days of filming when she had been in London and he had been in Derbyshire, powerless to do anything, and he saw the chemistry between them on film when he had been editing the Netherfield Ball scene.

He had been a little jealous; Lizzy had always been his and his alone, but as he had sat in the air-conditioned comfort of the editing suite with Thelma and Dylan, piecing together the intricate jigsaw of shots, the key pieces of the story, he could see the small glances and looks between his close friend and the mother of his child. They were unnoticeable to anyone else, but he could see the tiny sparks of something there, recognised the way she looked at Benn because it had been the way she used to look at him.

"Who is he with this week?" she said, not wanting to look up, not wanting to acknowledge the way he was looking at her, knowing that he would know exactly how she felt.

"Haven't you heard?"

Lizzy shook her head.

"He's –" Matthew held his breath. "He's seeing Sarah Delancey."

She looked at him nonplussed, "Sarah Delancey?"

"I'm sorry, I thought you knew," he laughed nervously, "I thought we could laugh about what a horrible cow she is."

"Benn is dating Sarah Delancey? What?"

"I didn't say dating. He might just be sleeping with her for all I know."

"It's the same thing... is he okay?"

"It's really not the same thing. But yeah, he's fine. Tired."

"He's not drinking anymore, is he?"

"Not that I know of, but it's nice that you care."

"Just because you don't see someone, it doesn't mean you stop caring about them or wanting them to be okay."

"I know that," he put his arm around her, pulling her in close. "Look, you will be able to talk to him at the premiere, and he will be back at Pemberley for some filming soon."

"Here? Why?"

It would be okay at the premiere because Imogen and Harriet would be there, but she didn't want to have to deal with him *here*. Why did it have to be Sarah Delancey? She could have coped with it being anyone else at all – Rosie Schaffer, Jenny Graves – but Sarah Delancey was not good enough for Benn, wouldn't love him in the way he deserved to be loved, would parade him around like a trophy husband rather than an actual human being. The more that Lizzy thought about it, the more she realised that the feelings she had for Benn Williams, the ones she thought she had buried, were emerging zombie-like from the ground.

"He got asked to do that history programme you like."

"Which one?"

"The one with the woman and the things, the... family one."

"The Story of My Life?"

"Yeah, that's the one. I'm not sure what they have discovered but they asked Joyce to film here. I think it's probably to tie in with the film, but you should ask him about it yourself."

He slipped on his shoes and put on his coat, his driver was still waiting downstairs, and it was only a short trip back to the comfort of the Armitage Arms and the warmth of his girlfriend.

"I don't think so."

"Send him a message. I think he might need it."

"Not if he's busy sticking it in Sarah bloody Delancey he doesn't!"

"Lizzy, you were the one who ended it with him. What did you expect him to do?"

"I..." she couldn't think of anything. The words gone.

"Lizzy, all men are broken pottery... all of us. Benn tried so hard to stick himself back together, but I think he needed you to hold the pieces."

It has been an insurmountable task that she had asked of him, she realised that now, and her heart ached at the thought of him struggling and alone. No wonder he had fallen for the easy, carefree and attentive nature of Sarah, who had known him before, who could love him again in all the ways she knew he liked. There would be no point waiting for temperamental and indecisive Lizzy Darcy who pulled him in close and pushed him away when he could have a media-savvy woman straight away who knew everything to say; who would look good on his arm and be good in his bed. Sarah wasn't a nice person, but at least she was consistent.

"Stop overthinking it, Lizard."

"I'm not," she snapped out of it.

"Yes, you are. Look, this thing with Sarah, it's not serious, trust me on that. I know Benn and this…it's not real."

"How do you know it's not real?"

"Because I saw the way he looked at you."

"I blew it with him, didn't I?"

"I don't think so, but you will never know if you don't ask."

"I hate it when you're right."

"It's not very often. Let me have this one."

They would be good for each other, he thought. He could see them together in his mind's eye and they looked right; Benn and Lizzy, Lizzy and Benn. Matthew knew that there were not many men that he would trust with his oldest friend, the mother of his only daughter, but he knew that Benn was capable of making her happy in ways that he would never have been able to.

He turned the brass lock of the door, walking out into the cold frostiness of the hallway and then down the twisting staircase at the back of the house. The journey was quick, and it was a relief to get in out of the cold night air and into the warm bed; Tamsin pulled his arm over her sleepily as he clambered in and he was asleep before his head hit the pillow. The insomnia that had tormented him for the past fifteen years had finally been defeated with the quick flick of a divorce court lawyer's pen.

Rupert

Colonel Fitzwilliam had never felt cold like this before in July, had never expected that war would be as brutal and as horrific as it was turning out to be. He had been called a hero, but there was nothing heroic about this conflict. Night was falling over the trenches and he could hear the constant noise of thousands of men all beating against each other, all shuffling and freezing and trying to keep their stiff upper lips intact, despite the memories and the visions of the horrors they had already seen.

Rupert had been told that he was a good soldier by his commanding officer, a Trinity man called Fothergill-McHeath who knew his cousin, George Darcy, and wondered why both men were fighting on the front when they could have had comfortable office jobs based in London. Rupert knew though, deep inside, that he wasn't good, he was simply lucky.

He walked through the trench, past 'Piccadilly Circus', 'Regent Street'; it was his last day on the line today, supervising his small brigade of men, although he supposed boys would be more accurate. A young lad called Ernest; supposedly eighteen, but quite obviously no more than fifteen was crouched on the parapet, his skinny legs perched, his head low as he observed No Man's Land. He was changing duty with an older man called Sampson, who had a magnificent moustache and a murderous glare, who hoisted himself up and got into position with a grumble.

As the boy climbed down there was a mild pop as out in the distance a shell fired, they all braced themselves. The bang was loud as it exploded about a mile along the line. The ground shuddered, there were shouts, screams, moans, the sound of help running along the wooden duckboards that lined the ground. Thud thud thud thud.

"Sykes."

"Colonel Fitzwilliam, Sir" he squeaked.

"Are you alright?"

"Yes, sir. Keeping my eye out for the Hun. They are quiet today."

"They won't be for long, Sykes, we're getting near the end now and they know it," he pulled a hard drag from his cigarette.

"Do you think we might be home for Christmas, Sir?"

"If we all pull together, I think they might go to pieces."

"Home for 1918 would be nice."

"It would, Sykes. Just one more Big Push."

"Yes, Sir. One more push."

Private Ernest Sykes stared at the Officer in front of him; he had remembered reading about the heroic Lord Fitzwilliam, who had saved his brigade, fighting mercilessly to provide cover. He had been still in the schoolroom then, but he knew he wanted to enlist, do his duty for King and Country.

Ernest knew that in normal life he would never have known this man in front of him, but the war had a funny way of blurring the lines and he knew he would trust Colonel Fitzwilliam with his life, he knew he would gladly take a bullet for him. He wasn't scared of being killed – that would be a hero's death – but he was terrified of losing an arm or a leg. That would hurt, but dying? No. He wasn't scared of that.

"Is it going to be soon, Sir?"

"Yes, Sykes. Very soon," he was pensive, sad almost, looking out into the distance. "You will be scared, Sykes, and your friends will fall down around you like dominoes."

"I would go back for them, Sir. No man left behind."

"No, you have to keep going – you have to focus on getting to where you are meant to be. Don't ever look down and don't ever turn back."

"Sir."

Rupert fell out of it, it happened sometimes when he forgot who he was.

"I'm sorry, Sykes. Go and get a cup of tea, I'll do the round."

"Yes, Sir," he saluted very formally and trundled off down the line, his uniform too big, his helmet moving from side to side.

Rupert trudged through, only two more hours and they would be relieved. His day had started before dawn and he was tired now, weary. He could feel the cold right through to his bones, could no longer feel his toes, but a few days rest in a billet a few miles back from the line would right it.

He needed a bath and a good shave, and then there would be letters. He wrote letters every night, using pencils to scribble away his thoughts and then folded them all up carefully into the small, regulation envelopes. It had been three months since he had seen her, a splendid few weeks when he had been classed as unfit for duty after a gas attack nearly saw fit to end his life.

There was that luck again.

He had been sent back home to Belgravia, where his mother fussed over him, and Millicent came and read him stories, fed him soup and was generally a delightful creature. He could hear her now, singing away in his head; her voice both a comfort and a curse. He had asked her to marry him before he left for the front nearly three years ago, and she said no. Not because she didn't love him, she said, but because she didn't want him to worry about her when he had bigger things to concentrate on.

Things like staying alive, she had said as she locked the door and slid under the stiff cotton covers with him, showing him how important staying alive should be.

Now there were two reasons to stay alive, he thought with a smile.

The sky lit up with a bang and a fizz and an explosion. He saw Sykes running towards him, shouting, screaming, his arms flailing as he rattled down the line, the tin cup full of hot, brown liquid spilling everywhere.

What a waste of tea, he thought.

Then he heard the screams and felt a thousand stars falling on his skin.

And then there was nothing.

Everything Rupert Fitzwilliam was, or hoped, or dreamed, was gone.

Benn

Benn stood in the sunshine of Santa Monica; he had been in LA for too long now, accustomed to the heat, noticing the drop-in temperature, wrapping himself up in a hoodie and boots even though if it were this hot in England he would be walking around in shorts. Sarah had stopped to buy them ice cream at Soda Jerks, but he continued without her walking down the flight of wooden steps, holding onto the smooth metal of the handrail. The platform was busy with every slice of society folding up yoga mats and chatting amongst themselves as the session finished and he found himself walking against the flow of people, wanting to reach the end of the pier and feel the cool breeze of the Pacific against his face.

Leaning over the balustrade of the pier, he watched the crashing waves of the water below, white horses galloping towards an invisible finish line. He still had the little pineapple in his pocket, still used it as a lucky charm to reassure him when the struggles with his inner demons threatened to take over. Pulling out the tangled chain, he rubbed the links between his fingers, holding it tentatively over the water. It would be easy to drop it, to let it be swallowed by the ocean and disappear forever. But he couldn't do it, not understanding why the copper pineapple was so hard to discard.

"Hey, you're Benn Williams!" A young surfer with an all-over tan and dreadlocks walked past and waved. Benn nodded and smiled. "I like your beard, man. Henry Jones, woohoo!"

Benn had grown his beard again for the role of Oscar Menzies and this time he had been assured by a very expensive stylist called Vogue that it wasn't pubey. He also liked how the beard made him look like every other middle-aged man now, and it was less permanent than the huge breakup tattoos favoured by his contemporaries. They could walk about downtown shopping for groceries holding hands and no-one noticed, and he found that he liked being able to grab a coffee or nip to the bookstore without having to worry about waiting photographers.

Filming 'Lilac' had been strange because when he had imagined it, he had always thought that Lizzy would be there when he had done for the day; and he could take her shopping in Venice or come here to Santa Monica to paddle in the Pacific. But there was no Lizzy, and this was the way it was, and it was okay. It would do. But he wasn't happy, not properly, not deep down in his heart. He was existing. It wasn't that Sarah was a bad person, she just wasn't what he wanted, and he didn't know how long he could pretend she was.

Sarah was sitting at the table with two soft scoops sundaes and coffee. She didn't really like ice cream, or Santa Monica come to think of it. Benn was staying in this grotty little condo in Venice and she had no idea what she was meant to do there. He was over at the end of the pier looking gorgeous and handsome as hell; he really was like a fine wine, getting so much better with age. The sex was great too, she would have to send Madeleine Tennant a bunch of flowers or a Jo Malone gift set because he was so much more giving than he had been at Cambridge, so much more aware of what it took to please a woman, and now he was super-rich and famous too. It would be just like before. Her bag vibrated. Benn's phone.

LIZZY: Wanted to make sure you were okay. Please call me if you are not.

Sarah smirked to herself a little as Benn turned around, smiling as he walked towards her. So, Lizzy Darcy wanted to get herself back into Benn's good books, did she? Too late, she thought, as she deleted the message.

"Did my phone go?" He asked, spooning a mouthful of ice-cream into his mouth.

"Yeah," she said, "crank caller."

@CaliGOirl436 Saw @OfficialBenn on #SantaMonicaPier this afternoon. Looks HAWT. #Spotted #OohMrDarcy **@QueenieCaro** *Is @OfficialBenn dating @LadySDlny Very cosy today on Sunset and Vine*

1837

The house in Norfolk was small. Not in the usual homely way as was the house at Longbourn or even the parsonage in Yorkshire occupied by her Aunt Mary, Uncle Hughes and their little regiment of boys; but small in that it felt confined, each room seeming to get tinier and tinier as she was led to her rooms in the guest suite. Mabel had been shipped to the house with her companion, Mrs Sedgwick, at the beginning of May. Felham Manor was a small estate near the seaside town of Cromer, and it had only been with strict instructions and careful planning that Fitzwilliam Darcy's only daughter had been allowed to travel to the county. Even now the thought of young girls in seaside resorts, with the temptations of fragranced gentlemen and handsome sailors made her father visibly blanche.

The journey had been arduous as they had bounced and bobbed along on the roads that led to the coast, but it was who was waiting at the other end that kept her focused on the weeks ahead. Her brother, James, had been given two months of leave from his commission about the ship HMS Envoy and would be sailing into the quay at Great Yarmouth within the next few days. Mabel had not seen her brother since he joined the navy six years ago; she had been fourteen, merely a girl, and now here she was nearly twenty-one and ready to be presented at court the following season. Likewise, James Horatio Darcy had been twenty – young and eager for adventure – now he would be a hardened sailor of twenty-five.

She wondered if he would have skin the colour of walnuts by now, crinkled and creased by the hot sunshine; would he smell like cinnamon and opium, his uniform scented with the heady fragrances of the ottoman markets, his voice husky with the rum of the Bahamas and the salt of the sea air. Imagining Captain Darcy aboard the ship darting about the Caribbean had given their mother palpitations, but it had given Mabel dreams that she knew were nigh on impossible.

A bell was sounding somewhere in the house, and outside in the hallway, she could hear the Wyndham daughters – three silly fluttery girls with a predilection for fancy dresses and hair that looked like confectionary – running down the corridors. Mabel sighed, rolling her eyes at Eleanor in the mirror, who was dressing her hair in the absence of any ladies' maid being available. Her room was called the Rose Room. It didn't smell like roses, it smelled damp and unaired; the only allusion to its name a small row of plasterwork roses in the cornicing. It was a tiny, dark room, but she must appear grateful.

The family was polite and accommodating, obviously honoured to have her staying with them. She could tell by the way they had paraded their small retinue of servants out on the front steps to greet her as she arrived in the barouche after seven days of travel. Their eldest son, Peter, had made an advantageous match with the youngest daughter of the Earl of Bentick, Maria Framingham, and they were due to marry within the month.

Mabel's mother and father were due to attend, travelling up from the house in Grosvenor Square and back to Pemberley for the summer. They would then collect her from the house of Lord Suffield in Cromer, where James would travel to once he had reached Yarmouth.

"I do not understand why I cannot meet James directly from the ship, Papa," she had whimpered pitifully one evening after dinner before the ladies retired to the drawing room. "It makes the whole visit overly complicated and I do not wish any imposition on the Wyndhams."

"Nonsense," Darcy dismissed her whining with a wave of his hand, it had been a laborious journey from Derbyshire, and he was not of the disposition this evening to launch into a debate with his daughter, however much she may prompt him.

"Papa!"

He pretended he hadn't heard her and rose from the table, Mabel glanced at her mother, who raised an eyebrow and returned back to her conversation with Emily Warner, who glanced over with prying eyes and a meddlesome countenance. She followed him into the hallway, and he turned, a deep sigh escaping from his mouth.

"What is it, Mabel?"

She folded her arms defensively. There had been enough battles with her father recently for her to know well enough that she must always protect herself against attack.

"I know you will disagree, but I feel that as I have been presented…" he started to interrupt her, but she ploughed on, "it would be acceptable for me to meet James in Yarmouth."

"Absolutely not! I do not understand why we are having this discussion once more when I have already made my feelings entirely clear regarding this matter, and when preparations have already been made."

"Papa, you made these plans without consulting me," her voice raised an octave and she could see that his mood was darkening with every word.

"I do not have to consult you, Mabel," the words stabbing the air, "the arrangements will continue as planned, and you will remember your position and your place."

The words were final, a sentence passed in judgment. Darcy disappeared into the smoking room, the door closing firmly behind him. She cried out in frustration and stamped her feet against the marble-tiled floor of the house in Grosvenor Square, before smoothing her gown and joining the ladies in the drawing room with a smile on her face.

"Did your father change his mind," Elizabeth whispered softly to her daughter upon her arrival in the room; out of earshot of Emily Warner and Emma Gerard, whom she knew would be angling for any ounce of gossip from Derbyshire House.

"Of course not," Mabel frowned, "but I have to keep trying."

"Perhaps you don't have to challenge him on everything," she soothed. "Papa has only ever wanted what is best for you."

"Papa seems intent on showing me the world, simply to make me aware of everything that I cannot have."

"Oh Mabel, you do have a tendency for the dramatic," she gestured for them to sit on the pink silk ottoman. "I think you get that from Grandmama."

"Quite possibly, although Aunt Lydia definitely inherited her nerves."

Elizabeth tried to stop a little laugh. Her youngest sister went into mourning for twice the length of time required by polite society after the death of their mother a few years earlier.

"I cannot promise that I will change his mind regarding your visit to Norfolk, but I think perhaps he may be able to be convinced about the plans for next year. I could suggest that you stay with Aunt Fitzwilliam and Uncle Richard until we arrive, I know you are eager to enjoy the society, but I know that Papa always prefers to arrive fashionably late for the start of the season..."

"Thank you, Mama."

Mabel smiled. She had read her mother's story, knew that even though she was Elizabeth Darcy now, that the obstinate Miss Bennet, with her fine eyes and muddy hems, was still hidden underneath the respectable shimmer of silk and sapphires.

"Your father has always liked an argument, so I may as well oblige him this evening."

Elizabeth rose from the ottoman and summoned Staughton to fetch Darcy from the smoking room; she disappeared into the hallway and the low rumble of voices could be heard until, noticing Emily Warner's intrigued expression, Mabel went over to the pianoforte and delighted the guests until her mother returned with a triumphant smile on her face and her father stood defeated in the hallway, before returning exasperatedly to his guests. Fitzwilliam Darcy always found it hard to deny his wife anything and it was a fact that she often used to her advantage.

It was cold tonight, even for Norfolk in May, when the rush of salty air drifted over the fields. Percy Wyndham sat reading in the library after dinner; he did not care for the masculine bravado on display in the Cabinet – the lavish room furnished with pictures and artefacts that his father William had brought back from the Grand Tour, his travelling partners being Fitzwilliam Darcy and a man of lower rank called Wickham, who had died at Waterloo – and so came here to find his next literary conquest. The door creaked open, a flurry of noise and giggles, the ruffle of silk and taffeta, and he saw the Darcy girl standing there, dressed in a gown of blue and silver, breathing a sigh of relief.

She didn't see him, hiding as he was in the corner of the room in the wing-backed chair, and she flounced over the window to gaze out, before huffing and puffing into the book room. He viewed her with great humour; she was a wonderfully fine girl, he thought, with dark hair piled upon her head and a spark hidden behind her eyes. She was clever too; he had heard her debating on the slave trade of the Americas with his father earlier, and then she had played a rather astonishing rondo on the piano, much to the chagrin of his three sisters.

He watched as she dragged the book from its place on the bookshelf and positioned it on the large table, and herself on the comfortable green chair that matched the modern décor of the room.

"I must say, Miss Darcy, your piano playing was exemplary. If you were intending to embarrass each of my sisters in turn, then you did a sterling job."

It was Percy, the second eldest Wyndham, his deep voice burnished with a flattering tone that was obviously well-practiced, living as he did with three sisters of little to no talent to recommend them.

"My apologies to your sisters for the discomfiture that I have unintentionally subjected them to."

"Unintentionally? Miss Mabel, I am not a simpleton. I can see exactly what you were attempting to do…" He walked into the book room, languishing at the door. "Next time you should maybe sing in French too, that would really vex Penelope."

"Would it? For I am more than happy to oblige."

"Almost certainly," he eyed her with curiosity.

The atlas was huge, splayed out now in front of her. She had recognised the gold Pemberley bull on the spine, and inside the hard-woven cover, snagged and faded with age, was the nameplate of her father, his clumsy teenage cursive firmly scrawled denoting ownership.

"Our fathers and a gentleman called Wickham travelled into Egypt and Greece for their Grand Tour, so you should blame Emperor Napoleon for their over-zealous scribblings."

He pointed to the annotations that Darcy had made in his youth; the party had eventually ventured down further into the east than any other Englishmen had before; recovering Greek marbles, Egyptian treasures, and purchasing length of luscious fabrics from the Arabs.

"Wickham? He was my Uncle. My father always spoke kindly of him, but I am fully aware that he was a bit of a scoundrel."

She had listened intently when she was younger, perched on Darcy's knee as he had recounted the tales of his adventures, gripped in wonder and admiration at the exploits of the man she called Papa.

This was the nicest place in the house, away from all the giggling and shrieking about hats and dresses, and how beautiful the new young Queen was, how excited they were to travel to town for the coronation. She blamed her upbringing; a house full of boys was never going to encourage conversation about muslin, and her mother was much happier walking around the parkland than travelling to town to engage their modiste in the preparation of gowns.

"What secret adventures are you planning?"

Mabel closed the book furtively as if she were plotting something forbidden. Percy had been, she found, a quiet port in a storm of noise and they were free to converse easily, given that he was already engaged to a dreary girl from Rutland called Flora, who had a titled father and a dowry of twenty thousand pounds.

"I'm trying to see what route my brother might take on his way back from the Indies," she proclaimed with a confidence he admired. "I'm attempting to calculate when he should return to port."

He walked over to where she was sitting, placing himself comfortably on the chair opposite, turning the atlas around and studying it carefully. Mabel eyed him curiously, he was quite handsome close up, and he smelled like pomade and cologne; he stood about a head taller than her but was a large spread of a man with a smile that filled his whole face.

He smiled often, grinning at her from across the room when she ended up caught in conversation with his mother, or a small wry smile, like the one this evening, when she gave his sisters a thorough drubbing after she had overheard them calling her unfashionable, he had looked at her as if he was terribly amused. She liked the feeling of camaraderie that it gave her, an ally in an enemy camp. He glanced up, she noticed that he had a faint scar above his left eye, she wondered where it was from.

"Surely you have already heard word from your brother regarding his approximate arrival at Yarmouth."

"I have," she muttered. "I am simply impatient to see him."

He observed her carefully; there was a little crease that appeared on her forehead as she concentrated, focusing intently on the map of the continents, the trade routes between the Caribbean and their very own sceptred isle. Percy knew that James Darcy was set to arrive four days hence, mentally he had calculated how long she had left as the family houseguest.

"Do you require me to accompany you to Cromer? I have business there this Thursday week."

She couldn't concentrate when he was so very close, her focus became blurry around the edges.

"I am not aware of any preparations that have been made," she said politely. "You will need to ask your father to speak to my companion."

"Well, that's decided then." Marking out the quickest plot with the sharp brass compass, he wrote down the numbers quickly on the border of the page, "I will take you and your companion to Cromer. From my jottings here, I am fairly sure that your brother will arrive home on time." She checked his sums, and once in agreement with them, she nodded her approval.

Percy got up from his seat, and gently placed his hand on her shoulder, giving it the vaguest hint of a squeeze. He had never touched her before and she felt a jolt run down her spine; it was something that she had not experienced before, and it made her instantly aware of the goosebumps on her arm.

"Once more unto the breach, dear Mabel," he smiled forlornly as he grabbed a book from the shelf and wandered back towards the cackling and laughter emanating from downstairs.

She watched as he stepped out of the book room, waited for the gentle click of the door signalling his departure and finally breathed.

Percy Wyndham made Mabel Darcy feel nervous, and she didn't know why.

The coach clattered along the coast to Cromer; a short distance of two and a half miles. Mrs Sedgwick, sitting next to Percy Wyndham, observed the young pair closely. Mabel had dressed her hair up high upon her head, a cupcake tier of curls adorned with bows and clips – the young girl acting as lady's maid at Felham finally attending to her – and she was wearing the new dress and jacket that had been sent up from London the day before by her mother. It was the deepest emerald green, trimmed with accents of gold and there were little peacocks embroidered into it in a vibrant, blue thread. Eleanor thought that Mabel looked entirely beautiful, and she could tell that the Wyndham boy thought the same and was obviously half in love with her. She glanced over, her charge seemed nervous as she gazed out of the window, fiddling with her kid gloves, constantly opening and closing her purse.

And then there it was; the vast expanse of the water spread out before them – glittering and blue under the May sunshine, Mabel inadvertently rose to her feet, her hands on the edges of the barouche, her face looking outward towards the sea. She had never seen anything so marvellous and declared so with shrieks and giggles, as she turned to him and said that it was so perfectly wonderful.

Percy watched her with delight, Mabel was proving to be something else entirely. He wondered what it would be like to wrap his arms around her as they travelled together in the coach, to hold her hand in his and allay any uncertainties she may have; but he knew that any ideas he had in that respect would come to naught, his engagement to Flora had been publicly announced in The Times and she had already ordered her wedding trousseau. It was all too late.

Elizabeth was excited to see her second eldest son; she was wondering how he must have changed. Darcy was currently reading the paper as best he could in the carriage, he looked stern, the moustache he had grown did not sit comfortably on his face and resulted in him looking constantly angry, and he refused to wear his spectacles, which vexed her greatly. They were both excited to see James again and Elizabeth personally could not wait to have all her children back on dry land and at Pemberley, even if only for a short while. She could smell the saltiness of the air, could hear the gentle caw of the gulls as they flew overhead. Darcy looked up from his paper and smiled at her, before reaching over and taking her hand as the carriage pulled along, the rhythm of hooves clattering against the cobbles as they reached the coast.

The billiard balls clunked against each other and Darcy, firmly ensconced in the house at Cromer, realised that he was losing to his wife. His second eldest son laughed from the corner of the room as he watched his parents battling each other on the smooth green baize.

"Lizzy," he walked around to where she was standing as she studied her next move. "What do you suggest we do about the Wyndham boy."

James rose to his feet, taking a long drag of the cigar, a deep gulp of the port. "It's obvious to anyone concerned that he has a great affection for her, and she for him."

"Obvious to everyone except your sister," Elizabeth said, as she shot for a cannon and missed, "I don't think she even comprehends the idea that her behaviour towards him is inappropriate."

Darcy eyed up his cue ball, hitting it will a firm precision and potting the red.

"How can she fail to see it?"

"Do you mean the affection or the impropriety?"

James was enjoying spending time with the man whose adventurous spirit he had inherited.

"Oh, I don't know!" He snapped, as the ball bounced off the edges of the pocket.

Elizabeth stood with her cue in her hand like an African tribeswoman, "I think both go together, but I don't think Mabel would do anything to purposely cause offence to anyone. She grew up with brothers, she probably regards it as a sisterly affection."

"Mama," James placated. "You are being rather generous in that assertion; my sister is not a fool."

"No," she sighed. "But she is a young woman in love, and people in love do very silly things with little regard for the opinion of others."

"Elizabeth," Darcy turned to face his wife, "she has been walking through town accompanied by a gentleman she is not related to. You cannot compare that to anything else."

"I can compare it to my sister running away to marry without the consent of our father."

"That was different," he dismissed her with a wave of the hand, she hated it when he did that.

"It was the same, Fitzwilliam."

Elizabeth used his Christian name very rarely, only when she was cross or disappointed. He preferred it when she was cross.

"Aunt Lydia ended up marrying Wickham though," James said, downing his port, feeling as if had come home and walked straight into the pages of a dramatic novel.

"At great expense!" Darcy walked over and poured himself a large brandy.

The financial implication of arranging the marriage of Lydia Bennet and George Wickham had cost him dearly, but the money was not the issue with Mabel. Elizabeth leaned over and lined up the ball; striking with precision she scored a cannon, two more points for a win. She looked over at her husband gleefully.

James clapped loudly, "oh well done, Mama!"

Darcy rolled his eyes as his wife placed the cue ball back on the table. He was scared for Mabel; Percy Wyndham was protected by his engagement, his daughter had nothing to protect her but her name. Any hint of impropriety or loss of virtue would mean that despite her dowry and her connections, Mabel would be cut from society, would never find a man to marry. His wife had just potted the winning shot.

"I think we both know what needs to be done, Darcy," Elizabeth placed her hand on his shoulder, and he leaned down and kissed her on the forehead. "We have to separate them as soon as possible before there is further deepening of this affection."

He downed his brandy and then directed his address to his son. The boy who he had thrown up in the air giggling gleefully on the lawn at Pemberley was now a man; made deep golden by the sunshine, he was tall and broad and although his countenance was very much like Darcy's own, he could sense his wife's lightness and humour dappled across the boy's personality like sunshine.

"James," he said firmly. "You will take Mabel back to Pemberley tonight."

"Tonight? But I…"

He had already made plans with a delicious red-haired girl from the inn with a lovely smile and a welcoming bosom.

"Do you concur?"

James clipped his cigar, nodding in agreement. "I will ask Manning to prepare the coach at once."

Elizabeth stood and looked at her husband as James left the room.

"She will hate you for this," she said as held his hand tightly in her own. "Are you prepared for the wrath of Mabel Anne Darcy?"

He sighed, poured himself another brandy.

"She will thank me for it soon enough," he lamented, "when Percy Wyndham is married to another and she only has a faded collection of poems and sketches to look back on."

"I don't think Mabel would succumb to such a flirtation as easily as you think."

"She has filled her head with unrealistic expectations of love, lifted directly from the pages of novels."

"Novels are not a terrible thing, my dear. Our own courtship was hardly typical."

"I was not engaged to another, therein lies the difference" Darcy stood to look out at the dark waves crashing against the beach below. "If only she had met Percy first, I would have no qualms about—"

He was interrupted by the slamming of the door, the screech as Mabel pounded into the room with a face like an incoming storm.

"How dare you decide what is best for me!"

She ran towards him, pounding her fists into his chest. He held her wrists tightly, restrained her, shouted.

"Do you have any idea what you are doing, Mabel?"

"I am following my heart," she shouted back, matching him in tone and volume, "I am doing what you did!"

Elizabeth ran over to try and envelop her daughter in her arms, to calm and soothe her as she had done so many times before but was pushed back.

'You are both hypocrites," the girl screamed. 'You want me to do as you say and not as you did.'

"That was different!"

"How was it different, Papa?"

The loudness of her voice caused Fielding to wince, and the elderly butler retreated to the edges of the room.

"In many ways!"

"Not at all! You know yourself that a marriage to Mama was beneath you. If your father had been alive, he would never have allowed you to marry someone of such inferior rank! At least Percy is of the same sphere, I think you forgot that you were a Darcy when you went to Hertfordshire!"

"Mabel," Elizabeth warned. "You go too far."

"I don't go far enough," she screeched. "Maybe I should go all the way to Scotland and get married where I do not need your consent or approval."

"This is not about my approval!" Darcy roared.

"This is most certainly about your approval!" She spat the words out in anger, "if you loved me then you would want me to be happy! But instead, I have to do as I am bloody well told."

He recoiled at this, everything he did was for his family; to ensure the continuation of their good fortune,

"I do want you to be happy, that is why I am doing this!"

"If you wanted me to be happy, you would let me be with whom I choose!"

It was a battle of wills; each Darcy equally matched, each as determinedly stubborn as the other.

"You cannot be with someone who is promised to another. Has he said he would break the engagement with this girl?" He searched her face for confirmation, finding nothing. "Percy has to marry her. He has no choice."

"There must be a choice, what if he had made me an offer?"

"Has he made you an offer, Mabel?"

She shook her head, bit her lip, "what if he had?"

"Mabel," her mother pressed, "has Mr Wyndham proposed to you?"

She stood there, indignant, the watching, worried eyes of her parents burning into her skin, wondering if they knew.

"Because if he had," her father said, "then it would not be valid. Percy is already betrothed to another. In the eyes of the law, he is already married."

Darcy understood his daughter well enough to know that there was something she had not revealed, but he hoped that this information would help her realise the error of her ways, that the promises of men were not always honourable. He watched her absorb his words, watched the realisation of the situation wash over her. She looked up, studied his face carefully. Mabel was so much like her mother.

"Is there nothing to be done?"

"If there was, I would be offering it to you willingly."

"But surely, Papa, *surely* there is something you could do."

Darcy shook his head as he wiped the tears from her cheek, his heart was breaking for her.

"Please, could I see him once more, just to say goodbye?"

As much as his heart ached for her, he knew that he could not allow her to see the Wyndham boy again.

"I don't think that is wise, but you can send him a letter informing him of your intentions if you wish."

Darcy sat with his daughter on the sofa at the edge of the room, pulling her in close, he held her tightly, stroking her brow, listening to her sobs and protestations.

Mabel and James climbed into the coach as the clock struck ten that night, the roads were smooth, and the sea air was cold on her shoulders. She had left the letter on the dresser, asking her mother to ensure that it was delivered after they had departed. The coach trundled through the narrow streets, the smell of salt and sand clinging to her pelisse. Mabel nestled into her brother's arm and he comforted her with tales of the Caribbean and ships until he could see the faintest hint of a smile on her face.

She knew that leaving Cromer was the best thing, she wasn't one of the silly girls from her books, she was Mabel Darcy and she was aware of her responsibilities to her father and her family. Norfolk had been a glorious escape from Pemberley and Grosvenor Square; she had felt free, uncaged, let herself fall head over heels in love with a man who was practically married to another. It was frivolous and foolish, and it would be her great regret.

It would take a while, James thought, until she overcame this loss, but she would be alright, Darcys always were. His commanding officer said he was like a cat, always landed on his feet, and Mabel was the same. In the meantime, 'The Wyndham Woes', as the brothers Darcy had been referring to it in their correspondence, distracted him from the news he needed to tell his father; all about his life in Port Royal and the Catalan woman with the sweet smile and kind heart, who had made him a papa to three tiny girls who had olive skin, almond-shaped eyes and Spanish that rolled off the tongue.

Percy Wyndham received her words the following afternoon. He had never expected that she would fall in love with him, but she had, kissing him at the end of the wooden jetty in Cromer as the waves crashed at their feet. He had never known that love could feel like this; there had been the wenches at the whorehouse who had pleasured him and make him shudder with delight, and the girls of his youth who had flattered his ego and pleased his eye, but Mabel had been something else entirely and he hadn't understood it, would never understand it now because she was gone, leaving him to his fate.

Twenty-Five

At nine o'clock sharp, the first of the team of polishers and pluckers arrived at their suite in The Dorchester. Lizzy had read once, on the Instagram post of a famous actress, that it took a village to get red carpet ready, and it was true. She had completely underestimated the amount of time it would take, and it was only now, seven hours after they had started, that the Lady Elizabeth, the Lady Imogen, and the Hon. Harriet Darcy were ready to glide into the waiting car to attend the London premiere of Pride and Prejudice.

Lizzy couldn't quite believe that she was looking at her own reflection in the floor-length mirror. The dress had a tight bodice, and pulled in all her wobbly bits, thanks to the amazing sucky-in underwear that she was wearing like a shield. It had little capped sleeves with sequins that looked itchy but were smooth on her skin, and the skirt flared out from her waist, over 10 metres of organza cascading to the floor, embroidered with tiny golden deer.

She had been bronzed and highlighted so that her arms were luminous and toned, and she had no idea what they had done to her face, but she was a real-life Snapchat filter. Her father had pulled some jewels from the deposit box at Coutts, a glittering selection of necklaces and bracelets that had belonged to the women of the Darcy family for his daughters and granddaughter to wear, although Lizzy knew that his main reason for visiting the bank was to carefully collect a very important piece of jewellery.

The Duke of Derbyshire had proposed to the love of his life at Mr Darcy's Pond, up out in the park one dusky summer evening. He had thought about it a lot, wondering if he should even consider asking her to be his wife - he was quite happy to spend his evenings holed up with her in the small cottage on the outskirts of the estate. They had spent nearly nine months doing normal couple things, and she told him off for leaving socks on the living room floor or feeding the dog too many scraps from the table.

He often found himself glancing over at her like a lovelorn schoolboy, and she would look back at him shyly before cracking a tea towel whip on his bum with a carefully timed attack. He hadn't bought a ring, didn't want to present her with something from Tiffany or De Beers, she would consider them too flashy, too much. Instead, he knew that he needed to outwardly declare his devotion with something steeped in the history of the family she loved and which he hoped she would want to be a part of.

The ring he had chosen once belonged to his great grandmother and was as reasonably modest as a piece of Darcy jewellery could be. There was a square emerald at its centre, which was surrounded by smaller diamonds. It was classic and understated, and it suited her perfectly. He hadn't needed to say the words, they had already been hanging unspoken in the air; quietly, carefully and with gentle kisses to his face, Joyce Hutchinson, crying happy tears, accepted his proposal. Their own relationship was now a small, but intrinsic part of the story that Pemberley would continue to weave long after they had gone.

Lizzy hadn't known which jewels to choose; they all seemed so grand and so heavy. In the end, she had chosen a simple hair barrette that had been made from Lady Anne's necklace, the diamonds and sapphires sparkled in the middle of her tamed curls, which were now straightened into the most elegant of up-dos. She stepped softly into the glitter-encrusted shoes and walked into the living room of the Penthouse.

Harriet was dressed in a stunning pink empire cut gown, with a diamante band pulled across her waist, her own curls tied back into a fishtail plait, dotted with tiny pearls throughout, and an antique hair clip from the vault, dotted with tiny rubies in the shapes of flowers entwined into her hair.

"Oh Harriet," Lizzy murmured. "You look absolutely beautiful."

"You too," she walked over and nuzzled herself under her mum's arm, feeling safe and excited and a whole other host of things.

"Woah, watch what you're doing, Lizard – you'll ruin all this hard work!"

Imogen, with her legs long and lean like a baby gazelle, was wearing the highest of Louboutins and a tasselled twenties style dress that had been edged with an iridescent thread, catching the light in the most magnificent of ways. Her hair, now its natural warm blonde, was curled and pinned with a shard of diamonds, and she looked as if Vivienne Westwood had kitted out the cast of Chicago, all Gatsby but with the hint of a hidden dangerous underbelly. It had been a year since she had left London, and she was preparing for a comeback, but it would be different this time. She was clean now; she was in control and she knew deep down in her heart that she would never lose herself again.

Lizzy thought that film premieres would be a lot more glamorous than they turned out to be; whilst she did capture the attention of the press standing awkwardly on the red carpet, they were more interested in real celebrities despite taking a few pictures of the stunning silver gown. The photographers did, however, go wild for Lady Imogen – who hadn't been seen for months – and the barrage of noise and lights was immense. Lizzy felt Harriet's arm on hers and they were all whisked inside by assistants and handlers.

'Lady Elizabeth, what a fabulous dress!' called a busty sparkly orange lady from the other side of the room, as she pushed her way over. "I'm Wendy and I will be pointing you in the right direction for the evening."

She began to lead them over to a sectioned off area, where Harriet recognised a few reality stars and poked Lizzy to draw attention to them being in the presence of actual famous people. There was a loud hum of people as the room began to fill.

"I feel really overdressed," Lizzy said as she swished through the crowd.

"You look amazing, Lizzy," Imogen assured her, squeezing her hand three times.

"It holds over two thousand people, of course," Wendy wittered, "but only a very small percentage of them have anything to do with the film."

"Who are they all then?" Harriet asked.

"Competition winners, regular people who have bought tickets, that kind of thing," Wendy reached another velvet rope, "but you don't have to worry about that."

Despite spending most of her childhood on film sets and fraternising with film stars of varying brightness, Matthew Wickham's daughter got positively starstruck by people from Big Brother or The Only Way Is Essex. Imogen spotted Jonty, the son of the bread billionaire, with whom she had a televised tryst during her brief stint on Babes of Bayswater. She grabbed Harriet's hand and pulled her over to meet him, her niece blushing furiously as they all posed for selfies.

Abandoned by Harriet and Imogen, Lizzy pushed her way to the bar – not an easy thing in a massive dress – and ordered herself a pink gin cocktail, which was conveniently called 'Wet White Shirt'. She was messaging Debs and sipping it through a straw when the roar of applause and cheers from outside caught her attention. Craning her neck over the sea of people, she saw Benn Williams and the honey-blonde, coiffured Lady Sarah Delancey. He was so different – more polished, much more handsome even without the sideburns – wearing a tuxedo and a smile he was completely, totally, every inch the Hollywood star and she felt her stomach do a flip. She was torn between wanting to hide from him whilst at the same time wanting him to acknowledge her. Ordering another cocktail at the bar, she texted Deb for moral support.

DEBS: Just stand there and look fabulous, I've looked online and Sarah Bitchface's dress looks shit.
LIZZY: Hahah, really? Looks alright from here.
DEBS: No. Shit. He doesn't look like he's having any fun.
LIZZY: He hates these things.
DEBS: Lizzy, are you going to speak to him?
LIZZY: If he speaks to me.
DEBS: Don't do that. Speak to him!

"Are you ready to go through now, Lady Elizabeth?"

Wendy magically appeared, gesturing for her to follow her. Lizzy turned her phone off and signed it over to the security staff, who also wanded her before letting her pass through into the auditorium. The screen was playing a phenomenal drone-based advert for Pemberley itself, which was part of the Historical House Society's promotional campaign to capitalise on the film. Directed to her seat, she could hardly take her eyes off the screen as amazing sweeping shots of the estate were shown on the screen, accompanied by a soaring, bespoke soundtrack. She never forgot how special her ancestral home was, but sometimes she needed reminding of how vast and varied the whole estate was.

As she was finding her seat, marked 'Lady Elizabeth Darcy' she noticed the polished, highlighted and impossibly tiny figure of Sarah Delancey moving down the aisle. She glanced down quickly at the seats either side of her own – on her left was 'Harriet Darcy' and on the right, the seat next to her was marked with a sign – 'Benn Williams'.

"Lady Sarah," she said, in her Lady Darcy accent. "Long time no see, how are you?"

"Hello Lady Elizabeth," Sarah said, as she squeezed past her. "Nice dress. Last season?"

"Oh, don't be ridiculous, Lady Delancey," Imogen interrupted, "you know as well as I that Lizzy's dress is bespoke."

"It's definitely something."

"It's definitely fabulous, and you're simply jealous because your dress is clearly from *Whistles*," Imogen had no intention of letting Sarah Delancey bully her sister.

"It may be off the rack, but it's the same one that the Duchess of Cambridge wore at Ascot, actually."

"Oh, it's hideous *and* second-hand? I didn't know that you had fallen on such hard times, Lady Delancey."

Sarah positioned herself in Benn's seat, angled herself towards Lizzy.

"Hard times? Oh yes, because I'm the one who has been sent packing up to Derbyshire for the duration, Imogen."

"At least *our* ancestral home is still a home where one can be sent for respite. I imagine it's impossible for you to achieve any kind of rest or relaxation at… what do we call Lancingham Park now? Oh yes, Mr Fizz's Fun World and Menagerie."

Both women stared at each other, like two warring lionesses on the savannah. Sarah's face was as red as her dress.

"Okay, let's stop this," Lizzy tried to stop this escalating before it all ended up on Twitter. "Sarah, you look beautiful as always, and I really love your dress."

"Benn thought so earlier this evening too. Although, I must admit he much preferred it when I wasn't wearing a dress at all."

"Pardon?"

"You heard what I said, Lady Darcy," she stood and moved to her own seat, "keep your hands and text messages away from my boyfriend. There's a good girl."

The lights began to lower as Matthew, Benn, and Jenny appeared on the stage to introduce the film. Imogen leaned over and tapped her on the arm, she turned sharply.

"What the fuck was that about?" Imogen mouthed, as Matthew announced the start of the film.

"I have no idea," she mouthed back, with a roll of her eyes and a bright smile

As the film began, he quickly walked down the aisle, gently excusing himself past those already seated, Harriet and Imogen jokingly tutted loudly at him and he grinned at them both. Lizzy had to stand to let him past her metres of organza. He squeezed past her, avoiding her eye, he was so close that she could smell his aftershave, could smell the faint tinge of alcohol on his breath.

Sitting in the seat next to her, he tried to avoid all bodily contact, as if she were a crazed fan that he didn't want to encourage. At one point his finger had accidentally grazed hers, and she sensed that little spark again. It was small but powerful, and she knew that he felt it too because he moved his hand away far too quickly.

1940

The young boy looked up at her with eyes as wide as saucers, he couldn't have been much more than seven, dressed in his smart shorts and a cream hand-knitted jumper with a red stripe at the bottom, he scratched the back of his leg with the sharp buckle of his shoe and instead of relieving his itch, it had just caused a scratch which hurt more than the itch had itched. He had his hands in his pockets, holding tightly to a small, polished pebble that his mother had given to him off the beach that morning as the sun was rising. She had smelled like toasted almonds and cigarettes, and the faint scent of perfume infused in the comforting blue jumper that she had been wearing as she hugged him tightly in their house on Fleetwood Road.

Earlier that day forty-seven children had marched across St Pancras Station with a banner emblazoned with the crest of Earls Hall school. They had been handed two sticks of barley sugar for the adventure – it was always called an adventure – and it was only as the train was pulling away that they realised their parents were crying as they waved goodbye.

"Can you play cricket? Your jumper looks like one my son used to wear when he was at school."

He shook his head quickly, his hands nervous as he picked the skin around his fingers. The lady in the black suit spoke funny, he thought. She sounded like the woman off the wireless who introduced the songs his mother sang to when she thought nobody was about. He nervously looked around the room, hearing the ominous tick of the huge clock at the opposite end. The room was cold, even in September and he wished that the large fireplace was lit, although it was so big that he suspected the heat would be immense. His attention moved back to the lady in front of him, he had noticed her hair first; had never seen a lady with such yellow hair, curled on top of her head, her red lips pursed as she continued to question him.

"Well, young man, as you do not play cricket, would you like to learn?"

He nodded quickly, as she wrote his answer down on the precisely cut, official-looking card; the kind that had been neatly printed the year before in preparation for this very event.

"And what is your name" she smiled kindly. "I can't very well call you 27486 for the duration, can I?"

She said something under her breath to the round-faced lady sitting next to her, and he was fascinated by the scarf she was wearing, it was made from an animal he didn't know and the cold dead eyes of whatever it was stared at him with unseeing eyes. He had never seen one of those in Southend, but then again, he had never seen a house this big back home in Essex either.

"I'm Thomas Bingley, m'lady," he said in a small voice.

"Bingley, eh? Well, that's a name I think we will remember," she chuckled to her friend.

He smiled wanly, not understanding the joke.

"Right Master Bingley," she said in a very official voice. "You can give your things to Miss Blake here and follow Peter to the parlour for some supper."

The round-faced lady with the ginger hair took his suitcase from him, but he was reluctant to give up his bear. She reached for it slowly, taking it from him gently.

"Don't worry, Thomas," her voice was kind. "I'll look after him for you until you get back from your supper."

The twelve children billeted to Pemberley were accompanied by their schoolmaster, a broad, handsome gentleman called Jonathan Sykes. He originally hailed from Preston but had moved to Southend to be with a woman he didn't end up marrying. He had been seriously injured in the last war and was consequently excused from service the second time around, wearing a patch to cover the hole where his eye once was, the residual scars streaking across the right-hand side of his face like a roadmap.

Millicent discovered that he was good at cricket and had studied at Brasenose College with her brother, George. They shared memories of their lost companion, wondering what he would be doing now. She told him about the death of Albert, and he shared the story of his own brother, Ernest, who had signed up at fifteen and broken their mother's heart when he returned with only one leg. Mr Sykes and Lady Darcy became firm friends, talking about anything and everything as they worked the grounds, digging up the intricate sixteenth-century flowerbeds to plant potatoes and carrots, and smoking like chimneys.

Hitler's bombs failed to materialise, and by the summer of 1940, most of the children had been summoned back home by their parents. Only two boisterous chattery girls, Laura and Charlotte Jones, remained, along with Thomas Bingley. He was getting good at cricket now and could either be found in the grounds practising or in the library, absorbing as much information as he could, as he dusted the books as part of his daily chores, lining up the Pemberley bulls in a row.

Mrs Reynolds, observing the Jones' girls making the fire, scolded them for constantly chattering and not concentrating on their work. 'If thou don't shut thee rattle. I'll belt thee tabs!' she bellowed in the strong Derbyshire accent that she only ever used in front of them and never in front of Lady Millicent.

The news of The Blitz reached Pemberley in dribs and drabs, for the most part, they were sheltered away in the grounds and it was only occasionally that they heard the faint drone of bombers overhead making their way to Manchester or Liverpool. Then the casualties started, and the three Pemberley evacuees were moved to the Wyatt Tower, where Mrs Reynolds stood guard over their small rooms at the top of the house, the beds in the long gallery filled by the wounded young men who were shipped in from the battlefields of France to the makeshift military hospital at Pemberley with alarming regularity.

Thomas often found Lady Darcy in her study – the compact panelled room that adjoined her bedroom - she was often tired after so much organising and planning, and he would sneak down to the kitchen to bring her tea and a biscuit, quietly knocking on the door before he entered. Sometimes she would ask him to join her and they would put a record on the gramophone, dancing around the small room as she lit a cigarette whilst pulling him into a twirl.

Her hair wasn't as yellow now, he noticed, and small flecks of silver were pushed back behind her ears, but she still wore red lipstick and smelled like his mother.

Twenty-Six

His girlfriend had left early, plagued by the noise and the raucous dancing, blaming a headache for her early departure, but he knew it was because he had been distracted and vague, not paying enough attention to inane conversations she was dragging him into. He had always known that Sarah Delancey had purposely reappeared in his life, that there was nothing coincidental or destined about meeting her in the Tesco in Clapham. She had *never* shopped in Tesco before, didn't really venture south of the river if she could help it, but he was lonely, aching with a longing that he couldn't quite explain. Sarah might not have filled the gaping void within him, but she was helping him forget it existed.

He knew that Lizzy was going to be at the Premiere. Harriet would never have let her not attend, and they were all in attendance, the three Darcy women, laughing and sparkling and charming everyone. He was happy to see that Imogen was back to herself, had noticed how grown up Harriet was.

The after-party, on the roof terrace of a trendy hotel in Shoreditch, was hot and busy, with a constant push and pull of people talking and congratulating themselves. The music – an eclectic mix of 60s psychedelia, 80's cheese, and 00's anthems – was loud and thumping, the room vibrating with the bass. Harriet and Imogen were dancing wildly, enjoying themselves ridiculously, and he watched Lizzy grin as her sister pulled a very famous and serious actor onto the floor during The Time Warp. He wished she had been there with him, so he could laugh with her, dance with her, but all hope of that had gone now.

Because he had moved on. He had a girlfriend.

Walking out onto the roof terrace, he pushed through from the warmth and heat of the party into the cooling rush of the winter air. If it had been summer, the balcony would have been heaving with people; but it was December and the cold was drifting in, turning the air icy. There she was, smoking a cigarette, diamonds twinkling in her hair and sparkly shoes on her feet. He suddenly felt a strange longing to see the bee shoes which made her wiggle when she walked, hips swaying from side to side like the animated temptress from a 1950s cartoon. He hadn't expected her to be there, was sure he had seen her a few moments ago in the middle of the back-patting throng standing at the bar, when Matthew had waved at him, Tamsin hanging off his arm looking devilishly glamorous in emerald green. Surely this meant something, surely if he believed in such nonsense this would be a sign.

"Lizzy," he said, the words stuck in his throat. "I meant to tell you before, you look beautiful."

Dropping the illicit cigarette on the floor, she stubbed it out with super-high heels and a twist of the ankle. Wearing skinny jeans now and a dark blue wrap dotted with tiny silver stars, he thought she looked like an edgy millennial Princess Diana.

"All a grand façade of contouring and Spanx, I'm afraid. You know I don't look like this in real life."

"You look better in real life."

"Thank you, you are always wildly generous with your compliments."

She did look beautiful, but he wanted her fresh-faced and mad haired; curled up next to him on the sofa in pyjamas with llamas on them, feeding him cheesecake, teasing his acting methods.

"Are you not cold?" he asked softly. He could see the little hairs on her arms, standing to attention like a regiment of foot soldiers.

"Absolutely freezing, and I look like the prow of a ship." Her eyebrow arched and, a soft smile crossed her lips.

"Lizzy," he said quietly. "I'm sorry."

"You have nothing to apologise for," she frowned.

"I do."

She gestured for him to move closer, stand with her under the lamp that was doling out mediocre heat. He was acutely aware of the soft golden hue of her skin, the faint smell of ginger biscuits and regret.

"You don't need to apologise to me, Benn."

They stood there, both staring straight ahead, the shot of whiskey he had necked earlier was wearing off now and he suddenly felt vulnerable.

"I think I need help."

"You should ask your *girlfriend*."

The last word made him wince.

"You're right," he said, after what seemed like a lifetime had passed. "Maybe I should."

He turned and started to walk away, and she felt that she couldn't let him leave without saying something.

"Benn," she said, louder than she thought.

"Yes?" His heart was beating in his chest, pounding away.

"You were brilliant."

"Thanks."

He obliged her with a very Regency bow and left. As the door closed behind him, the noise of the party escaping, she wished that she had said something different.

The car journey back hadn't given him enough time to process his thoughts, but he knew what he needed to do. All he could think about was Lizzy, stood there in diamonds and silk, trembling with cold; beautiful, silly, caring, soft, warm Elizabeth, who had haunted his dreams for the past year, whose face he had seen glimpses of in every woman he had dated. Elizabeth who he had disappointed, who he had hurt irreparably without realising. As he walked inside, with a nod from the doorman and the soft shuffle of his oxfords on the tiled floors, he knew that he couldn't go straight upstairs, couldn't face Sarah and her questions and her rage. He headed towards the sanctuary of the bar.

She was waiting for him, impatiently texting – he could feel the pulsating vibrate of the phone in his pocket - and she would be getting gradually more annoyed. It would result in an argument, where they would shout and argue, and she would throw things before softly turning to him and kissing him roughly as they fell onto the bed and had cool, technical make-up sex which he wouldn't enjoy, but which seemed to placate her enough to make her more pleasant the following day.

Sarah could be nice, she could sparkle, and sometimes she made him laugh. They still had the same friends from Cambridge, a similar social circle, but he didn't want to introduce her to his children, and even in the past, he had never introduced her to his mum. It was only a small feeling he had, but when he was with her, he felt as if she saw him as a trophy to be displayed rather than a person to be loved. There was something about it that left a bitter taste in his mouth every time she kissed him in public, or when he noticed how tightly she held onto his arm in front of photographers.

He ordered a whiskey, the familiar mahogany smoothness of it dripping down his throat like nectar and before he knew it, he was ordering another. He heard the voice in his head, warning him against it, and he ignored it. Doubles now; another, another. The world was blurring slightly, and he moved to the slippery comfort of a booth. Soft jazz was playing in the background and, unknowingly, he obnoxiously clapped as the pianist finished his rendition of 'The Way You Look

Tonight'. People were looking at him now, small ripples of recognition, and he posed for a selfie with a flock of leggy hens, chatted about the cricket with a group of City boys, told an inappropriate joke to a couple on a date who awkwardly laughed until he wandered off, hiding again in the splendid sanctuary of the Bar at the Dorchester. He needed fresh air now, and maybe a cigarette. Maybe two cigarettes. And a kebab.
But first, there was something he needed to do.

It was 2am when she found him slumped in a pile at the staff entrance, his jacket was tucked under his head, his trousers undone. There was drool down his chin and he stank of booze, cigarettes and chilli sauce; by his side was a half-eaten muddle of chicken and salad, partly wrapped in paper, the contents spilling out onto the concrete. A few waiters stepped over him as they clocked off for the night, a receptionist was taking a picture when she got there. She paid her £50 to delete it. The concierge had let her know where he was, had known that she had been looking for him, and arranged for a discreet car to collect them from the rear of the hotel.

"It's only because I respect the memory of the late Duke, Lady Darcy," he said in plummy tones, "we can't have this type of behaviour here."

"I understand, Nigel, and I deeply appreciate your care and attention. I will make sure that my father is aware of your service."

"Thank you, Lady Darcy," he enunciated as he helped her drag the film star to his feet.

Disturbed by being moved, Benn roused enough to vomit all over Nigel's highly polished shoes. Lizzy gave him a handful of notes and an apologetic smile.

The orange tinge of streetlights crept through the chinks in the heavy jacquard curtains, as he woke up, he instantly forgot where he was or how he got there. She was on the bed next to him, on top of the covers, a blanket draped over her. Even in sleep, he could still see the gentle jut of her chin, the frown on her brow and he leaned over tracing it with his fingertip just to make sure that it was her. She stirred a little in her sleep; quickly, gently, he clambered out of bed in search of a bathroom.

The shower was hot and powerful as he washed the night before off his skin, an inexplicable hint of chilli sauce dancing around his cuticles. There were clean towels and posh soaps, and he wondered what his mother would say about this bathroom with its sparkling ceramics and glistening chrome. Dry and warm, he climbed back under the cover. She stretched long and hard, her pyjama top pulling up tantalisingly high, opening her eyes she smiled warmly at him.

"Good morning."

"Morning, you should go back to sleep."

"I'm awake now. How is your head?"

She leaned over to pick up her phone, checked the time. It was really early.

He grimaced, "probably not as bad as it would have been."

She sat up in front of him. Even half-asleep, she was still beautiful to him. It wasn't simply the way she looked, it was the way she was.

"Where are we?"

"We're in Chelsea. This is my mum's house, I inherited it from her, I guess. They rent it out usually, but it's been empty for a while."

"Thank you. I appreciate it."

He reached over and placed his hand on hers.

"I didn't know where else to bring you, there were too many people at The Dorchester and this seemed like a good idea, but it looks like I've kidnapped you."

"You rescued me."

"Sounds better than kidnap, I suppose. I should have rescued you before," she murmured. "I wish you had told me that you were drinking again. I was just so cross that I read about it in the paper, but after I rang you, I was just furious with myself for not giving you a chance to explain. I should have flown to LA, I should have helped you."

"I thought I was okay when I got out there, being with you made me think I was okay. I thought it would be okay to have a drink. One drink."

"It's never just one drink."

"I know that. Seeing you last night made me realise what a fucking mess I made of everything, I –"

"I asked too much of you. I should have helped you rather than ignoring it, rather than walking away."

"I should have told you, but I was embarrassed," he said firmly.

"I would have stopped you."

"You wouldn't have been able to stop me."

"I would have tried," she said. "I *should* have tried." There was a pause as she thought carefully what she wanted to say, how she wanted to phrase it. "It's not about me, it's not even about you. It's about Esther and Anya."

"The girls?"

She nodded.

"I don't understand."

She didn't want him to feel sorry for her. She didn't want his pity, but she needed him to know her truth.

"My mum took an overdose, they think," she swallowed hard. "They didn't tell me that for a long time, didn't want me to know, because she didn't leave a note, so we never knew why she did it, or even if she meant to. I like to think that she didn't, and she just…"

She held her breath for a moment, summoned up the courage to carry on.

"When you told me about the Tube, I knew you wouldn't have thought about writing a note or giving a reason," the words rattled out of her like machine gunfire "and Esther and Anya, they are older, they would *remember* you. They would always want to know *why* you did it, they would always want to know if it was something they did, or if there was *something* they could have done to stop you."

Silence.

An awkward vacuum of nothingness.

"Fuck."

He had never even considered the brutal truth of it; that he would leave his children confused, his family devastated and uncertain.

"I didn't want you to drink, because I knew it would make you feel that way again, and I didn't want you to feel that way ever again. All I could think of was that I didn't want them to not know you. I didn't want them to always wonder why you weren't around."

He pulled her close into him, felt the shudder as her well-rehearsed façade crumbled.

"Please don't cry, please don't cry because of me," he pleaded. "I'm such a useless, selfish bastard."

She held him as tight as she possibly could, thinking about what she needed to say to him, all the words that she hadn't said to him when she should have.

"After what you told me, I should have been there for you, and I wasn't." This was the ugliest of cries. "I knew something wasn't right when you were in LA, I could tell."

"You couldn't have known. Lizzy, this is not your fault. You are not to blame for this."

"I am," she was nodding her head, her eyes puffy and red, her usual tone taking on a little whine.

"No," he was resolute in this statement, she could see his jaw clench. "This is something I have to fix, and I will. I promise you."

He placed his palm flat against hers, interlinking their fingers.

"Palm to palm is holy palmer's kiss," he whispered, a remembrance of the night when they saw the stars. "I'll make this right, Lizzy."

"But it's too late now, for us, isn't it?"

She was clean-faced, wearing pyjamas, her hair everywhere, her eyes sad because she thought that all hope of them had gone, and he felt an overpowering rush of love for her.

"Lizzy – my lovely Lizzy - it would never, ever be too late for us."

He watched her process the information, uncertain if she believed him or not; but then, as if she had gotten caught up in a moment that she couldn't get out of, he felt her lips on his. It was tentative, unsure, and she opened her eyes wide and all at once as if she had forgotten what she was doing, pulling back.

"I'm so sorry... you have a girlfriend."

"I don't."

"But what about..."

Without thinking about it, he kissed her. It was deep and dreamy, and he could feel himself get lost in the magical wondrousness of all of this. He wasn't entirely sure that he even awake, feeling as if he was at home in his lonely bed, fitfully dreaming about her. But it was real because here she was, running her fingers through his hair and making him feel as if he had never been kissed before. He needed to stop thinking about it, he needed to just enjoy it.

Lizzy was aware that her face was still hot from tears, but she wasn't even thinking about that. She was thinking about how Benn's hands were moving onto her waist, pulling her towards him. She could feel the gentle warmth of him against her, the gentle urgency, and all she was aware of was that she did not want this to end.

Under the sheets his hands moved tenderly, hesitantly, under the thin t-shirt; he felt the smoothness of her skin, the soft arc of her body. He touched every fragment of her until finally, slowly, he was moving inside her, and he felt her push against him as they held each other tightly, before falling to the sheets, sated and alive.

She curled up against him, her head on his chest, her hair in his face; as he drifted off to sleep, he swore to himself that he would always remember the image of her glistening up at him, the way her curls surrounded her face like a halo, the way she had bit her lip to stop from crying out.

A few hours later he awoke suddenly and dressed quickly, knowing full well that the scent of her was still lingering on his skin. In his jacket pocket, he felt the reassuring shape of the pineapple necklace. He curled the chain around his finger, placing the copper pendant on the pillow next to her. It had always been hers really, he just hoped that one day she would forgive him for what he was about to do.

When she woke up a short while later, Benn was gone, and his phone was going straight to voicemail.

1945

Thomas Bingley had been looking through some old atlases that he had found whilst rummaging about in the tower, where he was trying to keep out of Lady Millicent's way. A man from the War Office had come to visit and so Pemberley was stood to attention. The gold bull on the spine that he recognised from the books in the library was tarnished but still guarding the flaking cover and the fading illustrated pages. The letter was hidden between a map of Egypt and Persia and he removed it slowly, inhaling the musky smell.

My Dearest Elizabeth,

If this poorly formed letter is now in your hands, then I have taken my leave of this earth and left you alone in it. Do not cry, my dearest, for I would hate to think that sad thoughts of me would cause a frown upon your face when our love walks around in each of our children – the-enduring inheritance that we have bequeathed to Pemberley, and our grandchildren who will continue the legacy that we created.

Ours has been a rewarding life together, through the best of times and the saddest of times, but everything bad was easier to overcome with you by my side, and every beautiful occasion was made sweeter knowing that I had your hand to hold.

I am so grateful that you gave me the opportunity to prove to you every day that I was the gentleman worthy of you, and I sincerely hope that this life of ours has been as wonderful for you as it has been for me. We have built a strong family who have known what it is to grow up in a house filled with love and laughter, and my dearest wish is that there will always be Darcys at Pemberley, in the home we have loved so dearly, to continue our legacy.

Please know that however my end has occurred, my last thought will have been of you – of you dancing and laughing with a fire in your heart and a spark in your eyes. You may now be a grand duchess, but to me, you will always be the impertinent girl with the fine eyes who captured my heart across a crowded assembly room.

Elizabeth Bennet, I have loved you, most ardently, until the end of my days and will continue to love you until, by the grace of God, we meet again.

My heart always has been and always will be yours.

Darcy

He ran his finger over the parts where the words had become smudged, seeping into the page, the sharp lines of the letters blotting into the thick paper. Thomas was old enough to know that this letter had been cried over, teary drops of water falling onto the parchment and disguising the words – he squinted, deciphering what it said before folding the letter back up and carefully placing it back between the pages.

Thomas carried the atlas down the curve of the staircase, the woven cover accidentally bouncing off the plaster, before putting it back in its place in the library and returning the gilded bull to its literary herd. Inside, folded carefully, a lost treasure waiting to be found again.

Twenty-Seven

The yellow Mini darted up the driveway of Pemberley, over the hill, curling around the bridge, through the tall trees, fast and smooth in the curve of the landscape towards the house itself. Above them, the soft twilight of the stars illuminated the way, as the four women inside sang 'Total Eclipse of the Heart' as loudly as they could in the vast expanse of moorland that lay beneath the stately gaze of the Cage.

As they pulled into the visitor car park, they disturbed a few of the ancient red deer, who always ventured down after nightfall, perhaps trying to reclaim their lost land. The car came to an abrupt stop outside the small information kiosk, the doors opened, and Imogen fell out into a heap onto the floor.

"Fuckssake!!" she said exasperatedly as she struggled with the car seat, trying to let Harriet out of the back, as the smooth upholstery banged against her hip.

"Calm down, Imogen," Harriet warned as got out of the car and dragged her aunt to her feet.

Reaching the smooth path, the girls paused for a moment to remove their shoes and then began the slow walk up the steep hill to the house itself. Arm in arm, they began to sing again, their voices ringing out like a siren's call in the dark emptiness of the valley.

It was May, the air around Pemberley filled with the smell of the summer ahead; freshly mown grass, magnolias and the warmth of the air itself. The house on the hill was bathed in golden light, looking like a majestic wedding cake plonked on the landscape, its cornices and arches somehow transformed into sugarcraft in the darkness. In four weeks, the Duke of Derbyshire planned to marry for the third time, and this time he knew it was for real. The future Mrs Darcy, as she was choosing to be known for professional reasons, hadn't wanted a big fuss making, however, this evening had been her unofficial hen party.

Organised in the 'Georgiana' suite of the Armitage Arms, her future stepdaughters had arranged for family, friends and staff members, past and present, to attend and all were there to celebrate with Joyce, who had been overcome with emotion as she had been led into the room which had been decorated with soft pink roses, white lilies and dozens of fairy lights. It had taken three glasses of prosecco before she had finally relaxed and then danced with everyone, thanking them all profusely for attending, before falling asleep on one of the plush purple sofas, the glittery willy bopper headband still bouncing on her head. The willy headbands had been Imogen's idea and she had been immensely proud of them, whilst Lizzy had shuddered at the thought and tried to accidentally leave the bag behind in the flat.

"You did really well tonight," Maggie said, as they followed the younger women up the hill, "I think she really enjoyed it."

"She won't be saying that tomorrow when Imogen puts all of those pictures on Instagram."

"Maybe not," Maggie agreed.

They were halfway up the steep hill that led the way home. Maggie followed her cue and sat too, and they both stared up at the indigo sky, which was quietly dotted with stars.

"I had forgotten how dark it gets here."

"I miss you, Maggie."

"I miss you too," she said. "As great as London is, it's not Pemberley."

"Pemberley is home, Mags, it will always be here when you decide to come back," she reached into one of the bags they had brought back from the party and pulled out a small parcel wrapped in tin foil. "Cake?"

There was a silence again. Maggie knew that Lizzy was hiding something from her, she could always tell, would always know. She simply had to wait long enough for it all to come flooding out.

"How's Pete? Is he coming to pick you up tomorrow?"

Maggie had dated Peter Edwards on and off for years, and Lizzy counted him as part of the family, Harriet even called him 'Uncle Pete'. It looked as though they would never marry – Pete living in his own flat in Tooting, working as a DCI for the Metropolitan Police, and Maggie living and working at Pemberley – but they fumbled on and it seemed to work for them for a long time, until he wanted a future and a home with her, and she couldn't find it in herself to make the leap from her comfortable existence to something new and different.

It was the loss of Pete – the temporary split which saw her crying into her coffee far more often than she liked, ignoring the sad little glances from Kate in the ticket office – that pushed her to apply for the job at Austenation and move down south. He had proposed at the top of the Eiffel Tower on the eve of her birthday with a platinum solitaire from Tiffany's. He knew it had cost far too much money, but his mother had always told him that shrouds don't come with pockets, and Pete Edwards got down on one knee and popped the question as Margaret Jane Wickham accepted with the biggest of smiles. They had married quickly, quietly and without any fuss in the registry office at Chelsea and then treated themselves to afternoon tea and champagne at The Ritz before texting everyone to let them know the good news.

"Lizzy," she said with all seriousness. "Pete isn't perfect, he can be a complete arsehole sometimes, but I love him very much." She took Lizzy's hand, squeezing it a little, "I want you to be happy."

She rolled her eyes warningly, "I am happy, why would I not be happy?"

"Lizzy, I know that you think you're happy, but there is more to life than Pemberley; I think you need to leave for a bit, take stock of what you actually want. Maybe travel, take some of the book money and go on an adventure somewhere. Harriet is nearly all grown up, she will be going to university soon and what are you going to do then? You can't keep yourself busy by doing the Lady Darcy tours of the house six times a week, it's not enough. You've been rattling about since you left the office."

"Since I got sacked from the office, Mags. There's no point wrapping it up in pretty paper."

"Pemberley is a great harbour, Lizzy, you will always be safe here, but that's not why ships are built."

"Fucking hell, you're quoting Pinterest to me now... you really are drunk!"

"I mean it! You need to go your own way."

"Fleetwood Mac?" Lizzy raised her eyebrow and her laughing got louder. They pulled each other up of the pebbled pathway and made their way up the hill and into the house.

"I'm serious," Maggie said as they reached the oak door. "Pemberley was never designed to keep you locked up and prisoner, Pemberley was always designed to welcome you home. There are so many adventures waiting for you, Lizzy. Please go out and grab some of them before it's too late.'

"I will, Mags," she said, unlocking the door with a clank. "But first, let's have some tea. I'm absolutely parched!"

Maggie snorted loudly and the happy sound of their laughter echoed around the courtyard as they climbed the stairs to the flat in the tower.

1859

Mabel Darcy was forty-three years of age when her husband, Henry Fitzwilliam, Earl of Matlock, received two accidental shots to the head whilst out hunting with a party who had ridden up from town. She was thankful that they had been blessed with four beautiful children; the heir to the earldom, Richard, who had the Darcy countenance and the Bennet humour, and three other strong, healthy boys.

Henry had been Mabel's friend since childhood, his gentle manner and their shared adoration of the poetry of Shelley and Byron gave them a common interest. Their parents had been of the conviction that an affection had formed between the two, and tentative plans had been put in place when they were both still in schooling that one day the families of Darcy and Fitzwilliam would unite. Mabel wasn't convinced; Henry was a good friend, but she didn't think he would ever be able to love her like the prince in her storybooks loved the princess.

When she was twenty-two, her younger brother Francis confided in her one windy, thundery December night as they both stayed up reading late in the library at Pemberley, the windows rattling against the roar hitting them from across the Peaks. He had looked at her, scared, unsure; she had never seen him like this before, he was always so certain, so arrogant in his opinions, that she knew it was something serious.

"What is the matter, please tell me…" she begged, as he cried on her shoulder.

In the end, she hadn't been too shocked – she was a modern woman of the world after all, she thought - and she held her younger brother close. His soft brown waves burnished with hints of red curling behind his ears, his dark grey eyes almost molten as he held onto her, as a sailor would hold onto a mast in a storm.

"How can I overcome this, sister? How can I ever make it right with my own conscience?"

"Everything will be alright," she soothed. "I understand."

He pushed her away, "you will never understand!"

Never one to be intimidated by the rage of her brother she dragged him towards her and held him tightly.

"I do understand. I understand the seriousness of the sin you believe you are committing, but I am not of that belief and neither should you be."

Mabel understood that love was love in whatever form it came in and she would do anything to make her brother happy, that she would always do anything to make him happy.

"Will it be alright," she asked her Mama, who was brushing the lugs from her hair. The firm pull of the bristles made her feel very young again, even though at this time the following evening she would be Lady Fitzwilliam and a wife.

She looked up at her mother's reflection in the mirror, Elizabeth saw the look of fear and hesitation pass across her daughter's face. She recognised it clearly as it was the same look that she had seen on her own reflection over twenty years ago on the night before her own wedding.

"Of course, even if you love someone it is normal to feel apprehensive," she continued to brush the girl's hair. "You do love Henry very much, don't you Mabel?"

She wasn't very sure on how she should answer this, not wanting to reveal to her mother the indifferent love that she felt for the man she was about to marry. This was not the romantic love that she had dreamed about when she had read 'Emma' or 'Pamela', there would be no George Knightley or Mr B waiting for her at the altar.

"I hold him in very high regard, Mama."

Elizabeth placed her hands on the girl's shoulders, addressing her through the mirror.

"If you are unsure about any of this, you do not have to press ahead. I will not think less of you if you decide not to marry Henry."

Mabel turned on the stool, "I think I am simply apprehensive, Mama. It is a very big undertaking when one does not always fully comprehend the complexities of marriage."

"You do not have to fully comprehend marriage to embark upon it. Did we provide a good example for you?"

"You and Papa are always wondrously in love, even when you disagree or fight, I know that you don't really mean it…"

"I always mean it when I am cross with your father! The older he gets the more pompous he gets, and he needs someone to remind him of it every now and then."

"You remind him of it very often I think, Mama. You are so very lucky that he loves you a great deal."

"It's not luck, Mabel," she said, selecting a burnished orange gown from the selection being offered by Betsy. "Marriage is hard work, even for your father and me. There are sacrifices that we both make to ensure the happiness of the other. As you know, he hates the music of Mozart, whereas I could happily listen to it being played constantly, and I, well… I…."

"You don't like how Papa thinks he is better at billiards than you."

"Well, he isn't better than me, but for the sake of a happy household sometimes it is beneficial to let him think he is." She smiled, "your Father may have had an easier life with another lady from a better family, but I do not think he would have had a happier one."

Betsy started to pull and pin Mabel's hair into a cascade of curls, piled on top of her head, decorating it with tiny pearled clips and a twist of lilacs. She watched as her mother glided about the room, picking up objects, studying them. Mabel forgot sometimes that this had not always been her mother's home, that she had first entered the house as a visitor, viewing the splendour of it all as an outsider.

"Was it hard moving to Pemberley from Longbourn? It must have seemed huge compared to there, I so disliked it that one winter when we were all cramped together visiting Grandmama."

"It was difficult, of course; but Pemberley has always been so very welcoming. It was the running of the household that was the hardest part, but your father ensured that I had lots of help."

"I have positive nightmares about moving to Waddingham, I know I will be able to run a home, but…being a wife."

"You will have your tour first, you will be able to get know Henry properly, and all of the other things will fall into place."

The thought of being alone with Henry Fitzwilliam was the thing that was worrying Mabel the most. They were very good friends, possibly the best of friends, but imagining him kissing her in any other way than on the cheek, made her feel positively nauseous. She knew of the expectations of the marital bed; had prodded her two years wed cousin Charlotte for all the intimate details, which had been shared in letters and over deep conversations when she stayed at the house on Grosvenor Street, but the thought was truly horrifying. Especially so when she considered that she would have to do it more than once, that she would need to provide an heir; firstly, a boy to inherit the vast and ancient Fitzwilliam fortune, and then more children to ensure the continuation of the line.

As their lady's maid, Betsy, fastened her grandmother's jewels around her neck, all she could feel was the weight of the expectation and it made it hard to breathe.

"Mama, I don't think I can go ahead with this."

She threw herself into the warm, comforting embrace of her mother, holding onto her tightly in the bedroom that had been her sanctuary. There were tears falling down her face as she sobbed over and over that she didn't want to do it. Elizabeth pulled her closer to her, feeling the sobs rattle through her body. She gestured to Betsy, who left the room immediately and returned quickly with the Master.

Darcy had granted Henry Fitzwilliam permission to marry his only daughter for two reasons. Firstly, as the oldest son of his two cousins, Richard and Anne, he was assured of his pedigree. Secondly, he was a single man in possession of a large fortune and in want of a wife. He would, of course, always want his daughter to marry for love, but even with her substantial dowry, it would always be beneficial for Mabel to make a prudent marriage to a wealthy man. He walked into the room with a sour look on his face, it smelled like powder and lavender, the smell of women getting ready for the evening; Mabel was crying on the bed, Elizabeth holding her, looking at him with a questioning face, unsure what to do.

What, he mouthed to her.

I don't know, she mouthed back.

"What on earth is all this nonsense about, Mabel?"

The girl looked up at him slowly with a red, tearstained face. To him, she was instantly transformed once more to the mewling babe in the cradle and his heart felt a pull of longing to comfort her. She walked steadily over to him and he enfolded her in his embrace. He glanced over at his wife, who shook her head gently, their marital shorthand telling him what he needed to know.

"Now, my dearest, what is the matter? Surely nothing can be so bad to cause such agitation."

"Papa, I don't..." she stumbled with the words, "I don't think I should marry Henry. I do not love him like you love Mama."

"Mabel, love grows with time. I understand your apprehension, marriage is a big undertaking for anyone, but Henry is nice and well-educated, you will be happy with him."

"I know I will be happy with him. He is a good friend, and I like spending time with him, but I cannot see myself as his wife. I cannot imagine dancing with him in the way you dance with Mama or holding him tightly and looking at him in the same way that Aunt Jane looks at

Uncle Charles. I cannot see that future for myself with Henry, and that frightens me. I do not love him like a woman loves a man."

Darcy sat down on the bed, the embroidered coverlet sent over by one of the Bingley girls the summer before, knowing as they did Mabel's complete ineptitude for needlework. He studied the girl standing before him, hardly believing that the small child, who he had taught how to ride on a small pony, was now a fully-fledged woman preparing to wed. She reminded him so much of Elizabeth, but there was also a soft remembrance of his mother in her that danced around the periphery of his memory.

"If you do not wish it, then you do not have to proceed with the marriage, or you can extend your courtship for a few more months if you prefer. But Henry is a good man and he although he might not be outwardly demonstrative, I think he loves you and holds you in very high regard."

"I think I'm simply overwhelmed with it all, Papa."

"Marriage is overwhelming," her mother whispered. "I was petrified."

"Petrified of me?" Darcy had never known this.

"No, scared of becoming Mrs Darcy of Derbyshire. We place so many pressures on ourselves I think as women. I assure you that all those fears disappeared when I saw your father at the altar. I knew that even though there were challenges..."

"There were many challenges," Darcy interrupted, his wife throwing him a disparaging look and continuing.

"...that I would be able to overcome these because he was by my side. Everything was much easier knowing that I had a companion in life who would put my needs and wants above his own," Elizabeth took her husband's hand. "Although he only listens when he wants to and will eat all that we have of anything sweet if we let him. This is how you got so portly, darling," she patted his tight waistcoat with a smile.

Mabel smiled too, and her mother sensed that there was a little bit of lightness now.

"You have to remember," he said sincerely, "that Pemberley will *always* be your home; even though you will be the Mistress of a much grander house -"

"And it is much, much grander than here," Elizabeth smiled, "although obviously not as wonderful."

Darcy looked at his daughter with a serious expression on his face, "Mabel, you can *always* come home if you need to."

She nodded gently, brushed the curl back behind her ear, the huge Fitzwilliam sapphire glinting on her finger.

"I'm sorry," her face was brighter, "I feel much better now. I am sorry for... all of this, and now I have delayed us all getting ready for our guests."

"Not at all, my beautiful button." Darcy kissed his daughter on her forehead, before leaving her to complete her preparations with her mother, glancing at his wife for confirmation that he could leave everything in her capable hands now.

"Your father is very gracious, Miss Mabel, for I am at least half-hour behind in my toilette."

"Mama, I know I shouldn't, but I still wonder about..."

"I know you do, and I understand what you gave up," Elizabeth was softer now. "I think I understand this decision you have made, even I do not fully comprehend your reasons for it."

Mabel sighed gently, "I have accepted that Percy Wyndham is lost to me, that no amount of pining for him will alter that fact."

"Henry is a very handsome, very clever gentleman; he might not be a Captain Wentworth, but you have to remember that all of those heroes in your books were written by women and the reality is that men are not always as demonstrative in their affections, or as eloquent in their admissions of love. Miss Austen was always very good at coating everything in a deeply romantic veneer, she embellished your father to a great extent, but I suppose I am to blame as it was all based on my own recollection of events."

"She did write him very well indeed. I can see why women fall in love with Mr Darcy, he is so very honourable" she agreed, "not very much unlike Papa at all. Now all I need to do is be as happy as you are."

"Happiness is not always immediate, Mabel. Sometimes happiness sneaks up on us from around a corner."

"I am ever hopeful, Mama."

The celebration dinner went ahead on time and as planned and there was much feasting and merriment as Pemberley celebrated the impending nuptials. She laughed joyously as the Darcy and Fitzwilliam parents took to the polished wooden floor of the ballroom. Her father had always told her that to be fond of dancing was a certain step towards falling in love, but she had failed to see how they had ever fallen in love dancing the rigid, complicated dances of their youth. Looking at them now she knew that Fitzwilliam and Elizabeth Darcy were the epitome of the romantic love that she would always long for, the love she had found and lost, the love that she would never have again.

Fitzwilliam Darcy walked her down the aisle as proud as could be, a smile etched across his face for the whole day. As his only daughter, Mabel held a special place in his heart and in the dark days after her birth when his dearest Elizabeth was beyond his reach, the little sparkle in the baby's eyes kept him optimistic for the future. The delicate, blonde gentleman with the blue eyes that glittered like jewels and the tight little mouth that pursed like a rosebud, stood at the end of the aisle, looking nervously around as she floated towards him in a light pink gown, with frills to the arms which she found overly fussy. Meanwhile, she could see Francis standing there, smiling at her, grateful that she was keeping his secret safe, protecting his life by sacrificing her own.

Despite their unusual arrangement, Mabel and Henry had loved each other very much. She found something ultimately fulfilling in being married to your best friend, and she had never had to worry about Henry taking a mistress or not confiding in her. They were equal in every way and she knew that she had been envied by other women in their set, especially Florence Cadwallader, a lady constantly fretful of her own husband's infidelity, who complained heartily about her lot when she took tea on the terrace of the house at Wakefield. Mabel gazed out over the endless, rolling pastures that surrounded Waddingham. If only they knew the sacrifice a woman had to make for such security, she thought as she sipped her tea.

In the still room, the stone room hung with fragrant bunches of wildflowers and filled with the scent of rosemary, Mabel kissed Henry's cold face and said her goodbyes. She couldn't bear to imagine the pain that would have ripped through his body as his spine snapped into pieces, or the trauma of the jarring wound to his skull that had meant that even though she could identify him, it was obvious that half of his head was missing. Bowdler had not wanted the mistress to see her husband like this, had wanted to shield the lady from the gruesome sight, but she had insisted, cleaning the body by herself as her last duty to a beloved husband.

The butler at Waddingham had known Henry Fitzwilliam since he had been in the cradle, had glimpsed his peculiarities and his queerness when he had returned home from school, had witnessed the particular intimacy with the Darcy boy firsthand, and then there had been others. He felt worst for the Missus, he wondered if she was aware that her husband was…well… like he was. Bowdler also knew that this was no accident; that the shots with which the Earl had been hit were too precise, too calculated. Sitting in the pantry in the bowels of the house, he took a small shot of whisky from the stores, fully aware that his master had been killed in cold blood by the group of men currently drinking his brandy and sleeping under his roof.

She returned to the house to let her children know their father was dead. Richard, their eldest son, not quite thirteen and now the Earl of Matlock was petrified. It seemed as if he might drown under the burden of responsibility, and she held him tightly in her arms until the sobs echoed away, leaving him looking young and frightened even in sleep.

In the hallway of the grand house that she called home, the stain of her husband's blood on her gown, the brittle coldness of the night crackling on her skin, Mabel fell to her knees as the grief and the loss and the pain poured out of her, powerless to keep it all contained. She cried for her husband, for her brother James who was lost to the ocean, and for her dearest Mama and Papa. She cried until there was nothing left but noise and anger at a world that had left her so alone. She stayed there until the sun began to rise.

Then she stood up.

Twenty-Eight

The long gallery was humming with people and noise and the soft click-clack of boots and shoes on the wooden floor. It was a warm day and visitors had flocked inside, escaping into the breezy coolness of the building and the new Wartime at Pemberley exhibition. In the bay window, a woman was busy scolding her toddler, using a gentle but firm voice, as he threw himself on the floor, an older couple meandered up the stairs gently holding hands as they chatted softly, a couple of teenagers in walking boots and t-shirts looking serious and reading everything, a middle-aged woman and her daughter speaking in hushed tones.

Now displayed in large cabinets and on oversized display boards, the collection of photos and artefacts, found hidden in a cupboard down in the bowels of the house were giving visitors an insight into how life at Pemberley continued during both World Wars. Boxed up and categorised, detailed and documented in her great-grandmother's spindly, firm handwriting, were journals, diaries, pictures, records, and hundreds of glossy black and white photographs on thick paper. Lizzy's favourite was the picture of Millicent and Jonathan, standing in the Dutch Gardens, busy planting broad beans and onions – him resting his boot on a spade, whilst she grinned up at him wearing dungarees with her hair tied up in a scarf. But it was the picture of the first wave of evacuees – Pemberley Easter Hunt 1940 – that she found the most poignant; wondering how many of those little faces, grinning at the camera holding Easter baskets with their knobbly knees visible, survived the bombardment that they returned to.

The clippings and cuttings in the paper always referred to Millicent as 'the mother of the Duke of Derbyshire', rather than as a person in her own right. Despite Pemberley being preserved in English literature, the threat of abandonment and demolition in the post-war years had always been a very real danger, and she knew that Millicent, with her clever mind, had been the reason for its survival. Funny, Lizzy thought, how the Darcy women were only ever mentioned in relation to the men that they married or gave birth to. Millicent had never married, always danced to her own tune and had probably been the happiest of the most recent of her line – running her home, raising her children and doing it all wearing a string of pearls and a full-face of make-up.

Winston, injured and discharged, returned home in the summer of '43, he had been serving in the RAF – flying out over Dusseldorf on a targeted raid one September evening, trying not to think of the hundreds of innocent civilians below who were unlikely to survive the night; later limping home on a tank leaking fuel into the sea, they had crashed into a field on the south coast. Winston had felt the intense pain as his lower leg shattered, he would walk with a limp for the rest of his life because of it, but as their squadron sat silent and still, battered and bleeding, they called out with laughter and relief grateful to be alive under the starry skies of England.

Thomas Bingley, orphaned by the stray bomb that fell on the house in Fleetwood Road, never went back to Southend. Instead, the Darcys took it upon themselves to pay for his education and he was admitted to Eton at the start of Michaelmas Half 1946. He eventually played cricket for Derbyshire and lived in a small house in Lambton with his wife, before teaching PE and Geography at a local grammar school. They had raised three daughters, one of whom they named Millie after her godmother, who had stood proudly at the font in a hat trimmed with feathers and a fox fur stole.

The Jones' girls never stopped talking or cleaning fires badly and, after working with the Land Girls for the latter half of the war and providing Pemberley with much-needed supplies and amusement, they returned to the remains of their homes in the suburbs of Manchester. When Winston opened the house up to the public in the early seventies, Laura Jones paid the entrance fee and caught the shuttle bus up the drive towards the house that she had lived in for most of her childhood. She found herself overcome with happy memories as she sat in the servants' hall with a cup of tea, remembering the moment that Lady Darcy had told her that she wasn't being separated from her sister as she had feared, but that they would be living in this house from a storybook, the mornings when she cried for her mother and Mrs Reynolds would snuggle her close until the tears stopped, and the day they all found out, huddled around the wireless in the drawing room, that Hitler was dead and the war was over, all cheering with honest, thankful joy. Laura, now Mrs Palmer to the class of infants that she taught in Hyde, found herself quietly weeping as her husband averted his eyes and passed her a handkerchief.

Jonathan Sykes never went back to Essex, instead, he proclaimed loudly one autumn afternoon in 1944 that he had found his soulmate and companion of his life in the Lady of the House. They would live at Pemberley together for the next twenty-two years, where he would always make her morning cup of coffee himself and insisted on calling her 'm'lady' when she acted pompous in front of him, much to her great vexation. But he would hold her close at night when she screamed out in pain; the residual damage to her body from the treatment in prison catching up with her in small, agonizing ways; the nightmares that haunted her every so often, screaming out in terror as the sight of Emily being pounded to death by the King's horse was pulled into her dreams as she watched on powerless.

Sometimes the greatest love is found in the small, quiet moments of the night, the gentle cool hand on a burning fever.

He died the night before the World Cup Final, peacefully and without drama in his own bed, which cast a rather sombre shadow on the celebrations of the following day. Kenneth Wolstenholme blared out from the small television set in the corner of the stag parlour as England made a play for the goal, "they think it's all over!"

"It is now," said Millicent, jutting out her chin and refusing to cry, despite the sad looks and pitying glances from her friends and family. She sat silently writing at Fitzwilliam Darcy's desk, making plans for the funeral - three loaves, two tins of ham and a Victoria sponge.

Millicent didn't stay sad; she was a Darcy and it simply wasn't good form to grieve for too long. She had had three romantic loves in her life, and she was grateful for all of them, but the greatest love affair she had embarked upon was that with herself – she had lived so many lives, all of them remarkable in their own way, each one defining who she was at that moment in time. There was nothing to regret, nothing that she felt she had missed.

As she climbed the stairs up to her small bedroom for what would be her final night on earth, she hoped that she would be remembered by those whose lives she had touched, even if it was in the most unremarkable of ways.

Lady Millicent Augusta Darcy died in the early hours of what turned out to be the hottest day of the year. She was such a kindly mistress, Staughton had said to the coroner as they covered the body in a sheet and took her to the local chapel of rest; always down to earth, would do anything for anyone. It was a good old life, Mrs Reynolds nodded in agreement, as she packed a small bag for the funeral home with the clothes Lady Millicent had requested. Don't forget the red lipstick, Kitty had reminded them, she will haunt us if we let her go without that.

The room had become much busier now and John had signalled over from the other end that someone was looking for her. The elderly gentleman with the flash of white hair and the wide smile, he called her over and she embraced him warmly. He walked with a cane now but was still as firm and broad as he had been in his youth.

"Hello, Lady Elizabeth. I must say, this is all very grand, isn't it? Who'd have thought it of us, eh?"

"What do you think of the exhibition, Mr Bingley?" She asked as she caught his wistful look, "do you think my great-grandmother would have approved?"

"It's very impressive," he confirmed, before he admitted with a sheepish smile, "Lady Millicent would have thought it a big old fuss over nothing really."

As he looked around the long gallery, standing in almost the same place where his bed once stood, he felt a sudden rush of emotion for the long-lost days of his childhood. If he concentrated hard enough, he was certain that his old body could still smell *Shalimar* and cigarettes, could still hear Lady Darcy singing 'Wild Women Don't Have the Blues' as the gramophone crackled.

The Story of My Life

Mabel Fitzwilliam-Darcy, the prematurely widowed Countess of Matlock, had five sons and no daughters which was, perhaps, the best outcome for a woman of her rank. The youngest was a boy called Albert, who was born six months after his father's death. He was named after the venerable German prince who had married the British Queen and who would die on his namesake's second birthday.

Albert grew up healthy and strong, not tied down with the expectation attached to his older brothers. He went to Eton and Oxford, as was the family tradition, before marrying a lady called Maud Oxley, a buxom woman of middling appearance with a small dowry and a large chip on her shoulder. Taking charge of the family mills in Lancashire, Albert moved the family to a beautiful red brick building called 'Hartfield' on the outskirts of Manchester, where Maud blessed him with two children and the light side of her temper.

Albert often wondered about his only son, Walter, a small disagreeable child who had nothing to recommend him. Despite being well-educated, the boy loitered about the house until a job was found for him in the Ancoats Mill. Walter Fitzwilliam felt that working was an unnecessary chore and he saw it as a mere diversion to the real business of entertaining and visiting his clubs in London.

Albert collapsed one afternoon during a meeting regarding staff pay increases. It was preferable dying with his face down on the boardroom table than looking at the gnarly, red face of his wife, he thought as people realised what was happening too late. The world faded out of his vision until all he heard was the distant, unsure voice of the young Doctor.

'I don't think he's going to make it.'

Walter took advantage of his newly inherited wealth and married with undue haste, much to the disdain and disapproval of his mother. The new Mrs Fitzwilliam, a nineteen-year-old actress called Audrey Duncan, was famous for her role as Miss Pretty, but Maud thought she had bad manners, a dubious reputation and was not good enough for her eldest boy, regardless of how young, pretty and flaxen-haired she was. She gave birth to their first child soon after the marriage. Leonard was a bonny, bouncing boy with a placid temperament and a head full of ringlets.

"You need to chop those off", Maud said, "he looks like a girl".

"No, we need to dance, don't we, Lenny!"

Lighting a cigarette, she twirled around the living room as Leonard giggled with glee. Audrey hadn't expected Walter to fritter away his inheritance; trying to maintain the lifestyle of his peers from school whilst not having the talent, business acumen or income to sustain it. Without the security of the job in the mill at Ancoats, Audrey and Walter ended up virtually destitute and living in Maud's spare room. She raised Leonard quite singlehandedly, under the watchful eye of her mother-in-law, and earning a few quid here and there recording jingles for the radio, whilst her husband entertained himself with floozies down in London or tarts up in Manchester. Audrey didn't mind as much as she thought she would. Amazing how one's expectations lower once one is married, she thought, scrubbing her silk, monogrammed underwear in the kitchen sink with dish soap.

Leonard worked hard at school and showed a natural flair for languages, teaching his mother swear words in Spanish and passing the eleven plus with flying colours. He earned a place at the local Grammar School and his grandmother celebrated by dropping down dead as she iced his cake, scattering a confetti of royal icing sugar and currants over the floor. Death was no excuse for extravagance, Iris thought, as she picked the dried fruit up off the dusty floor with sore, rough hands, placing it back into the jar for another day. The war might be over, but rationing was still in place.

Walter passed away peacefully in a hospital bed one June afternoon in 1955. It was cancer, he said to a fellow patient as they smoked cigarettes stood outside in dressing gowns, the same one that had taken good King Bertie. He had nothing to leave Leonard, apart from an old pocket watch with a worn engraving on it that had belonged to one of his ancestors, he couldn't remember which one. It was an heirloom, Walter had told him as he pressed it into his hands that cool summer evening, both knowing that he wouldn't live to see autumn.

Audrey lived a year longer before being hit by a trolley bus on her way to work. The contents of her bag spilled over the road and her pink felt hat, crumpled and creased, lay forlornly under the wheels.

"Oh look", said a passer-by, "it's that actress who used to be Miss Pretty".

"Not so pretty now", said another, as they watched the ambulance men lifting the bloodied remains of Audrey onto the stretcher and carrying her away.

Leonard, now orphaned and alone, found refuge with a distant cousin of his father's. She couldn't offer him anything apart from a day's pay for a day's graft and lodgings in the stables, but he accepted gleefully, waving goodbye to Aunt Iris who was putting Hartfield up for sale and planning a move to Swindon.

The house had been big and cold, but he had enjoyed the good meals and working on the land. Using the family names and utilising the Old Boys network, the cousin found him a job at the Home Office, and he progressed quickly, entering the British Foreign Service; he was based in Libya and then Bangladesh, before being transferred home for a regular desk job at an office in Manchester, where he could commute to his little semi-detached on the outskirts of Bury.

Leonard married Margaret and they had one son, Derek, who was a commensurate disappointment; the path of his life decided when he failed the eleven plus and was shunted towards the local secondary modern, where he was barely adequate at anything. Still, the watch in his pocket kept ticking, and as time moved on, Derek met Lynn and they had two sons and a daughter. Leonard loved being a grandad and he recognised something of himself in the youngest boy and encouraged him with particular favouritism.

It seemed like only a few years had passed, but before he knew it the boy had graduated from Cambridge and everyone thought he was destined for great things. On graduation day, he pressed the small, smoothed pocket watch firmly into his palm, and his youngest grandson had held it in his hands, feeling the faint outline of the dedication that had once been engraved upon it: *Unum factum ex multis*. One made out of many.

The older man didn't care for the boys chosen career path, but he trusted that everything would be alright in the end and he offered his continued support: paying for the rent on the grotty bedsit in Mile End or taking them out for tea whenever he ventured to London. He paid for headshots and riding lessons, attended revues, festivals, and plays, he even suggested a new stage name. He needed something catchy, the agent had said, it was the nineties after all. Leonard pondered on it for a while as they drank milky coffee from chipped mugs.

"What about Benn Williams? That has a nice ring to it!"

"Yeah, I like that," the boy agreed, as they sat in the rented room that smelled like Turkish meat and Dettol.

A family tree has roots that run deep and strong, but the branches of it spread out far and wide, the leaves falling through time and reappearing in the most unlikely of places.

Twenty-Nine

Lizzy heard the clock in the long gallery chime its delicate melody, sounding out ten am. The house was due to open in half an hour and she was currently rummaging about in the small cupboard in what was once her old bedroom, trying to find a box of leaflets needed for her tour this afternoon. She loved the familiarity of being back in the Knights Bedroom and if she thought about it hard, she could still smell a hint of Impulse, stolen cigarettes out of the window, burning wood from when she singed the windowsill with her hair straighteners. The bed was still here, although it had undergone intensive restoration work, never to be slept in again; and the nail glue had finally been removed from the fireplace, although she had heard that it took nearly three weeks to gradually work it away.

Pulling out the box of leaflets, she walked along the north corridor and down the staff stairs towards the stewards' room where a small huddle of volunteers, gathered with brews and biscuits, waiting for the briefing from Hannah who would let them know what was happening for the day. Lizzy walked in late, halfway through the schedule, excusing herself and hovering around the door until the announcements were finished and the Thursday team went to their positions in various rooms around the house. Placing her box on the table she grabbed a biscuit and sat down, this room used to be the mahogany room, it still was depending on which plan of the house you checked or the age of the member of staff you spoke to. She opened the two-hundred-year-old sash window onto the view of the reflection lake, the peaceful morning breeze drifting in off the hills, carrying the scent of roses down from the garden near the Orangery.

"Lizzy?"

Hannah brushed back into the room, hurriedly making a cup of tea as she gathered clipboards and feedback forms under her arm, "they're doing the filming in the library, so you will need to cut that from your first tour this afternoon, that okay?"

Lizzy glanced back into the room distractedly, her eye taken by the small ducklings faltering about on the edge of the lake.

"What filming is this?"

Hannah, busily grabbing for a radio and checking the schedule for something more important shouted back as she left the room.

"The Story of My Life."

Lizzy felt her heart immediately palpitate. The door clunked shut and then reopened as Hannah walked back into the room to slurp her tea.

"I am so dippy today! It's the thought of Mr Darcy being about ten metres away from me all afternoon."

"He's going to be here *today?*"

"Yeah – did they ask you about it? We didn't think you would be bothered," she swigged the last mouthful, "he's signing autographs and books in the Servants Hall for staff, I am so excited! He was FIT as Darcy... I mean, UFFF...You must have met him when they filmed here, right?"

"Yeah," she said hesitantly, her heartbeat in her fingers. "Yeah, I met him once or twice."

"So LUCKY!" Hannah whined, "trust me to start work here like three weeks after they finished filming... the most exciting celebrity I've met so far was Jemima Lancaster, and she was nice, but she wasn't Benn frickin Williams!"

She disappeared out of the room, leaving an empty cup and the radio on the table. Lizzy stood there; still, unable to move, her heart almost beating out of her chest. If she closed her eyes, she could still feel the touch of his hand on her skin, could smell the soapy warmth of the crook of his neck, could hear the low growl of his voice in her ear.

It was lunchtime when, armed with a book, she escaped through the throng of people in the bright gallery and trudged down the north staircase emerging out into the warmth of the May sunshine. The courtyard was alive with people; children running about, HHS members queuing to have their cards scanned for entry, volunteers and staff and everyone bumping together in this great crowded hum of noise. She politely excused herself past a very large man with a very large dog, who was arguing, albeit fairly graciously, with Kate from the ticket office, and then quickly skirted around a loud, American couple who were asking if Colin Firth was about to emerge from the Lake in his wet white shirt. She heard one of the new ticket girls say lightheartedly, 'only if he's escaped from my handcuffs', and it made her laugh, even if the Americans were unimpressed.

She had already seen the production crew setting up in the Library, only a small team today, and the HHS historian who had contacted Joyce about the Fitzwilliam connection, but she had yet to see him. She didn't have to wait long. From her viewpoint next to the Orangery, she saw the Volvo pull up to the gates, watching with eager eyes as he was buzzed in.

Standing at the edge of the doorway to the library, she excused herself to the few members of the crew who were pushing past her. There was only a small team, and the historian from the HHS archives in London, who had brought boxes of information with her. And then there he was, sitting in the bay window of the library, being gently made up by the lady with the red hair, who she now knew was his sister-in-law, Lucy.

He looked different to how she had remembered him looking – he had never really looked like he did on movie posters or on the TV, but his face seemed a little thinner, and he had grown his beard again. He was wearing a smart white shirt and blue jeans, but instead of looking casually well-off as usual, he was tired around the edges. She wanted to run over and hug him, to tell him that everything was alright now, that everything would be alright if they were together, but she couldn't do it and she knew why. Because it would be hard, and scary, and perhaps this long time without any contact had been the universe telling them both that it was a bad idea. He glanced over in her direction and she bolted behind the door frame, trying to avoid Graeme who was walking down the stairs. Politely she tried to dodge out of the way, but it was too late.

"Miss Lizzy," he boomed. "How are you this fine Pemberley morning?"

He stopped dead at the bottom of the staircase, right in front of the doorway to the library. Caught between a velvet rope and a throng of brownie guides on a visit with Brown Owl, there was nowhere to hide, and she stood there like a frightened deer waiting to be hit by a minivan.

"Hello Graeme," she said graciously to the doorman she had known forever. "I'm wonderful, how are you?"

"All the better for seeing you, Miss Lizzy, are you here to relieve me or are you doing something more important?"

"I'm just…" she noticed that Benn was definitely looking over at her now, removing the napkin from under his chin and getting up from his seat, "…it's…erm…"

Graeme was confused, "are you okay?"

Benn was walking towards her now, and she needed to get away. "Yes, but if you would just excuse me…"

The older man nodded consent amiably before he was accosted by the brownie leader who was currently doling out information packs and pencils to the small hoard of smiling girls.

Lizzy moved through the crowd into the bright gallery where she then escaped down the side staircase, into the entrance hall, and out the front door. The courtyard was full of people still, even in the warm hum of the late afternoon, and she moved through the crowd and back into the house the wrong way around.

Benn knew he would see her; there was a flash of dark hair, a red polka dot dress, and then she was gone. He felt his heart flip a little, but then the excitement was replaced by fear. Fear of the unknown, fear that she would reject him and send him on his merry way. A long time had passed and although he was sure she would understand, he wouldn't blame her if she told him to get lost. He would try and lay his best hand on the table; he would have to hope that it was good enough.

"Are you ready for this, Mr Williams?"

"Call me Benn, please…" he said, with his characteristic charm.

This project had been so interesting, especially given the family connections that had emerged in her research. Felicity Kruger, the senior curator of the HHS archives, didn't know if he was aware that he was a descendant of Fitzwilliam Darcy, but she did know that this was going to make amazing television, and if she got to spend the afternoon flirting with Benn Williams then all the better.

"And how do you feel about discovering that you are, in fact, a five-time great-grandson of Fitzwilliam Darcy…?" Felicity pressed, as they sat at the large round table in the library with all of her discoveries presented before him.

"Well, obviously it's a little overwhelming…"

Benn had not expected this. He had thought the 'The Story of My Life' would flag up something vaguely interesting, they wouldn't have asked him to do it if it didn't, but this was absolutely mad. No wonder the production team had been so eager to film at Pemberley – it made complete sense now. He could see from the carefully plotted family tree that he was related to Fitzwilliam, and through that related to Lizzy. He was a Darcy, of sorts. He looked around the library, focusing on the small golden bulls glinting in the sunlight, and he wondered how many of them were still missing, replaced by the imposters.

"Do you need a minute, Benn?"

The director called over from behind the camera. Pulled out of his daydream, Benn smiled flirtatiously at Felicity who was looking at him expectantly.

"So,' he said never taking his eyes off her, "what you're saying is that of all this I could have been *Master?*"

It was cheesy, he knew that, but this was television and he had watched enough episodes of this programme to know what he needed to say. Felicity's laugh fluttered across the table towards him, and she blushed slightly, the colour of her cheeks rising to a gentle pink which matched her cardigan.

"Well not quite," she said, knowingly. "Your great-great grandad – Albert Fitzwilliam – was the grandson of Fitzwilliam Darcy through his mother, Mabel. So not only are you related to our lovely Darcy family here, but you are also a distant cousin of Dennys Fitzwilliam, the current Earl of Matlock."

"Not bad for a boy from Bury, is it?"

He searched the paper in front of him, following the curve of the family tree down to his own name and those of his daughters underneath it. Looking across he could see Lady Elizabeth Darcy marked across on the paper, all small parts of the same family.

"Were you not aware of this at all before you started filming the iconic role?"

Felicity's serious face was quite amusing; she had a pointed nose and drawn on eyebrows, her tightened smile highlighted by a pearly pink lipstick. She was looking at him intently, he would need to answer her.

"I mean, Mr Darcy's descendent playing Mr Darcy is quite special," she pressed

"Yes, yes of course it is, but this is the first time I've ever seen this." He was genuinely surprised. "My grandad once told me about staying with a cousin in Derbyshire, but I never really expected him to have stayed here at Pemberley."

"We looked through the Pemberley Archives and here we have a picture of Leonard Fitzwilliam, he's probably about nineteen here, with Lady Millicent Darcy."

Felicity pushed over a faded black and white photograph of a young Leonard standing with an older, but still glamorous Millicent – all smiling as they played croquet on the front lawn, the towering grandeur of Pemberley standing behind them; still the same, still as constant.

"Right, take five everyone." Christian shuffled his papers seriously, before jumping up from his chair and walking around looking important. "Guys, can you set up for the interview? Check the light balance in there too. There's a lot of gold, a lot of sunshine and I don't want any lens flare. I'm not JJ fucking Abrams! Get a few fillers of the lake too – Leanne can you add a note for the V/O writers to stick a line about Colin Firth popping out of it?"

Benn looked at Felicity questioningly.

"Saloon?"

"We have another set of shots and a little bit with Harriet Darcy. She's the daughter of Lady Elizabeth. Don't you know her already? I'm sure Matthew Wickham is her dad."

"Harriet?"

"We asked for Lady Elizabeth, but they couldn't schedule her in. She's very busy apparently. Harriet is just as good though, really nice girl."

"Yeah, I know Harriet."

"Oh, so you do know the family?" Felicity glanced over the edge of her reading glasses. "Shouldn't take too long."

Benn Williams had walked into the saloon, flirting and chatting with the lady from the HHS, who was obviously smitten with him. Harriet thought he looked older, a bit more worn around the edges; he was a bit fatter than she remembered from when filming had ended, but she knew how much he loved desserts, so she wasn't surprised. Harriet didn't like his beard, and she didn't like the way his eyes were tinged with sadness. He looked strange in his normal clothes; even when he had been at the flat almost every night it felt like one of those days at school where teachers wore their normal clothes, and she didn't know if she would ever get used to seeing him without a cravat and sideburns.

The filming had been really interesting, and she had learned a lot about Mabel Darcy. She had always wondered what had happened to the larger than life, romping girl who had bounded down the stairs, of course, she knew the facts – written down in books and on the internet – but she didn't know the stories, and that was all everyone ended up being in the end.

"I can't believe you never told me your real name was Bennet Fitzwilliam," she grinned at him, as they were positioned on the red velvet sofa, microphones being carefully removed by a production assistant with an ever-present frown.

"You would have taken the piss."

"Of course I would! We're family now, *Bennet*, you can expect a *huge* amount of piss-taking." She smiled, but he didn't smile back, not in the same way anyhow. "Does my mum know you're here today?"

"Not sure," he shrugged. "I guess she does."

"Would you like to come up for tea?"

He focused his attention to the papers on the table in front of them. But she saw the shift of something across his face, almost as if he was scared to say something out loud.

"Come and see us, later on when all this is done."

"I don't think I have the time, Harriet. I'm sorry."

"You're here to sign books for HHS staff and film *this*, so unless you have something outstandingly good planned for your evening at the Armitage, then I'm sure you can let me cook you some tea." Harriet did not like it when people interfered with her plans. "You can see my mum too, and you can go and flirt on the roof, or whatever it is you do"

Benn couldn't think of anything he would rather do than sit on the roof of Pemberley with Lizzy Darcy, laughing and joking and discussing all of the books he still hadn't read.

"Do you think she would be happy to see me?"

There was a moment and Harriet Darcy saw Benn Williams with the sad look behind his eyes and the mournful mouth, how even though he was flirty and charming with Felicity, she could tell that he was decidedly un-Benn-like.

"I know she would."

"Okay. Then yes, but only if you think it's a good idea."

"I do."

Harriet knew that her mum thought that being a Darcy always meant choosing responsibility over anything else. Harriet didn't, because she knew that being a Darcy meant choosing love over everything else, every single chance you could. She could see time and time again throughout history where her ancestors had done just that, and she could see no reason why they should all stop doing it now.

"Okay," Christian jumped down from his chair. "We've finished here, Benn are you alright to jump in the van with us to Waddingham?"

"Where's that?"

"Wakefield," Christian was busy concentrating on a wedge of papers on his clipboard. "It's the Fitzwilliam family home. It's where Mabel Darcy lived." He looked up at Benn, handing him a sheet with information on. "Did you know her husband was gay? He's like your grandad or something, isn't he? You're lucky to be here at all!"

This was not part of the plan, he hadn't planned to jump in anything and go to Waddingham, but he supposed it would be interesting to meet the Earl of Matlock and get shown around his ancestral home.

Felicity chirped in, eager to get his agreement to the trip.

"Dennys Fitzwilliam said that he can meet us there — we can introduce you." She noticed his reluctance, "It won't take long, just a few shots. Maximum three hours, I promise."

He nodded his consent before walking over to the window where Lucy had reappeared after the filming had finished. She was looking radiant as ever, and he could see the faint outline of the bump containing his new nephew, who was due to arrive after Christmas.

"Off to Yorkshire then?" She wiped the make-up from his face, "best thing to come out o'Yorkshire is the road! That's what your mum always says anyway!"

It was a running joke in the family of how proud Lynn was of her Lancastrian heritage.

"Best not tell her that we might all be from Yorkshire then, eh?"

"She'll disown us all!"

It didn't take three hours. The traffic on the M62 ground to a halt just before Leeds. the Earl of Matlock left the house around six-thirty unable to wait any longer, by eight they were being diverted off the motorway and onto an A road somewhere near Huddersfield. He should have known that nothing in life was ever straightforward. Pemberley was in darkness by the time he unfolded himself from the cramped conditions of the production bus; up on top of the house he could see the lights from the flat blazing away and he wished more than anything that he lived there so he would be home by now.

He had been away for so long, but he had thought about walking up the curling staircase, feeling his hands against the chalky plaster, and sitting down on the couch next to Lizzy, wrapping his arms around her. He wondered if would be too late now to knock on her door, wondered if she would be happy to see him. He stood there, looking up at the Tower, trying to get up the nerve; but confidence got the better of him and he changed his mind, turning on his heel and back towards the car.

Lizzy rose from her seat in the stone porch, where she had been waiting, the chain of the pineapple necklace she had treasured for the last few months tangled in her fingers. As he walked away, she watched him intently, hoping that he would look back.

He didn't.

1867

Mabel Fitzwilliam recovered from the death of her husband in a manner most ill befitting of ladies of her generation. Whilst she wore black for twelve months as required, she was determined to do something worthwhile with her life, something that would make a difference. It had been enough for her father that she had made a good match, but her mother had always wanted more for the girl who had lived.

She packed up her youngest children and left the house at Waddingham which was fast becoming a catacomb of grief, a shrine to a lost life. She visited Egypt, America, the Holy Lands, collecting artefacts and treasures, venturing further than most women in an age where a woman could be Queen in her own right, but where women were still deemed as the possessions of their husbands. She documented everything in the detailed and extensive travel journals that she would eventually become famous for, blazing a trail across the globe in a manner befitting the only daughter of Fitzwilliam Darcy and Elizabeth Bennet.

At the age of fifty-three, she returned to England and the house in Derbyshire as the guest of her nephew, Fitzwilliam. He introduced his fabled aunt - the great Lady Explorer, her skin the colour of walnuts, the smell of oud and rose oil surrounding her - to his new bride. The lady came from a Norfolk family, he said, perhaps she knew of them; the Wyndhams. The newest Duchess explained how her mother had died when she was eight, how her father had never remarried, despite being still relatively young. Clementine, wanting to ingratiate herself to her newest and most famous relative opened her locket to show a tiny painted miniature of her father, wondering if there was some prior acquaintance. Mabel shook her head gently as she sipped her tea.

After dinner she retired to the library, the room still smelled like her father; she was pleased to see his bulls all standing to attention, his chair still by the fireplace. She ran her finger along the row of books on the middle shelf, all still present and correct, and pulled out the atlas that she had brought home nearly thirty years ago.

Flipping through the pages, she traced her finger over the calculations that had been made in the margin, of the route that her dearest Papa had travelled, his handwriting still there, still present, his indelible mark on the world.

There was a letter, hidden between the pages, her father's large, wax seal still intact. It was addressed to her mother. She had expected to find some solace in the words, but all she found was the evidence of the ardent and unending love that she had admired for her whole life, and whilst she was comforted by the firm handwriting of her dearest Papa, it simply made her regret some of her earlier decisions.

Dabbing her tears from the paper, she folded the letter firmly and placed it back in between the pages of the atlas. Her mother had died three years before her father, passing away quietly in her own bed in the room that overlooked the lake. It had been quick, and for that she had been grateful, holding her mother's hand as she slipped into the next world. Comforting her father as he sobbed as if his life was over. Fitzwilliam had been interred next to Elizabeth in the church at Lambton, together for eternity, their final resting place marked with a simple dedication.

It had been nearly ten years since her father crashed out of the world, seven years since her brother Fitz had died suddenly, and unexpectedly in the night. Francis took the matter in hand and provided guidance to the young boy who was now in charge of the vast Darcy estates and business interests. Walking down the bright gallery, she was certain that she could still hear the echo of her father, his voice clear and strong, as his watch ticked away in her pocket, and sitting in the window seat, she was certain her mother's effervescent laugh was ringing across the courtyard. Mabel read 'Pride and Prejudice' often, and it amused her to know that the rector's daughter who had stayed at Pemberley one summer had immortalised her parents forever in the pages of a novel.

Newly arrived from the coast, Percy Wyndham had stepped off the train at Lambton not knowing that she was at Pemberley, not knowing that the feelings he had buried deep within him would re-emerge when he saw her. He had married Flora knowing that it was wrong; hated how she pandered to him, never challenged him. When she died, he barely noticed her absence, and he had despised himself for that. Mabel had been lost to him, and when they had met at social engagements, he saw the sadness pass across her eyes for the future that they could have had.

When news of her husband's death had reached Norfolk, he was determined to find her again; but by the time he arrived in Yorkshire she had already left, and the house was shuttered until the teenage Earl was ready to take up his inheritance. Once again, she had slipped through his fingers but now, in the library of her childhood home, here they were.

"Lady Fitzwilliam-Darcy," he bowed a stiff awkward bow to the woman in the turquoise dress. "How delightful to find you here."

"Mr Wyndham, how are you?" She felt her voice raise an octave at the end. "It has been many years since we last saw each other, has it not?"

"Indeed," he moved slowly towards her, watched as she placed her book down on the table. "It has been a lifetime. Mabel…".

"Percy," she glanced her fingertips across the top of his hand. "I have missed you."

"I think," he turned his hand so that his palm lay flat in hers, "that I may have missed you the most."

Mabel Darcy was always brought up to remember who she was and the protocols of polite society, but right now, at this moment, she felt herself fall into Percy Wyndham's embrace. The scent of rose oil and cinnamon permeated his soul, and he knew that fate was finally batting for his team.

"I never should have let you go," he breathed into her curls, now peppered with grey. "I should have fought for us."

She took his face in her hands; he was older now, much altered to anyone else, but the only face she could see was that of the handsome boy who she had fallen in love with such a long time ago.

"No," she beamed, "can you not see? This is all as it was meant to be." She pulled away from his embrace, walked over to the fireplace.

"All of these years apart?"

"All of these years becoming who we are now; imagine the stories we have to tell each other and the adventures we have already had. The adventures that are yet to come."

"I think I fail to understand your meaning."

"Mr Wyndham, if I recall correctly you once made me an offer of marriage a long time ago, and if I recall, I never gave you an answer."

"Do you have one now?"

"I have considered your proposal most sincerely and I am inclined to accept it."

Mabel finally married Percy Wyndham at the age of fifty-four; they had eighteen blissful years together in the house at Cromer, where they sailed out to sea and ate crabs straight from the shell. In the three corridors of the bright gallery, the exhibition about her life told the story of a fearless woman who defied society's conventions; on the walls hung the artefacts that she had brought back with her, the illustrations she had made of the places she had been to, the clothes she had worn and finally, in pride of place, the newly discovered atlas that had belonged to her father and where she had plotted and planned her journey in the library at Pemberley. Sometimes we need to travel to far-flung places, reach the furthest corners of the world, to realise that everything we are looking for is waiting patiently for us to return to shore.

Benn Williams on love, 'Lilac', lost family history, and letting go of his inner demons.

By Francesca O'Toole

Benn Williams walks in looking every inch the Hollywood superstar you would expect, but I am genuinely surprised to note how different he looks. Gone is the tense, stretched out actor who used to appear for interviews looking like a coiled spring. We have met before, and the former Henry Jones has always been short and sharp; barking out answers to questions and sending through a list of demands before his arrival, but today he meets me in his local coffee shop, relaxed and amenable as he excitedly tells me all about his new role in the dark, twisting tale of Oscar Menzies, the brooding protagonist of the eagerly anticipated 'Lilac'. Understandably we have to talk about his role as Mr Darcy in 'Pride and Prejudice', last year's adaptation directed by Matthew Wickham. It was a sumptuous production which won Jenny Graves her first Leading Actress BAFTA for the role of Elizabeth Bennet and saw Williams surpassing Colin Firth in the hot, regency hero stakes. "You always know that playing Darcy is a big thing," he says, as we order Eggs Benedict and coffee, "but you never really understand it until you actually put the shirt on." He, of course, referring to the 'wet shirt' scene which saw him reveal a cotton-covered glimpse of his MI6 super spy physique and which caused Miss Bennet to get suitably flustered. "Matthew wasn't sure if we were going to use it, but it's pretty much a given now that Mr Darcy gets damp," he grins with a twinkle in his eye.

> "You always know that playing Darcy is a big thing."

Williams was on location for nearly six months despite Mr Darcy's brief appearances in the film, 'I was going through my divorce and it was a very difficult time." He looks wistfully out of the window and his jaw clenches. I ask him if he is still friends with Madeleine Tennant, his former wife, and mother of his daughters, Esther and Anya. 'We plod on with it, we get along. It's gone past the point where there is anger about it. Life is too short to hold onto that kind of animosity, so we don't.' Tennant, 42, is currently on hiatus from her role as Lady Rebecca in ITV's 'Haringey Place', and due to give birth to her baby with new husband, French financier Antoine Pelletier, any day now. Benn attended the wedding. 'It was an odd feeling, because when we got married, I honestly thought that we would be together forever – we spent enough money,' he says, referring to the elaborate event that was featured in 'Hello' and saw both Tennant and Williams receive criticism from fans, despite the magazine fee being donated to various charities. 'But Madeleine is happy, and Antoine really is a great guy,' he pauses, and I realise that there is a full stop here. He isn't prepared to reveal any more about this.

Filming in LA for two months probably accounts for his tanned, relaxed look, despite Lilac being filmed on a shoestring budget. 'There was absolutely no money for it whatsoever, I was working for scale and it didn't even cover my expenses, but there is something so brutal about the way this story has been told, that I couldn't not do it.' The forty-three-year-old turned down the lead role in Jimin Jampol's 'Galaxy of Empires' to star in the low-budget shoot. 'Gainsma Quince is an iconic character, but there are twelve books in the series, and it would have been a massive commitment. I was away from home for nearly three years in total when I filmed Henry Jones, and it was bloody hard work. There is something about a job like that. It takes its toll on you, physically and mentally.' We finish our breakfast and order more coffee, Williams flashes his famous smile at the waitress. 'But Lilac was different.'

The film, currently showing at Sundance, weaves the tale of Oscar and Janey, a brutal reworking of a classic Hemingway novel, repackaged and re-located to the frontline of the war in Afghanistan.

There is no happy ending in 'Lilac', but Williams likes that. 'There isn't always a happy ending to stories, sometimes you are just left in the middle of a chapter wondering what happened, not sure how it should have ended, and I liked that about this story.' And the sex scenes? There was an initial furore regarding the film due to the explicit storyline and Williams' insistence on casting an age-appropriate actress for the role of his lover, Janey. 'It would have been easy to have chosen a brilliant, younger actress – because there are so many talented women out there – but Oscar and Janey are the same age, they are middle-aged, and it felt dishonest of me to show Oscar as this older, damaged man prancing about with a hot, young thing.' The part of Janey went to Jemima Lancaster, 43. There is no doubting the chemistry between the old friends who are both veterans of the Cambridge Footlights. 'It was great working with Jemima again and I feel that we bring a wonderful sense of honesty to the story. It's very raw, very passionate, and it needed that because the story that Catherine [Lawson] has written is so brilliantly pure.'

Currently in rehearsals for 'The Importance of Being Earnest' at Manchester's Royal Exchange, Benn will be playing Lady Bracknell, 'who doesn't want to screech 'a handbag??', he grins, "and I get to wear a bustle, how amazing is that?" Williams has

"We can all get to the point where we hit rock bottom…"

been back 'up north' for other reasons too. His family tree has recently been researched for celebrity genealogy programme, 'The Story of My Life' and the team discovered a lot of hidden history. The episode is due to air in a few weeks' time, and both Benn and the BBC are keeping details under wraps, although released promotional stills show Williams in the gardens at Pemberley. 'It's ridiculously interesting and revealed some amazing facts,' he says, with a smile on his face. So, how did he get on with the famous Darcys during his time at the Derbyshire estate? 'They are a surprisingly down to earth family,' he says, and it is clear from Instagram posts shared by Harriet - daughter of Lady Elizabeth Darcy, bestselling author of 'Most Ardently', and Benn's close friend, Matthew Wickham - that he spent a lot of time with them whilst there. 'They are very private, but Harriet is like any other teenager. She is a lot of fun.'

And what about Darcy wild child Lady Imogen? The troubled socialite has been out of the spotlight for the past year, but recently re-emerged on social media to raise mental health awareness. Her suicide attempt was well documented in the tabloids, despite the family's attempts to keep it out of the press. 'We were in the middle of filming when Lady Elizabeth received the phonecall. It was a harrowing time for all concerned, really touch and go.' His relaxed mood shifts slightly, 'but it can happen to any of us. We can all get to the point where we hit rock bottom.' Williams reveals that he has been receiving treatment for alcoholism, 'it got to the point where I hit rock bottom too, and I stayed there. I stayed there for a long time, until something happened that made me

realise that I needed to stop. Well, two things actually.' I ask him what he means, and he retreats slightly before emerging with confidence, 'I nearly threw myself in front of a tube train and I was stopped by a stranger. He literally pulled me back onto the platform. I don't know who he is, but I want to thank him.' He takes a large mouthful of his flat white, 'suicide is the biggest killer of men under forty-five in the UK, and I hope that by sharing this it might help someone else. Even if it is just one person.' I realise, sitting there in a coffee shop in Manchester's northern quarter, that it is taking a lot of nerve for Benn Williams to sit here and tell me this. 'I am not immune to feeling as if there is no escape. A person very dear to me once said, 'it's never the answer, but it can sometimes be the question' and that rings very true.'

So, is he on the road to recovery now? 'I'm getting there, slowly but surely. It's not a sprint, it's an endurance race, but I like the person who I am without alcohol. He's actually quite nice.' I wholeheartedly agree. 'And I met someone too.' He tries to be coy about this, but it just blurts out of his mouth. 'She made me realise that what we do has a ripple effect, it's not just about one person.' Is this lucky lady the new woman in Benn Williams' life? 'I hope so,' he smiles, 'but I have to convince her that it's not a completely terrible idea!' He rises to leave, but not before giving me a massive hug. 'Fingers crossed, Fran,' he says, as he walks off.

As I watch him disappear down Shudehill, I realise that I'm really rooting for him.

The Importance of Being Earnest' runs from 15 May – 27th July at the Royal Exchange, Manchester. 'Lilac' is released on the 24th June nationwide.

HARRIET: Mum, you need to read The Guardian. Like now. Go online. Read it now.

DEBS: Fuck me, did you see the interview? Did you read it? Fucking hell. Fuck fuck fuck. AMAZING.

IMOHOHO: OMG LIZARD, WTF??? He loves you, he LOVES you!! Benn Williams is like 100% totally in love with you.

MAGS: Lizzy. It is NOT A COMPLETELY TERRIBLE IDEA.

MATT: What more does the man have to do??

BENN: Hey you.

Lizzy lay on the floor of the Saloon, above her the gold embellishments on the ceiling sparkled in the early morning light. She couldn't sleep, had come downstairs the wrong way, sitting on the steps of the grand staircase until the sun began to rise, hoping that Hortense Holland wasn't out for a ghostly stroll, and now she was here in Mr Darcy's grand reception room as the sun appeared over the hills, the rays glinting off the lake.

Over the fireplace, the picture of Mabel Darcy in her wedding gown looked down at her, strange to think that she was Benn's great great great grandmother, that they were both leaves from the same tree. The wax cylinder recording crackled to life, looping on a timer that had been set too early and which nobody had fixed yet. Mabel's voice, all at once eerie and firm, sounded out in the room where her wedding banquet had been held.

"We are all islands alone, but that does not mean we cannot be traversed every now and then."

It was as if Mabel was reaching out to her through time because she knew now what she needed to do.

LIZZY: Hey.

Thirty

The Lady Darcy tour was due to start at twelve; an intimate guided tour around the house led by Elizabeth Darcy herself. Guests were guided down passageways and up staircases that they would probably never have known existed, before being led to the saloon and given the chance to step out onto the balcony as Darcy and Elizabeth would have done.

The group moved down the corridor of the bright gallery, the vibration of twelve people moving all at once causing the glass cabinet to shudder and clink and then the lid of the Chinese spice jar to join in with the chorus. They moved to the bottom of the grand staircase and she went through her prepared spiel of how George Darcy had been marched down these stairs as he was arrested for treason, how Lady Hortense Darcy had met an untimely end at the foot of them, and how Mr Darcy himself had personally selected the carvings and embellishments.

"And most recently," she continued, "the house was the location for the filming of Pride and Prejudice and, if you've seen it, you will probably remember the staircase as being the centrepiece of the final scenes where the happy couple return to Pemberley after the wedding."

"Oh yes," trilled a plump, enthusiastic woman stood at the front. "This was where Darcy took her by the hand and led her upstairs with the candle in his hand."

"That was so romantic," swooned another less plump but more orange lady, who was pointing at a portrait of the real Fitzwilliam that hung on the staircase wall. "I recognise that picture!"

"And he said, *"Let me show you, Mrs Darcy, that being Mistress of Pemberley might be something,"* and then he kisses her!"

"He kisses her right here next to the bannister!"

The orange lady moved past Lizzy and a flustered woman wrangling two children and threw herself onto the staircase in the manner of the fictional Mrs Darcy.

"And then she says… '*Oh, Mr Darcy, you are very fortunate indeed, for you appear to have wed the happiest and luckiest woman in England*'," they laughed in unison, both doing pitch-perfect impressions of Jenny Graves.

"I don't remember that being in the book."

A voice piped up from the back of the crowd, pushing to the front Benn Williams seemed slightly dishevelled. He caught her eye, just for one quick, unsure second. But it was enough.

"Oh, it should have been," said the plump woman, who did a double-take.

There was a shriek from a few more of the ladies on the tour, and he was surrounded in a hubbub of noise, signing autographs and taking pictures. Lizzy watched as he smiled and charmed and made love to them all, and she found that she was smiling with them.

She began her ascent up the stairs, slowly making her way past the people taking pictures. The tour paused momentarily so that people could take pictures on the grand staircase or choose a regency bonnet or top hat from the selection. She stood to one side, out of the way.

He walked up the stairs towards her, pausing slowly, hesitantly. He wasn't sure how he was going to approach this, wasn't sure how he could. But he knew he had to say something, knew he had to see her and ask, because if he didn't then what would have been the point of it all.

"Lizzy."

"Hello."

Her voice not as loud as usual, as if she had the wind knocked out of her. She wondered why he looked so unhappy and then she felt those familiar prickles again, couldn't quite tell if they were good or bad - was he trying to tell her that really this wasn't a good idea, that this was another false start, that this was all they would ever amount to.

Benn knew what he wanted to say, but he couldn't quite figure out how to get the words out of his head. So, he decided, amidst the noise and the rumble of a busy Pemberley day, that he would start at the beginning.

"These last twelve months have been the worst months of my life," he said, looking out of the window. "The best thing I can take from them was that morning with you."

"The morning with me?"

"Lizzy, the way I drink is not normal. I know that now. It changed me, and I was tired of not being me and being a different person; you made me remember who I am. I read a lot – drinking took that away from me, took my concentration – but I've read so much. I read your book," he saw her blush slightly, "it was brilliant."

He reached for her hand and was happy to note that she offered it willingly. It was good to feel the grasp of her fingers in his hand and held them like he was a little boy holding onto the string of a shiny balloon that he never wanted to let go.

"Lizzy, I didn't stop drinking *because* of you, but what you said made me not want to start again. It made me realise that there are other things that are more important." He could hear his heartbeat in his head, knew he had to be honest. "And I had to come back and tell you all of this so that when I did you would know."

When she spoke, her voice was small and unsure, and there was a wobble to it.

"What would I know?"

"It was all for you, Lizzy. I needed to be the man worthy of you. I think I am now."

"You always have been," she said. "It just took me a while to realise it."

Standing close to him now, she could see the straight little scar above his eyebrow that he got on a zip wire during Freshers Week, the dimpled mark on his forehead from where he had chickenpox, the red spot on his lip where she knew he had been biting it because he was nervous; all of the little parts of his story written across his face.

"Benn, I made a promise to myself that I would tell you how I felt, because, I don't want you as a best friend. I want your laugh, and your grumpy moods – because I love the way your face scrunches up when you're cross. I want to support you in what you want to do, I want us to be a real team – and that can be making your tea for you, or watching the cricket with you, or travelling around the world with you. But I want you to end each day knowing that I have your back because I know you have mine."

She scanned his face, could see the turn of his mouth twitching slightly, and she continued, knowing that once everything she felt for him spilled out, she would never be able to gather it back in and hide it away again.

"I want your cold feet on my thighs in bed, and to hold you as you fall asleep, I want us to work on things together and things apart. I want all of this. I want all of you, the bad bits, the good bits, the infuriating bits. *Everything*. I think I've always been yours, and I think you've always been mine too. It was just a question of timing."

Lizzy held her breath, she had never done this before, never been so open and honest. Maybe it was genetics, or maybe it was simply that she feared rejection. She didn't know the reasons, but she did know that she had spread out her dreams under Benn Williams's feet, and she was hoping that he wouldn't tread on them.

There was a moment of silence, but then he smiled, a massive complete all across his face kind of smile.

"I want that too!" He immediately felt as if all the worry and the weight of the last few years had been lifted from his shoulders. "I want your bedhead and your sleepy yawns, I want your cleverness and your silliness – you are the most amazing woman I know. I want us to travel to places that we've never been to and I want to make hundreds of thousands of new memories with you, and maybe even make some babies with you. I want you to meet my kids, I want you to meet my *mum*!"

He wondered if he was getting a bit carried away with himself, and he knew that there were people looking at them now.

"You have burned in me like a furious fire for this whole time...and I'm sorry," he squeezed her hand, "I'm so sorry for all this time that we have wasted, for all this time we could have already had."

She closed her eyes and dipped her head, placing her forehead against his shoulder, breathing him in. As the tingles passed through him, he thought of all the missed opportunities, and he knew that he couldn't – that he wouldn't - let anything come between them again. There was a look, an understanding, a promise.

"Elizabeth Darcy, I want a future with you, whatever that entails. If you have a plan, or if we just make it up as we go along...You see, I'm not the way you found me, I'll never be the same."

She was looking at him with a confused look on her face and he immediately felt as if he had done something wrong.

"That's Hall & Oates."

The orange lady with the massive smile laughed, "Mr Darcy is trying to woo you with Hall & Oates?? Hey, Paula!" she shouted down the stairs, "Benn Williams is trying to chat up Lady Darcy with Hall & Oates!"

"What?" He looked confusedly from Lizzy to the orange woman.

"It's a song!" The lady began to sing, slightly loudly and off-key. "What I want you got, and it might be hard to handle..."

The recognition streaked across his face and he laughed at himself, unable to stop smiling at Lizzy. The orange lady grabbed him for a quick selfie before grinning excitedly at them both and shuffling off to the long gallery.

"I told you I was bad at this," he laughed.

"I think you're awesome at this," she beamed back, "and you know I'm never wrong."

"Neither am I, so that bodes very well for the future!"

She leaned in towards him, stretching up on tiptoes to kiss him on the nose.

"I love you, Lizzy, I mean it. Proper love, not acting."

There. He had finally said it to her face, rather than practising it in his rear-view mirror. Now all he could do was watch and wait.

"Bennet Fitzwilliam, regular man on the street, I suppose because you were so sincere," she teased, "that I should tell you that I love you too… and I've said it out loud now, so it's real and everything."

A massive grin – his famous Hollywood smile – spread across his face.

"Do you hear that?" He shouted over the bannister to the visitors below. "She loves me!"

There was cheering and clapping from the gathered audience as Lizzy threw her head back laughing. The sound fell like sunshine into his soul as he pulled her close and kissed her on the staircase of the house that played a part in both of their histories, his heart full of love and hope, and his arms wrapped tightly around his dearest, loveliest Elizabeth.

"Do you think they're going to stay there all day," Paula said to her friend.

"If that were me," the older lady laughed, "I think I'd stay there for the rest of my life!"

Epilogue

Lizzy gently padded through the hallway, the stone floor warm against her feet on the summer morning – she walked past the sideboard with its collection of pictures in a mismatch of frames; her favourite was the one of her and Benn at her dad's wedding. They were standing together, his head pressed gently against hers, her arms around his shoulders, his hands on her waist. It was a perfect moment of tenderness and happiness, captured accidentally and now printed forever. Another showed Harriet at her College Ball, dressed in emerald green and gold, next to her Imogen was throwing her leg up in the air, smiling with glee; pictures of Esther and Anya, no-longer little girls but teenagers blessed with their mothers looks and their fathers humour; Joyce and Hugh at the villa in Cap Ferrat sipping champagne and looking fabulous; Charlie and his boys on the balcony at Pemberley, and at the front in pride of place was a small photograph of Lizzy and her mother, taken at the house in Chelsea the day before her fourth birthday.

Joyce Hutchinson retired at the end of the season. She left Pemberley under the watchful eye of a new management team, who loved the house almost as much as she did. Hugh took her travelling and they spent summers in France, surrounded by their blended family of children and grandchildren. Eventually, Mrs Darcy got used to being called 'Your Grace', but she did thoroughly reprimand her husband once when he nipped to Harrods for a box of teabags. She never got used to wearing a tiara at formal events, but she did get used to being loved deeply by the man she adored every single day. Their wedding had been small and simple, held in a semi-private part of the garden which seemed to have been designed to naturally lend itself to the occasion; Joyce had walked down the aisle with her sons on either side as the scent of the rose garden planted by Lady Anne Darcy floated towards them.

"Hello, you," he said, unable to believe they were finally doing this.

"It's about time," she laughed, as she took his hand.

Later in the evening, as the families sat in the marquee that had been erected on the west front lawn, Charlie would declare that this was a love story that had been forty years in the making. Joyce had smiled at Hugh, all at once the reverent twelve-year-old who had visited Pemberley with a papery guidebook and now as Lady Darcy, her own history now written into that of the house that she loved – not just as the woman who had managed it for so long but now as part of the family who had built it. Pemberley had always been magical, an enchanted castle hiding away in the peaks and valleys and as Hugh pulled her onto the dancefloor, she knew that whilst the journey to get to this point had not been easy, she was stepping into her destiny knowing that every choice had brought her to this moment.

They danced under the twinkling fairy lights hanging from the roof of the marquee as their loved ones stood cheering from the sidelines. She saw Gareth and James, the two boys who had grown into men almost overnight, both fathers now to adorable children; Charles and Joseph Darcy – both handsome and so very tall, looking like their father; Harriet, the girl she had known since birth, blossoming into a true descendant of the Darcy women who had gone before her; Imogen, stronger than she appeared and radiant in the evening light. And then, happy, laughing and completely incandescent, there was Elizabeth, being held tightly by the handsome actor who was looking at her as if she was the most precious thing in the world.

Sam and Imogen broke up just after Hugh's wedding, but they remained firm friends and were often found wandering up to the Cage together or hanging out in the Ranger station. It was only when Imogen got accepted onto a course at a college in Preston that Sam realised what he felt for her, declaring himself in front of everyone at the Staff Summer Party after two fruit ciders and sambuca. Imogen wasn't sure what she felt but decided that she was happy enough in Derbyshire – her boarding school accent even gaining a soft northern twang, which she quite liked.

Imogen fully believed that fate had smiled upon her that terrible evening, when tired and empty, she hadn't realised that she was drifting off into the light before being brought crashing back to earth; she was meant to return to Pemberley, was meant to start the new chapter of her story in the historic lands that had belonged to her family for centuries, and now she had a new job there, helping to protect and preserve it for years to come. Welcome home, she thought, every time she crossed the railway bridge and juddered over the cattle grid, not just the place where she lived, but the place where her heart resided.

Harriet loved the little flat at the top of the tower and didn't see any point in moving her life across the county in cardboard boxes for nine months of the year when she could easily commute to the Textile Design course that she was undertaking at the University of Derby. With the approval of her mum, she changed her name to Darcy-Wickham. Granny Wickham had never known how much her mum had pushed Matthew to put his name on her birth certificate, how much she had wanted him to recognise the baby who was his mirror image as his own, and he hadn't realised how much he had wanted it until it was too late.

Now nearly eighteen years later, Harriet embraced it and the family branches of the Wickhams and the Darcys became more permanently entangled and written down officially on the Darcy family tree. Living together in the small flat, Harriet and Imogen were often seen driving a little too fast down the driveway in the yellow Mini, singing Wannabe by the Spice Girls and drinking coffee out of travel mugs as they headed towards campus.

Matthew stayed in Malibu with Tamsin, her fame in the US eclipsing his own and reducing him in some ways to the position of holding her handbag whilst she pouted and smiled for the cameras. She was still devoted to him and, despite the reservations of a few close friends, they worked as a couple, with enough love and mutual respect to build something truly solid. He spent lazy days writing, giving himself a few years off, wanting to spend time with his children.

He was as surprised as anyone when his little pet project, written in ten days and filmed on a budget by a small production company, was nominated for the Academy Award for Best Original Screenplay, and even more surprised when he won. Linda, still his stalwart and confidante, asked for more money, better benefits, and a bigger office, already anxious for the busy years ahead.

Maggie and Pete welcomed their daughter, Jeannie, named for her nanna, into the world at ten past midnight on Christmas Day morning. Pete was instantly besotted, and Maggie would later confide to Lizzy after copious amounts of Pinot G that she didn't realise how much she loved him until she saw how much he loved their daughter. Maggie took a senior role in the northern Austenation offices and the family moved back to Lambton into a cottage that had once been occupied by a Bridget Wickham, which seemed like too much of huge coincidence for the whole move not to have been predestined. Pete rolled his eyes at his wife and put the kettle on for the removals men.

Benn finally won an Academy Award for his role as Oscar Menzies. Audiences and critics agreed that it had been his best work and he semi-seriously declared in his speech that his career had now peaked. Over the next few months, he read fewer scripts, took on less work and decided that he had spent too much of his life away on location. He went back to theatre; it had always been his first love and there was something about standing on a stage in front of an audience and feeling the immediate emotional response that kept him safe and grounded in a way that hiding on film sets in trailers had never been able to do.

He found interesting and unique tales and constructed narratives that truly made people think, he started to direct. It was his production of 'Cat's Paw' by a new writer, Louisa Garrett, that caught the attention of critics – it moved to the larger theatres of Manchester, then the West End, before winning an Olivier Award and professional acclaim for the man whose portrayal of Mr Darcy had been called 'oversentimental and brooding' by the film critic in the Daily Mail.

Despite the success, Benn continued to base himself at the small theatre in Buxton, where people gradually forgot that he had ever been in the movies, where his face blended into the crowd on the high street and people only occasionally asked him if he had been on Coronation Street. He also loved the convenience of being able to commute from the house hidden near the entrance of the Pemberley estate, never too far from the woman who would hold his hand at night whenever he reached for it.

Lizzy found that it was always a lot of fun when the man of your dreams was in your bed, or kissing you on the staircase in some grand, romantic gesture like the film star he was, but it was always a bit disconcerting when you realised that he liked to leave dirty socks on the bedroom floor, loved cricket to a level of boredom and would argue about practically anything if you let him get away with it, especially if he thought it would get you riled.

Sometimes he would swan about the house in a majestic manner, huffing and puffing; she would laugh with Esther and Anya which got him even grumpier, before sending him off to his Man Cave at the bottom of the garden whilst they ordered pizza and watched a film without him. He would return a few hours later and she would pull him into his place on the sofa, throw her legs over him and stroke the curl behind his ear until he nuzzled her gently and they would go to bed. The girls would roll their eyes at each other and turn up the volume on the television.

She never did go back to a law office but did write another book. And another, and another. Her books become bestsellers. One was turned into a TV series, and there was talk of a film. Lizzy found that the ideas came to her quickly, and she found inspiration around the world as she travelled far and wide with Benn, following in the footsteps of his great-great-great-grandma. It was a trip that the BBC were desperate to film, but an offer they declined. Some things were meant to be private and this was definitely one of them.

The happy couple would go for long, meandering walks across the parklands watching as the wind brushed through the grass, the light catching the rustling blades; the spectral image of imagined rabbits darting across the moorland. Laughing, talking, giggling they would walk back to their house in time for dinner with their dog, Jethro, who had been adopted by them after a heated discussion where the extended Fitzwilliam-Darcy-Wickham family all had differing opinions.

The kitchen would be filled with children and sisters, all gathered around the large table, eating and playing games until Lizzy would lose too much money at Monopoly and tell them all to go home, Harriet shrieking with laughter, Anya defending her in French, Esther kicking her dad under the table whilst he called his girlfriend a bad sport, and she stormed off in a huff. He would later find her reading a book, placating her with coffee and cake, and by doing the washing up, which was, he found, always the quickest way to her heart.

It was nearly midnight amid the celebrations of the Pemberley New Year's Eve Ball when, casually and without ceremony, he presented her with a sapphire ring that had belonged to Mabel Darcy and removed from the Darcy family vaults for this very occasion. For a man who had done this before he felt strangely nervous. He knew that he would never be her firsts in so many things. He knew that he had come too late, when all these things had already been woven into her, were already lines written in the book that he had read, and he loved the woman she was because of all the firsts that had already been, but he wanted her lasts in whatever form they came. His gaze had never wavered as she nodded yes, and they kissed until the clock struck twelve and the tune of Auld Lang Syne echoed out into the courtyard. Benn knew that the happiness he had been looking for was stood before him in sparkly bumblebee shoes.

They celebrated their nuptials in the small chapel at Pemberley the following May, much to the delight of the press who reported 'Mr Darcy and Lady Darcy's' wedding alongside a picture of Colin Firth, obviously. They honeymooned in Paris and nine months later found they were starting all over again

Austen Fitzwilliam-Darcy had his father's mild-mannered temperament, unlike his sister Evelyn, who arrived a year later, kicking and screaming and very much like her mother. It had been hard at first - the sleeplessness, the night feeds, and then entertaining a toddler whilst holding a newborn, and there were arguments and shouting matches and the occasional storming out- but when Lizzy looked at her husband, sleeping on the couch, with their daughter on his chest and their son nestled in the crook of his arm, Billie Holiday crooning in the background, she knew that she would not change any of this; that this was where she was meant to be, raising another generation of Darcys on the ancient hunting lands.

It was a glorious Derbyshire morning, and the steady stream of visitors were already beginning to arrive; Austen was out in the garden, running and jumping on the lawn, Benn had been up early with Evelyn, a pile of bacon sandwiches and a pot of coffee were already on the table and she grabbed one before cheekily ruffling her husband's hair. It was light again, but he had grown out his curls, which she loved, although she was still dubious about the beard, however much fancy beard oil he put on it. He quickly grabbed her hand, leaning in for a kiss, before passing her the Cath Kidston scarf that had been merrily drying on the line.

It was going to be a busy day.

A family tree has roots that run deep and dark into the earth that supports it, trailing its way through history, the branches weaving and wending their way through time itself, the leaves sprouting, blooming, falling, before returning to the ground and sustaining the tree with life before the never-ending cycle begins again.

It was all here in the crook of the land, in the reflection of the stream that trickled down from the peaks, in the arching curve of the hills that had dominated the geography of the land for centuries before Piers D'Arcy had claimed it for his own.

And so, it was as it would always be, the players would change, but the gentle sweeping route through the landscape would lead them all back home, layer upon layer, year upon year. The house nestled in the valley would continue to weave its magic into the family who loved it. Pemberley would always remain as constant as the stars in the sky.

Matilda

The woman rode to the summit of the hill overlooking the land; she had ridden here for nearly two days straight, banished to the rough country of the high peaks.

Edward had never forgiven her husband for his earlier treachery and treason, and this was the perfect punishment, gift-wrapped in the form of a feral wilderness that he hoped would destroy them all.

Matilda looked down on the land before her, resolute and decided; the King may have buried the D'Arcy family in the bitter soil of Derbyshire, but he did not realise that they were seeds.

The world consists of tiny stories powered by the beat of the human heart.

about the author

Sara Smallman lives and works on the outskirts of Lancashire, in a cluttered but vaguely tidy house that she shares with her two children.

Volunteering at Lyme Park for the National Trust, she constantly finds inspiration in the characters who lived there, especially in Thomas Legh, who is her historical man crush. She is adamant that if you learn about him, he will become your historical man crush too.

Sara has a degree in Screenwriting from the University of Central Lancashire and is like Lizzy Darcy in that she is quite sure that gin and cake will right any wrong.

Controversially, Matthew Rhys is her favourite Darcy.

'Becoming Lady Darcy' is her first novel.

acknowledgments

You all know who you are, you don't need me to validate you.

Thank you for the support, the kind words, the late-night messages, the helpful hints, the dubious googling, checking the smut/cheese ratio, the soundtrack suggestions, the copious amounts of tea, the listening to me rant on, the reading of tiny script on tiny screens, for keeping me laughing, for buying me gin, for giving me hope, for being the world's best cheerleaders.

K & O, you keep me OK. Love you to Pemberley and back again.

Lady Penny's Cheese Pie

Millicent, nicknamed Penny by her American-born mother, was perhaps the most infamous of all the Darcy women to live here at Pemberley during the last century. Arrested several times, she was a prolific and somewhat combatant suffragette, causing damage to the properties of her father's friends and serving time in Holloway. During the First World War, she trained as a nurse, working in the military hospital at Dunmarleigh, as well as driving ambulances for the medical corps. This expertise was called upon again when she ran the officer's convalescent home, based at Pemberley during World War Two, in addition to rehoming a number of evacuees from cities hit by German bombing raids. In later years, she would take over the running of the Darcy business interests, including Stratton Mills and local newspaper publisher, Mercantile News. Following her death in 1969, her son Winston, the 10th Duke, discovered her memoirs and diaries, including her recipe for cheese pie, which became a seasonal favourite in the Pemberley tearooms.

FILLING:
3-4 onions
50g best butter
400g floury potatoes
200g Lancashire cheese
50g strong cheddar
1 tsp English Mustard powder
100ml double cream.

PASTRY:
150g plain flour
150g self-raising flour
Salt
150g best butter
1 beaten egg, to glaze

- To make the pastry, tip your dry ingredients into a good strong bowl. Add your butter and squish between your fingers. When it gets to nearly breadcrumbs, stop. Splash in a touch of water and mix gently until it begins to clump. Bring together and leave to one side.

- The inside is what makes this pie special. Chop your onions. You must use new onions for this as old ones will not melt down. Add roughly 200ml water and butter. The onions should reduce into an onion puree. Do not allow them to colour.

- Boil your potatoes in salted water until soft. Leave to cool and mash them. Add your onions, potatoes, cheese, cream, and mustard to a bowl and mix. Season to taste, white pepper is always preferable.

- Roll out your pastry, a 20cm pie tin is ample. Add the filling and pie lid. Glaze your pie with the beaten egg and then bake in a hot oven (190c/170c fan/gas 5) for approx. forty minutes or until golden. Serve with a light salad, Mrs Reynolds' Beetroot Chutney and a large glass of good red wine.

30846989R00265

Printed in Great
Britain
by Amazon